W9-AQH-120

DISCARD

Date: 1/10/19

LP FIC HOPKINS
Hopkins, Ellen,
A sin such as this

PALM BEACH COUNTY
LIBRARY SYSTEM
3650 SUMMIT BLVD.
WEST PALM BEACH, FL 33406

A SIN SUCH AS THIS

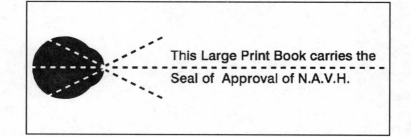

This Large Print Book carries the
Seal of Approval of N.A.V.H.

A Sin Such as This

Ellen Hopkins

THORNDIKE PRESS
A part of Gale, a Cengage Company

Farmington Hills, Mich • San Francisco • New York • Waterville, Maine
Meriden, Conn • Mason, Ohio • Chicago

Copyright © 2018 by Ellen Hopkins.
Thorndike Press, a part of Gale, a Cengage Company.

ALL RIGHTS RESERVED
This book is a work of fiction. Any references to historical events, real people, or real places are used fictitiously. Other names, characters, places, and events are products of the author's imagination, and any resemblance to actual events or locales or persons, living or dead, is entirely coincidental.
Thorndike Press® Large Print Core.
The text of this Large Print edition is unabridged.
Other aspects of the book may vary from the original edition.
Set in 16 pt. Plantin.

LIBRARY OF CONGRESS CIP DATA ON FILE.
CATALOGUING IN PUBLICATION FOR THIS BOOK
IS AVAILABLE FROM THE LIBRARY OF CONGRESS

ISBN-13: 978-1-4328-5862-9 (hardcover)

Published in 2018 by arrangement with Atria, an imprint of Simon & Schuster, Inc.

Printed in the United States of America
1 2 3 4 5 6 7 22 21 20 19 18

This book is dedicated to the truth, and to those who value it enough to seek it out.

Cleansing

Barring blizzard or virus,
she goes to church every week, sits
with the choir, in the front row,
all robed in green and a slight air of
    hauteur.
She looks her pastor in the eye,
smiles at his absolution.

Accepts communion.

She sings like an angel,
her Sunday friends say, cool blue
soprano lifting off the scale, toward the
    king
of forgiveness, carved above the altar.
She looks, they think, like a weary
    Madonna,
amber eyes, set deep in alabaster.

She goes home, cleansed.

Stands at the window, wonders
what her Sunday friends would say
if she told them alabaster was nothing
more than sandstone, born lucky.
She tucks her Good News
beneath the latest *Cosmo,*
turns on the computer to open his e-mail.

Come to me.

A sliver of her wants to resist,
to tell him he's only a tiny footnote
on the master plan. But most of her
will give him anything he demands.
She is a lemming on the precipice, drawn
to the dark song of surf and not afraid to
   jump.

She walks through his door.

Hers is the beauty of a goddess,
he thinks, with golden hair and eager
skin, so in need of discipline, fresh
from her Father's house.
Yes, you look like a goddess, he says,
but you fuck like a demon.

Turn around.

The sliver screams, "Run!"
The lemming falls facedown
on the bed, submits to the tide,
the ebb of silk and the flow of leather.
His flesh into hers, she surrenders
to the surge, exhales tears, and goes home.

In need of cleansing.

ONE

Every honeymoon comes to an end, romance segueing into marriage. I should know. This is my fourth. It wraps with the bellow of a horn and a barely discernable reverse braking motion as the *Radiance of the Seas* docks in Vancouver. I take a deep breath, exhale regret that we must now return to the day-to-day minutiae. Alas, I bore too easily.

It's been a lovely two weeks, up to Seward and back again, a double cruise. Our stateroom suite was gorgeous. The food was amazing. And every excursion, from Skagway to Ketchikan, was a bold undertaking, though the cumulative effect was an uncomfortable reminder that my right knee hasn't totally healed from last winter's surgery.

Admittedly, small irritations marred the trip. Cavin's onboard gambling became a distraction and, if not for a late almost-breakeven win, might have made a substan-

9

tial dent in his personal bank account. Discovering your new husband has quirks you didn't know about is one thing. Finding out one of those idiosyncrasies could wipe out your assets is another. I spent the bulk of my lifetime building financial stability. Love will not ruin that. Whether or not games of chance will ruin love remains to be seen.

Having invested around twenty times as much into this trip as the average couple, Cavin and I are afforded Royal Caribbean's Enhanced Program privileges, including priority departure ahead of the mass exodus. I reach for his hand. "Ready?"

He tugs me against his chest, rests his chin on top of my head. "Not really, but we don't have a choice." He tilts up my face, cool green marble eyes locking on mine, and his kiss swears he loves me. Love. Such a hard thing to accept when it takes forty-one years to find it. Love. Such a hard thing to give when you're not sure how to define it, let alone how to translate whatever watery meaning you can dredge up into action. This is the closest I've ever come, however, and I'm determined to explore this novel territory.

Truthfully, I can't believe I fell for him so hard, so fast, not to mention under such ridiculous circumstances. I mean, there I was, lying on a gurney in the ER after a serious fall skiing, when in saunters this doctor, going over my X-rays. My first impression was he was cute, in a careless way, his wheat-colored hair a bit too long and his scrubs slightly askew. But his bedside manner was marvelous — humor cloaked in physician talk that put me instantly at ease, despite the bad news he delivered about dual ligament tears and meniscus shredding.

Then he pulled back the sheet to examine my leg, and when his hand touched my knee, electric sparks danced from patella to groin. That was enough to make me ask for his number. Next day, we were dating. Six months later, we were married.

As we're given the "all clear to disembark," I slide his arm around my waist and press his hand in place.

He leans down, murmurs into my ear, "Afraid I'll lose you?"

"Afraid you might wander off."

"Never. At least, not permanently."

That stops me, but only momentarily. "To be clear, I don't give second chances."

Wisely, he remains mute.

Our luggage was collected earlier and will be delivered to our hotel, which is directly across the street from the Canada Place Cruise Ship Terminal. We have to clear Canadian customs, so I'm glad our enhanced privileges allow us to leave the ship ahead of some two thousand unenhanced passengers. It's a short wait, and Cavin has already filled out the necessary forms. We have nothing to declare, as the stuff we bought came from Alaska, so is considered US goods, simply passing through on its way back to the lower forty-eight.

Regardless, for some inexplicable reason, the customs agent decides to be a jerk. "What is your reason for entering Canada?" Do they just randomly decide to be shitty to some people?

"Uh . . . because the *Radiance of the Seas* dropped us off here?" offers Cavin.

Mr. Customs shifts in his seat. The last thing we need is a problem. I lean forward, allowing a tempting glance just beneath the scooped neckline of my sweater, and can't help but smile when his eyes immediately drop.

"Unfortunately, we can only stay in your beautiful country overnight," I say.

He never even looks up. "Shame. Hope you'll visit us again." Aaaaand . . . he passes us through.

Ten paces beyond, Cavin snorts laughter.

"Wow. You really know how to use those things to your advantage."

"Jealous?"

"Of the ability? Yes. Am I worried about losing you to an overzealous Mountie? Hardly."

"I wouldn't be overconfident. Dumpy, bald customs agents are no competition for a gorgeous surgeon. But if there's one thing hotter in the saddle than a doctor, it's most definitely a cop, and Royal Canadian Mounted Police are the hottest cops of all."

"I suppose I'll have to apply for a position, then. I've heard it's very competitive. Do you think a medical degree will give me an advantage?"

"Probably not, but your bedside manner might provide a leg up, at least if the commissioner happens to be a woman."

We reach the hotel lobby, which will fill in behind us very soon. When we booked the room, the desk clerk made it clear that this property is particularly popular with the cruise ship crowd, both coming and going, a fact that's confirmed by the unavailability of our room for at least three hours while housekeeping tries to catch up.

"We'll keep your luggage safe until check-in is possible," says the annoyingly dimpled girl behind the counter. "Meanwhile, enjoy some sightseeing. City tour buses leave every half hour, right across the street. Or, if you're so inclined, you could rent bicycles and ride over to Stanley Park. It's a must-see."

Stuffing ourselves into a packed tour bus does not sound appealing, so we opt for the bike rental shop. The place is busy, and we occupy our wait time touching each other in ways inappropriate for a public venue.

When it's finally our turn, the geeky clerk (Tristan, according to his name badge) grins. "Newlyweds?" he guesses.

I smile. "What gave us away?"

"You're too comfortable with each other to be dating. But you're too, uh . . . interested in each other to have been married very long."

Cavin glances around surreptitiously, lowers his voice. "Sounds like our Witness Protection Program disguises are working perfectly."

We all laugh as Tristan hands Cavin a form to fill out and takes his driver's license and credit card. Once the paperwork is handled, he offers directions to Stanley Park. "The main bike path is along the seawall," he says. "It's one-way, counter-clockwise, flat. But if you want more difficult and less crowded terrain, I'd try the interior trails through the big trees. Here, I'll give you a map."

He unfolds it, marking trailheads with asterisks and restaurants with arrows. When he hands it to me, there are a couple of circled areas.

"What are these?" I ask.

Tristan winks. "Less frequented areas of the park. In case you'd like a few private moments, if you get my gist. Your bikes are in stalls thirty-four and thirty-five. Oh, and the helmets are over there. They're mandatory in British Columbia."

As we start toward the protective headgear, Cavin whispers, "Better check the visors for hidden cameras. I think ol' Tristan is a little too helpful, if you get my gist."

Cavin might have been kidding, but as improbable as the idea might seem, I go ahead and give the helmet a thorough once-over.

As we reach the bikes, my cell buzzes. It's a text from my niece Kayla. *Who's Sophia?*

My jaw drops. The very mention of that name is like a slap in the face. How would Kayla know anything about Sophia?

Cavin's ex-fiancée is producing a show in Reno, only an hour from our Glenbrook home. He swears I've got nothing to worry about, but her proximity displeases me, despite the ugly reasons for which he broke up with her.

If I thought she was a knockout in the old pictures Cavin still kept in his office over a year after they split (the ones I pouted about until he put them away), I couldn't help but be impressed by her in the flesh — tall, with coltish dancer's legs and dark spikes of hair, tipped silver, that make her look even younger than her thirty-one years. That she's a decade younger than I is only one reason I hate her.

The fact that I ran into her in *my* house, after she'd just screwed Cavin's teenage son (again!), proves the woman owns no moral compass whatsoever. Eli is clearly smitten, and she's obviously happy to use him. But for what purpose? Is the boy really that great in bed, or is it just an excuse for her to stay near my husband?

Cavin notices my consternation. "What is it?"

I show him Kayla's message.

"Don't look at me," he says. "Eli must've said something. Stirring shit, as usual."

Eli *is* a champion shit stirrer. The question is, why *this* shit?

TWO

It isn't far to Stanley Park, a thousand-and-one-acre jut of forested land surrounded by water — Vancouver Harbor on one side, English Bay on the other. The seawall bike path is famous, and this being an absolutely sumptuous day, it's packed with families on outings. As we maneuver the loop, avoiding small children who haven't quite mastered their handlebars, I can't help but think about Sophia. And Eli.

I never wanted kids, never invited one to inhabit my home. But I wasn't given a choice. Eli landed on our doorstep after expulsion from a pricey boarding school. His infraction? Hacking into the admin computers and improving his classmates' grades. For a hefty price, of course. He couldn't live with his mother, as she's currently in Dubai with her diplomat husband for at least a year.

Eli is a study in contrasts. On first glance,

he's a gawky boy. Get to know him, however, and you discover unexpected maturity. He's a self-avowed partier and troublemaker, yet nevertheless maintains a 4.0 GPA. He's either brutally honest or masterful at deceit. It's hard to tell because he and Cavin often spin the same basic premise in totally different directions. And that is maddening because, while I want to always believe his father, often Eli sways me.

Cavin brakes his bike, pausing at a trailhead to consult the map Tristan provided. "I've got an idea. Come on."

He leads the way on the flat dirt track aptly named Beaver Lake Trail, because that's where it takes us. Not that Beaver Lake is much of a lake. More like a water-lily-choked swamp. Just beyond the point where the soupy water thickens into mud, we cross a small stream and soon after that the Stanley Park Causeway. Now we have three choices. Straight ahead on flat ground. Left, downhill. Or right, uphill on Bridle Path.

Cavin opts for the most difficult route, up a very steep stretch through ferns and cedars. He studies the landscape and eventually stops, walking his bike well back off the path toward a dense copse of trees. When we drop the kickstands, he reaches for me. "Let's play a game."

Seriously? "Like what?"

He kisses me. Hard. Rough. Leaves me breathless. "How about Red Riding Hood?"

"What's that?"

"Hide-and-seek with a twist. If I catch you, I eat you."

Okay, he's piqued my interest. "What if you don't catch me?"

"You can eat me."

"You still have to count to one hundred."

He closes his eyes. "One, two . . ."

I sprint back into a dense cop of woods, losing sunlight as the boughs close in. I zig right, zag left, try not to leave an easy trail.

Cavin is still counting, "Ten, eleven, twelve . . ."

Deeper, deeper, loping into the shadows, where I succumb to a sudden luscious shiver of fear, a rare treat. Was this what R. R. Hood felt as she wound through the trees, a lupine threat on her heels?

Breathing hard, I stop. Assess. Realize I'm not exactly sure which way is out. Everything looks the same. Well, that was stupid. Quite unlike me. Caution is something I learned a very long time ago and honed over the years. I listen intently but can't hear Cavin counting.

Something rustles in the brush.

"Hello?"

No answer but a crackling of twigs and dried leaves. I plunge behind a curtain of ferns, heart drumming against my breastbone. Movement again, heavy footsteps disturbing drifts of fallen needles. Bear? Deer? Tristan? Some random forest dweller, hungry for a fuck?

"Goddamn it, who's there? Cavin? Is that you?"

Just off to my left is the tall, hollowed-out stump of a huge cedar, lost in one of the big windstorms that felled many of the old-timer trees. I bend to peek inside it, ascertain there's nothing there, and just as I start to tuck myself in, hands close around my throat from behind. Tighten, thumbs pushing against the pounding pulse.

Self-defense. There's a move . . . no . . . can't remember. I bring my own hands up, but when I try to pry my attacker's fingers off my neck, he barks, "Don't fight me, Red. This will barely hurt at all."

Cavin! Jesus. What the hell? Who is this man, and what, exactly, is his game? His teeth rake my neck, biting hard enough to cause pain, if not blood. And for some insane reason, the mad rush of near panic serves as an aphrodisiac. I'm either going to die or come.

"Stop." It's a weak attempt and the word lodges in my throat.

"Shut up."

He forces me facedown onto the thick cushion of forest vegetation. Briefly, I hope there's no poison oak or ivy or whatever might grow in these woods. But any thought of rashes vanishes as soon as he yanks my leggings and panties to my ankles, then all the way off. My instinct screams *get away.* Do I listen? Or wrestle it and trust the Big Bad Wolf only wants to play?

"Luscious," he says, caressing the rounded contours of my butt, and that is closer to the man I've come to know.

"Cav—"

A hand clamps over my mouth. "Do not talk." He lifts himself over me, moves my hair to one side, and lowers his lips to the back of my neck. Again, there is a brilliant sink of fangs.

I force myself to stay calm, but now he slides his spare hand under my belly, lifts the lower half of my body off the forest floor and toward his face. "I will devour you." He burrows between my thighs, tongue tracing the slick path to the hard, round knob, and when it responds to the pull of his mouth, there is a small snap of incisors there, too. I'm moaning, "No," but he knows I mean yes, and even if I didn't, there's no stopping him now. When he pushes his fingers inside me — one, then two, then three, four — there's no resistance, only wet invitation.

Cavin flips me onto my back, pulls my shirt up over my head, shuttering light and trapping my arms in the long sleeves. He nips the length of my body, not enough to open skin, but I might discover bruises later. "Don't come until I say you can."

I lay wrapped in darkness, head whirling with semideviant sex, inhaling the scent of dampish earth and sharp evergreen incense. I hear him slither out of his jeans, and now he crosses my wrists, pins them over my head. He enters me, thrusting fiercely and growling like a rutting wolf and I learn something new about my husband. Also myself, when our mutual orgasm elicits my completely unscripted scream.

He withdraws but doesn't immediately free my hands. "We should play this game more often. I kind of like you helpless." He smooths my shirt back into place and kisses me softly before releasing me completely.

As I follow his unhesitant lead straight to the bikes, I'm listing slightly. And as we start back toward the city, I sort through my unease. The only other person who engaged me in alternative play was Jordan, and it was always with tacit consent. Cavin's game was a surprise, and not totally pleasant. When I finally escaped my mother's abuse, I swore forevermore to remain in complete control. Marriage cannot — will not — change that.

We are almost back to the rental shop when I miss a shift and the pedal resists and my not-quite-healed knee does something strange. It doesn't exactly pop, not like it did when it gave way on Ellie's, a black diamond ski run well within my realm of expertise had it not been for a skier hitting me from behind. But it does . . . wobble, I guess.

When I brake to a stop and slip off the seat, I'm careful to put my left leg down first. Still, a slight sideways motion as I park the bike shoots a hot electric bolt through my patella.

"Shit!" The word fires from my mouth, drawing Cavin's attention.

"What's wrong?"

"Nothing," I lie.

"Tara . . ."

"It's just . . . I think I worked my knee a little too hard."

"Let me see." He kneels and rolls up my legging, does a quick exam. "It feels solid but it's starting to swell. We'll ice it at the

23

hotel. Can you walk okay?"

"Of course."

The bravado is short-lived, though I try to disguise my discomfort. When my limp becomes noticeable, Cavin wraps an arm around me and lifts so I'm mostly strolling on air. Rather than wait for the line at the desk, he sits me on a chair in the lobby and goes over to the concierge, who shoots me a sympathetic glance.

Twenty minutes later, I'm settled on a big chair in our room, with my leg elevated and chilling nicely. Cavin orders room service, then digs in his suitcase for his Percodan stash. I accept one and by the time our dinner arrives I'm comfortably numb. After a glass of wine I'm comfortably numb enough to start humming the Pink Floyd song bearing that name while we try to find something to watch on TV.

Cavin's cell phone interrupts. He glances at the caller ID, excuses himself, and pulls off into a corner for a short, perhaps contentious, conversation. I hear snippets ". . . still in Vancouver . . . I know . . ." Long interlude, and then ". . . till tomorrow . . ." When he signs off he doesn't wait for a query. "Sorry about that. It was my service. I guess one of my patients is overanxious about a script refill."

Seriously?

"Couldn't you just okay that from here?"

"I don't like to prescribe without seeing blood work."

I hold up the bottle of Percodan. "You did for me."

He grins. "I've been known to make exceptions." He comes over, refills my glass, lifts the ice pack from my leg, and examines my knee. "Swelling's down. How's the pain?"

"Percodan with a wine chaser? What pain? Seriously, though, I think I just overworked it."

"Well, take it easy for the next couple of days. I'll make an appointment with your orthopedist for you when I get back tomorrow. You sure you'll be okay? As I recall, those Russian Hill stairs are steep."

The plan is to fly into San Francisco tomorrow. From there Cavin will go on to Reno and pick up his car at the airport, where we left it two weeks ago. I'll stay in the city a couple of days, then drive my BMW to its new garage in Tahoe, with a quick stop at my sister Melody's house in Sacramento to drop off the Alaska trinkets we bought for her family.

"I'll be fine. To be honest, I miss the city."

"Enough to make you change your mind

about selling the house?"

I've considered and reconsidered, so the answer comes readily. "No. I love it, of course. But it's a possession rooted in my past, and that's where it belongs. When I crave the Pacific, there's always your place in Carmel. I've been considering where to reinvest my equity. I was thinking Park City, or maybe Jackson Hole."

Cavin smiles. "Some place to ski other than Heavenly?"

"Yes, but both are beautiful in the summertime, too. And who knows? Maybe one day you'll get tired of Tahoe. Either location would have the need for a sports injury expert."

He doesn't comment, and I don't mention the fact that, other than possibly the online type, gambling isn't available in either place.

And neither is Sophia.

THREE

I'm in the backseat of a limo, and when the driver exits the freeway into familiar neighborhoods, the barest hint of nostalgia threatens. It isn't the coast that I've missed — I've had my fill of ocean recently. But there is something about the opulent Americana that satisfies some appetite. I can manufacture happiness anywhere, but it comes easily here.

At least until I arrive home and find the garage doors are open. Apparently the real estate agent is showing the house. Yes, that is Carol's job and I asked her to do it, but I'm displeased to come across strangers traipsing through my rooms.

I pay the driver and make my way up the precipitous garage stairs. Passing the wine cellar door, I make a mental note to compare what's left in inventory with the list I made after a break-in convinced me extra caution was required. I've done everything I could externally — updated the alarm system and hired a security service — but Carol does have access. So does Charlie, the university student I hired to play boy Friday after my accident. He still checks on the house from time to time, and will until it sells.

That possibility seems more concrete when I crest the main floor landing and overhear the current prospects and their agent talking bottom-line price. "I work for the seller," says Carol, stating the obvious. "The best I can tell you is to put in an offer. But properties like this are few and far in between, and what she's asking is more than fair, so I don't think she'll budge much."

"Ahem." I announce my presence. "I won't budge at all. I'm quite fond of this place, and in no hurry to sell."

"Oh!" Carol startles. "I, um . . . didn't expect you." She is cool, and likely displeased with my frankness.

"Just a short visit." I redirect the dialogue toward the potential buyers, a thirty-something couple, couture-dressed and quite obviously showing off expensive jewelry. Silicon Valley is my guess, old money or tech-built new. Either way, I'm not impressed. "Hello. I'm Tara Lattimore.

I'm happy to answer any questions you might have."

Carol introduces the couple — Peter and Julie Baird. They follow me into the living room, tossing out relatively benign inquiries. How long have I lived here? What about the neighbors? Why do I want to sell? Now Julie asks, "Who did the interior?"

"My decorator was Sandra Bloomberg, but I did the actual design work." I glance around the room, which looks a bit naked sans my favorite artwork, already hanging at the lake. Still, my ego inflates. I love the look we created.

"Ah. I see."

Hardly the compliment I expected. "Would you like Sandra's number?"

"Oh, no. I'd bring in my own person, someone intelligent and quirky. But thank you."

I hate her. Instantly. Sincerely. Would strangling be too severe?

Peter seems to intuit my reaction. "You've got a beautiful home. We'll definitely talk it over." He tugs his wife toward the kitchen, where the two real estate agents have been conversing quietly.

The idea of *Julie* defacing my house makes me livid. If she wants the opportunity, she'll have to pay for it. I reach for my phone, send Carol a text: *Tell the Bairds we just got a full-price offer.*

I hear the chime of her cell in the next room. It takes a minute to get her response: *We did?*

Back at her, a straight-out: *No.*

Game on, Julie.

I wait for them to leave, then claim my kitchen. Charlie has diligently scouted the farmers' markets for me, delivering everything I need to make eggplant parmigiana, plus a loaf of bakery-fresh bread. He also left a couple of bottles of a lovely Sangiovese sitting on the counter. I open one, pour a glass, and consider dinner.

The dish must be served straight from the oven, but I can do the prep work now. As I slice Spanish onions, I'm reminded of the first time Cavin visited here, just a few days beyond the dawn of this year. We'd had two dates at Tahoe after my accident. He'd been called into the city to deal with Eli's headmaster, and stopped by. It was the first night I cooked for him. He brought Cristal champagne and ended up spending the night. We hardly knew each other then. How much do we know each other now?

Once the tomatoes, onion, carrot, and garlic are simmering, I slice the eggplants, arrange them in a baking dish, and grate fresh Parmesan. And now a low pulse in my knee signals it's time for another painkiller. Cavin left me with Percodan, but I opt for ibuprofen instead. The last thing I want to encourage is dependency.

Cassandra and Charlie arrive a little after six. When they ring the intercom, the security camera shows them all over each other and giggling about it. Interesting couple, my socialite best friend and the cash-strapped college kid who originally struck me as gay. I buzz them in, and up they come, bringing the party with them.

"Sidecars?" suggests Cassandra, who holds a bottle of Prunier cognac, to pair with Charlie's Solerno blood orange liqueur.

"Why not?" I amble over and give her a hug. "Charlie, would you mind bartending? Oh, and could you please sprinkle the bread crumbs over the eggplant and put it into the oven? Twenty minutes on the timer." I take Cassandra's arm, steer her into the living room. "I see you and Charlie are still, uh . . . enjoying each other."

She plops onto the sofa and I sit on the adjacent chair. "Oh yes. Such youthful enthusiasm! How about you? I take it your honeymoon was enjoyable?"

"Major understatement. Have you ever been to Alaska?"

"Um, no. A nice, mellow Caribbean cruise would be my style. But then, you've always been more the rugged adventurous type."

That draws an amused chuckle. "Yeah, rugged. But even if that's true, I'm afraid my adventurous days are over for a while. Seems I might have reinjured my knee."

"Oh, shit. Too much rough sex?"

She's joking. So why do I feel like she's been peeking in my bedroom windows or maybe through a bike helmet viewfinder? I parry, "No, nothing as fun as that. Most likely I pushed the rehab a little too hard."

"You'd better slow down, girl."

I roll my eyes. "I just got married. I've already slowed down considerably."

"Yeah, and how has that worked out for you in the past?"

Depends on how you look at it. My first husband, Raul, hit a tree skiing. Despite my accidental role in his death — spiking his cocoa so he'd nap rather than flirt with his young ski instructor — I'll always value the leg up he gave me. Without his intervention, I might still be stripping in Las Vegas. Instead, he gifted me with a college education and an extremely large trust fund, plus the knowledge to invest wisely and form a long-term financial plan that continues to suit me well.

Jordan, husband number two, is currently serving federal time for some underhanded deals he made as a US senator. Glad I divorced the cheating rat well before I might have been implicated. Instead, I turned him in. He should've known better than resorting to blackmail to try and force my silence. I'm only vindictive when cornered.

Finally, Finn, whose punishment for infidelity was the community property problem divorce brings. His generous settlement, which included all equity in this house, was stimulated by his need to eliminate controversy. He was taking his company public at the time, and having founded it on "Christian principles," leaving his wife for a younger woman — one who happened to be pregnant with twins — wouldn't have played well on that stage.

Twenty years of failed marriages has left me older, wiser, and wealthier, and that's what I tell her.

"I still think you're crazy to marry again. Marriage is like slow death."

Charlie interrupts, drinks in hand. "Dinner's in the oven, the bread is sliced, and the table is set. Let's get buzzed!"

The conversation segues to Inside Passage scenery and aerial glacier landings. Charlie's grandfather, we learn, is a stellar fly fisherman, and the two of them have long planned a trip into the Alaska interior to catch some trophy-size rainbow trout.

"I thought farmers' markets were the extent of your outdoorsmanship."

Charlie grins. "Never judge a man by his suave demeanor."

"I'll try to remember that."

The timer sounds. We move to the table and are halfway through our eggplant when I get the text from Carol: *Just heard from the Bairds' agent. They came in at 5.25M.*

Little shivers creep up my spine — the thrill of upping the ante. I text: *Tell them the other buyer countered, too. I'll preempt for 5.5.*

I apologize for the interruption, then explain, "That was my Realtor. I got an offer."

"Full price?" asks Cassandra.

"Better than. Quite a bit better, in fact."

"Aw," says Charlie. "I was hoping it would take a while to sell this place."

"Who says it's sold?"

"You're not taking it?" Cassandra is incredulous.

I shake my head. "I asked for more."

"Jesus. How can you take a chance on losing that kind of money?"

"It's a bluff, Charlie. You watch. They're

still at the table."

"Remind me never to play poker with you."

"The problem with any game of chance is you must have the ability to keep betting until you win."

We skip dessert, unless you count sidecars, and since we've almost emptied the bottles they brought, I send for Lyft to take them home. Once I've locked up behind them, I take a moment to touch base with Cavin. Funny he didn't call. Oh, wait. There's a text: *Arrived safely.*

That's it?

His cell goes to voice mail, so I try the home number. It's Eli who answers, "Hey, Mom."

"Your mom is in Dubai, remember?"

"Okay, Stand-in Mom."

Close enough, I suppose. "May I please speak with your father?"

"He's not here."

"Do you know where he is?"

"Nope. He *was* here, I guess. When we got back from the store, his suitcase was next to the door. But no sign of Dad."

"Okay, well, tell him I called and I think I'll be vacating Russian Hill very soon."

"Ah. That's too bad. I love that place. In fact . . ." He lowers his voice. "Wish I was there with you right now. I could give you a foot rub while we watched the fog licking the bay. But since I'm here instead, try to have a great night without me."

"I'll do my best."

The echo of Charlie's earlier comment is a bit unsettling, as is the innuendo.

Truthfully, Eli is maddening. I'm generally good at reading people, but that kid is perplexing, not to mention brilliant at wordplay. At seventeen, he can almost hold his own with me. It will be interesting to see how he matures.

Suddenly, unreasonably lonely, I decide another drink couldn't hurt so I finish off the cognac, with Lithium station grunge and Henry Miller for company. Still no word from my husband, so I message him: *Where are you?*

Rather than trek upstairs for a last night in my memory-laden bed, I settle on the couch, with the window above it cracked to let in a trickle of the mist-drenched San Francisco night.

Mist.

Fog.

Licking.

As my eyes close, it's Eli I'm thinking about.

.

FOUR

The alcohol allowed deep sleep, sans dreams, or at least any I remember. I must have spaced the drinks far enough apart for my body to metabolize them well, because I wake refreshed, and with no hint of hangover. It does take a minute to remember where I am and why I'm sleeping on a couch, very much alone. That doesn't bother me. I like my solo energy.

The morning brings the expected news, and better. Not only did the Bairds say okay to the 5.5 million, but they also agreed to handle the closing costs. This brings both a sense of immense satisfaction and a "holy crap" moment when I consider the implications of letting go.

It lets Finn off the hook for this mortgage, and we can cut ties completely, something that benefits him and his barely beyond-adolescent wife.

I'll likely never again live on Russian Hill.

The only real property I'll own will be the community property Cavin and I will share.

The last makes me a little queasy. Regardless, I told Carol I'd preempt for that price; they matched it and then some. The one thing I won't do is renege.

I wander through the house. What will I do with the furniture? Store it, I guess. Funny, because as much as I would have thought I cared about this stuff, I don't really, despite the fact I picked it out personally. It suits my taste, but I'm not attached to it at all. Something shifts inside me, and in a sudden unsettling instant, I am a stranger here. I want to leave today.

When I reach for my phone to call Carol, I find Cavin's response to my message last night: *Grabbed drinks with a friend. Night got away. Love you.* Time-stamped: 2:22 a.m. The night got away, indeed.

A question crosses my suspicious mind. Two, in fact. Where did the night get away from him? Tahoe or Reno? And was this friend of his male or female?

I consider an interrogation but decide against it, and also against informing him that I have changed my travel plans. I'd rather surprise him. I stash my irritation, dial the real estate office, and ask for Carol. "I decided to go on home today. Can you have the paperwork ready this morning?"

She says she'll be over before noon. Hungry for that commission, and even splitting it with the other agent, it's going to be major, as will the capital gains tax. Better put in a call to my accountant.

Charlie arrives at ten o'clock sharp, as we arranged last night, to box the best of what's left of my cellar. He comes upstairs for the inventory list. "I brought six cartons. Think that's enough?"

"The BMW's trunk wouldn't hold much more than that. I put asterisks by the ones I'm most concerned about. Oh, FYI. Not only did the Bairds remain at the table; they also sweetened the pot."

"You're kidding me." He studies me long enough to realize I'm serious. "Remind me never to play any games with you."

"You have learned a valuable lesson. Now, if you'll excuse me, I'm going to take a shower."

Charlie heads down to handle the cellar and I enjoy lathering with familiar fragrances in the guest bathroom. When I step out of the shower, I discover I left my overnight case in the other room, so I wrap a big bath sheet around myself and go in search of clean clothes. Towel dropped on the floor, I'm just stepping into lacy panties when Charlie reappears.

He gives a low whistle. "Wow. Nice picture."

I don't really care if he sees me in the buff, so I dig for a bra and present him with a simple question. "You're all finished with the wine?"

"Six cases of vino in the trunk." He watches me fasten the hooks and eyes with undisguised interest.

Vaguely troubling. I try to divert his attention. "Tell me about you and Cassandra. You love her?"

He snickers. "Nah. I mean, I don't know. I like being with her. She's fun and hell on wheels in bed."

"Is that so?" I slip a peasant blouse over my head. "Well, I'm glad she hooked up with a nice guy."

"Nice guy? Kill me now."

"What's wrong with that?"

"A nice guy is roughly the equivalent of a decent girl. They're like comfort food. Satisfying, but in all the wrong ways."

My response is laughter, something he seems to take wrong. He crosses the floor and words materialize: "I just want to eat you."

"What are you doing, Charlie?"

He stops only inches away. "Hopefully

what you want me to?"

"What made you decide that?"

"Well, Cassandra said you sleep around, and I think you're hot, and you did let me see you naked, so . . ."

Cassandra? Really? Why would she feel the need to discuss my sex life with Charlie? I've never revealed her secrets. What else has she said about mine?

I look him straight in the eye. "Charlie, when I was single, I absolutely slept around. But never while married, at least not without tacit permission, and one of the few requirements I've ever had of lovers was that they weren't emotionally committed to someone else. I value morality, at least my definition of the word. My moral sense won't allow me to sleep with you, both because of Cavin and also because you regularly fuck my friend."

Ex-friend. I'll have a word with her later.

He takes a big step backward. "I'm sorry."

"Apology accepted."

"No hard feelings?"

"Miscues, that's all. Nothing to be pissed about. Oh, there's the intercom. Would you please buzz Carol in?"

She comes strutting upstairs wearing a suit that has seen better days and a ridiculous grin. "Congratulations! Game well played."

The only thing more irritating than her dated wardrobe is her disingenuous chatter. "Let's step over to the dining room table. May I see the paperwork, please?" It doesn't take long to absorb. "Pen?"

"But don't you want to go over —"

"I'm not new to real estate deals. Order the inspections. We can close whenever. I assume the Bairds will qualify for the financing they'll need. As soon as I know that's the case, I'll take care of moving my possessions. Anything else?"

"I guess not. But, to be honest, I've never had a client who was so self-assured."

My patience is going, going . . . "Your job is to make sure everything is copacetic, yes? I hired you because I believed you were competent, so unless you're telling me you're not, let's get on with it."

I sign the offer and send her on her way. I could still change my mind, but I won't. Indecision is no one's friend. Forward momentum, that's always been my goal. Nothing past tense is worth hanging on to.

I'd almost forgotten about Charlie, who's still sitting in the living room, waiting for a check. "Holy shit," he says. "Why were you so short with that woman?"

"Was I?"

"You were brutal."

"Nah, not even close. Curt, maybe."

"But why?" he asks.

"Some people rub me the wrong way."

"I vow to always rub you the right way. Oh, and don't take that literally."

I reward him with a smile. Start toward the office to retrieve my checkbook. Remember it's no longer here. Go in search of my purse instead. Hand him a hundred in cash and dismiss him, quite likely for the last time.

Also quite likely for the last time, I carry a cup of coffee out onto the deck, sip it as I listen to familiar sounds — the bark of my neighbor's dog, car engines fighting the steep grade, jets in and out of SFO. I won't miss any of that. What I will miss, something of great value to me, is the absolute privacy I've enjoyed, living here alone. Cassandra might have been right. Maybe I was crazy to get married again. Time will tell.

I finish my coffee, wash the mug by hand, unload the dishwasher, and put everything away, the way I would were I simply enjoying the city for the day. Then I close the window, lock the doors, and turn on the alarm system, all as if I'm just leaving on another trip instead of going home. How long will it take for Tahoe to truly replace San Francisco as "home"?

FIVE

It's Sunday, so traffic heading toward the Sierra Nevada is light. I get to Mel's a little before one, which might be good except she's not here. It's Graham who answers the door. "Come on in. They'll be home from church soon." He steps back to let me by.

As always, no love between us, it's awkward being here with Graham. I paint on my socialite fund-raiser face in favor of playing the shrew and follow him into the kitchen. "I was about to have some iced tea," he says. "Sit. Can I get you something?"

"Tea would great. No sweetener, please."

"Of course not."

I ignore the slightly disparaging tone and watch him pour two glasses from a big pitcher stamped with a smiling solar face. "Is that really sun tea?"

"Beats me." He hands me a glass, sits

across the table, and stares out the window at his golden retrievers playing in the backyard.

I wait, but when it becomes obvious that's all he's got to say, I break the silence. "So, how are things?"

Such a simple question generally nets an equally uncomplicated answer like "pretty good, thanks." Or, in the case of someone like Graham, who has probably uttered one hundred (mostly unkind) words, max, to me over the last ten years, a plain old "okay." Unreasonably, I sense a lot more coming.

He clears his throat. "Things are incredibly fucked-up right now, Tara. But thanks for asking."

How am I supposed to respond to that? "Sorry to hear it. Anything I can do?"

"Nope. I'm afraid all the money in the world can't fix some things."

Normally, I'd jump on the offensive, but something in his voice makes me pause. I study his face. Age has tempered his sharp handsome features, softened them with a few extra pounds and a network of crisscrossing channels. "Well, I don't have all the money in the world, but even if I did, I wasn't suggesting bailing you out of financial difficulty. But if I could refer you to someone or, I don't know . . . offer an ear? The figurative kind, of course."

He actually rewards the small joke with a shallow grin. "Tara, you and I have labored relentlessly to build a history of mutual distrust. Altering our relationship now would seem . . . immoral."

I have to respect his command of the English language. Too bad we don't like talking to each other. "Yeah, well, though few enough people believe this, I happen to have a strong sense of morality. . . ." Am I seriously defending that twice in one day? "So I won't offer advice again, unless you ask for it."

He lowers his gaze, starts to say something, but hesitates, and I wonder if he might actually take me up on the offer. Instead, he says, "Do you ever wonder where we'd be if things had gone differently twenty years ago?"

The question, out of the blue, takes me aback, and I struggle to find an answer. Punt, I guess. "It's my policy not to look backward, Graham."

"So, no regrets?"

"Regret is a luxury I refuse to indulge."

"Regret as luxury?"

"Anything that slows you down is a luxury. Anything that forces you to linger."

His head tilts to one side. "And that's a bad thing?"

"Not necessarily. But I've only got so much time, so if I'm going to tarry, it won't be with something painful."

He's still processing this when the garage door opens. Melody pushes inside, laughing over her shoulder. Graham and I jerk our attention away from each other and redirect our focus in her direction, something she can't help but notice. It gives her pause. Her eyes travel side to side, Graham's face to mine.

"You're back," she says simply as two of her daughters traipse in.

Graham and I both stand. He picks up his tea. "If you'll excuse me, I'm going to check on the Giants game and let you engage in woman talk."

I direct my woman talk toward the girls. "Hello, ladies. How was church?"

"Holy," jokes Suzette, setting a grocery bag down on the counter.

"Boring," adds Jessica. At just-turned-thirteen, she doubtless thinks everything is boring, though she's probably right about church.

Mel gives me an assessing once-over. "You look great. Tell me about Alaska while I fix us some lunch."

"Skipping," says Suzette.

"She's diiiiiiieting," taunts Jessica. " 'Cause she's so fat, you know."

"Join us at the table anyway, please." Mel shoos the girls to go change while she starts working on an Asian chicken salad. "So, what were you and Graham talking about?"

"Nothing much. Sun tea. Mutual distrust. He seemed . . . subdued."

"Think so? He has been distant, but that's nothing new."

"I'm going to sit, if you don't need help. I've been having knee problems."

She gestures for me to take a seat. "Bad problems?"

"Not sure yet. I'll find out when I see my doctor."

"Not too bad, I hope. I was going to ask if you wanted to hike Half Dome with me this fall."

"Half Dome? As in Yosemite?"

"Yes. I've never done it, and thought it might be a good challenge."

"Melody, you don't hike. And have you ever even been to Yosemite?"

"No. Stupid, huh? I mean, it's not so very far from here. And I have been taking some day hikes. Trying to exercise more, ward off middle-age flab."

My sister *has* shed a few pounds, and

there's something different about her demeanor, an unfamiliar air of confidence, evident in her posture. "Huh. Half Dome. You are full of surprises."

"I turn forty in October. I decided to celebrate with an adventure."

Wow. I never figured Melody for the midlife-crisis type, but if she is, she's going about it all wrong. "How about an adventure in Paris? Or Sydney? Or Monte Carlo, for Christ's sake. I mean, I love Yosemite, but jeez, Mel. If you're going to start living at forty, start living *big.*"

"Half Dome is pretty darn big, you know."

Melody, ambitious. Graham, polite. What is happening in this house? Only the kids seem semi-normal. A couple of them, anyway. The oldest is noticeably absent. "Where's Kayla?"

"You don't know?"

"If I did, would I have asked you?"

She turns her back on the napa cabbage she's been chopping, faces me, and drops her eyes level with mine. "Last I heard she was shacking up with Eli."

"What?"

"She's been at Tahoe since you left for your honeymoon."

"No one said a word to me!" Who the hell thought that would be all right? And why isn't Mel upset? "You're okay with this?"

"Look, Tara. I've got enough stress in my life. I've decided not to let things I have no control over upset my spiritual harmony."

"Spiritual harmony? Next you'll tell me you've taken up yoga."

"I have, actually, and maybe you should try it. Tapping into your inner power allows you to shed negativity from your life."

"Negativity like your daughter?"

"Exactly. Kayla's eighteen, technically an adult. I could try and influence her choices, but she doesn't have to listen to me, and in fact she didn't much listen to me before she turned eighteen. Anyway, I figure Eli is a fling, and it will fizzle once Kayla starts school next month."

The San Francisco Art Institute. Right. The college of her dreams. The one Graham and Mel can't afford to send Kayla to, but I can, so I offered to cover the insane tuition as a Christmas gift. I had to pull major strings to get her accepted, considering her less-than-stellar grades. I take a couple of deep breaths and encourage my blood pressure to lower. This situation is temporary, unless . . . "She still plans to go, right?"

Mel shrugs. "As far as I know. You'll have to ask her."

Oh, I most definitely will, and I'll make damn sure she doesn't change her mind. I went out on a very expensive limb for that girl, going as far as asking for Finn's help. He has a friend on the board, Larry Alexander, who's working to funnel my tax-deductible contribution into a scholarship for Kayla. Larry's a gold-standard connection, one I won't have severed due to my overwrought niece's infatuation with my stepson.

Jessica comes running back into the kitchen, all dressed down in comfy shorts and a T-shirt. Graham and Suzette are right on her heels. At the interruption, it comes to me. Kayla's question about Sophia. No wonder she wanted to know who she is.

"Is lunch ready?" Jessica exhales. "Strangely, 'Jesus healing lepers' talk makes me hungry."

"Jess!" exclaims Mel.

But we all smile, and the heat is off Melody, at least for now. Still, as she arranges plates on the table, the interaction between her and her husband is curious. Graham is unusually attentive and doesn't aim a single barb in my direction. Mel doesn't seem to care. Maybe she doesn't even see it, but considering the chill factor in the past, his relative warmth is disconcerting. How could she not notice?

Think I'll stir the pot a little. "Hey, Graham. Did you know Mel's planning to hike Half Dome for her fortieth?"

He has to work very hard not to let Asian chicken salad fall out of his mouth.

"What?"

"Really?" says Jessica, grinning. "That's so cool. Can we go camping, too?"

"Oh, a family trip. Even better," I tease.

Melody shoots me an evil glare. "You can't miss school to go camping, Jess. Anyway, I haven't made any solid plans yet. Just considering."

"Yosemite is gorgeous in October. Perfect weather. No crowds to speak of, not even on weekends." I'm not sure why I feel the need to work Graham up, which is absolutely the net effect of this exchange. Maybe I really do like him better when we're trading insults. Old habits die hard.

His expression is priceless. Half confusion. Half irritation. I expect a forward assault. Instead, he retreats. "Well, let me know when you make up your mind." He returns to his lunch in silence.

"Hey, before I go, I've got Alaska souvenirs for everyone. Be right back."

I left them in a bag by the door. Tees for the girls. A shot glass for Graham. And an unusual sweater for Melody. July is the wrong time of year in Sacramento to try on wool, but Mel goes to do exactly that while Suz and Jessica admire the sparkly killer whales on their shirts and Graham studies the logo on his glass.

"Yukon Kate's House of Ill-repute. Is this a personal recommendation?"

The girls miss the joke. I go with it. "Absolutely. I was in charge of auditions."

He actually laughs, and now I'm creeped out. I believe his psychosis is showing. Timing it perfectly, Melody returns, looking slim and svelte in musk ox. Graham rewards her with a wolf whistle. "Those workouts are paying off."

Mel ignores the remark completely and directs her comment toward me. "I never knew wool could be so soft. Almost makes me wish for winter." Says the woman who wears a thick down powder suit to ski and still gripes about the snow.

"I'm glad you like it." I glance at my watch. "Better go. Still have a drive ahead. I'll let you know what the doctor says about my knee and we can discuss October. Walk me to my car?"

"Tara, it's ninety-five degrees out there. I'll melt in this sweater."

True enough. "Okay. I'll text you."

Heat trails, in fact, shimmer off the asphalt. I start my car and crank up the air-conditioning, and while I wait for it to cool, I message Melody. *Srsly. What's going on with Graham and you? That was a compliment, you know.*

She must have been waiting, because the reply comes right away. *Too little, too late. Fuck Graham.*

Did my sister just say "fuck"?

For two decades, Melody has defined her life by her marriage. Her husband and children have meant absolutely everything, and stability was her prime objective. After the chaos of our childhood, I understood that.

Even choosing a career as a technical writer instead of a journalist or novelist was all about playing it safe. Mel has always loved words, especially poetry. That is one of the few things we have in common. That and music, our childhood escape when our unstable mother was in one of her evil moods, brought us closer together.

Early marriages put us on separate trajectories, but I've done my best to support her in whatever ways I could, with or without Graham's blessing. I've also encouraged her to take chances, especially if they added excitement to her staid existence.

Still, our annual ski trip has historically been the most audacious outing of her year. So, hiking Half Dome? Improbable. And the whole "fuck Graham" thing?

Impossible.

Six

There are several routes from Sacramento into the Tahoe Basin. I choose the most direct between Mel's and home, turning off the freeway in Truckee and heading south on Highway 267. Passing the Northstar ski resort, I can't help but recall the last time I went this way, a few months ago.

Melody was driving me to my scheduled knee surgery at Barton Memorial Hospital, and we'd been discussing Kayla's illicit activities, including her marijuana habit. "Yes, I've smelled it on her before but have tried to ignore it," Mel admitted. "I'm sure it's just a phase, and besides, to tell you the truth, she's easier to get along with when she's a little buzzed."

That was so unlike my sister, or at least my concept of her, that I had to rethink what I knew about her and came to the conclusion that it's impossible to know anyone completely. We all have our skeletons, and they don't always rattle their bones loudly enough to draw outside attention. I'd really like to peek in Mel's closet right now, just to see what's jangling in there.

She's alluded to problems with Graham for a while, and considering his usual surly demeanor, I've always supposed the fault to be his. His recent spare-time activities — starting a band, weekend gigs, not to mention a solo trip to Las Vegas — indicated some sort of midlife adjustment, at least to my suspicious mind. But what if it's Mel who's reassessing? Trading the tried-and-true for risk taking? It's hard to picture.

The changes in her are enigmatic, really. On one hand, she started attending church regularly a few years ago, after refusing religion for most of her adult life. On the other, apparently she sanctions her daughter not only sleeping around but also moving into my stepson's bedroom for the summer. Will the real Melody Ann Schumacher please raise your hand?

As I'm dropping down the hill into Kings Beach, another part of my Kayla-centric conversation with my sister surfaces. I said I assumed, with or without marijuana, the girl had enough sense to use birth control. "She's been on Depo-Provera for almost two years now," said Mel. "One shot. Twelve weeks of protection."

Wonder when she last visited her doctor. A pregnancy now would be a most unwelcome development.

Summer tourist traffic chokes the highways. It's bumper-to-bumper, sightseer speed, frustration building with every mile. I tune into a mellow radio station, try to relax, and remind myself that only a few short months ago, I was still a visitor here, too. I'm sure I pissed off my fair share of locals, putting along and gawking at the lake view. It's as stunning as ever — aquamarine closer to the rocky shoreline, emboldened to indigo out where the water grows mountain deep. But I've seen it before.

By the time I get home, I'm a downed live wire, sparking irritation. The feeling subsides a little when I turn off the highway and onto the road that winds up the hill opposite the lake, snaking through tall Douglas firs and sugar pines. I roll down the window and inhale the sharp sweet scent of conifers, signaling I've arrived.

This is definitely not San Francisco, a shiny, diverse city that can't be ignored when you're there. Its storied history surrounds you, enfolds you. Sometimes it swallows you.

Each neighborhood wears it differently but reflects the influx of immigrants and American settlers drawn to California opportunity.

Some of those people passed by here, crossing the Sierra on their migrations. Few enough stayed, and those who did were tough. Today, Lake Tahoe boasts no real cities, just small towns dotting its shores. Tourists flock to the area seasonally for winter and summer recreation, which is why the locals prefer spring and autumn.

We live in Glenbrook, which is more neighborhood than town. It's so not Russian Hill, where the houses are tall, relatively narrow, and sandwiched closely between the neighbors. Our home is wide, with street-level parking on the top floor of two, rather than at the foot of three. Its sprawl is probably close, square-footage-wise, to what I enjoyed in San Francisco. But rather than modern, this place defines "Tahoe chic," with log pillars, cedar siding, river rock accents, and windows that look through the forest down to the lake on the south side, away from the road. And the wooded property offers plenty of space between the people who live in either direction and us. I enjoy the breathing room.

I pull into the driveway, where Eli's Hummer is carelessly parked too far toward center. I manage to wrangle the Beamer into the narrow slot he left for me, but I can barely squeeze out the door. We'll have to come up with a better system. Oh, I know. Eli can park on the street.

Good thing I'm not expecting a fancy welcome, because no one greets me at all. "Hello?" I call once I'm on the far side of the threshold. "I'm home."

Nothing.

I can hear the bass of Eli's music downstairs, too loud for him to have heard the meager sound of my voice. And if he and Kayla happen to be "busy," I'm sure I'd be ignored anyway. "Cavin? Andrew?"

Zilch. No response from my husband, nor from his dad.

Annoying.

I carry my purse back to the master bedroom, find it neat and the bed made, but no sign of Cavin, who's not in his office, either. Or outside, at least not anywhere I can see from the deck. I go to the head of the stairs, yell down, "Is anyone here?"

No answer.

So, fine. I'll check the lower level, even though I hate going down there. It's so . . . so . . . boys-in-the-basement, with Eli's room, the game room, and two guest rooms, which have only housed Andrew as far as men go, all below. The music grows louder as I descend, some dubstep mix that wouldn't be so bad at a lower volume. I knock on Eli's door. "You in there?"

I expect some response. A slow shuffle across the floor. The creak of bedsprings. Something. Anything. But no. Is he (are they) asleep, this time of day? Mid-act? Wearing earplugs? Should I go ahead and peek inside? Oh hell. Why not?

Empty.

Unreasonably, anxiety prickles. The paranoia of a few months back, when I was getting threatening anonymous messages, dissipated once their source — my crooked politician ex-husband — was discovered and sent to prison on an unrelated charge. I have nothing to be afraid of. So why the sudden trepidation?

I explore the floor. Every room is devoid of human presence, though it looks like someone was enjoying the pool table earlier. Mostly drained beer bottles trash the wet bar, along with paper plates littered with cracker crumbs and bits of cheese. Okay, obviously some alien spacecraft happened over and decided this totally dysfunctional family was worthy of probing. Screw it. They'll either beam back down intact or I've got the house to myself.

Back upstairs I trudge. It's wine time for sure. I'm in the kitchen, opening a bottle, when Cavin and Andrew come through the front door, carrying groceries. "You're home," says Cavin. "I didn't expect you until tomorrow."

"Thought I'd surprise you."

"Not a bad thing," comments Andrew. "Good to keep a man on his toes."

Indeed.

Cavin deposits four shopping bags on the counter before welcoming me with a kiss. "Meant to get to the store earlier, but there was a Yankees game on, and Dad's a fan, so we watched downstairs while we shot some pool."

"Hard to be a Yankees fan some days," complains Andrew as he sets his own bags down and starts to empty them. "Which is why I'm also a Padres fan."

Why did I assume both my SUV and Cavin's Audi were parked in the garage? I never even looked. Sloppy detective work. I'd make a terrible PI. "Can I pour either of you gentlemen a glass of wine?"

"I'll handle it," offers Cavin. "You relax. How's the knee?"

"Could be worse."

"Roger managed to squeeze you in on

Wednesday afternoon, and I scheduled a preappointment MRI, CT scan, and X-rays for Tuesday, so we'll have some hard data back."

A sigh escapes. "I'm seriously not ready for more poking and prodding."

"Don't blame you. But let's take the cautious route."

I sit on a bar stool at the kitchen island, where I can watch the men work. As Andrew replenishes the refrigerator, Cavin fills three glasses and puts one in front of me before starting dinner. Steaks, it seems. "Where are Eli and Kayla?" I ask.

Cavin doesn't even inquire how I know she's here. "Downstairs, I think. Sounds like it, anyway."

"They're not, actually. When I got home and no one seemed to be here, I went looking for signs of life. I didn't see them."

"Strange. Pretty sure they were here when we left."

"They were," says Andrew. "When I changed my shoes I could hear them talking. It was a rather heated discussion."

"Hope he isn't out hiding her body in the woods," jokes Cavin.

"Or she isn't hiding his," Andrew counters.

"Touché."

"Before they get back from wherever, would either of you like to explain why she seems to be living here?"

"Not living, exactly," says Cavin. "Just hanging out for a few weeks."

Andrew blushes. "My fault completely. Eli told me you knew about their relationship and didn't have a problem with it."

"No, it's not your fault," argues Cavin. "You know how convincing Eli can be, Tara. Dad didn't have a chance."

"And no one thought to inform me? I had to find out from my sister."

"I didn't know myself until this morning. By the time I got home last night everyone was already in bed."

"Really. And what time was that?"

He eyes me warily. "Around two."

Clearly, this conversation could deteriorate quickly, so Andrew says, "If you'll excuse me, I'll clean the grill."

Once he's out of earshot, Cavin asks, "You're not angry because I went out last night, are you?"

Am I? Why should I be? If I wanted to go out, I would. Why should it be any different for my husband? I soften. "Not unless you mortgaged your soul to cover your blackjack chips."

"My soul remains debt free." He offers an

awkward grin. "Except to you, of course. On a scale of one to ten, how mad are you about Kayla?"

"Maybe seven. I realize it's a temporary arrangement, at least if she follows through with school, and if she doesn't, I'll probably bury her myself."

"You almost sound serious."

"I almost am. I value my privacy and dislike sharing my possessions, except by explicit invitation."

Generosity isn't my best thing.

"I'll keep that in mind."

Cavin is lighting the grill when Eli and Kayla come wandering up through the trees. They're holding hands, but her body language tells me she hasn't exactly forgiven whatever his infraction was, and when they climb the back stairs to the deck, I can see her eyes are puffy and red.

Eli spots me on the lounge chair and disengages from Kayla. He stomps across the deck, and for about the hundredth time I wonder how someone that slender can weight his feet so heavily. He bends and his lips whisper across my forehead. "Welcome home."

The gesture catches my breath. "It's good to be here." As he straightens, I can't help but notice my niece's icy glare. "You all

66

right, Kayla?"

"Fine." But she stares at her feet, which I interpret as a signal that she isn't okay at all.

"You want to talk?" I nudge.

"Not really."

"I think we should. Let's go inside."

"Take it easy on her," says Eli. "She's fragile right now."

"Whose fault is that?" she snaps, and I'm almost surprised when she trails me back into the office. I sit behind the desk, and she takes the comfortable rocker. "What happened?"

Even in the failing light, her sudden blush is obvious. "He . . . he . . . wanted me to do . . . stuff I didn't want to do. When I wouldn't, he said he was going to drive down to Reno to see his ex, because she'd do anything he wanted, and maybe I should go with him to observe how it's done. So then we had a big fight and I ran out the door and he came after me."

"So you know about Sophia, then?"

Understanding dawns. "*That's* who Sophia is?"

"Yes. You still didn't know?"

She shakes her head. "I thought maybe Sophia was . . ."

"What?"

"Code word for you."

"Oh my God, no. Why would you imagine that?"

"One time he told me 'Sophia' taught him to appreciate older women. When I asked who she was he said to ask his dad."

"I still don't understand."

She draws herself up, tall and stiff-backed. "You must have noticed Eli's crushing on you. He talks about you all the time."

"That may or may not be, Kayla, but I'm no threat to you. Sophia, on the other hand . . ." I shrug.

"So, what does she have to do with Uncle Cavin?"

I give her the short-and-not-so-sweet version.

"Seriously? That's sick!"

"It is what it is. Look. Is it possible you and Eli simply aren't compatible? I mean, you hooked up awfully quickly."

"Sometimes the best hookups are fast hookups."

"Define 'best.' "

Zero hesitation. "Hot. Fun. No strings."

"Okay, no strings. So why bother to fight? Walk away."

"Sounds simple enough, yeah, except sometimes you fall for the guy. That doesn't always happen to me, but when it does, he's always the bad-boy type."

Eli definitely qualifies.

"But bad boys generally don't want commitment. They want no-strings hot fun."

"Yeah, but I thought Eli was different. He's so together for his age."

"Together? Are you referring to the Eli who lives downstairs?"

"Uh-huh. He's got his future mapped, unlike the other guys I've gone out with, and they're all older than Eli. At least he doesn't want to serve lattes forever, or deal drugs to get by."

"Kayla, the last time I spoke with Eli about his career goals, he was vacillating between professional hacker and gigolo."

A bit of a stretch, but she gets the point and grimaces. "He said you were trying to convince him to go to Le Cordon Bleu. But he's focused on that interdisciplinary studies program at Sierra Nevada College. It sounds pretty awesome. If art wasn't my thing, I'd consider it myself."

"You're talking about the one that combines ski resort management and outdoor adventures leadership, yes? But you've never cared about snow or winter recreation. I thought you hated cold weather."

"It's never too late to learn to snowboard. And with the right person to keep me warm inside, subzero outside would be okay, especially if it meant being with someone I love."

I look her straight in the eye. "Kayla, you aren't giving up on the Art Institute, are you? Because, even discounting my very large investment, I'd be extremely upset if you sacrificed your dreams because of a guy. Any guy, let alone one who tries to coerce you to engage in sexual activities you're not comfortable with."

"Don't worry, Aunt Tara. I plan to show up for orientation right on time." She cocks her head, perhaps listening for a spy in the hall. No sign of intrusion, she lowers her voice. "You know, if he'd been patient and hadn't made that disgusting threat, I might have gone along with his little game eventually. Outdoor adventure may not be my thing, but I'm usually up for the indoor variety."

"Whoa. Too much information, Kayla."

And inappropriate, considering our relationship and the fact that we've had intimate conversations only a time or two.

Worse, now she's got me wondering exactly what Eli's little game was.

SEVEN

It's a sterling Sierra evening, the sun just below the treetops as Cavin and Andrew put the steaks on the grill, which is fragrant with smoking hickory chips. We'll eat outside, on the big redwood table at the edge of the deck, overlooking the forest floor. With the earlier upset settled, Kayla and Eli are demonstrably affectionate as they shuttle silverware, plates, bread, and salad from inside. An outsider looking in would think we're the perfect extended family.

We are all well practiced at disguising dysfunction.

I have to admit the small gathering is kind of nice — too many people to accommodate bickering, but not enough to make conversation impossible. I rarely experience this particular dynamic and it's so comfortable that I'm pretty sure it won't last long.

The meat cooks quickly, and when Cavin sets a sizzling platter midtable, Kayla remarks, "God, those smell good. Glad I gave up on the vegan thing."

"How long did you go?" asks Andrew.

"Two weeks. Did you know veggie burgers stink?"

"I could never go without meat," says Eli. "I am a carnivore. . . ."

The word flashes me back to Stanley Park and the twisted game of hide-and-seek. Is cannibalism genetic?

A weak howl lifts me from my reverie. In real time, Eli has proven his appetite for meat by biting Kayla's neck hard enough to draw her vocal protest, which he discounts. "Yum," he says. "Delicious."

Cavin flashes a disapproving frown. "If you must eat your girlfriend, please do it in private."

Everyone freezes, not quite sure if he's serious or not, or if the double entendre was purposeful. But then he laughs, freeing us to follow suit, and I change the subject.

"Kayla says you've decided to apply to SNC for sure, Eli. Have you given any more thought to Squaw Valley Academy?"

"No. Why would I?"

"Just seems like a better choice for senior-year college prep."

Not to mention it's a boarding school.

"Don't worry, Mom. I've got it handled. I

72

talked to my counselor before Whittell let out for summer. You'll approve of my schedule because it will keep me very busy next year. Calculus. Forensics. AP English. US government. And psych."

"Psychology? Still doing research?"

Before the honeymoon, he loaned me a book he'd been reading: *Confessions of a Sociopath.*

He smiles at the inside joke. "Self-help, remember?"

Eli and I chuckle, mystifying the rest of the table, if I'm reading their faces correctly. "Anyway," I interject, "we have some time to talk about school. The next few weeks will be jam-packed, though, between doctor visits and tying up loose ends in San Francisco." I turn to my husband. "Oh. Forgot to tell you. Russian Hill sold. I signed the offer this morning."

Cavin congratulates me, then adds, "I expected it to take longer."

"Me, too." This is not the time or place to discuss the details.

"But it will still be yours for a month or so, won't it?" asks Eli.

"Something like that. Why?"

"I was hoping Kayla and I could spend a few days there before she starts school. Any chance of that?"

"Doubtful. Even if the timing worked out, I couldn't take a chance on you calling up some of your old Athenian friends for a party."

He might have gotten kicked out of the Bay Area academy, but that doesn't mean he isn't connected to some of his former classmates. In fact, I know he's still in contact with Cassandra's son, who was in trouble at the same school for drinking and cyberbullying. Taylor even came to our wedding.

"Like I would?"

"Eli, if you trashed the house preclosing —"

"You really have to learn to trust me." He reaches across Kayla, resting his wrist on her forearm as he strokes my hand in a quite intimate way.

She tosses her arm, effectively flinging his hand away from mine. "Don't throw that word around, Eli. Trust is something you earn."

"Trust is something you cultivate," Cavin corrects. "You can earn it short-term, but maintaining it takes dedication."

"Ahem. Please pass the salad," I say, mostly as a way to keep everyone's hands in their proper place. Around it comes, and as it does, I continue, "Anyway, I have to figure out what to do with the furniture. Storage for now, I guess."

"What about the 'Vette?" asks Kayla eagerly.

"She's giving it to me," answers Eli.

The smile falls from Kayla's face. "No way. You already have a nice car."

"I am absolutely *not* giving the Corvette to Eli, or to you, either."

"But I need a car." Kayla actually tips her lower lip into a pout.

"Not in San Francisco. It's a hard city to drive in. But even if you did, it wouldn't be that one. No, I'll have to sell it."

"Hey, Dad . . ."

"Absolutely not, Eli. Your mother, stepdad, and I discussed what would be the best kind of vehicle for you, and chose the Hummer because we figured all that metal wrapped around you was a good idea. Fiberglass? Not so much."

"Carbon fiber, actually. They haven't been fiberglass for years," I say. "But your father's point is valid. The statistics are grim enough for boys your age dying in automobile accidents. The Hummer is a tank, but it's relatively safe."

"But —"

Andrew clears his throat loudly, circumventing the pending argument. "How much do you want for it? I always told myself when I hit a certain age I'd treat myself to a sports car. I've got a finite amount of time left. If not now, when?"

"I looked at Kelley Blue Book a few weeks ago, when I first thought about selling it. It's worth forty-five thousand. I'd take forty from you."

The grin that pops up on his face could only be described as sly. "Thirty-eight?"

"Sold."

"You don't want to counter?" Andrew seems genuinely disappointed.

"What's a couple grand between friends? Anyway, the car served a purpose at the time I bought it, but I'm beyond my midlife-crisis phase now, thanks to your son."

"That's very good to hear," says Cavin. "But should you consider reentry, please let me know and I'll work very hard to change your mind."

"Well, I'm glad the Corvette will be in good hands. Now all we have to do is get you to San Francisco. Can you change your return ticket home?"

"It'll cost me, but not as much as the car's costing me. And the drive down the coast home will be worth it. Wait. It is a convertible, right? And what color is it?"

"Silver over midnight blue. And yes, it's a

convertible. Are you sure you don't want to look at it before you commit?" I'd never buy a car sight unseen. "Tell you what. You drive it on home and send me a check if you like it."

"And if you don't like it, it's mine," says Eli.

He's only half joking.

As the light fades, the evening chills and we move inside. Kayla and Cavin do the dishes and Andrew goes to call the airline, leaving me alone with Eli, who sits next to me on the couch, close enough so his knee kisses mine. I suppose I could move. But, then again, why?

Apparently he wants to talk semiprivately because he forces his voice very low. "So, are you mad about Kayla and me?"

"Why would I be mad?"

"I don't know. I just thought it was a possibility."

"Listen, Eli. I will definitely be pissed if Kayla doesn't start school, but your relationship doesn't bother me."

He looks at me earnestly. "You're sure?"

"Do you *want* me to be angry?"

"Kind of, yeah. At least a little jealous." He brushes my cheek with the back of his hand. Just the barest touch, for only a second.

Highly inappropriate.

Sexy as hell.

I meet his gorgeous eyes — the gray-dappled green ones he inherited from his father and, as I noticed at dinner, his grandfather, too. "Jealousy is reserved for people with low self-esteem. Does that sound like me?"

"Not on your worst day." He taps my knee gently with his. "It's awesome you're home. It was boring as hell without —"

"All finished!" Kayla interrupts, hustling into the room and wiping what's left of the dishwater on her shorts. But now she takes notice of the unique energy passing between Eli and me, not to mention his proximity. Her smile dissolves. "What's going on? Are you talking about me?"

Eli starts to say no, but this might as well be out in the open. "Yes, in fact, we were. Eli asked if I was angry about your relationship."

"Oh. Well, are you?"

"No. I mean, I was miffed that he invited you to stay here without discussing it with his dad and me first. But if the two of you hit it off, who am I to complain? Especially since it doesn't seem to bother your parents."

"Yeah, well, they're all wrapped up in their

own problems. I wasn't sure they'd even noticed I left." Kayla starts in his direction and Eli wisely stands to let her take his place on the sofa. But when he moves into the adjacent chair, she plops into his lap.

I wait until they arrange their various body parts to ask, "So what's up with your mom and dad?"

"Beats me. Regular married-people stuff, I guess. Either they're arguing or they aren't talking at all."

Eli snorts. "Marriage, defined. Kick me if I ever consider it, will you, please?"

"Oh, I don't know," I say. "Marriage has its advantages."

"Some people make it a career." Kayla sneers.

I do believe she was referring to me.

Andrew crests the stairs. "No problem switching the ticket, and they only charged an arm. I get to save the leg for next time."

"Text me your flight information and I'll arrange for Charlie to pick you up at the airport, take you over to the house, and let you into the garage."

"I'll drive you to the airport in Reno," volunteers Eli.

Kayla glares. "And I'll come, too, to make sure there are no unauthorized stops along the way." She stands, stretches her hand toward Eli. "Let's take a walk before it gets dark."

Eli agrees, and as they head toward the door, he slips an arm around her waist, dangles his hand along her outer thigh. In turn, she encircles his back with her arm and they bump hips. The gesture reminds me how young they are and stirs a murmur of envy. While there's much to be said for experience, discovery is more exciting.

Andrew notices me studying their departure. "Interesting couple, eh? Dissimilar halves that somehow create a workable whole."

"Dissimilar, definitely. Workable, I'm not so sure. But hey, youth is all about making mistakes. Too bad so many kids insist on big ones, especially when it comes to partnering."

"True. But sometimes they get lucky. I did, at least for a while."

Ooh. He opened the door. "How old was your wife when she died? I mean, if you don't mind talking about her."

"Not at all. She was thirty-six."

"Wow. So young. I'm sorry."

"Don't be. It was a long time ago." He closes his eyes. "She was something when we first met — a truly amazing girl. Why she chose a boring guy like me, I don't know, but I was determined to keep her. I'm happy for the time we had, although things got bad near the end." Now he straightens, blinks. "I take it you know about Maureen's mental health issues?"

"Yes. Cavin told me."

I don't mention the fact that a private investigator informed me first or that I had to pry the details out of my husband, who encouraged me to hire the PI to look into his background before I agreed to marry him. Of course, he'd previously secured the services of one Dirk Caldwell to investigate me, something I found out about quite by accident. The timing of that, very early in our relationship, raised some suspicions. (Did he fall for *me* or my money?) But Cavin swore it was only to circumvent surprises similar to those that drove him and Sophia apart. I came up clean. The detective I hired discovered Cavin once had a large IRS debt, now satisfied, and the fact that his mother had committed suicide.

"There was no hint of her illness until her first pregnancy," continues Andrew. "After she had Cavin, she suffered mild postpartum depression, which was successfully treated with medication. But when she got pregnant with Paul, she refused her meds, and after he was born her depression blossomed into full-blown bipolar disorder. Post-Pamela, she was never right again."

"Sounds like she shouldn't have had kids."

"Probably not. But she loved children. Especially her own, though it became impossible for them to see it. Brain chemistry is fascinating. I've often wished I'd focused my research there. We've come a long way in our understanding, but there's still a lot we don't know."

"At least we're not blaming it on demon possession anymore."

"You'd be surprised how many people still do."

"Still do what?" This time it's Cavin who's interrupting.

"Nothing," I say. Not sure he'd appreciate our discussing his mother. "Where have you been, anyway?"

"Just going over my schedule for the week. It's going to be busy."

"Well, at least I'll be out of your hair," says Andrew.

Cavin glances at his watch. "Padres and Dodgers are playing, Dad. We missed a couple of innings, but I'm game to watch the rest if Tara doesn't mind."

"Not if you don't mind me taking a bath and reading."

The deal is struck.

It Is Not the Darkness

The evening
has no teeth,
cannot rake
itself against
our skin, open
us, bleed us out,
draw infection in.

A shadow
has no claws,
cannot rend flesh
from bones, nor crush
them beneath
its weight, petrify
them into stone.

Where, then,
comes this fear,
rooted fast in childhood?
Why, when lights
go dim and soft
black curtains close,
why do young ones cry?

The moon, eclipsed,
carries no curse.
It is not the night that makes
us scream. It is the monster
caged inside, the terror

that escapes when
we open up to dream.

EIGHT

The summer glare off Idaho desert over-
whelms my eyes. I stare at the tail end of an
old Ford pickup fishtailing over the hard-
scrabble ground, moving away as fast as its
ancient engine can take it. It burps and hic-
cups, and the scent of burning oil embraces
hints of tobacco and booze. "Fuck off,
Mom," I call after it. "I prefer the company
of buzzards."

They circle overhead — huge black
wraiths, waiting. Waiting. Waiting. Patient
bone pickers. "I'm not dead yet, you bas-
tards." But it's ninety degrees out here, and
she left me without a drop of water. It won't
be long.

I start in the general direction of home.
What home, I'm not sure, only that I seem
to belong there. My feet sink in the soft
sand. That is, when they're not tripping over
the chunks of basalt and rhyolite that litter
the landscape. This must be what it's like to

be walking on the moon. And now I've got that Police song playing in my head. I sing to the vultures as I stumble along, hoping my legs don't break, either.

What's that? Coming this way. No, lurching. That's the verb I want. Lurching toward me, with arms extended, zombielike. As it nears, I can make out the face, though it's starting to rot, and that smell hits me first. "Kayla? What happened?" But she doesn't answer, just keeps moving closer, crunching on something that sounds like bones, and I can't let her touch me because I'm sure her condition is contagious. I reverse motion, but as I turn away, I notice two more figures far behind her, traversing the sand in similar fashion. One male, one female, I think, and though I can't see their features, I'm sure I know them.

I wheel.

Run.

Sprint.

Leak sweat from every pore.

I'm tempted to glance behind me but don't dare slow. I use my other senses instead.

No detectable footsteps.

No sharp intake of crypt smell.

No crunching of bones.

I must be outpacing them.

But now I hear a clunking old Ford 302 closing in on me. It passes on my right and skids to a stop, and the door jerks open. "Get in." The words exit a cavernous hole where my mother's lips used to be. The skin peels back from her jawbone, and one eye socket is vacant. The eye that remains wobbles as it stares, and I cough on a scream. Beside her on the passenger seat, what's left of our old collie, Liz, is gnawing on a very live snake whose fangs are useless against a corpse buried twenty-five years ago.

"Come on," commands Mom-zombie. "Climb in back. They'll be here any second."

I don't want to, but I do, just like when I was little, because I know things will be worse if I disobey. I swing a leg over the side of the bed, flop inside, and huddle against the cab. "Where are we going?"

"Stupid girl. To the moon." She slams the door shut, punches the gas pedal.

As the truck picks up speed, everything blurs and the heat bellows. Suddenly, we jet into the sky, arrow through the orbiting buzzards, and rise up, up, toward the pale lunar shadow. The atmosphere thins quickly and I wheeze it in until it is no more.

Fighting for oxygen in a vacuum, I feel

my lungs turn inside out, and . . .

I spring upright, desperately gulping in air and seeking substance in the present. Drapes of darkness. Silken silence. The scent of my husband, who doesn't stir within his envelope of deep sleep. A subtle throb in my knee, as if it's been fighting the sink of desert sand.

But no buzzards.

No snakes.

No walking, driving, teeth-snapping cadavers.

Another flickering nightmare set in the Idaho moonscape and starring my mother. And like most of them, as insane as it was, this one captured elements of truth. Chromosomes host some contagions.

I leave Cavin to his own dreams and creep from under the covers, into the night's embrace. There will be no sleep for a while. I tiptoe to the bathroom to pee and search for a painkiller. Ibuprofen might quiet my knee, but a taste of poppy could whisk me back into the arms of Morpheus at some point tonight. Meanwhile, I'll take my book into the living room. A soft wash of moon through the window guides my way into the hall. Once I've cleared the threshold and closed the door, the light is shuttered.

I shuffle along, mostly blind, but my ears

pick up human interaction outside. The sound trickles in through the open sliding glass door, and it takes only a few seconds to identify Eli and Kayla, having sex. They don't seem to care if someone hears them. Wonder how they'd feel about someone watching.

I should back away, hide my eyes. Instead, I'm compelled forward, moving soundlessly on bare feet. With the house steeped in shadow, moon glow spotlights the scene on the deck. Kayla is on her hands and knees, facing the forest. Eli kneels behind her — thankfully shielding the body parts that would be incestuous to view. But I can see one of his hands, knotted in her hair, pulling her head back so her face turns up toward the star-sequined sky. They perform as if on camera — his hard thrust and slow withdrawal eliciting her low growl of pleasure.

Stop watching.

Turn away.

Go back to bed.

But I can't. I'm perversely fascinated. It's not like I've never witnessed people having sex before. I mean, right out of high school I worked at a Vegas strip club, and while I never interacted that way with a customer, plenty of the girls did, often right there for all to see. But those ladies were "seasoned," to be kind, and their clients were mostly out for cheap thrills. The act, bought and paid for, tended to be drunken, fast, and dirty. Nothing I wanted to see.

This, however . . . I can't *not* watch. It's an unfolding. Raw. Unpretentious. A little clumsy, even. For all Eli's older lover claims he's "all man," the truth is he's just a boy. And though I know Kayla has been intimate with at least a couple of guys, she's every bit as inexperienced. The two are relying on instinct. Pure animal drive, like big cats called by nature to mate for the first time.

I expect Eli to finish quickly. Instead he brakes himself, more mature than I believed, coaxes Kayla onto her back. I sink to the floor as close as I can get to the door without them noticing my presence and lean against the wall, watching Eli's hands travel the length of Kayla's legs. When he reaches her thighs, he pushes them apart, burrows his face between them, and it's all I can do to swallow the moan that has lodged in my throat. I'm a sick, sad voyeur.

Lust-fueled, he enters her again, missionary-style. All lion now, he fucks hard and fast, and when her growl blossoms into the roar of orgasm, I don't need to touch myself to come, too. I catch my breath, the sound barely audible, but enough to make Eli twist his head slightly, left ear toward the open door. I can't see his face, but I suspect he's smiling. Unreasonably, I am, too.

He rolls off Kayla, lying next to her and holding her hand, and I realize I've got a small problem. Eli might suspect my presence, but I don't think Kayla does, nor should she. Slowly, quiet as a sigh, I scoot my rear end sideways along the hardwood. This proves a stealthy means of transportation, thanks in no small part to the silk of my robe. The green perfume of marijuana drifts in from outside and follows me into the hall. I have a couple of minutes to complete my escape.

Once I'm out of sight, I push myself up onto my feet, too quickly. Suddenly and forcefully, I'm reminded of the problem with my knee. Despite the lovely opioid haze I've been enjoying, pain spasms from shin to groin.

I am an idiot.

You are a voyeur.

Who knew?

I close my eyes and wait for the sizzling in my knee to subside. Eventually it does, though a quick check informs me the joint is ballooning. Ice, that's what I need, and at this point I refuse discretion. This is my home, and I'm certainly allowed a trip to the kitchen. I turn on the light in the hallway to announce my approach and allow them to cover up the essentials, and I underline the fact that I'm here by saying, quite loudly, "If you're going to smoke that stuff, the least you could do is shut the door so it doesn't stink up the house."

There is movement on the deck as Kayla tries to cover up. Eli doesn't bother and in fact is quite content to let me peek, going as far as to stand and reach for the door handle, his entire package in full view. "My bad," he says. "I thought everyone was asleep."

I try to keep my eyes above his waist, but the temptation to compare him to Cavin is massive and I succumb. Eli definitely inherited his father's exceptional asset. He smiles at my interest. Kayla, however, isn't amused. "Put some clothes on, Eli. Don't be disgusting."

But her injured look targets me.

I leave them to work it out while I locate ice. My head is in the freezer when I become aware of someone standing behind me. I extricate a gel pack, which is preferable to cubes because it will fold around my knee, working equally on all sides. Then I turn to face Eli, who is half-dressed. Thankfully, it's the shirt he's lacking.

"Sorry," he says, appearing anything but.

"About what?"

"The weed. I forgot it offends you."

I shrug. "It doesn't really offend me. I just prefer not to have an illegal substance in my home. And I'm sure your father feels the same way."

"It's not illegal anymore, and you apparently haven't discussed it with Dad. Before Nevada approved recreational use, he actually encouraged me to apply for a medical marijuana card."

Oh, that's a regular truckload of manure. "Medical marijuana for what condition, exactly?"

"Migraines. Well, cluster headaches, to be more accurate. I don't get them often, but when I do they drop me hard, and they come for consecutive days. Thus, the name."

"I know. Finn used to get them. Now, if you'll please excuse me, I need to go sit for a while."

Eli glances down at my leg, which my robe has opened enough to reveal. He parts it even farther, touches a spot just above the offending joint. "Does it hurt?"

"A little," I admit.

"Maybe you should try some weed." His

fingers tiptoe upward.

I allow them to linger on my thigh, then back away, cinch my robe closed. "Yeah, probably not. But thanks for the suggestion."

He doesn't move to let me by, so I push past him and can't help but notice how he's bulked up in the past couple of months. He must be lifting weights or something. He also wears the musk of sex. "You should take a shower."

"What for? I like how it smells. Besides, we'll do it again when we go to bed."

Why does that bother me?

I wander back to my own bed, toss both robe and gel pack, and shake my husband from whatever dreams he's wandered into. "Fuck me."

Like he has a choice.

NINE

Despite the pharmaceutical aid and a luscious round of semideviant lovemaking, sleep did not come easily last night. Cavin rolled over and dove straight back into the Land of Nod, but all I could do was lie there listening to his pillow-muffled breathing, envious of his ability to switch off whatever voices live inside his head. I probably dozed off around three. Even so, when the bed stirs at six a.m., so do I. Three hours isn't much sleep, but it will just have to do.

Cavin kisses me, goes to shower before work. I throw on an oversize shirt and some shorts, hustle into the kitchen to make coffee. I'm enjoying a cup on the deck, listening to the squawk of jays and chatter of squirrels, when Kayla comes out, sipping her own steaming mug. She sits on the next bench over. "Can I ask you something?"

"You may always ask."

"Is something going on between Eli and you?"

"What do you mean?"

She considers her approach. "He's attracted to you."

"Think so? Well, I guess I should be flattered."

Wrong answer. Her body stiffens and I swear something dark shadows her eyes. They take on the color of a gathering tornado. "Is the attraction mutual?"

The only plausible answer is stern denial. Does she expect anything else? "Why would you believe it was?"

"I don't know. Maybe if you didn't wear slinky lingerie around the house . . ."

Cat and mouse with my niece. Honey, the cat always wins. "Um, look what I'm wearing, Kayla. But if you're referring to last night, I woke from a bad dream and couldn't go back to sleep. Rather than disturb my husband, I threw on the nearest robe and went to read. I had no clue anyone else was awake, let alone smoking pot in the nude on the deck."

Her face flares scarlet, but she doesn't apologize. "Weed lowers inhibitions. I was trying to be more adventurous, remember?"

"Yes, well, I can understand that. But it's not my fault I happened to catch the tail end of your little adventure. If you're expecting privacy, a bit of caution might be prudent."

"I'll keep that in mind." Her voice is cool. "Though I might say the same thing to you, considering Eli plans to live here for a while."

"Kayla, this happens to be *my* home. How I dress or behave here is totally up to me. If that worries you, it's your problem, not mine. I certainly don't have to defend myself to you."

She doesn't answer, but her grim expression tells me she's stewing.

"Listen, Kayla. Jealousy is a quick path to implosion. You and Eli haven't been together long enough to build much trust, but it's something you'll have to work on if you want this thing to last. Believe me, I have no desire to come between the two of you. My husband takes exceptionally good care of me, and I don't tolerate infidelity within my committed relationships, on either side of the marital bed."

Her demeanor tempers. "I'm not sure monogamy is a human trait."

I have to smile at that. "It requires superior intelligence."

"Is that the secret? I thought it took sobriety."

"So if it's important to you, why do you keep hooking up with stoners?"

"Good question."

Inside, her latest stoner crests the stairs into the living room, carrying a large suitcase. He clomps into the kitchen, where Andrew joins him a few seconds later.

"Looks like they're getting ready to leave. Shall we go in?"

"We'd better. Eli will want breakfast."

Wait. What? "You do realize he's been feeding himself for years, right? In fact, he's quite the talented cook."

"I know, but I don't care, and he kind of expects —"

"Screw that, Kayla. If you want his respect, don't beg for it. Demand it. Subtly, of course. Tell him you've heard he's amazing in the kitchen, and you'd love it if he'd cook for you. In fact, you'd reward him. It's all in the way you play the game. Eli's used to winning. Turn the tables. If nothing else, it would be fun, and you've got nothing to lose."

"I could lose him."

"You could."

Choices. Brutal honesty or tempered guidance?

Eli eliminates the decision, yelling, "Hey, K-K, would you please come in here?"

My hackles lift. "K-K?"

"Cute, huh? I've never had a nickname before."

"Cute? You realize it makes you sound about three years old, right?"

And God help the person who tries to nick the name Tara.

Kayla pouts. "I like it. It makes me feel special, like he made it up just for me."

Ridiculous. "Ask him to make up your breakfast. If he does, you're special."

But when we go inside, as Kayla predicted, Eli requests, "Could you whip up an omelet? We should be out of here in twenty minutes or so."

I glance at Kayla, who shoots me a helpless look in reply, then starts toward the kitchen. "Hey, Eli. Did something happen to your hands?" I ask.

He actually studies them. "Uh, no. Why?"

"I just wondered because I've personally witnessed your culinary expertise. Is there a reason you can't whip up your own omelet?"

As always, he's got a ready answer. "Why would I want to, when I have someone who'll do it for me?"

Temper.

Inhale.

Temper.

Exhale.

I force my voice low and cool. "Eli, your utter lack of respect for Kayla disheartens me. You are quite capable of cooking your own damn breakfast, and I don't appreciate you treating her like hired help."

"It's okay," interrupts Kayla. "I don't mind."

"Fine, *K-K*. If you insist on being a doormat, I won't tell Eli to quit wiping his feet on you. But when you're choking on the dirt, remember it was your choice and don't come crying to me. Now if you'll excuse me, I need caffeine."

I push past both of them and stomp into the kitchen, where I pour a second cup.

When I turn, I find not only the offending couple but also Cavin and Andrew staring at me as if assessing whether or not I need a ride to the nearest psych ward.

The only one I look in the eye is Eli. "What?"

He shrugs. "Nothing."

"Then scrub that stinking smirk off your face or give serious consideration to boarding school." Now it's Cavin whose eyes mine meet, but he has nothing to add, so I take my coffee back outside, pausing only to tell Andrew, "Please come say good-bye before you leave. I've enjoyed spending a little time with you and hope we will find an excuse to do so again in the near future."

I sit in a wide patio chair, facing the forest so I don't have to watch Kayla play housewife. Then again, what would I expect, considering Melody is her example? Mel, who bakes bread for her family before embarking on ski trips, despite the fact that they'll all exist on fast food diets while she's gone. Mel, who roasts both a turkey and a ham for Christmas dinner because her kids love turkey and her husband claims it makes him queasy. Wonder what she's got simmering lately.

The sliding glass door opens behind me and even without turning I know it's Cavin by the sound of his footsteps and the soap scent lifting off his skin. "I've got to go. Can I do anything for you first?"

"Yes. Could you knock a little sense into your kid?"

"Hey, if I thought violence could accomplish it, I'd break out the nunchakus. Unfortunately, the kind of sense you're talking about needs to be programmed in childhood. I'm afraid it's much too late for Eli."

A huge sigh escapes me. "Oh, well. There's always poison."

Cavin lifts my hair, kisses my neck. "Just don't get caught. I like having you around. Life imprisonment would be a colossal waste of an exceptional woman."

"First, I'd die before I'd rot in prison. Second, I don't believe I've ever heard anyone actually say 'colossal' before." Good word, if a bit unwieldy, and that is an even better word. In fact, colossal things tend to be unwieldy.

"Enjoy your day, stay off that leg, and I'll see you anon. Anon — how about that word, huh?" He starts to leave, hesitates, then adds, "I might be late. Lots of catching up to do. Are you okay with making dinner, or should I bring something?"

"No worries. I just elected Eli to handle dinner. In fact, would you ask him to come out here, please?"

It takes a few minutes for the boy to comply, but finally he wanders out onto the deck. "Dad said you wanted to talk to me?"

"Yes. I'd like you to stop by Whole Foods while you're in Reno. I miss having one close by. If you don't mind, I'll make a list. Oh, and I'm expecting you to cover dinner tonight, with or without Kayla's help. Your father's working late and he ordered me to rest my knee as much as possible until we get a verdict back. That's okay, isn't it?"

I dare him to say no.

But he doesn't even look consternated, so I guess he's forgiven or forgotten my earlier outburst. "I guess. I mean, sure, if you need my help. So, you know, I was planning on stopping by Guitar Center, too, so Kayla and I will be gone most of the day."

"Guitar Center?"

"Yeah. My guitar's been calling to me lately, but the strings are shot."

"That's right. You told me you played. Why the renewed interest?"

"I've got ladies to impress." He inches closer. "Hope you were impressed last night."

I look him directly in the eye. "I'm sure I don't know what you mean."

He shrugs. "No problem. I don't mind an audience."

The conversation is disrupted by Andrew's appearance. He glances at his watch.

"We should probably hit the road, don't you think?"

"Yeah, we should," agrees Eli, backing away. "Wanna just text me your list?"

"Sounds like a plan. Oh, there will be perishables, so be sure to come straight home."

"Yes, Mom."

I wince at the word.

He smiles at the wince.

Turns and goes inside.

Andrew comes over and gives me a hug.

"It was a pleasure getting to know you. I promise to be kind to your car."

"Your car," I correct. "The two of you will make quite the pair. Be sure and bring her for a visit sometime."

"Will do. Take care of yourself, and my son and grandson, too."

"That's okay." It's Eli's turn to interrupt. "I can take care of myself. But here" — he hands me my phone — "text me, and keep icing that knee. Hard to keep up with us young'uns with a limp."

Eli winks.

Andrew laughs.

And I laugh, too, because what else is there to do?

After everyone leaves, I send a substantial grocery list to Eli via text message, then decide to read on the deck. I'm currently between books, so I randomly pull one off Cavin's bookshelf. It's Ray Bradbury's *Something Wicked This Way Comes*. I generally don't choose genre fiction, but for some reason this one calls to me, and I find myself sucked in immediately.

Having perused the jacket, and being somewhat familiar with Bradbury, I understand that the approaching carnival has sinister overtones. The foreshadowing is excellent, and the characters very well drawn. I've just reached the part where old Tom Fury peeks in the shop window, to see the woman made of ice, when something feels off.

I realize I'm ridiculously on edge from this silly book, which I put down so I can survey my surroundings. What was it that bothered me? I see nothing out of the ordinary beyond the railing. I listen intently but can hear only the chatter of birds and the chuff of wind in the treetops.

It was only something sensed. Intuited. But I could've sworn someone was watching me.

Trust your instincts.

I'm not sure where that sentiment rose up from, but it's good advice. I retrieve the book and go inside where invisible eyes can't find me.

TEN

Eli and Kayla manage to get Andrew to check-in with plenty of time to spare. They conquer the extensive shopping list I sent, delivering everything home before possible spoilage. They shuttle in bags, put everything away, and refuse to let me help. If they had any personal problems between morning and late afternoon, it's not obvious beneath the ridiculous grins plastered to their faces. I begin to suspect it wasn't just guitar strings Eli picked up in Reno.

I left it to him what to do for dinner. He's a genius in the kitchen — says he taught himself as a means of survival, since neither of his parents was around much when he was a kid — and, in fact, I suspect it's his one marketable skill. At the moment, he's got Kayla playing sous chef, dressing an impressive salad while he flash sears some beautiful ahi steaks. "You might use a little soy sauce to season them," I suggest, watching him from my barstool perch.

"Hey. You appointed me cook. I've got this covered, unless you decided you want the job after all."

He leaves the soy sauce in the cupboard, and instead chooses a squeeze of fresh lime, chili powder, and a pinch of salt, plus garlic and cilantro to flavor the olive oil in the frying pan. It doesn't take long to cook tuna rare, and he's slicing it when my phone rings.

"Tara?" It's Mel. "I wanted you to know we've moved Mom into hospice care. Her cancer has metastasized and she doesn't have much time. I'm driving down to visit her and want to take the girls. You're welcome to come, too, if you've changed your mind about saying good-bye."

"I haven't." I hated being around my mother when she was healthy. Seeing her all chewed up by radiation and pretty much helpless? Wait. Maybe. "I still can't believe how fast this happened."

"Neither can she. She's in total denial. But if the doctors have given up on her, I think we have to as well. There's a steep monetary incentive to keep treating her."

"So why did they stop?"

"I told them to."

Boom.

"But how is that even possible?"

"Mom signed a durable power of attorney, naming me as her agent. I couldn't find one good reason to continue radiation. Her few possessions will have to be liquidated to handle the insurance deductibles, which would've just kept piling up, regardless of the imminent outcome."

My sister is full of surprises. Rarely have I heard such resolve in her voice.

"She has medical insurance?"

"Seems so. She's not quite old enough to qualify for Medicare, but Medi-Cal — that's California's Medicaid system — covers her."

"And she agreed to hospice, even though she doesn't think she's dying?"

"Truthfully, she's so doped up, she's in no condition to agree or disagree. Tara, you know if I thought treatment would give her more quality time on this earth, I wouldn't have made this decision."

"It's okay, Mel. I'm positive you've done the right thing. Not like it's easy to pull the plug on someone."

At that, Eli and Kayla put the brakes on the kitchen prep. "Who's Mom pulling the plug on?" asks Kayla.

I offer the name our mother requested her grandchildren call her, "June." It's matter-of-fact, but it's not like Mom is close to

Mel's daughters, or any of us.

I wrote her off decades ago. She was never a real mother. More like an incubator for my sister and me, one who resented every single minute she was forced to spend with us. If her brain was wired for love, I never saw a hint of it. The last thing I needed in my adult life was a psychotic parent draining my money and energy.

Mel, I guess, has kept in touch, but with Mom living in Rialto with her trucker-of-the-month, it's mostly been by e-mail or phone, with the occasional drop-in visit from Mom, who has always insisted Mel's girls call her June rather than Grandma.

"Oh," says Kayla. "Right."

I return my attention to the phone in my hand. "I thought you wanted me to help with the paperwork."

"Honestly, it would have been a waste of your time. I just went to one of those online legal services and printed out what we needed. It was a no-brainer. She made a living will, which I haven't seen yet, but how complicated could it be?"

Very true.

"So, when are you leaving on this pilgrimage?"

"I'd like to go tomorrow, and I'll need to

pick up Kayla. Is she around? Can I talk to her?"

Oh, this should be good. I hand over the phone and observe the emotions in Kayla's expressions, which change with Melody's responses to her short bursts of dialogue:

"When?"

Disbelief.

"Why do I need to go?"

Puzzlement.

"But I've only got a few weeks until school starts."

Irritation.

This time, whatever Melody says takes a while. Finally, Kayla spits, "Fine!"

Full-blown rage.

Anger pulses in her temples. She shoves the phone back into my hand, and I find no Mel on the other end. "Did you hang up on your mother?" I ask.

"She's just so unreasonable!"

Eli, who isn't exactly clued into the drama, inquires, "What's the matter?"

"I guess my grandmother's dying," huffs Kayla. "And Mom wants to drive all of us down to Southern California to pay our last respects."

"What's wrong with that?" Eli seems genuinely confused.

"Nothing, except I don't have any 'first

respect' for June. I barely even know her. And the idea of an eight-hour trip, cooped up in a car with my sisters and mom, is enough to make me crazy. She wants to leave tomorrow, too. Said she'd pick me up around nine."

"What about you?" He aims the question in my direction. "Are you going?"

I shake my head. "I know June too well, and don't have any respect for her, either. But that's not really a secret, is it? Let's eat."

The terse subject change lasts only long enough for the kids to carry plates and silverware to the table. Eli and I dive in, but Kayla picks at her salad, fuming.

"Stow your pissy attitude and try the ahi," I suggest. "Like I said, Eli's a pretty great cook, and this is outstanding."

Eli shoots me an appreciative wink, but Kayla responds, "Not hungry."

"You were hungry before your mom called," he observes.

"Yeah, well, the idea of death isn't a great appetizer." Her eyes roll up from her salad, drill into mine. "Maybe as a main dish . . ."

The little hairs on the back of my neck lift in warning. "What does that mean?"

She looks down again immediately. "Nothing. I just can't find a decent reason to go."

"You don't really have to," says Eli, deflating slightly. "You're eighteen. She can't tell you what to do anymore."

Fact is, Mel hasn't been in charge of Kayla for a while now, any more than Cavin can control Eli, who actually broke into my San Francisco house "just for fun" and pretty much comes and goes here at will, all expenses paid by his parents. Same goes for Kayla, who I've witnessed sauntering into Mel's house after a three-day bender with her previous boyfriend, expecting no questions asked and certainly no consequences. A little respect is called for, but all I see in either of them is a bloated sense of entitlement and, in Kayla's case, a troubling dependency on her partners.

"Hey, Eli," I nudge. "Would you mind finding a decent bottle of something red and opening it for me? I believe your father left the wine boxed up in the office until he gets the racks built."

"Sure thing," he says. "But only if you'll share."

I shrug. "Depends on which vintage you choose."

"Selfish."

"Of course. But not about everything." I wait till he's out of earshot. "So what's the real problem, Kayla? Surely it's not the travel, and you'll only be away a few days."

She stares at her plate. "It's just . . . I don't trust him."

"With me?"

"Not you specifically."

Uh-huh. But I'll leave it alone. "Look. The best way to keep a guy interested is to act like you don't care what he does. Then he'll wonder what you're up to, too. Mutual distrust can create a powerful connection."

"You're just saying that."

"I mean it. Anyway, what's the point of digging your fingernails into someone who isn't masochistic?" Okay, the reference was a bit esoteric.

"I don't get it," says Kayla.

"Why try to hang on to a person who's determined to stray? You can't demand fidelity. If he really cares about keeping you, he'll be anxiously waiting for your return. If you have to worry about what he's doing behind your back, dump him, unless what he can offer you is worth the concern. There are lots of men in the world. Eventually you'll catch the right one."

"But what if Eli is the right one?"

"Then he'll pass the test and all will be well."

At the sound of his approaching return, the conversation dies and Kayla actually picks up her fork and takes a bite of tuna.

"Yum. This *is* good."

Eli arrives in time to hear the compliment. "Hey, I'm not just great in the sack, you know." He places a bottle on the table in front of me. "One glass or three?"

It's a pricey Bordeaux. "One, I think. Even if it wasn't among the more expensive bottles, your father should be home any time now."

"(A) like I told you, my mom doesn't care if I have a glass of wine with dinner, so I highly doubt my dad would. And (B) selfish."

"(A) like I told you, I'm only selfish about some things. And (B) let's ask your dad when he gets here. Meanwhile, would you mind playing sommelier?"

"Whatever I can do to please you, Lady Tremaine." Eli goes to the kitchen for a corkscrew and wineglass.

"Who's Lady Tremaine?" asks Kayla when he returns.

"The wicked stepmother in *Cinderella,*" he explains.

"And how did you know *that,* Eli?" It definitely piques my curiosity.

He grins and opens the Bordeaux. As the cork nudges out, he says, "I know many things. But in this case, I wrote a paper comparing the original Grimm version, the

Disney representation, and the movie *Ever After.* Only Disney made her a wuss, by the way."

"This was at the Athenian?" I ask.

"Yeah. Honors English. We had to pick a classic fairy tale and compare it with modern versions."

"So, why *Cinderella?*"

"I liked the name Aschenputtel?"

Kayla looks confused. "What?"

"That's what the Grimms called her. And she was kick-ass. *Ever After* was closer to the original. Drew Barrymore rocked that part. All women should be like that — strong, assertive, not afraid to go after what they want."

I glance at Kayla, who is none of those things, and wonder if the message sank in at all. Probably not, but maybe it will, and a few days away from Eli can only help. Still, to underline it, I ask, "Do you really mean that, Eli? I thought you preferred the kind of girl who'd wait on you."

Kayla shoots me an "I want to kill you" look.

Eli doesn't notice, because his gaze meets mine head-on. "If waiting on me is a means to an end, that's one thing. If it's a personality flaw, that's another. I want someone who's not afraid to be my equal; who might

115

challenge me, even."

Wow. If that didn't get through, nothing will.

"Are you up to challenging him, Kayla? How assertive are you?"

Something surfaces in her eyes, something sinister. Her hand lunges sideways, snatches at Eli's arm. "Assertive enough to fight for what's mine."

Eli and I both are stunned into momentary silence. He recovers before I do. "Hey. First of all, I don't belong to you. People can't own people. You're definitely worth keeping around, though."

The girl is unstable, but at the moment I'm feeling uneven myself. Part of me wants to applaud her. The bigger piece wants to make it very clear she could never be a match for me, if that's where she was going, and I have to believe it was.

Clarity. Fight fire with facts masquerading as weak humor. "Eli's not all that, anyway, Kayla —"

"What the fuck?" interrupts Eli. "I'm all that and a whole lot more than you could ever imagine. I happen to be *experienced.*"

I ignore him. "But if he matters to you, damn sure stand your ground."

"Don't worry," she snarls. "I plan to."

Well okay, then.

We've just about cleaned our plates when Cavin gets home. The clock claims it's after seven. He's definitely put in an extended day and, wondering how often this might happen in the future, I realize I'll need to make a new friend or two or, even without the burden of friendship, find someone to hang out with every now and then. Someone other than Eli.

"Looks like I missed dinner," Cavin says, scouring the leftovers in the kitchen.

"Don't worry," Eli calls, "there's plenty for you."

Before long, Cavin appears with a plate of food and a glass in need of wine. "I haven't had a bite since breakfast, and I'm starving. Who cooked? This looks great."

"I did," volunteers Eli.

"Hey, I helped," reminds Kayla. "And I helped with the shopping, too."

God, I wish she wouldn't sound so desperate. "That's true. You did. And I'm grateful to both of you." Now I turn my attention to my husband. "Long day. Hope it was uneventful."

"Tedious, actually." He fills his glass to the brim and, before he takes a sip, bends to collect a kiss. "I think I'm ready for another honeymoon. Can we leave tomorrow?"

"Sure," quips Eli. "You two run along. We'll take care of everything here for you."

"Including my patient load?"

"How hard could it be? Take two Vicodin twice a day, see you next week."

Cavin snorts. "As if it could be that easy."

I clear my throat. "Even if it were that easy, unfortunately, I believe I'm scheduled for an MRI in the morning."

"Crap. That's right." Cavin sits and goes to work on his belated dinner.

Eli stands. "Well, if you'll excuse me, I'm finished here. K-K?"

My hackles rise. "Why must you insist on a pet name? The one her parents gave her is perfectly fine."

Kayla jumps to her feet. "It's okay, Aunt Tara."

Way to challenge him, girl.

"Since your mom will be here first thing in the morning, you should probably throw a few clothes into a suitcase tonight, don't you think?" I ask.

A scowl pinches her face, and I see what she'll look like when the years whittle lines around her eyes and mouth. More Graham than Mel in her middle age, I think.

"Yeah, I guess so."

"Good idea," says Eli, sliding an arm around her shoulder and pulling her close.

"That way we won't have to wake up too early tomorrow, and that means we can stay up later tonight. Let's have some fun."

He leaves it to Cavin and me to decipher his meaning, which isn't exactly hard to do. Once they've disappeared down the stairs, Cavin comments, "I take it your sister is picking up Kayla?"

"She is." I give him the details of Mom's condition.

"Are you sure you don't want to go along? I can postpone those tests for you."

"I'm positive."

He sips his wine, mulling something over in his head. Finally, he says, "Toward the end of my mother's life, I thought I hated her. She'd deteriorated into quite a horrible woman, though once in a while a glimpse of her good side managed to shine through. But once she was gone, I wished I'd tried harder to interact, or at the very least told her I loved her once in a while. I still wrestle with guilt."

Guilt is mostly lost to me, denied by brain chemistry. I don't think I miss it. "There are a couple of major differences. One, my mom doesn't have a good side . . ." Even the relatively sane part of her was mean as hell; the half fueled by her borderline personality disorder was off-the-charts vicious. "And, two, telling her I loved her would be a lie, something I have zero need to go out of my way to do."

"I hope you don't come to regret your decision."

"Don't worry. I won't."

Regret and guilt are interlinked.

ELEVEN

My tests were arranged for ten a.m., so I'm happy when Melody arrives a little ahead of schedule, at quarter to nine. I'm expecting her, and the coffee is hot and fresh when the doorbell rings. When I open the door, my jaw drops.

"Oh my God. What did you do?"

Her hair, which she has forever worn long and naturally silver, is cut very short and dyed close to its original copper red, with blond highlights. She grins. "Like it?"

I move to one side to let her in. "I . . . I . . . Yeah, I suppose I do. I just never thought this day would come."

"I got tired of the same old look, the operative word being 'old.' "

"I always thought it was rather attractive on you. Plus, gray hair has become the 'in' thing now, you know. So you were really just ahead of the trend."

"Guess I'll have to start a new trend, then.

Is Kayla ready?"

"I haven't seen her yet this morning, but I'll go check. Want a cup of coffee while you're waiting?" I start toward the kitchen.

"The girls are in the car, so I probably shouldn't. Although, it does smell inviting."

"Just brewed. Come on. Might as well amp up for your drive. I'll pour you a cup and you can take it to go if you don't finish it before Kayla makes an appearance. Do you want me to invite Suz and Jessica in?"

"We'll never get out of here if you do, and they've got their phones for entertainment. They'll be okay for a few." She follows me into the kitchen. "So, how's married life? And where is your husband?"

"Cavin went into the hospital early. He has back-to-back surgeries this morning. And so far, married life is pretty darn good, despite his hectic schedule." Of course, he returned to work only a couple of days ago. I could very well grow weary of it.

"I suppose I should be grateful Graham's just a lowly pediatrician. His hours are relatively steady."

Right, so she can expect when not to expect him. I locate a travel mug in the cupboard, point to the Mr. Coffee. "Help yourself. There's milk in the fridge and sugar on the counter. I'll go check on Kayla."

I rotate too quickly on the wrong leg, forgetting the state of my knee, which screams at the mistake. "Christ!"

Almost supernaturally, Eli materializes at the top of the stairs. "You don't have to be so formal. All my friends call me JC," he jokes.

Kayla appears seconds later, overstuffed backpack in hand. "Mom! What did you do to your hair?"

"She decided to update her image," I tease, wiping pain tears from the corners of my eyes.

"Really? Well then, she'd better let me take her clothes shopping," replies Kayla. "Those jeans are, like, ugh."

She has a point.

Mel joins our loosely assembled group, coffee in hand. "I'll have you know these are Old Navy."

"Right. Old lady Old Navy," says Kayla, giggling.

She's not too pissy, anyway. At least not until Melody suggests, "We should probably hit the highway. We've got a decent drive ahead of us."

At that, the girl's demeanor changes. "I'd fucking better get shotgun."

Our heads swivel and Eli demands, "Why's everyone staring at me? I didn't teach her the F-word. Come on, K-K. I'll walk you to the car."

Mel shoots me a "what the hell?" look.

I shake my head. "Beats me. She claims she likes it, that she's never had a nickname before. I've told them both how I feel about it. Now I think he's just doing it to spite me."

"Why would he want to do that?"

I borrow the explanation Charlie once provided for Eli's unpredictable behavior. "Entertainment."

Melody smiles, but then she sobers. "Is there anything you'd like me to tell Mom?"

I mull it over for a minute or two, but the first thing that comes to mind is the latest dream I had about her. "Tell her to beware the zombie apocalypse."

"Seriously?"

"Seriously, tell her I wish she would have tried harder to be a decent mother, that trying to connect with someone after relentlessly driving them away for decades is impossible on any real level. Tell her she never gave us a chance, that if it wasn't for personal ambition we'd probably be waiting tables or stripping for a living. Tell her I feel sorry for Will because he's just another in a long line of losers she's used and abused as meal tickets, with a little good lovin' tossed in for dessert. Tell her science is right. Smoking's bad for you. Tell her I don't forgive her, and her offer to forgive me isn't only unnecessary. It's laughable."

Melody opens her mouth to object. Closes it again. But finally, she says, "You've told her all that before."

"True. But I want her to know death changes nothing."

Bam. Sounded heartless, even to me. But considering my mother is largely responsible for my lacking a heart to begin with, every sentiment was fair.

"I think I'll just stick to the zombie apocalypse."

"Probably the best plan." I consider small talk, but she's anxious to get on the road and I've got an appointment looming. "Will you be dropping off Kayla on your way home?"

"I'm sure that's what she'll want."

"Plan on staying long enough for a real conversation. I mean, if you want one and Graham doesn't mind. We can take the girls to the beach or something."

"I'll definitely consider it. And I don't care what Graham thinks about it."

Hmm. That's different, too. Has my little

sister finally grown up?

I escort Mel to the front door, and when I open it, we find Eli and Kayla on the front step, lip-locked, with all four hands in highly inappropriate places. "Ahem. You two might not care what the neighbors think, but I do. Save the foreplay for behind closed doors."

"Not only that," Mel says to Kayla, "but your sisters are watching."

"Hey, they have to learn this stuff sometime, don't they?" Eli's tasteless joke lands with a thud.

Mel's glare could level a linebacker. "I don't subscribe to the 'watch it live' theory of sex education, thank you very much. Now if you'll excuse us. Kayla?"

The girl actually jabs her tongue into Eli's mouth as a good-bye gesture. Mel stalks off, pretending not to notice, but I've got a feeling it will lead to some intense communication once they're in the car. Now *that* might be entertaining.

"Enough already," I tell them. "Don't keep your mother waiting, Kayla."

With a massive, melodramatic sigh, she finally joins her family for the long, slow ride to hell. Eli doesn't wait to watch them drive away, but instead goes straight inside, with me on his tail.

"Don't you think that was rather inappropriate?" I know it's a mistake the second it slips from my mouth.

"I don't see what the problem is. We had all our clothes on."

"Look. The last thing any mother wants to see is some guy groping her daughter."

"That's a rather broad statement. Some mothers actually offer their daughters up to potential gropers."

Okay, he's got me there. Still. "Well, Melody isn't that kind of mother. You might show her more respect."

He looks me straight in the eye. "I will. Since it matters to you. Now, want some breakfast?"

"You're offering to cook for me?" He nods, and I'd like to take him up on it. But now I glance at my watch. Nine twenty. "Sorry. Can't. I have to be at Barton by ten."

"Maybe tomorrow, then."

"Maybe. But, hey, since your day just got less complicated, would you take responsibility for dinner again? After being poked, prodded, and otherwise violated, I don't think I'll be in the mood."

"Any preference as to what I make?"

"Nope. There's plenty of stuff to choose from. Surprise me."

"Okay. But wait. Can I ask you something?"

Uh-oh. I hate when someone prefaces a question by asking if it's all right to ask it. How can you respond except with something like "I guess"?

"Will you really not feel bad when your mother dies?" Eli's a go-directly-for-the-jugular kind of kid.

And I'll be direct with my answer. "No."

"Is that the sociopath in you?"

"No. It's the ritually abused little girl."

He grins. "I can't imagine you as a little girl, but I suppose you were one once." He reaches out, touches my arm with the very tips of his fingers. "I'm sorry your mom is so fucked up. Kind of makes me wonder what *her* childhood was like, though."

Jesus. I hate when he sounds like an adult.

Truthfully, I don't know a lot about Mom's early years. I never met my grandfather, who was stationed at Mountain Home Air Force Base when he played the knock-up-a-local-girl-then-get-out-of-Dodge game, or at least that's how the story went. My grandmother raised Mom solo in Glenns Ferry, Idaho, though she apparently cycled through a string of men, one of whom ultimately drew a steady bead and shot her through her left eye in the heat of an argument. I was four or five when that happened, so I did have some contact with her beforehand, but not much. I best remember her lying in her unadorned casket, a waxy-skinned mannequin with an eye patch.

Grandmother wasn't close to Mom, who rarely discussed how she was raised, though it's obvious enough whose examples she emulated.

Did Mom inherit borderline personality disorder from her own mother?

Possibly, although BPD could have been carried by Air Force Dude's genes.

Was Mom abused?

Maybe. In fact, I'd say it's likely.

Does that make me any more forgiving of her?

Not even remotely.

Twelve

The battery of tests I'm subjected to is more than extensive. It's exhausting. A very nice, very young clinician does his best to keep me distracted with some awful jokes as he observes my alignment while weight bearing and watches my gait for a "dynamic varus thrust," whatever the hell that is.

"Varus and valgus may sound like Greek gods," explains Drew, "but the terms have to do with the way your lower leg aligns with the upper leg through the knee. 'Varus' means the tibia/fibula point toward the midline of your body. 'Valgus' means the tibia/ fibula head away from midline. Think about being bowlegged (varus) versus knock-kneed (valgus)."

More useless medical lingo to store away. "Actually, I think 'varus' sounds like a disease. 'Valgus' sounds like something you'd see in *Hustler.*"

Drew laughs. "The odds of *Hustler* paying

130

me to expose anything aren't very good, I'm afraid. Okay, hop up on the table." At my gigantic eye roll, he amends, "Not doing much hopping lately, I guess. Let me help."

He gives me a little boost and then examines my skin for signs of infection before checking range of motion, patellar mobility, and overall muscle strength. He names the tests as he goes: Lachman, pivot shift, posterior drawer, sag, dial. And that's just the beginning.

Next comes a full set of radiographs, taken from every angle, some with me standing. Another noisy MRI — this time with rock music in the headphones to keep me from going crazy. And finally, a CT scan, which apparently gives a better indication of "bony architecture" than the MRI, which is all about the soft tissue.

"There are many reasons a reconstruction might fail, if that's even what's happening," Drew tells me as he wraps things up. "I'll spare you the boring details, but surgeon error is only one possibility. You might have rehabbed too hard and reinjured it, or it could be that something was missed in the initial diagnosis. Dr. Stanley should have a pretty good idea of what's going on when you see him tomorrow."

"I doubt you could have missed anything

this time around. In fact, I can reasonably state that no one has ever been quite this familiar with my knee before. Not even my husband."

"Well, that's a shame," he responds. "Other than a fair amount of swelling, it's a very nice knee."

Bedside manner is everything.

It's close to one by the time we finish, so I stop by Cavin's office to see if he wants to grab a bite or something. The reception desk is unmanned. Rebecca must be at lunch. "Hello?" I call toward Cavin's closed door. "Anyone home?" There's no response, so I crack it, peek behind. Empty. Could he still be in surgery? Considering how long it took just to run some tests, I suppose he very well could be.

Mildly disappointed, I leave him a simple note: *Stopped by. Sorry we missed each other.* I'm on my way out when my attention is necessarily drawn to a familiar person on her way in. All heads turn at the entrance of Genevieve Lennon, who, though her famed beauty is fading, will always remain a member of the supermodel club.

I've known her for a decade. We first met at one of Jordan's campaign dinners. He knew lots of the "beautiful people," and she and her entourage certainly qualified. My first impression of Genevieve was "breath-taking," a term I rarely apply to other women, including models. At twenty-nine, she was already beyond industry prime, I suppose, but that didn't bother me. What did was my instant attraction, and it proved to be mutual.

Before I married Raul, I slept with a couple of women — strippers at the Jel-lybean Club. I chalk up those encounters to youthful curiosity and a sincere hunger for the kind of comfort only sex can provide. At that point, the club's customers had pretty much turned me from men, all of whom, it seemed, only wanted to get off as quickly and cheaply as possible. Those girls were coarse and crude and satisfied my appetite without forming any real attachment.

Genevieve was different. I'd believed my draw toward women a passing fancy, so the mad jolt of lust I felt the first time I met her shocked me. I've never been one much for gossip, but during the height of her career it would've been impossible to be unaware of Genevieve Lennon, whose exotic good looks graced magazine covers from *Vogue* to *Sports Illustrated,* and whose famed excesses gave her spreads in the *National Enquirer.* Before we actually met, however, I would've discounted her as just another hollow celebrity.

To say she isn't fueled by conceit would be a lie, but there is substance there as well as beauty, and the combination was irresistible. With Jordan's explicit approval, Genevieve and I entered into a sexually charged part-time liaison that lasted for almost two years. Jordan's only requirement was being allowed to watch a time or two. It didn't feel like cheating, with his permission. Only later did I learn that was meant to distract me from his personal infidelities.

After Jordan and I split and I met Finn, I let Genevieve know the nature of our relationship had to change. We've remained friends, though not close, and she's continued to support my fund-raising efforts over the years. I rarely revisit that window of my life and have never confessed it to anyone. What's interesting is how often she and I seem to run into each other in unexpected places. Like today, for instance.

"Tara," she says when she sees me. "What a surprise, not to mention a coincidence. So happens I'm here to consult with your husband."

"Really?"

"Well, yes. I often come up to the lake to enjoy the Shakespeare Festival at Sand

Harbor. Have you been?"

"Once, several years ago. I imagine I'll go every summer now, though."

"If you'd like to attend, please let me know. I'm a patron, and the director happens to be a good friend, so tickets are not a problem."

Sounds uncomfortable. Not watching a play on the beach, which is a lovely experience, and I enjoy Shakespeare. But spending an evening in such close proximity to Genevieve, with my new husband along? "Thanks for the offer, but I'm not really sure. I mean, besides me, it would be Cavin and probably Eli as well."

"Eli?"

"Cavin's son. He's almost eighteen."

"And delicious, I imagine."

Is her mouth watering?

Subject change in order. "You said you're here to see Cavin?"

"Tomorrow, actually. Today I'm just here for tests. I've been having some joint pain. Nothing major, but enough to cause concern. I'm hoping to rule out arthritis. Anyway, I remembered he specialized in orthopedics and thought since I'm staying in Incline I'd have him take a look."

Should this bother me? "Well, your timing is good. We've only been home from our honeymoon for a few days."

"I know. You were still gone when I called to make the appointment. I'm glad it worked out. Few things I dislike more than going to a strange doctor."

To my knowledge, she's met Cavin only the one time, at a charity event I organized in San Francisco. It's not like they're well acquainted. "All doctors are a little strange, within my realm of experience, anyway."

"Including your husband?"

"Especially Cavin. It only bothers me once in a while." I smile. "Oh, but diagnosticians tend to be solid — at least the one I had today was. Drew was exceptionally thorough."

"Good to know. And I suppose I should be on my way. I'm a couple minutes late now. Let's be in touch. You have my number, yes?"

"I do."

I suppose I should be gracious and invite her to dinner or something. Instead, I watch her slink away. Must be hard to slink when you're six feet tall, but she carries it off with aplomb. Funny, earlier I was musing about needing a local friend. Genevieve is not who I had in mind.

Even on a Tuesday, the traffic through South Lake Tahoe into Glenbrook and beyond is horrific. I've never spent much time up here in the summer before, and now I know why I've avoided peak tourist season. Vehicles clog every byway, and pedestrians taking risks make things even crazier. The eighteen-mile drive home takes almost fifty minutes, and by the time I finally park, my stress-worried shoulders feel like concrete.

They soften almost immediately when I go inside to find Eli out on the deck, slider open, playing his guitar. It's acoustic, thank God, and though I would have suspected he'd imitate some annoying brand of metal, he's strumming a Green Day song.

Not only is his fingering accurate; so is his vocal.

I'd considered putting in time on the stationary bike, but suddenly a glass of wine alfresco sounds like the better plan. And, almost unreasonably, it's something crisp and fruity and white I find myself craving. I don't feel like digging through my boxed cellar for a wine that will be difficult to locate, considering my usual preference for reds, but as I recall, Andrew was drinking a riesling on Sunday. Maybe he left some in the fridge.

He did!

Must be your lucky day.

Luck. I consider that while I fill my glass, and what I think is luck is a fragile gift and one you mostly create, like buying yourself the birthday present you truly want, rather than hoping someone else will read your mind or pick up on your hints and not quite surprise you with it. Luck is the by-product of ascertaining facts, assessing your odds, then positioning yourself in the exact right location to reach out and grab the golden ring.

No time for breakfast this morning, no Cavin to take me to lunch, I should probably nibble on something. Eli's Whole Foods run offers tempting possibilities, and I succumb to the lure of brie and whole grain crackers, plus maybe some fruit. When I search the bin, I discover a mango and make a mental note not to eat anything orange and risk an allergic reaction. I'll go for red instead and grab a handful of strawberries.

I take everything out on the deck, where Eli is now into "Bohemian Rhapsody." The boy can definitely sing. At my interruption, he stops. "No, keep going," I urge. "You're really good."

His face colors, but his smile stretches wide. "Think so?"

"I do." I reach for a strawberry, and that

reminds me. "Hey, I noticed a mango in the kitchen. You remember my allergy, right?"

"Of course. How could I forget the EpiPen episode? No worries. No suspect smoothies, I promise. It was Kayla who bought it, in fact. Think it will still be good by the time she gets back?"

"Probably. But if you want to eat it, go ahead. Proximity to someone enjoying a mango doesn't wreak anaphylactic mayhem on my system."

"Good to know, though I can take or leave mangoes. I'll save it for Kayla. She expects to be back by Friday."

Friday? Seems ambitious to me, but it doesn't really matter either way. "Well, if she doesn't reappear before the weekend, go ahead and do something with the mango. Just be sure to warn me first. Meanwhile, please play something."

"I'm taking requests."

"Everclear?"

He launches into an excellent rendition of "Volvo Driving Soccer Moms." The lyrics are amusing, but Eli's facial expressions when he delivers some of them make me laugh out loud. There's a single uncomfortable moment when he sings about being a dancer at the local strip club, but it dissolves as soon as he moves on. My days working at the Jellybean Club were a long time ago, and they did lead to my most fortunate marriage to Raul, but I'd rather not contemplate them. And I'd definitely prefer that Cavin, not to mention Eli, never finds out about them.

Even at this elevation, it's a relatively warm summer afternoon, and we move into the cool shelter of the house after an hour or so. "What have you planned for dinner?" I ask. "Hope it's not too heavy."

"I was thinking tacos. Chicken or steak, your call. With mango-free salsa."

"Steak. Definitely."

"Awesome. Oh, by the way, you'll have to take care of dinner tomorrow. I'm going to hang out with a friend in Reno. In fact, I'll probably spend the night so I don't have to drive home late."

"Really. I didn't know you have friends in Reno."

"A friend," he corrects. "You know who she is."

I do, and my cheeks ignite, along with the tips of my ears. "Not Sophia?"

"Who else? She invited me to see her new show."

He's got to be kidding. "What about Kayla?"

He shrugs. "She isn't here, is she?"

140

The kid has the morals of a horny chimpanzee, but that's the least of my problems with this whole proposed scenario. "Kayla's only been gone a few hours. When did you get this invitation?"

"It was open-ended. I called Sophia after Kayla left, and she happened to be free *mañana*." He interprets my body language. "You don't approve."

"Not of infidelity in general and especially not with Sophia. Don't you feel strange about sleeping with your father's ex-fiancée?"

"Not really. Why should I?"

"It doesn't seem a bit incestuous?"

He looks me straight in the eye. "Sleeping with you might be a bit incestuous."

Might?

I ignore the comment. "What about your dad's feelings?"

"What do you mean?"

"Come on, Eli. Surely he wouldn't be happy about this arrangement."

"Actually, I talked to him about Sophia and me. He said he doesn't care."

Impossible. "That can't be true."

"Why would I lie to you?"

That's what I keep trying to figure out. "All right, then. If it's okay by your father — and I really can't see how it would be —

141

what about me? You know it aggravates me for that woman to be attached so closely to this family."

"I understand. But I'll make it up to you."

"Oh yeah? How?"

"Tacos."

Tacos. Right.

By the time Cavin gets home, tired and more than a little hungry, Eli has prepared a huge spread: warm tortillas, freshly grated cheddar, shredded cabbage, chopped onions, and from-scratch salsa and guacamole. I'm thinking he's got quite an evening planned with Sophia tomorrow.

As Cavin washes up, Eli grills the steak, and by the time his father joins us in the kitchen, the meat is cooked medium rare and sliced. Cavin peruses the buffet. "I think Tara's right. You could make a career out of this."

Eli doesn't respond. Instead, he hands Cavin a plate. "You have to build your own tacos. I don't do grunt labor."

We sit at the table, considering topics for discussion, and before very long the conversation rolls around to my tests this morning. After reciting the extended list, I remember, "Oh, I bumped into Genevieve, on her way in for her own lab work. You didn't tell me she'd made an appointment with you."

"Sorry. It slipped my mind."

"Slipped your mind? Considering the shameless way she flirted with you at my Lost Souls fund-raiser (and right in front of me, no less) I'd think it would be foremost on your mind."

Cavin laughs. "You're not jealous, are you?"

"Who, me? Jealous of my handsome husband examining the oft-photographed limbs of a world-famous supermodel who just might be crushing on him?"

That, of course, piques Eli's interest. "Wait. Who are you talking about?"

"Genevieve Lennon," replies Cavin.

"No shit? You *know* her?"

"Tara knows her. I only met her once, at one of Tara's charity events."

"Lucky. Hey, I want to meet her. When's her appointment?"

That draws my gigantic sigh. "She's not that special, Eli. In fact, she's kind of a bitch."

"Who cares? Have you ever seen her *Sports Illustrated* covers? Anyway, most beautiful women are bitches."

"Including the one you're seeing tomorrow?" I steer the conversation toward Cavin. "Sophia invited Eli to Reno to see her new show. He said you're fine with that?"

Confusion clouds Cavin's eyes. "I know nothing about it, Tara. Why would you say that, Eli?"

"You told me you didn't care about Sophia and me."

"Wait. No. What I said was I didn't care about what happened between the two of you in the past because what's done can't be undone. I never said I was okay with you continuing to see her."

"That's not how it sounded to me."

As so often happens, it's like the two are conversing across parallel universes or something. I can't stand it. I require solid footing in *this* dimension.

"I need a beer," says Cavin, standing and grinding the argument to a halt. "Tara, can I bring you something?"

"I don't suppose you have a margarita handy?" Tequila, yeah, that's what I need. "Just kidding. Sparkling water would be fine, thanks."

What I'd really like is a truth-o-meter. I've always prided myself on my ability to discern deception, but these two have an uncanny knack for skewing facts to support their agendas.

"Water?" asks Eli. "You on the wagon since, like, an hour ago?"

"Just in the mood for clarity."

I don't offer a deeper explanation, and neither asks for one. Instead, silence swallows us.

No more talk of Sophia.

No more talk of Genevieve.

And that's fine by me.

THIRTEEN

My confidence rarely falters, but I find myself nervous as I wait to see Dr. Stanley, who managed to squeeze me in this morning, short notice, at the insistence of his colleague, my husband. "Squeeze me in," of course, means I could sit here for however long, nothing to do but read old magazines featuring sports injuries or check e-mail via smartphone.

Rather than do either of those things, I people watch and, when that grows tiresome, allow myself the luxury of closing my eyes to think about what transpired last night. It wasn't big in any real way, but it was a reminder to closely examine the connotation of words exchanged across the dinner table by the men in my life. That is, if I can consider Eli a man, and I'm not sure how else to think about him. Sometimes he seems all kid, other times, totally adult. Too adult, in fact.

The idea of Eli going to Reno to see Sophia seared into me all evening, and as Cavin and I got ready for bed, I straight out asked, "Why do you think Sophia insists on maintaining her relationship with Eli?"

"I really don't know, Tara. You'd have to ask her. But it seems to me like Eli's the one driving that train."

I wish that's all there was to it, but I intuited an undercurrent.

I pushed a little harder. "Doesn't it bother you, thinking about the two of them having sex?"

He tipped up my chin, bringing us eye to eye. "I do my level best not to think about it — or Sophia — at all."

I accepted that without comment. But when he almost immediately grew erect and requested head, I had to wonder if it was the spiky-haired nymph he pictured when he closed his eyes and came.

Conversely, what are the odds that Eli conjures images of me when he's having sex with Sophia? Kayla? Himself? And why would that question even cross my mind? I'm warped.

"Mrs. Lattimore?" Contemplation interruptus. "Dr. Stanley will see you now."

I follow the nurse, whose quite un-nursely name is Heather, back to an examining room. On the way, we stop at the scale, something I've managed to avoid for several weeks.

"One thirty-two," she informs me. "Not bad, after a two-week honeymoon cruise. I bet the food was amazing."

"It was, though I did try to be careful." Regardless, and despite heavy workouts, I managed to gain two pounds. At five foot seven, 132 pounds of mostly muscle is okay. Wonder what my body fat percentage is.

Once I ease up onto the examination table, Nurse Heather takes my blood pressure. One ten over seventy. At least that's good. Must be the red wine.

"I'll let Dr. Stanley know you're ready." Heather closes the door behind her.

Now comes that obnoxious sit-here-and-wait-hoping-the-door-opens-soon time period that's included in pretty much every doctor visit I've ever experienced. Good thing they don't charge by the minute; at least, I don't think they do. There aren't even any old magazines, and a sign on the wall requests, "Please don't use your cell phones," so I'm very happy when it's not more than five minutes before Dr. Stanley comes in.

"Let's take a look at that knee," he says matter-of-factly.

I'm wearing shorts, which makes it easy enough for him to decide I'm dealing with a fair amount of swelling.

"I've gone over the tests, reviewed the X-rays and MRI. The ACL graft does seem to be faltering. It's my opinion that you rehabbed too intensely and injured it. How much pain are you in?"

"Depends. Sometimes it feels like a knife's slicing right through it. Other times, I forget about it completely, and that can be worse because I might do something stupid like kneel on it. Then it feels like it's coming apart."

"I'll refill your pain med prescription. Other than that, since it *hasn't* actually come apart, I think we should take a cautious approach and brace the knee for several weeks, give it a chance to heal on its own. I'd urge caution as far as exercise, although we do want to maintain a healthy range of motion."

We? What's this "we"?

And that's it?

"So, you don't think another surgery is necessary?"

Dr. Stanley shakes his head. "Not called for. First of all, ACL revisions tend to be less successful than the initial reconstructions. Rehab takes longer and may not produce the intended results. If you continue to demonstrate knee instability, we can always revisit the option, but for now let's allow nature to take its course and see where we end up."

There's that "we" again. "What can I do as far as exercise?"

"Weight-bearing or swimming in moderation, and with the brace locked in full extension. Stationary cycling as tolerated. Come out of the brace a couple times each day for gentle stretching. You still have a brace at home, yes?"

"I do."

"Good. Let me see you again in a couple of weeks."

I should get a second opinion. Glad I happen to have one close by. This time when I visit Cavin's office, his receptionist is on duty. "Hi, Rebecca. I don't suppose my husband has a few minutes?"

"As a matter of fact, he does. He just finished up with his last patient a little while ago and his next appointment isn't until three. I'll let him know you're here."

I wander back to Cavin's office, where he's doing some paperwork, face tipped toward his desk. His hair has fallen over his forehead, almost to his eyes. When I come through the door, he looks up, sending most of it back into place, but a single strand remains. I make my way over, brush the wayward lock gently away. "Good afternoon, Dr. Lattimore. I think you need a trim."

He smiles. "I'll get around to it eventually. I always do."

"No hurry. I hear the unkempt look is all the rage. In fact, I kind of like it. It's rather endearing."

"There are worse things to be, I guess."

He tilts his chin up and I take the hint, kissing him full on the mouth and dipping the tip of my tongue inside. Hunger surfaces in his eyes.

"Wanna make out?" I tease.

"Rain check? I've still got two appointments this afternoon and must remain professional."

"Unkempt professional," I correct. "I'll agree to the rain check as long as it storms tonight."

"A regular hurricane, I promise. So, I take it you're finished with Roger? What did he have to say?"

"That's what I wanted to talk to you about, much as I prefer the flirty repartee. Dr. Stanley suggests I injured the allograft by rehabbing too hard. He wants me to brace the knee and play wait-and-see."

"Roger does tend toward caution."

"I was hoping you might go over the test results and give me your opinion. Not that I'm dying to have another surgery. But if it's the best course of action, I want to know."

"Of course. In fact, I meant to review them already. I've got a little time this afternoon."

I glance at the file he's working on, and of course it belongs to Genevieve Lennon. "What's up with her? Is she going to survive?"

"For quite a while, I'm guessing. Can't say more than that. Doctor/patient privilege and all. Oh, I gave her the phone number at home. Hope you don't mind. She said she tried your cell but you never returned her call, and she wants to talk to you about the Shakespeare Festival at Sand Harbor."

Irritation sizzles. "I wish you wouldn't have done that, actually. I was hoping to avoid her company."

"Really? I thought the two of you were close."

"What makes you say that?"

He shrugs. "She just mentioned that you used to . . ."

She wouldn't.

She might.

". . . spend a lot of time with each other.

Take vacations together and such. I guess I didn't realize that the first time you introduced us."

His tone is hard to read. Surprised? Hurt? Indifferent?

And how to respond?

With humor, that's how. I smile. "Life in the fast lane. Back when I was geared for speed."

He winks. "How fast *were* you, exactly?"

"Not nearly as fast as Genevieve. She was hard to keep up with. Exhausting, in fact. Eventually I stopped trying, especially after I married Finn, who was pretty much the tortoise to my hare. Not to mention Genevieve's cheetah."

"I can't imagine anyone outrunning you, with or without a bum knee."

"Bum? Ooh. Love that country-boy doctor-speak."

"You do?"

"No."

"Regardless, I think Genevieve has probably slowed down quite a bit, too. Don't you?"

"I think that's likely. Still, I had my reasons for allowing our friendship to cool."

The main one being that at one point she confessed she was in love with me. My marriage to Jordan was crumbling into oblivion.

I hadn't met Finn yet. I wasn't in the market for love, especially not with a woman. Men are malleable; love makes them more so. Women are manipulative; love doesn't mitigate that.

"Oh, honey, I'm sorry. She made it sound like you were anxious to see *Taming of the Shrew,* but you were worried about tickets for all of us. She said she scored four for this coming weekend and asked if we had other plans."

What part of "I'm really not sure" did she not understand? I would've sworn the implication was crystal clear. One of the problems in our enhanced friendship was always that we both insisted on taking charge. I had the talent; she had the clout. Even, but not.

I'm used to getting my way. Too often she was able to circumvent that. She enjoyed the game. I thought it tedious and I'm really not interested in playing it again.

"I don't suppose you said we did have other plans."

"No, because we don't."

My body stiffens and I draw it up very straight. "True."

"Tara, if I'd realized it was going to upset you, I would've happily lied. Genevieve Lennon means nothing to me."

Not his fault I may or may not be a little jealous of Ms. Supermodel, and I don't suppose spending one evening with her will ruin my summer. In fact, what I need to do is figure out how to leverage our relationship. "It's okay. I'll survive. Which night are we looking at?"

"Sunday."

Sunday. Good. Hopefully Kayla will be home by then, negating Eli tagging along.

And why the hell does the idea keep surfacing that he might somehow become involved with Genevieve? Like a thirty-something waning star would hook up with the seventeen-year-old son of a married doctor who she may or may not have set her sights on? Ridiculous. And even if it *did* happen, why should I care? The Eli part, not the Cavin part.

"Hello?" Cavin forces me back into real time.

"My turn to be sorry. I was just thinking about whether or not Kayla will be back from California, which would either require an extra ticket or omitting them."

"We could always buy a general admission ticket. Eli and she could sit in the back."

"Good point. Okay, then, I'll plan on Sunday. Do we need to pack a picnic?"

"Not with Genevieve's seats. Row one Adirondack chairs. Food and drinks arrive by waiter. All we have to do is choose our menu before Sunday."

Privilege has its perks.

FOURTEEN

When I arrive home, the first thing I do is check the mail. In addition to the massive amount of junk and minimal amount of actual paper bills, I find a couple of letters addressed to me. Very expensive letters, as it turns out.

The first is from Larry Alexander:

Greetings, Tara. I have arranged for your generous tax-deductible donation to the San Francisco Art Institute to accommodate the tuition of one Kayla Schumacher. Your niece's first semester fees are currently due. Please send a check at your earliest convenience.

On a more personal note, it has come to my attention that your ex-husband is considering moving his young wife and their twins to the East Coast, where they can be closer to his daughter (and by default, since they're partners, mine).

Were you aware of the move? Apparently they made the decision upon hearing that the Russian Hill home is currently in escrow. San Francisco loses luster with your departure.

All best, Larry

Well, at least he's nice about asking for twenty-five grand. The part about Finn prickles, however. Not that he's thinking about relocating his family. I can understand him wanting deeper connection with his grown daughter, who I never met. Seemed Claire didn't approve of our marriage. But considering the house only just sold, how can he know it's in escrow? Something to do with the mortgage, which I'm sure he's relieved to be rid of? Or maybe he has a spy in the real estate office.

The letter from my accountant is a bit more straightforward.

Dear Tara:

In looking at the possible outcomes regarding the Russian Hill sale, I suggest we send max quarterly contributions to the IRS. If I can find a way around the repercussions, as always, I will.

Has anything else changed regarding

income/expenditures? Will you be filing jointly with your husband for the current tax year?

Sincerely . . .

Wonder how far the total fifty-thousand-dollar-ish-per-this-year donation to the SFAI will go toward mitigating the Russian Hill sale? This is why I pay my accountant the big bucks, I suppose. Thankfully, his fees are also tax deductible. As for the joint filing issue . . . I'd better do a little research.

I consider digging the brace out of the hall closet but decide to wait for Cavin's input. Plenty of time to isolate the knee if that's the proper path. Meanwhile, I go ahead and put in some time on the stationary bike. Not too much tension. Speed instead. I give it an hour, watching an Ellen DeGeneres show featuring kids interviewing random people at amusement parks and a woman who invests the majority of her paychecks in building tiny houses for homeless people.

The segment reminds me I need to find a pet project, preferably sooner than later. My portfolio investments keep me well off financially, but they don't require a lot of mental energy, and I get anxious when I'm bored. But what kind of endeavor should I tackle next?

I've already devoted many hours into projects serving the homeless, whose numbers I doubt rank high among the Tahoe population. We're relatively isolated up here, and the weather would make too many months on the street undoable. Plus, with the high tourist count, I imagine law enforcement would find little patience for panhandlers. No, I'll have to investigate the lake elite and where they invest their tax write-off dollars. Perhaps Genevieve has some connections, and certainly Cavin does, and if those resources fail me, someone in my address book must have Tahoe contacts.

The workout initiates a decent sweat and stress relief, and only results in a slight ache in the patella. Maybe Dr. Stanley's right and it will heal on its own after all. I clean up and think about dinner and am starting toward the kitchen when the phone rings.

"Aunt Tara?" It's Kayla's whine. "Is Eli there?"

Uh-oh. "Afraid not. Have you tried his cell?"

"Of course. Over and over. He's not answering. Do you know where he is?"

Double uh-oh. But it's not my job to lie for the kid. "He's visiting a friend in Reno tonight. He'll be home tomorrow."

"Reno?"

"That's what he said."

"And he's staying overnight?"

"Yes. Apparently they're seeing a show that will run late."

"May I ask who the friend is?"

"Kayla, as far as I know, he's only acquainted with one person in Reno."

"Oh." Eloquence, in one two-letter word. I change the subject. "When do you expect to return? Eli said you thought Friday?"

"I did, but not anymore. Here, I'll let you talk to Mom."

The phone goes quiet for several long seconds, but finally Mel says, "Hello? Tara?"

"I'm here. Just looking for an update."

She exhales, forcing an audible sigh. "It's pretty awful. She's doped up out of her mind, so she's either asleep or ranting most of the time. She can't feed herself. Can't use the bathroom. Thank God for the hospice people, who handle all the dirty details. I'm glad I don't have to. It will be a blessing when she's gone."

What have I been trying to tell her? "So, how long are you staying down there?"

"Not sure. At least through the weekend. I'm trying to put everything in order before I go. Later today I'm going over to the funeral parlor to pick out a casket."

"Why bother? Burial is expensive. Have her cremated."

"She quite specifically wants to be buried."

"So what? Once she's dead she won't know the difference."

"No. But *I* will. Oh, and she wants to be buried back home in Glenns Ferry. I guess she bought a plot in the same cemetery where her mother was interred, which is weird, I know, considering their contentious relationship. It's all written down in her living will, which is handwritten but apparently valid."

"Do you need me to handle anything?"

"Thanks for offering, but no. She doesn't own much. In fact, there's nothing to cover the deductibles but a small life insurance policy and even smaller savings account. Other than that, some furniture and clothes, all of which can go to the Salvation Army. Oh, she does have an old beater. Rather than try to sell it, I thought I'd just give it to Will, unless you object."

He hung around longer than most of Mom's men. "No objection. If she's still able, you might have her sign over the title now. Either that or forge her signature and a bill of sale. No use arguing with the DMV if you don't have to."

"It's already taken care of."

My sister defines efficiency.

"What about the casket? Do you need some money to pay for it? Those things are expensive. And what about shipping it to Idaho?"

"I'll put it on a credit card and if you want to reimburse me some, that would be great. Will has already volunteered to handle the transport. Believe it or not, that man really seems to care about Mom, and not because he thinks he's in line for her junker truck."

Too little, too late, so sorry, Will. Wonder if Mom even cares.

Suddenly, a hideous scream erupts on the far end of the line, somewhere behind Melody, who says, "I have to go. She needs her meds. Is there anything you want me to tell her?"

I've worked very hard not to say a damn word to the bitch for over two decades. Mutual anger charged the few exchanges we've had. But with death hovering over her head, there isn't much left to be pissed about. I don't regret the silent years, and wonder how I'll remember her after she's gone. Will planting her in Glenns Ferry mitigate the Idaho nightmares? Will I think of her at all?

"Tell her bon voyage."

I think that calls for a drink, and what sounds good this afternoon is sangria. I've got a favorite recipe that calls for white peaches, which we happen to have, turning ripe. I dice three, put them in the bottom of a pitcher along with a little brandy and a half bottle of Grenache, and am topping the whole thing off with prosecco when Cavin blows in, tornado-like. His expression reads "disgusted."

"What's wrong?"

He comes straight over, puts his arms around me, and kisses me softly, denying the tenseness in his shoulders. "Are you finished with that?" He points to the sangria.

"Only just."

"Sit down. I'll bring you a glass."

Now what? But I do as instructed and watch him pour two tall tumblers, spooning some peaches into each. Then he joins me on the sofa. "So, I reviewed your test results. Spent quite a bit of time going over the films and digesting the tech's notes. I disagree completely with Roger. The ACL reconstruction is rupturing, and a revision is most definitely in order . . ."

I mostly tune out for the length of time it takes him to give me all the reasons my knee could be disintegrating. What it comes down to is he wants me to have surgery to repair the repair.

"In my opinion, a two-stage ACLR revision is necessary."

"What does that mean?"

"Two surgeries, around three months apart. The first would remove the old hardware, and bone would be grafted to fill the holes where the screws are currently in place. Once that heals, the second surgery would do what the original ACLR was supposed to."

"Sounds like an awful lot of downtime, not to mention physical therapy."

"Yes, and the PT could not be as aggressive as last time. You are a strong, stubborn woman, but, even with the revision, your knee will never be either of those again, and pushing it too hard would be bad all the way around."

"What if I forego further surgeries?"

"The knee will improve slightly, but it will always be prone to laxity. The odds of re-injury would be great, as well as the possibility of arthritis developing."

I don't know whether to be relieved, scared, or goddamn angry. I'm starting to feel like damaged goods. But mostly what concerns me is too many hours being housebound again.

Maybe you need a third opinion.

I treat myself to a refreshing sip of some very good sangria and reach for my husband's hand. "Would you do the surgeries? I'd want someone I can trust at the helm."

"I would definitely oversee the entire thing, even if my hands don't do the work. But don't worry. I won't let Roger in the OR. There are others I can call in."

"Will I be able to ski again?"

"Probably not this year. Possibly not without a brace. And definitely no more Mott Canyon. But yes, you'll ski again, and we'll ski together. I'm so looking forward to that."

"Me, too, and two years seems like a long way off."

"Sixteen months. Eighteen max, depending on Mother Nature. I'll still be here. Will you?"

"That's been my plan all along."

"Excellent." He takes a long pull off his glass. "And so is this concoction. What, exactly, is it?"

"White peach sangria. Just one of my many specialties."

"Let's finish our drinks and I'll show you one of mine."

He runs three fingertips along the pulse just beneath my jaw, down my neck, and into the scoop of my blouse, all the way to the rising beat of my heart.

"Here? Now? Before dinner?"

"Why not? We're alone in the house. Let's work up an appetite."

Suddenly I realize how few times we've indulged our libidos since we got back from our honeymoon.

What's up with that?

Middle age?

Marriage?

Now I'm parched.

Thirsting.

And not for sangria.

Dry Spell

You are like rain, forecasted
to quench a summer's thirsting,
thirst grown beyond easy need, to life or
    death.

I watch the clouds,
approaching windward mountains, slate
bruising black beneath expectation.

The western window
darkens as, laden, the curtain falls,
descends to veil peaks and rifts, draws
    nearer.

Is it thunder that I hear?
Or is the sudden rumble but the flurry
of hurried birds, on wing against unceasing
    drought?

One warm, wet spatter
stings the dust, stamps its ragged mark,
imprints a welt of hope upon the arid
    parchment.

Promise sizzles in the air,
wrapped in threads of ozone, electric
with desire so bold it borders ecstasy.

Claim this vacant sky.
Cast your shadow, speak to me in thunder,
throb against thirsting skin and flesh gone
    fallow.

Oh, give me rain!
Gift me with downpour, fill this empty
    well,
the reservoir drained to grit by lingering
    dry spell.

FIFTEEN

I despise being unsure. I mean, even of petty things, like whether to purchase an oversize bag because people will see I've bought the best or instead go for the one unnoticeable to thieves that also serves its purpose better because I only carry my wallet, phone, pepper spray, and the occasional lipstick inside it anyway.

But when it comes to major decisions, like whether to listen to the doctor who originally "fixed" my knee or take the word of another orthopedist — one who happens to be my husband — and tear out what's already there, then rebuild it again? I wish it were cut-and-dried, but it's anything but. It would be so easy to play wait-and-see — brace it, prop it, isolate it. But Cavin says I could limp forever. On the other hand, while surgical corrections, followed by months of physical therapy, might raise the odds of my participating in the activities I love, there are no promises. It's frustrating as hell.

All I know is, I want the knee right. Skiing isn't the only thing it's getting in the way of. My sex manual is currently a limited edition. In Cavin's relentless pursuit of coition sans patellar pain, he is careful. Too careful, when what I want is no-holds-barred recklessness.

The evening Eli stayed in Reno, our lovemaking was disappointing at best. The foreplay was good enough — Cavin is brilliant at cunnilingus, and I just have to find a comfortable way to lie, legs open in invitation, for that. It's nice. But nice is not what I'm after. My goal, that night and in the future, is dirty, nasty, bordering-on-demonic fuckfesting. Instead, any time I moaned, whether for the right reason or not, he was all, "Sorry. Didn't mean to hurt you." Then he backed off, though not completely out. He gave just enough effort to finish and pull away, satisfied, if not depleted.

High school sex déjà vu.

Except for the tongue.

High school boys hate oral sex.

Giving, not receiving.

So, if anything is making me lean toward saying okay to surgery, it's my desire to live out my life having lust-driven sex without worrying about popping my tibia sideways due to abnormal rotational forces. God, I sound like a medical dictionary.

I'm still mulling over the decision when Cavin and Eli get back from town. Eli wanted a new shirt to wear to Shakespeare tonight. "Something upscale casual" was how he put it. Something to impress Genevieve Lennon is what I'm thinking. Good thing South Lake Tahoe has an excellent little boutique that sells both men's and women's clothing; otherwise it would have necessitated another trip to Reno.

He didn't want to "bore us with the details" of his evening with Sophia, other than to say the lead actress in her show was sexy as hell, but not in a disgusting way. Like a boy his age would think anything involving scantily clad women on a stage less than three feet from his face was disgusting. As for what might or might not have happened between the encore and his return the following afternoon, well, he left that completely up to our imaginations.

When he got home, his pupils looked awfully dilated, and he was sniffling enough for me to notice. I wanted to quiz him about possible substance ingestion but thought better of it. After the fact wouldn't have meant a thing, especially if before the fact didn't mean a thing, either. Besides, my counsel in the having-to-do-with-Sophia department is quite obviously unappreciated. Actually, I don't think he appreciates my counsel about anything.

He definitely wasn't happy about me outing him to Kayla. "What did you say to her?" he demanded.

"All I did was answer her questions. She was worried because she couldn't get hold of you, and asked if I knew your whereabouts. I told her you were in Reno, visiting a friend."

"Why did you tell her that?" Anger swelling.

"Because that's what you told me. What should I have said?"

"You could have made something up." Temples visibly pulsing.

"Eli, I've made it clear to you that I despise dishonesty. Not that I've never lied, but it's rare. And I have absolutely zero desire to cover for you, especially under the circumstances. That would make me an accomplice to your deception. *Plus,* I'd be deceiving my own niece. I won't lie to family."

"Well, just so you know, she's royally pissed."

"Yeah, well, she should be."

"It doesn't bother you to piss off your family?"

"*You* pissed her off. But hey, I didn't mention the fact that we're all going out with Genevieve Lennon on Sunday."

That shut him up, at least about Kayla, who's supposed to be back sometime this week. Should be an interesting reunion.

The men come bustling in a little after three. Beyond clothes shopping, they've visited the barber, or maybe a stylist. Cavin's hair is cut quite attractively, with lots of short feathered layers. Eli's, on the other hand, is buzzed in back and on the sides, but he kept it long on top and is wearing it swept to one side. Young, but smart, and definitely handsome.

"Wow. The two of you spruce up pretty nice."

"All for you, milady," replies Cavin.

Eli flips his hair to the other side. "Not mine. This is completely about impressing Ms. Lennon. Maybe she'll help me get a modeling job."

The funny thing is, he probably could model. He's tall and slim, with just enough muscle to look built but not enough to look like he tries too hard, and Cavin has gifted him with handsomely carved features, not to mention those expressive eyes. "It's a dog-eat-dog industry, Eli."

"Yeah, but think about the perks!"

"Is that saliva leaking down your chin?" I tease. "Not real attractive."

"I'll be sure to wipe it off before I meet Genevieve." He pronounces it "Zhan-vee-ev."

"I'm sure she'll appreciate that, although I'm just as certain she's used to a fair amount of dripping drool."

Cavin clears his throat. "If you'll excuse me, I want to go shower. I don't know how it's possible for hair to get everywhere when you're wearing those big cape thingies, but I feel like it's clinging to every inch of my upper torso."

Eli fishes around in the shopping bag he's been holding. "Here's your Tommy Bahama, Dad."

He tosses a Hawaiian-patterned shirt, all in blue, to Cavin, whose face flushes slightly. "Couldn't help myself," he tells me. "It's not something I would ordinarily buy, but for some reason I like it."

"It's awesome," says Eli. "But not as cool as mine."

Eli's shirt is black, with a bold orchid print in lavender and mint green. Considering I've only ever seen him in T-shirts and Henleys, this is quite the departure. "Interesting choices. What got into you two?"

Eli grins. "Must have been the mango."

"Unusual side effect, but okay, and now what can I possibly wear to coordinate?"

"Grass skirt and coconut shell bra?" suggests Eli.

"Don't worry. I'll figure out something."

Cavin reminds us we're meeting Genevieve at the entrance at six. "It's not that far, but we should leave here no later than five thirty. Traffic and parking will be terrible. Oh, and if I were you, I'd wear the knee brace tonight. That sand is a bear to walk through even if you're perfectly sound, and you're not. Now, if you'll excuse me, hot water beckons."

Off he goes, but Eli lingers. "Dad says you're having another surgery?"

"Maybe. Maybe two, in fact. He thinks the ACL repair is failing and it's my best shot at approaching 'normal' again."

"Did you get a second opinion?"

"His *was* the second opinion. The first was that I rehabbed too hard and with proper bracing and PT the graft would likely heal on its own."

He cocks his head, studying me. "So why not wait and see? What if caution's the better course?"

There he goes again, sounding way too adult.

"Look, Eli, I trust your fa—"

"Maybe you shouldn't. Maybe he prefers you helpless."

The echo of Cavin's recent statement is bothersome. *I kind of like you helpless.*

Without waiting for a response, Eli turns on one heel and stomps downstairs. Not for the first time, he leaves me slightly askew. The boy excels at yanking my chain, but subtly, feeding me uncertainties I must bite on and chew to digest.

Why is that?

With the question very much on my mind, I wander back to my bedroom to change. Quandary. What do I wear to look sexy while sporting a decidedly unsexy piece of hardware? I draw on my rudimentary knowledge of fashion, choosing a billowy calf-length skirt in amethyst. I will draw attention upward to a form-fitting gold tank with a cleavage-revealing scoop. I may not have legs up to there like Ms. Vogue, but I've got her beat in the breast department, especially with excellent support keeping everything propped up into place. I devote a copious amount of time to skin care, makeup, and creating, with minuscule dabs of gel and mouse, perfect fox-red tresses.

Overall, it's a good look, a fact that's confirmed when Cavin finds me leaning forward to buckle a pair of flat sandals and rewards me with a low whistle. "Wow, woman. Talk about a stunning view."

I truly hope the attraction knotting us together doesn't fray in the future. "You like?"

"I love," he corrects. "And if we didn't need to go very soon, I'd show you just how much. But since we do, would you mind handing me my new Tommy Bahama? I still can't believe Eli talked me into it. I've never worn a Hawaiian shirt in my life."

"First time for everything, I hear. Besides, it becomes you."

It does.

Suddenly I don't want to share him with anyone. Not his receptionist. Not his patients. Not the Shakespeare Festival crowd. And definitely not Genevieve. "I think I want to kidnap you and spirit you away somewhere."

"Tara, we've only been back from our honeymoon for ten days."

"True. I suppose that's a bit unrealistic, huh?"

"Afraid so. At least until I retire. Then we can live a nomadic life if you wish."

There's something romantic about the

idea of trekking the world, touching down somewhere unique and staying for a while. On the other hand, I enjoy being alone and wonder if I'd get tired of coupling full-time. The half-of-a-whole concept might get tedious. Besides, I expect my partner to contribute financially as well as emotionally, and I doubt his retirement account will accommodate five-star travel. Plus, I like having a place that belongs to me — a place I can escape to, burrow into, hide out in.

"I believe there's an unwritten law that nomads require two functioning knees, so let's get me mended first."

"Amen to that. That skirt is pretty enough, but I prefer the way you look in something shorter. Just call me a letch."

"Okay, letch. Question before we go."

"What?"

"Do you really prefer me helpless?"

"You, helpless? That, my darling, is an epic oxymoron, any preference aside."

He'd better not forget it.

The evening holds few surprises. We arrive in plenty of time and, of course, Genevieve's skirt exposes way too many inches of her legs-up-to-there. Even across the parking lot, she's hard to miss, holding court by the gate, signing autographs for a gaggle of admirers. Cavin has the good grace not to stare too blatantly. Not so, Eli.

"Holy crap!" he exclaims. "That's one model who doesn't need airbrushing."

"You haven't seen her up close yet. She could actually use a little." Ooh, too catty. I retract my claws.

Eli jumps to her defense. "That's not very nice. I thought you two were friends."

"Not exactly."

"Well, you should be."

When Genevieve notices our approach, she dismisses her entourage and comes over to join us. I introduce her to Eli, who really should close his mouth.

He pushes in between her and me to shake her hand. "Hey, Ms. Lennon. Wow. I'm such a huge fan!"

Yeah, of her half-naked *Sports Illustrated* poses. God, could he be any more obvious? Should I offer a pen for her autograph?

Don't be ridiculous. He's just a kid and she's an icon.

"So good to meet you, Eli, and please call me Genevieve. Are we ready to go in?" She hooks Eli's elbow, steers him toward the entrance.

Cavin takes my hand, bends to put his mouth close to my ear. "Heaven help us, that kid's ego is visibly bloating."

We have to stop several times as people

who either know or want to know Genevieve say hello, but eventually we make our way to the VIP section, where an attractive young usher checks our tickets. Eli is so enthralled by Genevieve, he barely even notices the cute attendant, who escorts us to our seats. The low Adirondacks are front row, square center.

"Wow," exhales Eli. "What do you have to do to rate seats like this? Kill someone?"

"No," replies Genevieve. "You just have to donate a lot of money. Money is generally a better motivator than murder."

Before we can sit, a tall man with rather amazing silver hair makes his way through the crowd. "Good evening, Genevieve. How have you been?"

"Wonderful, thank you. Oh, allow me to introduce my guests. Austin, this is Cavin Lattimore; his wife, Tara; and son, Eli. Cavin is an orthopedic surgeon. And Austin is the executive director of the festival."

Austin reluctantly pries his gaze off Genevieve to give me an assessing once-over, and then meets Cavin's eyes. "Of course. So good to see you again, Dr. Lattimore. I wasn't aware you'd married."

Cavin looks slightly flustered. He takes my hand. "It was a relatively quick decision. But how could I let this one get away?"

The question rankles, though it sounds like a compliment. "To be fair, I wasn't running very fast," I say. "Literally or figuratively."

"How do you two know each other?" asks Genevieve, intrigued.

"My daughter Allison's a dancer," answers Austin. "Dr. Lattimore put her splintered tibia back together. Happy to say she's still dancing."

"That's very good to hear," says Cavin. "How long have you been in charge of the festival?"

"This is my second year."

"And Maryann?" queries Genevieve. "Is she here somewhere?"

"Not tonight. She had another function. My wife is involved with the Parasol Foundation," explains Austin. "It's an umbrella organization for several local nonprofits, including the Shakespeare Festival."

"Interesting," I say. "I've only just moved to the lake, after years of fund-raising work in San Francisco. If there's anything I can do to help out, I'd love to be involved."

"Tara does fantastic events," Genevieve adds. "I've attended several, and always leave a little poorer."

Austin reassesses me. "I'll be sure to mention your interest to Maryann. In fact, we're

183

hosting a postperformance party on Friday evening, mostly for festival donors who want to meet the cast. Would you care to join us?"

I glance at Cavin, whose expression says "why not?" "We'd love to."

"Great. You're welcome, too, Genevieve, if you'll still be around."

"I'm here another week at least. Why don't you send me the details and I'll forward them to Tara?"

"Sounds like a plan. Now, I'd better mingle. I hope you enjoy the performance."

The play is *The Taming of the Shrew,* not my favorite of the bard's offerings.

Too much deception and more than a fair amount of misogyny — thanks so much for that, Mr. Shakespeare. But it's performed well by a stellar cast, with the requisite humor to make the premise palatable. Even Eli laughs where he should.

Genevieve flirts with him. She flirts with Cavin. She does not flirt with me, at least not while flirting with them. But at intermission, when the guys excuse themselves to head to the restroom, she stays behind.

"Attractive men," she observes.

I don't feel the need to argue. "Yes, they are."

"I was surprised you married again. *And*

again. I thought Jordan might've soured you on the practice."

A small laugh escapes me. "Guess I'm just a glutton for punishment. As the old song goes, I've looked for love in all the wrong places. Hopefully Cavin proves to be the right place."

Genevieve sighs. "You know what Jordan told me once? That you were the only woman he ever really loved."

Let's put that on hold. "When did he tell you that?"

"Oh. I'm not sure if you were aware of it, but he and I saw each other for a short while after the two of you split up."

I shouldn't be surprised. "Really."

She slides her hand under the armrest and settles it on my knee. "Does that bother you?"

The sensual gesture is disconcerting, and it takes a couple of seconds to manufacture a question in response to hers. "Do you want it to?"

That draws a wry smile. "I probably did at the time, and I'm pretty sure Jordan's motivation revolved completely around revenge."

"I don't understand. It wasn't like he was interested in keeping our marriage intact."

"Love and immorality aren't mutually

exclusive. Know what else he said? That he wasn't sure you were capable of loving him back, or loving anyone, in fact."

There is no judgment in her voice, but it does pose the silent question: *Was he right?* The slow creep of heat across my cheeks suggests I should change the subject. I cover her hand, still a memory against my knee, with my own. "What about you? Any prospects for love?"

She shrugs. "Boy toys. Girl toys. Playthings. Insipid conversation and sex as religion. Funny how being not alone can in fact make you lonelier."

The men return and she withdraws her hand, and as the second act begins, I consider her last remark. She's right. There have been times when, surrounded by people, I've felt completely isolated.

Tonight is not one of those occasions.

Sixteen

I wake to the sound of a door opening. It's dark in the room, and steady breathing beside me tells me Cavin's sleep is undisturbed. I lie very still, listening to a soft scratching across the carpet.

"E-e-e . . ." It's a rasp, and the second syllable of Eli's name won't escape me at all. But even as I realize that, I understand it can't be him. The footsteps are almost weightless.

Terror grips me suddenly, holds me fast against the bed. I try to lash out, to kick, to scream, but not a single part of my body will move except my eyes. And they can't see anything out of the ordinary in the low pewter light of what must be predawn. Yet something — something! — is moving toward me, and it's carrying menace.

"N-n-o." Almost a word. "Lea—"

But it's not ready to leave yet.

Nothing there.

Nothing there.

Nothing there.

That's what I keep repeating, at least inside my head. Nothing there. Nothing that can be seen. Nothing of substance. Yet there's a force. A power. Energy. Something dynamic.

And it wants me.

Why can't Cavin feel it? Why can't he intuit the horror rising up from my gut like bile and gurgling into my brain?

My side of the bed depresses, like someone just sat beside me. She's reaching out. She?

Who?

What?

Her voice materializes from the gloom. "We have to go now."

Mom's gone.

Just a bad dream.

The pressure on my chest increases and I can barely find breath. It's like all the air has been vacuumed from my lungs. *Thump-thump. Thump-thump. Thump-thump!* My heart shrieks and still the weight increases. The more I fight, the more it grows, and after a while I can't hang on. Fade toward black.

I settle into a nightmare, find comfort there, because at least I know I'm dreaming. Melody and I are sleeping on a makeshift bed on the smelly floor of the closet of a motel room. We were scared when Mama shut us in here, but she said we didn't want to see what was going to happen. We hear everything.

The man grunting.

Mama moaning.

The man's voice rising, angry.

Mama begging. "I need another twenty. Come on, baby. I'll do whatever you want."

Something slapping skin.

Mama crying.

Something thumping against flesh.

Mama screaming.

Crashing. Thrashing. Something heavy hitting the floor.

Quiet, then sudden movement.

The closet door yanks open. "Come on. We have to go now. Fast."

As she hurries us toward our escape, I see the man, still naked, lying silent on the floor, a small trickle of blood on his forehead where the now-broken lamp connected. She pushes us out the door and across the parking lot, to where the pickup truck sleeps. I wait till we're on the highway to ask, "Did you kill him?"

"I don't think his wife got that lucky." Her voice is cold concrete.

And so is mine when I ask, "Did we get lucky?"

In answer, she pulls into McDonald's. After two days, bellies burning with hunger, we will eat tonight after all. I picture the stranger, a mannequin on that stinking motel room floor. Smile.

Suddenly, my body compresses again, only this time when I ascend from the depths, I look up into my husband's eyes, feel the dream-risen heat of his skin against my own. Relief relaxes me into his arms, and a vortex of need drives away every vestige of fear. Despite his weight, I can breathe again.

I inhale him.

Exhale me.

Into his mouth, a breath of us, wrapped up in a kiss too tender.

I want more, want him to take me, and encourage him with a tango of tongue and teeth. He understands, no words required, moves the dance lower. I arch my back, invite his hands to explore the knolls of my breasts, and the slow circling of his fingers lifts my nipples, ripens them into sweet, purple berries for the pluck of his lips.

"Bite them," I demand, and he does, but too gently. "Harder."

Quick bolts.

Exquisite pain.

Enough to waken Inanna, the queen of Heaven, sleeping within. Goddess of gentle rain and, equally, flood; of evening star and morning dawning; of war and ritual sex. Her lust infuses me now, threads my body, coaxes every nerve to full alert. Cavin throws off the covers, drops back toward the foot of the bed, and parts my legs gently, careful to put all the pressure on the left side. He kisses up the length of each, back and forth between them, and knowing what's surely coming next, an anticipatory moan escapes me.

I close my eyes against the morning light and surety of his motives and am instantly rewarded with the firm demand of his tongue. It knows me well.

All ghosts forgotten, I open myself to the heady perfection of my husband's practiced foreplay, and when he pauses before entering me, I beg, "Please don't stop." My hands explore the firm musculature of his derriere, settle there, and push.

Hard.

He's inside me.

Stretching me.

Filling me.

Rocking me.

Making me scream.

Anyone listening would think he was kill-ing me, but every hint of pain is perfect pain, and I match each thrust with one of my own until we build in unison to the ultimate cresting.

Mutual orgasm.

His, punctuated by distant thunder.

Mine, by epic flood.

I crumble back into his arms, and realize he's brought me to tears. "Thank you."

He strokes my hair, fingers tangling into the damp mess of curls. "For what?"

"Chasing her away."

"Who?"

"Mom. She wanted to take me with her." I confide the horror movie that recently played itself right in this very room.

His lips brush across my forehead. "Nightmare. Nothing more."

"I know."

It was a lot more than a dream, but I leave it there and allow myself the luxury of two minutes' respite, cushioned by his arms and buoyed by his spirit.

Finally, he rouses. "Busy day ahead. Better get it started."

"Okay, fine." I pout. "Don't worry about me."

"Tara, I see no need whatsoever to worry about you." He swings his legs over the side of the bed, reaches back for one more kiss.

Then he goes to the window, slides it all the way open, inviting the forest inside. "See? It's a gorgeous day. Not a cloud in sight. And no evidence of ghosts."

Cavin retreats to the shower and I go in search of a mega helping of caffeine to ward off any lingering spirits. Once the coffee is brewing I check my phone. Sure enough, there's a message from Mel.

Mom died just before midnight. She went peacefully.

The first part doesn't surprise me. I have little doubt she actually stopped by, hoping to take me with her. But I expected she'd complain about her departure. Wrestle the Grim Reaper, in fact, desperate to remain in this world. I find myself disappointed she exited so easily.

As has become my habit, I carry my coffee out onto the deck and immerse myself in the crisp Sierra air. Rarely did I have such an opportunity in San Francisco, where morning most often comes shrouded in Pacific mist, and not often did I rise before nine. Here, though Cavin doesn't expect it, I want to see him off to work. But even without that necessity, I enjoy the amenities offered in the mountains this time of day.

Chief among those is quiet, albeit punctuated by the varied voices of wildlife, busily attending their a.m. duties. But those fade into the grand envelope of woodland silence. I sink down into it and try to decipher the strange mix of emotions I seem to be experiencing.

My mother drew her last breath.

There's loss here, but I'm not sure why.

She's been dead to you for years.

There's regret here that I don't understand.

Did some sliver of you want connection?

Anger seethes, familiar.

If anyone deserved a truncated life, she did.

A wind of confusion mushrooms.

Why should you care that she's gone?

She was never there.

Cavin's voice startles me out of my reverie. "Hey. You okay? You're trembling."

My head bobs, on autopilot. I don't feel so okay but don't need to share that with him. "But so happens you were wrong about that ghost. I heard from Melody."

"Your mom?"

"Yes. She's gone."

I just hope she stays that way.

SEVENTEEN

It's an emotionally tumultuous couple of days. Melody handles the final details, turning whatever's left of our mother over to the funeral parlor to plop into the casket. I tried to talk Mel into the $995 Walmart low-end job, but the funeral director proposed a special deal on a prettier model, offering to toss in the gaskets that will keep water from leaking in. So, for the rock-bottom price of $2,250 plus applicable taxes, Mom's remains will rot just a little slower, with a satin pillow to cushion her head.

They swing back by the house on Wednesday afternoon, and Mel decides to take me up on my invitation to spend the night. It's uncomfortable all the way round, starting with Kayla, who arrives with a well-deserved chip on her shoulder. She storms through the door, defenses raised.

Eli has been preparing his alibi, which, of course, is a lie. But first he greets her with a very sweet kiss. "Hey, baby. Missed you."

Kayla does her best not to be swayed. "I'm sure."

"I really did. The house has seemed empty without you."

Oh my God. What a crock. The boy is shameless. And I do believe it's working. Kayla's shoulders drop just a little, as if tension is deserting them.

Eli continues, "Um . . . Sorry about your grandma."

"You didn't even know June."

"But you cared about h—"

"I didn't know her either. Not really."

"Oh. Well, I'm sorry anyway. Here, let me take your backpack."

She hoists it higher on her shoulder. "I've got it. Can we go downstairs? We need to talk. Now."

Yikes.

Mel and her other two girls stand in a straight line in the hallway, watching the scene unfold. We all wait for Kayla and Eli to disappear from sight before any of us dares move. As soon as they're gone for sure, the chatter begins.

Jessica, in her just-turned-thirteen, high-decibel squeal: "Ooh. She's so gonna dump him!"

Suzette, pretending to be worldlier than

her overprotected not-quite-sixteen years could possibly allow: "Okay by me. I'll take him on the rebound."

Jesus, now that I've invited them to stay over, what am I going to do with them? No wonder I avoided all this family stuff for so many years. "The guest rooms are downstairs, and so is the game room. You're welcome to check them out, although you might want to wait a few minutes until the fireworks fizzle out. Meanwhile, I guess you can watch TV up here."

"What about the beach?" asks Jessica.

"I did promise that, didn't I? We'll go in a little while, unless you want to stay another day, and then we could go tomorrow instead and hang out longer," I offer, certain Mel will want to get home.

So when Suz pleads for the extra time, it's something of a surprise that Melody agrees. "Oh, why not? It's just back to the tedium anyway, not to mention the God-awful heat. It's supposed to be, like, ninety-eight in Sacramento today."

"Graham won't mind?"

"Who cares?"

"Don't you think you should call him?"

Her head cocks to one side. "What business is it of yours?"

Whoa. Okay. "None at all."

I must've sounded hurt because she's quick to apologize. "Sorry. Didn't mean to be curt, but I don't answer to Graham."

Uh-oh. I really want to quiz my sister about the state of her marriage, but I'll put that on hold. "Okay, then, I guess it's settled. We'll probably have to run to the grocery store. And did you girls bring swimsuits?"

They shake their heads in unison. That would be a negative.

"We can pick some up while we're out. In fact, maybe we should just run those errands right now." Give the feuding couple some space. "I'll let Eli and Kayla know we're going."

I maneuver the staircase noisily, providing plenty of warning. When I pause outside Eli's bedroom door, it seems quiet on the far side, so I go ahead and knock.

Kayla giggles.

"Shh!" orders Eli, before responding, "Wha-at?" He's out of breath.

Guess his alibi worked.

"Sorry to interrupt. We're going shopping. Anything you need?"

"Yeah. For you to leave us alone."

Will do.

"Sure. But when we get back, the girls will want to use the game room. Please expect company down here. Oh, they're staying over until Friday, too. We plan to go to the beach tomorrow, and maybe take a ride on the *Dixie*. You're welcome to come along."

"Coming is exactly what I have in mind, although now I've got to start over."

Kayla snickers again, and I take the opportunity to retreat. I should be used to Eli's brutal bluntness by now, but it still catches me off guard. "Yeah, well, go easy. I'd hate for you to pull a muscle or something."

I don't wait for a response, and by the time I reach the top of the stairs, the others are waiting by the front door. "Everything okay down there?" asks Mel.

I wink. "A little too okay, if you catch my drift."

"Ugh!" exclaims Jessica. "Are they *doing it*?"

"Let's just say Suz seems to be out of luck as far as the rebound thing."

"No fair," jokes Suzette. "But what I want to know is how he got away with it. She's been mad for days."

"That boy is a well-practiced liar," I say.

"All men are liars," adds Mel. "Don't forget that. Now, you girls go get in the car." She watches them exit, and once they're safely out of earshot, she turns to me. "Can

I ask you something?"

"Of course."

"Who is Sophia?"

My cheeks burn instantly. "What?"

"We've been hearing about Sophia for days. Who, exactly, is she?"

Some information is meant to be held close to the chest, at least until there's no way around coughing it up. I wouldn't have shared this with my sister independently, but I guess she has the right to know, considering it's affecting her daughter so personally. I inhale sharply and exhale words.

"Sophia is Cavin's ex-girlfriend. He was planning on marrying her until he discovered she had a sizable cocaine habit and didn't mind enjoying several men on the side, one of whom happened to be Eli. She had moved to New York to produce some off-Broadway dance show, but she's currently back in Reno, which is where Eli recently hooked up with her."

Mel cocks her head. "But Eli isn't a man."

"According to Sophia, he's all man."

"How do you know?"

"Because she told me so. Eli actually brought her here a few weeks ago, and I arrived home unexpectedly. It was when you and I went shopping for the wedding and I decided not to stay over in Sacramento. Anyway, he ran into Sophia at the beach and thought he was safe enjoying her company in my house. I made it quite clear it had better not ever happen again, and then I asked if she couldn't find someone closer to her age to seduce. When I said Eli was just a kid, she happily corrected me."

"That must have been awkward."

"To say the least."

On our way to the car, Mel says, "I'd be livid if I ever came home to find another woman there."

"That would never happen though, right?"

"It'd better not."

We close the door on the subject as we get in the car and start toward town, the girls chattering contentedly in the backseat. When Melody finally speaks, it's with her usual good cheer. "Where are we going?"

"There are some shops in Heavenly Village that sell swimsuits," I suggest. "A bit pricey, perhaps, but I'm happy to spring for them."

"How expensive can a quarter yard of fabric be?" asks Mel.

Turns out, close to fifty dollars each. Both girls opt for bikinis and, surprisingly, so does Melody. In fact, I can't believe it. "I've never seen you wear anything less than a skirted one-piece."

"I've lost a little weight. I want to try it on, at least." She disappears into a dressing room. "Come here, Tara. What do you think?"

While she might not be *Sports Illustrated* material, she can definitely wear the bikini. "Wow. How much have you lost, anyway?"

"Almost thirty pounds."

"In how long?"

"A little over six months. It was my New Year's resolution."

"Whatever you're doing, keep it up. You look great."

She absolutely does, but for some reason, the phrase that keeps running through my head is "trouble in Paradise."

Swimsuits, beach towels, and UV-blocking sunglasses set me back close to three hundred bucks, and that doesn't include the sand-sifting mat, which adds another 150, or the gorgeous leather handbag I happen across. Replacing the one I've got, not even grown ratty as yet, is a three-hundred-dollar expense. The sunscreen we save for the grocery store.

Turns out, it's kind of nice having the girls along there. A hot little wave begins to pulse in my knee about halfway through, and I can send them off in search of things, which cuts time on my feet considerably. Plus, they carry everything in when we get home and volunteer to help make dinner. Of course, that's probably because Eli is playing chef.

Mel and I sit outside, where a breeze carrying hints of honeysuckle ruffles the evergreens. She sighs. "It's beautiful up here. I'd consider moving to Tahoe myself, once the girls go off to college."

"There are high schools around here, you know."

"Yes, but I wouldn't want to make them leave their friends."

Okay, this is a test. "Not to mention Graham's practice."

"Tara, if I ever move, it will be without a husband in tow."

"Sounds like something you've been considering."

Weight loss. New hairstyle and color. And, now that I'm really studying her, more makeup than I've seen her wear before. Maybe she's more than considering. Could it be she's planning?

"When I was at Mom's, I had a lot of time to think. Twenty years is forever to be with a person, and it would be difficult to dissolve our marriage, both emotionally and financially. So I'm not in a hurry to divorce Graham, especially not with a couple of children still living at home and the other less than two hours away. I'm just not sure he feels the same."

Inside, the kids are joking and laughing as they go about making dinner. Which is, I suppose, though I've no experience with it at all, the way a family should engage. It does make me wonder, however, what Eli said to Kayla to make her forgive him so easily. I think of Mel's earlier remark: *All men are liars.*

"Have you talked with Graham about your future, or possible futures?"

"We don't talk anymore. Mostly, we quarrel, if we happen to find ourselves in the same room together."

"Just throwing this out there. Lots of couples divorce and their kids manage fine."

"I understand that."

"So, what's the point?"

"I wish I knew."

"Happiness?"

"What's that?"

This can't be my sister, the eternal optimist, talking. Strange, only months ago, she wouldn't have been the one feeling this way. I would have.

"Can I ask a personal question?"

"You can always ask."

"Are you and Graham still intimate?"

Her expression reads vexed. "You mean do we have sex?"

"Well, yeah. It's kind of important, right?"

"Not to me."

"But you're only thirty-nine. You really don't care about sex?"

She inhales deeply. Exhales dramatically. "It's Graham who isn't interested, Tara."

That's what I figured. "Do you think he's seeing someone?"

"I don't know. Probably. Some questions are better left unasked."

"I disagree. Not one that important." Here's one I won't leave unasked, not that I expect a confession. "So, what about you? Have you ever considered sex on the side?"

Mel looks at me like I've lost my mind. "I'd have no idea how to go about that."

I smile. "Try joining a gym. It would help you get in shape for your Half Dome hike, too. Oh, by the way. I definitely won't be accompanying you. I'll be rehabbing the knee into the New Year."

Great segue. I'm tired of talking about Graham. And I can't comprehend the concept of celibacy before forty.

Regardless, we spend a very nice evening enjoying each other's company, not to mention some excellent food. Eli makes chicken cacciatore, which satisfies all of us on different levels.

Cavin, who missed lunch and is starving when he gets home, because Italian is his favorite, and there's plenty of it.

Mel, because the dish doesn't contain an excessive number of calories.

The kids, because they all contributed in some way.

Me, because we eat outside on paper plates, containing the cleanup, which I don't have to do anyway.

After that is accomplished, Eli and Kayla go for an evening walk. Cavin, sensing my need to spend more alone time with Mel, ushers the young ones downstairs to play pool and listen to music.

"I love you," I tell him as the exodus begins.

"I know," he buzzes into my ear. "And you can prove it later."

Melody and I watch them go. Wonder if she's jealous of our obvious sexual connection.

"He must have been a good dad," Mel observes.

"Not according to Eli. But Cavin's ex moved Eli away when he was little. I don't think he and Cavin did a lot of bonding."

"But they're making up for it now?"

I can't help but laugh. "Depends on your

definition of bonding, I suppose. More like testing, as far as I can tell."

"Sounds like most parent/child relationships."

"Maybe. I have nothing to compare it to." No children of my own. And as for my relationship with Mom, any sort of manipulating boundaries had to be done on the sly. Nothing like Eli's in-your-face style. And speaking of our mother, "Hey, forgot to mention Mom stopped by on her way to wherever."

Mel's head jerks in my direction. "What are you talking about?"

I repeat the story about the possible encounter. "Do you suppose, now that she's gone, the Idaho nightmares will stop?" They've been regular visitors for as long as I can remember.

"Pretty sure that's not how it works."

"I was afraid that's what you'd say. I'll probably always dream about Idaho."

"Idaho." The way she says it sounds like a preface, and apparently it is. "Just FYI, I've been considering going to Glenns Ferry for her burial."

"Why?"

"Closure."

"You've got to be kidding me."

Mel shakes her head. "I think the way to

eliminate nightmares is to confront the source head-on. Idaho is just a place. It's not responsible for our miserable childhoods. Now that the person who was is no longer a problem, it's time to find some peace. You're welcome to come along."

I swore I'd never go back there. But maybe she's right. "When are you leaving?"

"Monday. Unless Graham strenuously objects, and I can't see why he would."

"Are you taking the girls?"

"No. Facing down phantoms is best done sans teen drama."

"I'll think about it."

I can't believe it. But I will.

EIGHTEEN

Even more unbelievably, I decide to go. I book a Reno-to-Boise ticket with a Las Vegas layover that coincides with Mel's on her Sacramento–Boise flight, and reserve a luxury vehicle that will keep us comfortable on the approximately one-hour drive. That's all accomplished before Melody and the girls head home on Friday morning.

As promised, Genevieve forwarded Austin Colvin's invitation to tonight's party, along with an invitation to lunch next week. "There's something you should know," she said, "and it would be better to discuss it in person."

She refused further details. Nevertheless, I agreed to meet her on Monday. I remind myself to inform her I'll be out of town for a couple of days, and will have to reschedule, when I see her at the postperformance festivities.

Austin also left Cavin and me two will-call tickets for this evening's show, which happens to be *Cabaret.* The festival now alternates Shakespeare with a musical. Lucky me. Unlike *Taming of the Shrew,* this is one of my favorites.

Our seats aren't quite as good as those reserved for big donors. But they are close to center in the lower gallery, and right off the aisle, so it's easy enough for me to shimmy into one and stretch my leg straight if need be. Still, I make a mental note to send in a donation check very soon. I prefer food and beverage service to packing a picnic.

The cast is sensational, especially the young woman playing Sally. It's a treat to hear her vocals, and her dance is amazing. Cavin and I enjoy deli-bought sub sandwiches and made-at-home sangria. The evening is lovely, right up until intermission, when I spy a familiar form coming in our direction.

"Is that Sophia?"

Cavin follows the direction of my eyes. "I believe it is."

She's on the arm of an older gentleman, who acts quite proprietary. I wish we could avoid engaging them, but when they're around two feet away, she looks me directly in the eye before turning her complete attention toward Cavin. "Oh, hello, darling. Always a pleasure running into you."

Darling. I kind of want to kill her.

Kind of?

Cavin has little choice but to stand and acknowledge her with a quick kiss on the cheek. "You, too. Um, you remember Tara?"

I feel like an idiot sitting here, so I work my way out of the chair and onto my feet. "Nice to see you." The tone of my voice makes it clear she's the last person I want to see, and I plaster myself to my husband.

"Yes. Well. This is Maury Bernstein. Maury, this is an old friend of mine, Cavin Lattimore." She waits for the men to shake hands. "Maury and I are here scouting talent. We heard the female lead was incredible. She is, don't you think?"

We all agree on that, at least.

"Scouting talent for a new show?" I ask.

Sophia turns her focus toward me, and her eyes narrow. "Yes. Well, reviving an old one, actually, and bringing it to Stateline."

"Stateline? As in South Lake Tahoe?"

Her smile is tepid. "Exactly. Seems we'll be neighbors. Isn't that nice?"

It takes sheer force of will not to react in a manner that would make me look completely immature, not to mention feed her incredible ego. Before I can concoct a suitable retort, Cavin cleverly detours the dialogue.

"Well, I hope your scouting trip is successful. Tara and I were just about to hike over to the restroom. Enjoy the rest of the show." He takes my hand and steers me carefully away from our seats and across the sand. "You're fuming, aren't you?"

"Who, me? Why would you think so?"

"Something to do with the smoke streaming out of your ears?"

"Very funny." I don't know what more to say so I fall silent instead. It's not like her living closer should change a thing. Reno isn't that far away, so it isn't distance keeping Sophia and Cavin apart. He swears he's been over her for quite some time. He's married to me, and seems happy that way. Jealousy serves no good purpose other than to drive a wedge between people, and allowing someone like Sophia to sledgehammer my emotions is something I've always refused to do. I am, and will remain, in control.

By the time I'm finished in the ladies room, my temper is curbed, and stays that way through the second act. I've almost forgotten there's a problem, in fact, until we arrive at the Colvins' party to find Sophia and Maury there, too. "You've got to be kidding me," I tell Cavin.

"The point of this party was to schmooze with the cast, remember? If they're courting actors, it makes perfect sense."

It makes even more sense when I discover Maury and Austin went to college together. That information comes straight from Maryann Colvin, a matronly woman whose stately carriage, not to mention an exquisite teal silk Armani suit, endows her with a solid air of money.

Austin makes the initial introduction. "You remember Dr. Lattimore, dear?"

"Of course. Thanks so much for coming tonight. And you must be the new Mrs. Lattimore. It's a pleasure to meet you."

"Tara, please. And the pleasure is all mine."

Formalities accomplished, Austin adds, "Tara is the lady I told you about who'd like to help out on the fund-raising end. According to Genevieve, she's quite convincing."

Maryann takes my hand. "We can always use assistance encouraging donor generosity. Most people find it not their cup of tea."

"Not me. I definitely enjoy it, and do seem to have a talent for it."

"Why don't you two ladies talk, while Cavin and I circulate?" Austin suggests.

The men begin a counterclockwise sweep of the room and Maryann comments, "We're so appreciative of your husband's surgical skill. We quite thought Allison's injury would sideline her forever."

"He is amazing," I respond. "Professionally and personally."

"I understand. And you? What do you do?"

I offer my most winning smile. "I am independently wealthy." Which, I think, sounds better than "living off my investments."

"Rarely are people quite so blunt. It's refreshing."

"I prefer forthrightness to playing coy. I've worked hard and invested well. The fundraising is a hobby, one I spent years doing in San Francisco. Now I've moved here, I'd like to continue with nonprofit work. Housewifery is not exactly intellectually stimulating."

She laughs. "How long have you been married?"

"Six weeks, give or take. Cavin is what brought me to the lake full-time. So I just recently left the Bay Area, with its assorted baggage, both good and not so, behind."

I don't mention my husband's baggage, the prime example of which holds court across the room, Maury on one side of her and two cast members, including the promising young actress, on the other. Sophia's focus is clearly on the male actor, who responds as most straight, just-beyond-adolescent men might, with a hopeful leer. Wonder what exactly about said boys entices her thumbs-up or thumbs-down.

As I watch, Cavin and Austin pause to chat with her and her entourage. Even from here, it's obvious that my husband and Sophia have some sort of history by the familiar way they engage. She diverts her attention from the actor and focuses it completely on Cavin. He leans down to say something close to her ear, and when he straightens, she rewards him with laughter. Hope Maryann can't see the new plumes of smoke emanating from my ears.

"How do you know Sophia?" I ask, completely unable to help myself.

"Sophia?" She turns to assess where I'm looking, find context. "Oh, the woman with Maury? I'm not acquainted with her, but I believe Austin is helping Maury secure funding for some show she's producing. In addition to his work with the festival, Austin coordinates private sector investments. He's got a particular interest in arts projects, of course. He and Maury are old college chums and have in common a love of the theater, though Austin's leans toward Broadway, while Maury's runs more in the direction of burlesque."

"Yes, I can see that. Cavin and Sophia are old friends, too. Small world."

"It is, and the older you get, the more it shrinks."

That's what I'm afraid of. "If you don't mind, I think I'll go find a glass of wine." And reclaim my husband.

"Please do. The bar is in the next room. Why don't you give me a call sometime next week and we can discuss putting you to work."

"Sounds like a plan. I'm traveling to Idaho on Monday, so it will probably be closer to Friday."

"Whenever is fine. The foundation isn't going anywhere. It was lovely getting to know you. I'll have to thank Genevieve."

"She's not here tonight?"

"We expected her, but I haven't seen her yet. Oh, here comes your husband. If you'll excuse me, I'll leave you two newlyweds alone."

Off she goes in one direction while Cavin joins me from the other. "Everything good?" he asks.

I know he's referring to his close encounter with Sophia and tailor my response suitably. "Everything's just fine, except I'd like a glass of wine. Coming with me?"

"Of course. Sorry that took so long, by the way. That Maury sure likes to talk about himself. It was hard to break away."

"Really. From here it looked like Sophia was doing most of the talking."

"Tar—"

"But that's okay. It was good to have a few minutes with Maryann. Looks like I'll be doing some work for her organization. You don't mind, do you? I'm in need of a little intellectual stimulation."

Obviously relieved I let him off the hook, Cavin lifts my hand to his lips, kisses my fingertips. "I don't mind one bit. You stimulate your intellect. I'll take care of the rest of you. Deal?"

"Apology accepted."

For the moment.

We stay long enough to indulge in a glass of wine. I wouldn't label it "good." Apparently the Colvins don't feel the need to pander to a troupe of actors and their fans. Personally, I'd serve better, boosting the estimation of those in attendance, and write off the expense. No ego there, of course.

Wine consumed, mission accomplished, we are among the first to bid adieu to Austin and Maryann. Sophia and Maury remain. Genevieve has yet to appear. It being close to midnight, the road home is fairly quiet. The long unlit stretches make me glad Cavin is familiar with the highway.

It is along one of the dark, deserted segments I ask, "So, did you have any idea before tonight that Sophia was moving to Tahoe?"

Cavin considers for a moment, and I don't like that his ready answer wasn't a simple no. Finally, he says, "Eli told me it was possible."

"And neither of you thought you should mention it to me?"

"Tara, I'm never sure how much of what Eli says is truthful. As you well know, he thrives on provocation. I wanted to wait until I was certain before making you worry needlessly. And besides, whether or not she actually winds up on the south shore, it doesn't matter to me. I have nothing to hide from you."

That's what he keeps telling me.

Everyone has something to hide.

"Why would Eli confide that to you but keep it quiet from me?"

"Kayla is my guess. He figured you'd tell her straight off."

How do I play this one?

"She has a right to know."

"You're absolutely correct. She does. But should you or I be the one to tell her? Besides, she's leaving for school in a couple of weeks, yes? Time and distance might take care of it. And if you really think about it, how much of a threat to Kayla is Sophia? Eli is just the woman's plaything. She'll never be serious about him, nor he about her. Kayla has more to worry about from the girls Eli will see at school every day."

I mull all that over. Generally I favor logic over emotion, and his argument is totally rational. The problem is I become a party to a huge lie by omission. If Kayla finds out Sophia's here, and that I knew but didn't say anything, she'll be righteously — and rightfully — pissed. I despise being put in this position. Still, I don't have to make a decision tonight. "I guess you're right. We've achieved a small sense of harmony at the Lattimore residence. No use upsetting that fragile balance over a maybe."

"Glad you agree. And I'm happy tonight was successful for you."

"What about you? Did you meet any potential patients?"

He laughs. "This is Tahoe. Anyone who spends time here regularly is a potential patient."

It's almost one by the time we pull into the driveway, so I'm surprised to find Eli not only awake but also upstairs, looting the refrigerator. "Don't you know it's bad to eat right before you sleep?" I ask, setting my purse down on the counter.

He pops a Thompson seedless into his mouth. "Just a few grapes. I've got the munchies."

Of course he does. "Is Kayla still up?"

Cavin shoots me a warning glance, continues down the hall toward our room.

"Nope. She crashed an hour ago."

Okay, I could just stay quiet, but that's so not my style. "So, I have a question."

"Shoot."

"Why didn't you inform me that Sophia might be moving to the lake?"

He regards me with curious eyes. "I told Dad."

"But not me."

"I wasn't sure how you'd take it. Dad said not to worry, that he'd discuss it with you."

"Are you sure? He never said a word."

"I'm positive. But if he didn't tell you, how did you find out?"

"We ran into her at the festival tonight. She was delighted to share the news."

"Yeah, well, she can be a bitch, especially when she's buzzed. But like I've said before, a buzzed bitch is great in bed. Anyway, however you found out, I'm glad you know. Shit like that shouldn't be a secret between a husband and wife."

"Really? So Kayla knows?"

"No. But we're not married. Are you going to tell her?"

"Depends."

"On what?"

"On if I ever find Sophia in my house again."

He comes closer. Close enough to touch me. In fact, he rests his forehead against mine, looks me directly in the eyes. "You won't. I promise." Warm grape-scented breath infiltrates my nostrils and just as I think he'll kiss me, he takes a small backward step, sparking a fleeting moment of regret. "At least, not at my request."

"What does that mean?"

"I don't know. Just wondering why Dad wasn't more up front."

Spores of doubt release again like dandelion seeds, riled by the breeze.

Cavin would never bring Sophia here. He wouldn't dare. And why must I worry about that, anyway? "Your father said he didn't want to upset me needlessly and that Sophia's plans were still up in the air."

Eli's smile defines "wry." "Sounds plausible." He finishes his grapes. "I should go to bed. Anyway . . ." His fingertips meander softly along the length of my jawline. "I wouldn't worry. Sophia isn't half the woman you are."

He turns away and I'm glad he doesn't see the way he's made me tremble. What is wrong with me? He's a kid, and not just any kid. He's Cavin's kid. All sense of personal integrity crumbles in this moment. It took sheer strength of will not to purchase copious quantities of whatever it is Eli was selling. What happens the next time he comes knocking on the door?

Beyond that, the central question materializes. Why wasn't my husband up front with me?

I go to bed myself, where Cavin waits, skin hot from the wanting, to stimulate everything but my intellect. The whole time he does, I'm vaguely distracted by a little voice inside my head.

It's insistent.

Persistent.

And what it keeps repeating is:

Better watch your back.

Nineteen

Turns out the reason Genevieve never showed up at the Colvins' was horrific. As the Saturday morning headlines announced: FAMED MODEL CRITICALLY INJURED IN COLLISION ON MT. ROSE HIGHWAY. Apparently, she was driving way too fast down the mountain road when a two-ton truck turned out onto the highway in front of her little BMW roadster. There wasn't much left of the Z4, and what remains of Genevieve is currently in guarded condition at Renown Hospital in Reno. Doctors aren't sure if she'll live, and if she happens to, she won't model again.

The news hits me hard. Whatever our relationship has mellowed into, she was once a vibrant element of my life and a rare female friend. A snippet of conversation at *The Taming of the Shrew* was about how much she missed that.

"I wish things would've gone differently,"

she said. "You're one of the few people I've ever thought I could trust."

That surprised me. "Really? Why?"

"Because of your brutal honesty. Whether or not I appreciated your answer, I always knew if I asked you a question you'd respond truthfully. That's a rare thing in my world."

That was only eight days ago. Today, her world is an intensive care room, where she's fighting for her life.

I can't help but think about that as I steer my own BMW over the same stretch of roadway where her accident happened, on my way to the airport. I did my best to leave myself plenty of time, assuming I'd take Highway 50 all the way down into Carson City, then catch the freeway into Reno from there. But a brushfire up on the pass diverted traffic through Incline Village, and it's been slow going, something I'm grateful for, all things considered, as long as I reach the gate on time.

Luck is with me and I make my plane with ten minutes to spare. I still can't believe I'm doing this. Why the hell did I agree? It's a no-frills flight, nothing but peanuts for food, and I skipped breakfast, thinking I'd have time to grab a bite at the airport. But, no direct flights available, I've got a two-hour layover in Las Vegas. I can eat something then to absorb the alcohol from the two Bloody Marys I'm intent on consuming on the first short leg of my journey.

"Are you sure you want two?" asks the flight attendant, sticking her nose where it clearly doesn't belong. "You are aware we're only in the air another forty-five minutes?"

"I am completely cognizant of that, yes." I could tell her I'm going to my mother's funeral, elicit sympathy I'm not seeking. But I'm an adult, not drunk already, and not causing trouble. I don't have to explain myself.

Reluctantly, she hands me two bottles of vodka and a can of spicy tomato juice. "Fourteen dollars."

"Allow me," says the elderly woman beside me, handing her four drink coupons. "I'll have the same."

"Thank you," I tell the lady.

When she smiles, her eyes crinkle even more. "It's never too early for vodka, especially when you're going to Vegas."

Generally I discourage conversations with random seatmates, but she did cover my drinks, and it's not like I'll be stuck talking with her for hours. "Actually, I'm just passing through on my way to Idaho."

"Idaho. Never been there. Going home?"

"Believe me, you haven't missed a thing. I left there when I was a kid, and I've never gone back."

"Why now then? I mean, if you don't mind me asking."

"For my mother's funeral. Well, burial. Guess she still considered Idaho home."

"Oh. I'm sorry you lost her."

"Don't be. I'm not."

Vodka plus empty stomach equals too much information. At least it allows me to slip into silence. Pretty sure my companion is as uncomfortable as I am. We both concentrate on our drinks and manage to finish them before the snooty flight attendant comes around to collect our cups. By the time we touch down, I'm relishing a light buzz.

As we stand to deplane, I turn to the woman. "Enjoy Vegas. And thank you again for the drinks."

"No worries. I've got lots of coupons. I fly here regularly to visit my son."

"That's nice," I say as we start the slow shuffle up the aisle.

"It really is. We didn't speak for many years. His wife and I didn't get along, so I missed a great deal of my grandchildren's childhoods. She finally left him, and he and I reconciled, but that was time I can never regain. I regret not having tried harder to mend our relationship sooner. If an old woman can offer one word of advice? Hold on tight to the people who matter to you. Sometimes that requires forgiveness."

"I'll keep that in mind."

I do as I take leave of the woman and make my way into the insanity that is McCarran International Airport. Forgiveness. That is not something I understand, not even when my brain is less fuzzy. I've always considered forgiveness a sign of weakness.

Forgive, you invite whatever damage you originally suffered.

Forgive, it's like saying it didn't hurt so bad after all.

Forgive, it means you have to care in the first place.

And that is what I've always avoided.

It's also why there can be no forgiveness for my mother. I would've had to care about her in the first place. Or, perhaps much more accurately, she would have had to care about me.

I stuff that depressing thought and, as planned, text Mel, whose flight should have landed almost simultaneously with mine. *Just arrived, Gate C-14. Starving. Are you here?*

The answer comes immediately. *Taxiing in now. Arriving C-11.*

I glance around. *Meet me at Jose Cuervo Tequileria. I'll get a table.*

That proves easier said than done, considering it's twelve thirty and apparently everyone else has been dining on peanuts, too. I'm still waiting for them to clear a table when Melody comes puttering up. "Phew. It's wicked flying in over that mountain. The turbulence was scary."

" 'Mountain waves,' I believe those air currents are called. Fortunately, we only hit them as we circled to land. God, wouldn't it be the worst kind of irony to crash and burn on *this* trip, of all trips?"

"Jeez, Tara, what are you trying to do? Jinx us?"

I study my sister. "Don't tell me you're superstitious."

"Not really. But no use tempting fate."

"Do you read your horoscope, too?"

"Not every day."

The hostess informs us our table is ready, and we follow her to a small space near the back of the garishly colored room. She hands us menus, and before she can leave I ask for a Bloody Mary.

"Bloody Mary?" asks Mel.

"Considering the restaurant, I would have

ordered a margarita, but I already had a couple of Bloody Marys on the plane. Don't want to mix liquors."

"It's a little early, don't you think?"

"On another day, maybe. But it feels necessary today."

It takes forever, but our waitress finally arrives, Bloody Mary in hand. I'm glad I ordered it when I did. Mel asks for the taco salad and a Diet Coke. I go for carne asada. Protein, that's what I need. Steak. And vodka.

My drink is halfway gone by the time our meal is delivered, so the protein has some catching up to do. Mel grimaces at the first bite.

"What's wrong?" I ask.

"Nothing. It's okay. A little greasy, and fat is something I've been avoiding."

"Rule number eighty-two. Order basic fare at airport restaurants. It's hard to screw up a steak. Want half? It's good."

Mel shakes her head. "No. That's okay. I had breakfast, so I can just pick. You, however, need to eat if you're going to keep drinking like that."

"That's my plan. Hope you don't mind doing the driving once we get there."

"At this point, that's *my* plan."

We work on our food without talking for a

few minutes. Finally, Mel puts down her fork. "Ugh. Enough. So, I'm thinking we should go ahead and drive into Glenns Ferry this evening. Not much in the way of accommodations there, I'm afraid. I went ahead and booked us a room in one of the downtown motels. There are only two. Tomorrow night we can stay in Boise so we're closer to the airport."

"What time are they dropping her into the hole?"

Mel cringes. "Must you be so blunt?"

"Okay. Laying her to rest, if you insist on my being theatrical."

"Not theatrical. Just decent. One o'clock."

"Good. Then we don't have to be up early."

I finish every bite of meat, leaving the rice and beans, then dig the green olive out of my drink and eat it for dessert. By the time our waitress brings the bill, it's just about time to board. Good thing the gate is close. Between my knee and the relative frothiness inside my head, I'm not moving very quickly. It's also a good thing I paid extra for early boarding. Standing in line for the cattle call could be problematic.

We are comfortably settled in our seats before I check my phone for messages.

There's one voice mail, from Cavin. "In

case you haven't heard, Genevieve didn't make it. Sorry, honey. Touch bases when you get to Boise, okay? Love you."

Gone.

She's gone.

How is that possible?

I inhale sharply.

"What's wrong?" asks Mel.

"Genevieve Lennon died. She was in a car accident on Friday night and didn't survive."

"The model? Was she a friend of yours?"

"I've known her for years. In fact, we just spent an evening together at the Shakespeare Festival a little over a week ago. And she was on her way to a party where Cavin and I were when the accident happened. It's . . . mind-boggling."

"Life is unpredictable. It's one reason why people cling so tightly to faith, I think."

"You mean, like, faith in horoscopes?"

"Better than faith in nothing."

"Maybe. I doubt faith is something Genevieve suffered from, however."

And me? I'm allergic.

"Why? Because of her lifestyle?"

"More like her attitude. Hardly the stuff of saints."

Mel grins. "You can't judge a saint by her attitude. Some of the most dedicated churchgoers I know are not very nice on the surface."

"I thought that was the point. Being kind to others. Helping the poor. Caring for the sick."

"The point is salvation."

"Oh, right. Redemption by way of the offering plate. You know, if it's possible to buy Heaven without all that Good Samaritan hype, I'm not sure it's worth going. Think of the kind of people you'd have to spend eternity with."

"You're not interested in eternal life?"

Before I can answer, the intercom buzzes and our purser goes over the safety features of our Boeing 737. I'm glad for the interruption because I don't know how to answer Mel's question. Am I interested in eternal life? All the query does is lead to others.

Do I believe there is such a thing? The biggest part of me doubts it, though a little voice insists there must be more to human existence than eating, drinking, working, fucking, and finding a little fun once in a while, all leading up to lights-out forever.

If there is something approximating paradise, does it take church and Bible study to attain it? Logic insists otherwise.

If you're diligent about church and Bible study, but ignore basic principles like feeding the hungry and treating others the way you want to be treated, will you still find yourself on God's fast pass through the Pearly Gates?

Every fiber of my being insists no.

The plane backs away from the gate and pauses on the runway, and for some reason Mel feels the need to share, "I know this doesn't matter one way or the other to you, but toward the end, Mom asked to be saved. Hospice called in a priest, and he took her confession. One of the things she struggled with the most was the way she raised us. She said she wanted to be a better mother but didn't have the proper tools."

"Tools? She didn't have a functional toolbox."

"That wasn't her fault."

True enough, I suppose.

But forgiving her is still not an option.

TWENTY

By the time we reach Boise, I've gone from sloshed to napped-away-the-sloshed and am coherent enough to deal with the Hertz person, who seems very impressed that I'm willing to pay for a Chrysler 200 convertible when I could get an Impala for twenty dollars less per day.

It's five thirty by the time we pick up the car and hit the freeway. I let Mel drive, despite my relative clarity, and spend the first fifteen minutes or so congratulating myself on getting this far. The airport is on the edge of the city proper, and the interstate skirts it, so before long we are beyond traveler-friendly hotels and restaurants, past industrial monstrosities, and motoring across a vast expanse of nothing but scrub brush. "Just like I remembered it. Ugly as hell."

"I think it's got a beauty all its own. Stark, yes. But beautiful nonetheless."

"What are you talking about? There are pretty places in Idaho, but this is not one of them."

"To each his own. At least it isn't overpopulated."

"That's because no one wants to live out here. I mean, what would a person do? Cook meth? Anyway, could you go a little faster, please? It would be good to get there before dark."

"I don't want to get a ticket, Ms. Backseat Driver. Besides, what are you worried about? Vampires wandering the streets of Glenns Ferry?"

"I'd say bloodsuckers are a given."

She does inch up over the speed limit, and forty-five minutes into the trip, we're passing Mountain Home. "Do you want to stop for dinner?" asks Mel. "There will be more choices here."

"Not even. Way too many ugly memories there."

It's where we grew up, mostly raising ourselves while Mom chased after whatever men were available and interested. Sometimes they weren't even technically available. She brought more than one married man home and into her bed, and didn't try to hide it from us. Once in a while a pissed spouse would ring the doorbell. When I got old enough to realize that's who was at the door, I let them in. Served Mom — and the guy — right.

I have no doubt such experiences helped form my "no having sex with someone who's committed to another person" rule.

"I thought the point of this trip was to confront the personal demons haunting our past."

A huge sigh escapes me. "Look, Mel. I promised myself I'd never come back here, and yet here I am. One baby step at a time, okay? Besides, I want the true Glenns Ferry experience. Surely they'll have a bar serving burgers or something."

Excellent subject change, if I do think so myself.

"They do. I checked it out. And I guess as far as breakfast goes, the café attached to our motel is supposed to be very good, at least by small-town Idaho standards."

As dusk deepens, we exit the freeway, and an overwhelming sense of déjà vu smacks my face. I'm four years old again, and even though this is a brand-new vehicle, it smells like tobacco-tainted Naugahyde and Quaker State in need of changing. I sink lower into the seat, stare at the nearly deserted streets of the tiny town where our grandmother lived. We didn't visit often, and when we did it was usually because Mom needed something from her mother. Invariably money. "It hasn't changed at all."

"Not much," agrees Melody. "The cars are newer."

We drive straight down 1st Avenue, past a couple of ministorage places, some older homes, the Corner Market, and Sinclair gas, then pull into the parking lot of a motel that looks like it has seen better days. "This is it?"

"This one or one farther down that way." Mel points. "Don't worry. I read the Trip-Advisor reviews. The rooms may be small, but they're clean. And this one is walking distance to the café."

The woman behind the desk is very nice. Overly friendly, in fact. "I see you've got a reservation. Mostly we just get people stopping in off the freeway. You ladies don't look like the 'tubing the Snake River' kind of people. Going wine tasting?"

"Wine tasting?" I ask.

"Well, yes. We've got a wonderful little winery right over by the state park. Decent restaurant there, too. Oh, but you're only staying one night?"

I don't want to tell her it's all I can stomach. "This time, unfortunately. Guess we'll have to come back."

If nothing else, it deflects having to tell her why we're here. She runs Mel's credit card and seems very pleased that it cleared. "You can park right in front. Makes it easy."

Lord.

We thank her and go check out the room. Mel's description is accurate. Good thing we're only here for one night. I'm already feeling claustrophobic, and we've just brought in our suitcases. "Okay, let's get dinner." And drinks. Lots of drinks.

The evening is warm, not much of a breeze to temper the arid air. But it's only two blocks to the restaurant, which defines "down-home." There's a lot of memorabilia from the town's storied days as a major Snake River crossing and railroad stop. The tracks are located right across the street, in fact, and mainline trains still travel them daily.

A plump little waitress, Lena, hustles over to give us menus, which offer basic fare. Steaks, chops, burgers, sandwiches. Nary a rice bowl to be found. When in Glenns Ferry, eat as the Glenns Ferrians do, I guess. I order a barbecue burger, hold the cheese. Melody keeps the cheese and adds bacon.

"Some diet," I observe.

"Hey, I didn't eat my lunch. Besides, I

skipped the fries."

"Can I get you something to drink?" asks Lena.

"Give us a second, will you?"

Lena goes to put in our dinner order and I study the drink menu. There are a lot of beers, including local brews, but not much in the way of wine. I'd ask for a sidecar, but I'm pretty sure the bartender would have to go look it up.

"I'm thinking about one of these Idaho craft beers to go with my burger. Then something stronger for dessert."

"I should skip the alcohol."

"We are getting drunk together tonight," I insist. "It's only two blocks to stumble back to our room, and we need to celebrate."

"Celebrate what?"

"Losing weight."

"I won't keep it off if I drink too much."

"That isn't the kind of weight I meant."

"Wha—" She thinks it over. "Oh. You're talking about Mom."

"Exactly." I wave to our waitress, who really has nothing better to do than hurry on over. The place isn't exactly crowded. "We'll have a couple of lagers, please." They look to be the lightest brews. Don't want to fill up on beer.

Our food arrives in record time, and I

must say it's really good. The meat is juicy, the buns are soft, the tomatoes are ripe, and the lettuce is crisp. And the beer is really cold, if a little hoppy for my taste.

"I think I'll take a walk in the morning, if it isn't too hot," says Mel. "This is going to go straight to my butt otherwise."

"This time of year in Idaho, it's definitely going to be warm. Hope the cemetery is shady. I hate sweating at funerals."

"When have you ever sweated at a funeral?"

"Good question."

The only funeral I've ever been to was Raul's, and even though it was in Las Vegas, it was dead-on winter.

Lena clears the table, asks about dessert.

"Are you kidding? I don't know where I'd put it. We're moving to the bar, so can you bring the check over there?"

"You can keep the table if you want," Lena replies.

"I understand. But I'm in the mood to belly up, if you know what I mean."

"Sure thing. Watch out for Alvin, though. He'll talk your ear off if you let him. He's the one in the big Stetson."

Lucky us. The two empty bar stools just happen to be adjacent to Alvin's right side. Who cares? Maybe after a couple of drinks the man, who is sixtyish and definitely a local, will be amusing. Anyway, there are other men at the bar, so it's possible he'll talk their ears off instead of ours.

Except, no. Strangers in town always draw attention.

"Well, hello." Alvin tips his hat. "Haven't seen you ladies around here before. Welcome to Glenns Ferry."

"Thanks, Alvin." I sidle in next to him. Mel wouldn't handle overeager conversation as well as I can. Although, now when I turn to look at her, I see the guy on her right is about her age, and not bad to look at, beneath a handlebar mustache. Stupid move, Tara. You're out of practice.

You're married.

Who asked you?

"Do we know each other?" asks Alvin, stupefied.

I laugh. "No. Lena warned me about you. She said you are quite the ladies' man."

"Oh, she did, did she? I'll have to get after her for spreading lies."

"Bet she's not lying." Am I flirting with a guy old enough to be my father?

"Can I buy you two a drink?"

"Only if I can buy one for you after."

"Deal. Josh? These ladies are thirsty. Get your ass over here."

Okay, maybe there was a reason I sat next to Alvin, because Josh deserts the far end of the bar to take care of Mel and me. "What'll it be?"

"Don't suppose you could do blood-orange sidecars?"

Josh grins. "Would regular sidecars do? Most people around here prefer their drinks blood free."

I smile at Mel. "So much for the vampire theory."

Alvin looks confused. "Vampire theory? And what the hell is a sidecar?"

"Watch and learn," says Josh, reaching for a bottle of Hennessey. "A lot of cognac, a little triple sec, and a squeeze of lemon." Josh sets the drinks down on the bar, waits for us to taste them.

"Very good," I say after a long swallow.

Mel is more circumspect, sipping gently. "Oh. This *is* good, blood or no blood. Thank you, Alvin."

"Any time. Not like we get a whole lot of pretty ladies sitting here on a Monday night. You have business in Glenns Ferry?"

Strangers in a strange place invite questions. But I guess I don't mind. "We've got business at the cemetery. We're here to bury our mother."

"That's unusual. Not many get planted at

Glenn Rest anymore. Was your ma from around these parts?"

"She grew up here. June Cogburn?"

Now he looks stunned. "Junie."

"You knew her?"

"Well, yeah. We used to go together. Way back when, that is. And you're her daughters. Huh."

Okay, I'm borderline stunned myself. And Mel, who was chatting up that guy beside her, redirects her attention toward Alvin. "What year would that have been?"

"Let me think. I guess it must have been seventy-four or seventy-five. We were in high school."

"What was she like?" I ask, not at all sure why.

"Wild. Wild and troubled. Her home life was awful. I don't like to speak ill of the dead, but that girl's mother was what we used to call a loose woman. Oh. I probably shouldn't have said that to you."

"It's okay," soothes Mel. "We know."

I signal to Josh to bring another round, including a double bourbon for Alvin. I want to keep him talking because suddenly I realize he could be, or at least might know who is, my father. And wouldn't that be a crazy coincidence?

The whiskey does what it's supposed to

do. "Junie was a rebel, and she had every right to be. That man living with her ma, well, he was one mean motherfucker. Oh, excuse me. The whiskey's got my dirty mouth talking."

"It's okay. My dirty mouth fires up after a few drinks, too." I might even let it, here in Idaho, where it originated.

Alvin chuckles at that. "Anyway, that asshole beat up on both of them. Poor Junie used to come to school all black-and-blue. She said she was going to escape, first chance she got. And she did. Eighteen, she was out of here."

"But you didn't go with her?" asks Melody.

"She never asked me. Nope, she ran off in the middle of the night with Vince Cartwright. They didn't go far, not that there's too far to go in Idaho. Vince got him a mechanic job in Mountain Home, and they shacked up together for a while."

I'm not exactly sure how to pose the question that's hovering right there, unvoiced, in front of me. "I don't suppose she was pregnant when she left?"

"Hell no, at least, not by me!"

I'm vaguely disappointed. Alvin would make a decent dad, I think, not that I ever yearned to have one before. "Did you ever see Mom again?"

"Oh, sure. She visited her ma once in a while. In fact, I probably saw you two when you were little girls. Yes, I think so. I remember the red hair."

"Small world."

"Well, small town, anyway. Very small. You say you're laying Junie to rest tomorrow?" Alvin tosses back the rest of his bourbon.

"Yep. One o'clock." Yep. There I go with the Idaho. "May I buy you another drink, Alvin?"

"I believe it's my round."

Josh has already gone to work. Give the man a big tip.

"Hey, Mel. Suck it up. There's another one on its way."

"Oh, man. You two are going to get me sloshed." It's not really a complaint, because she slugs what's left of her sidecar. Interesting. Mel rarely lets her hair down.

Wonder if it has to do with Mustache Man, who's most definitely coming on to her and says, "Okay by me. A drunk woman is a fun woman, if you know what I mean."

I bristle, but before I can say anything, Mel answers him. "I'm not drunk yet, and I'm never very much fun. I'm married."

Alvin nods wisely. "Marriage, yep. That's definitely a fun killer."

Which busts up everyone at the bar. This easy camaraderie between relative strangers is something I'm unused to. Funny thing, to find it here.

Maybe you should've looked sooner.

TWENTY-ONE

I wake to the sound of a semi downshifting. What? Semi? My eyes open, try to focus in the dark room, blinds closed tightly. Where am I? I turn my head side to side, find a khaki wall on my right, an empty single bed to my left. Motel room. That's it. Glenns Ferry. That's right.

"Mel?"

But the bed where she should be sleeping is made, bedspread untouched and pillow plumped. Oh, man. That's right. I sit up, too quickly, and a hammering starts in my skull. We drank a lot last night. And Melody did get drunk. Sloppy drunk. And Mustache Man — Jerry, I think — actually talked her into going home with him.

Alvin was kind enough to escort me back here and never tried to get into the room. Sweet man. I even confessed I'd wondered if he was my father. Mom had me when she was nineteen. The timing was close to right.

He laughed at that. "No. Wasn't me. In fact, she and I didn't make it past second base. It could've been Vince, but I don't think Junie was much for fidelity, sorry to say. Damn. There I go again. I sure do feel like I've been telling tales out of school about your dearly departed mother."

"No worries, Alvin. Mom didn't hide her ugly side from us. In fact, we never saw anything else. I did what she did, left home at eighteen and refused to look back. Only difference was I made sure to never have children. Melody chose to, and she managed to break the cycle of violence. But it was mostly me Mom went after, and she was wicked mean. I understand why a little more now, so thank you for that."

"How did Junie die, if you don't mind me asking."

"Lung cancer."

He nodded. "She started smoking young. We used to argue over it. Never could stand the stink."

"Me, either. It was one of the best things about moving out on my own. Hey, you sure you and I aren't related?"

"Positive. I take it you and Junie weren't what you'd call tight."

"No, actually. We've barely spoken at all in the last twenty-five years."

"So how come you're here?"

"Closure."

We were at the motel by then. He waited for me to dig out the room key. "I might stop by the cemetery tomorrow, pay my respects. That okay?"

"Of course. Oh. One thing. That Jerry guy. Is he all right? I mean, my sister's not in danger, is she?"

"In danger of being bored to death, maybe. He's not the brightest fella around. Course I doubt it's his brain she's interested in."

"True. Hope to see you tomorrow, Alvin. Good night."

That was that.

But I did expect Mel back last night. The little alarm clock on the frills-free night-stand tells me it's 8:06. I get up — slowly — and dig my phone out of my bag, to find a text from my wayward sister. *Im ok. Staying over. Don want drive.*

If Jerry was half as messed up as she obviously was, I think that was the right call, though I'm still irritated that she left in the first place. What would I say to her family if she ended up dead, of boredom or anything else, in a stranger's bed? I text her back. *Going to breakfast. See you soon. Hope he had a big one and knew how to use it.*

I grab a bottle of ibuprofen, take it into the bathroom, and swallow three with tap water. One thing I'll say about Glenns Ferry. Buying bottled water here would be a waste of money. What comes out of the faucet is sweet and cold.

The headache fades as I shower and dress, and it's nothing more than a thin memory by the time I settle in at the restaurant. My coffee has just arrived when Mel comes through the door wearing yesterday's clothes, which somehow managed to avoid too many wrinkles, and a smile that says pretty much everything.

"That big, huh?"

"No, but he did know how to use it." Melody scoots into the chair across from me, signals to the waitress to bring the coffeepot over. Once she's holding a cup in her hand, she asks, "You're not angry with me, are you?"

"Why? Do I seem angry?"

"Other than the huge scowl, not at all."

"It's your life, Mel. I'm not your babysitter."

"But you disapprove."

I shake my head. "Again, not up to me. I would just caution you to remember every action invites a reaction. I don't want you to get hurt."

"Well, thanks for that, I guess." She sips her coffee, peruses the menu. Eventually, she asks, "How long till the guilt kicks into gear?"

"Don't know. Guilt is not in my vocabulary, and at this point I'd suggest excising it from yours, too. It's an exercise in futility."

"Programmed heavily by our mother."

"Probably why I resisted it so single-mindedly. Anyway, she's gone. Now you can expunge her, too."

"You make it sound easy."

"It is. All you need to do is remember what a snake she was."

Some snakes are rather beautiful.

Mel sighs. "Let's change the subject."

A-okay by me. "I'm surprised you made it back so early."

"Jerry had to be at work by nine."

"Work? Hope he wasn't as hungover as I was."

"Me, too. I got pretty wasted, didn't I?"

"I doubt we'd be having this conversation otherwise."

Mel must've worked up quite an appetite because when the waitress comes over she orders steak and eggs, with hash browns and toast. The portions are Idaho size. I manage to consume about half of an enormous Denver omelet, but Melody actually finishes every bite. I watch incredulously as she wolfs it down, wait until she's done to observe, "You should have sex more often."

"No kidding."

I think back to the ski trip we took in December and how on the way to Tahoe from Sacramento I mentioned picking up a guy in a bar. He turned out to be not so nice, and I had to threaten him with pepper spray to get out the door. Mel chastised me for being so reckless as to sleep with a stranger. I don't indulge that habit very often. Too easy for things to go wrong, like they did that night. But earlier in the day I'd discovered that the guy I'd been seeing, mostly as a plaything, was in love with a girlfriend I knew nothing about. One thing I refuse to accept is being cast in the role of "the other woman." It felt like getting even.

"If I ask you something, will you tell me the truth?"

She hesitates, but then says, "Uh, I guess."

"Was that, like, your first one-night stand?"

"Tara, how well do you know me?"

"Pretty well. At least, I thought so until Jerry."

"Don't you think I would've told you if I'd ever done something like that before?"

"Seriously? I don't know. And it doesn't

matter, anyhow. Another question. Would you ever do something like it again?"

Her cheeks blossom a lovely cherry color. Still, she looks me straight in the eye. "Who knows? I've heard it gets easier with practice."

"Did you aim that directly at me?"

Her simple answer is to glance away. But after a couple of beats she says, "Let me ask *you* something. Were you more surprised that I went for him, or that he went for me?"

I have no good honest response for that, so I'm happy when the waitress interrupts to ask if we'd like anything else. We decline and I hand her my credit card. As she waddles away, I ask Mel, "Do you still want to go for a hike?"

"Might as well. We've got a couple of hours with nothing else to do but watch soap operas."

There's a nice walking trail between downtown and Three Island Crossing State Park, basically the place where the Oregon Trail crossed the Snake River. It's tepid on the outbound, but by the time we turn around, the temperature is closing in on ninety degrees. I arrive back at the room dripping sweat.

I'm glad we went. We mostly walked in silence, breathing in air carrying scent unique to this peculiar landscape. Vague familiarity hit me square in the solar plexus, and each exhale brought the slow release of persistent recollections that have stalked me since I was little. This is where they belong, and hopefully they'll remain interred here, along with Mom. Funny, but now I can clearly see that she belongs in this place.

Mel and I take turns showering. It's my second of the day, but exertion sweat is stinky sweat, and we'll be sharing close quarters on the ride back to Boise. It's past checkout time when we finish, so we pack up our few belongings and head on over to the cemetery, where we find a semi parked out in front of the big wrought-iron gates.

The grave is open, a gaping hole in the prairie, and Will stands beside it, hat in hand. He looks up at our approach, and I'm surprised to find him tearful. "You both came. That's good. That's real good."

"Um, where is she?" I ask.

"She'll be here soon, arriving by hearse. The funeral parlor is in Mountain Home. She's been resting there since yesterday. I talked to the local priest. He's gonna say a few words."

Hearse and priest appear in tandem just before one, and so does Alvin, in a dark blue suit and polished cowboy boots. There are quick introductions all around before the casket is rolled graveside for the lowering. The priest's words are, indeed, few, the ceremony short and free of flowers.

"Bye, Junie. Godspeed," says Alvin at the end, and that seems as good a benediction as any.

Will stays behind to make sure someone's planning to close the grave. I don't understand his sadness, but it's palpable. "I think he really loved her," I comment.

"What did I tell you?" says Melody. "There must have been something good between them."

I can't reconcile Mom with "good." But I no longer think of her as evil. Alvin helped with that, and so did Will. They gave me a sense that she was human, at least at the beginning and ending of her life, and not completely responsible for everything in between.

Maybe that means you're human, too.

I'm really starting to wish that little voice inside my head would shut up for a while. I take the wheel for the drive back to Boise. We're halfway there when Mel, who's been totally silent and obviously lost in thought, finally asks, "Do you think less of me?"

Truthfully, I haven't been thinking about her at all. My mind's been grappling with the idea that I have one less person to hate, not to mention the one I've most despised, now that the dirt is settling back at Glenn Rest Cemetery. "Less of you for what?"

"For last night. I know how you feel about infidelity."

"Justified in certain circumstances. How long has it been since you had sex with Graham?"

"I don't know. Months."

"And how long since you've had sex that made you smile the way you were smiling this morning?"

No hesitation. "Years."

If ever, is my educated guess.

Silence balloons again, to the point of suffocation. I could suggest — one more time — that she dissolve her marriage, free herself to find someone to love her, honor her, and make her come regularly. But she's really going to have to reach that conclusion on her own. Hmm. Wonder how Graham would feel if he found out about last night? Pissed? Jealous? Would he shoulder any of the blame?

As if reading my mind, Mel says, "You won't tell Graham about this, right?"

"Who, me? Like Graham and I talk about anything, let alone something I have no right to disclose? Girl, that confession is completely up to you, and if you're intent on keeping your marriage intact, I wouldn't recommend it."

Methinks the guilt train is steamrolling down the tracks.

But now she says, "I kept Jerry's number."

"Why?"

Her shrug is audible. "In case I ever come back to Glenns Ferry? I have no idea."

I don't voice my opinion that sex should rarely be the ultimate goal. Better to utilize it as a catalyst. It's a powerful means to an end sought. I do, however, try to assuage her conscience a little. "Hey, Mel? Don't beat yourself up. Lust is simply a dynamic of human nature."

"Lust is a sin. Not only that, but a deadly sin."

A little late to worry about that now. "There are seven of those, I've heard. Everyone succumbs to at least one over the course of their lifetime."

We pull into the Hampton Inn near the airport midafternoon. Hamptons are rarely my first choice, but there aren't a lot of others, and this room is a hundred times better than the one we stayed in last night. Mel decides to take a swim in the indoor pool. I tell her I'll join her in a few, but I want to touch base with Cavin.

I call his office first. His receptionist informs me he had to go home to deal with something but offers no details. I try his cell, which goes to voice mail. "Just me, checking in. Hope everything's okay."

I didn't bring a swimsuit, but I do have some shorts and a tank top that will work. I'm ready to catch up with Mel at the pool when Cavin calls back.

"Hi, honey. How did it go?"

"As good as it could. We planted Mom, and before you know it, she'll be fertilizing a fresh patch of grass. Believe it or not, I even met a man who used to date her. He gave me a little perspective, and I managed to silence a ghost or two."

"The trip was worthwhile, then. I'm happy to hear it. But I want you home. I'm definitely missing you."

"Is everything okay? Rebecca said you had to leave work early?"

"Oh. Right. Nothing major. I had a cancelation and some free time, so I had the Escalade smogged and registered. The notice came in the mail."

"Thank you, but I could've managed it."

"You don't mind that I drove your car, do you?"

"Of course not."

Except, I kind of do.

Ghosts

Even a small bed is too big, alone.
She lies half-awake, draws stuttered breath,
listens to memory's bittersweet drone,
wonders if silence comes cloaked in death.

Not quite awake, she draws stuttered
    breath,
promises shattering on her pillow.
She wonders if silence comes cloaked in
    death,
as her storm clouds begin to billow.

Promises shattering on her pillow,
she conjures the image she cannot dismiss,
seeding her storm clouds. They billow
with the black remembrance of his kiss.

She conjures the image she cannot dismiss,
summons the heat of his skin on her skin,
the black remembrance of his kiss,
desire, abandoned somewhere within.

She summons the heat of his skin on her
    skin,
opens herself to herself, in disguise,
recovers desire, abandoned within. Heart
beating ghosts, she closes her eyes

And opens herself to herself, in disguise,
listens to memory's bittersweet drone.
Heart beating ghosts, she closes her eyes,
knowing her small bed is too big, alone.

Twenty-Two

The trip home is uneventful, other than for a slight delay on our first flight due to a late-arriving crew. Still, we have plenty of time in Vegas to make our connection. I promised Mel I'd skip the alcohol this morning, and she guilt-tripped me into avoiding it last night, too. Instead, after dinner, with the sun solidly down, we dropped the top on the convertible and cruised slowly through the prettier streets of downtown Boise.

When I mentioned the fact that Cavin had registered the Cadillac without my even asking, she commented, "I doubt Graham would even know how to manage it. That job has always fallen to me. Of course, since I work at home, my time is never completely my own."

"You could simply refuse to handle all the minutiae."

"I could, but then it wouldn't get done."

"You sound like me."

"More and more. I'm not sure if that's good or bad."

"Well, I've got a decent idea what Graham would say."

"I do, too. He'd say you're a rotten influence."

"Hey, what's a big sister for?"

We left it exactly there.

Mel and I catch separate flights to separate cities to return to our separate homes, with one new thing in common — at least a small sense of sympathy for our dearly departed mother, thanks to Alvin and Will. As Melody and I part ways, I tell her again, "Make yourself happy, would you, please? Life is too short to feel consistently dissatisfied and divorce only stings till the final papers are signed."

And sometimes it doesn't sting at all.

I arrive at the house late afternoon. Eli and Kayla are outside on the front step, smoking something decidedly not tobacco. They don't even try to hide it when I pull into the driveway and exit the Beamer.

"Why are you doing that out here?" I demand.

"It's too windy on the other side of the house," explains Eli.

"So why not confine it to your room, like you usually do?"

He shrugs. "We needed a little fresh air. My room smells a little . . . musty."

He means musky.

"Well, I'd prefer you don't announce your bad habits to the entire neighborhood."

"No one around but us juvenile miscreants," he jokes.

"What's a miscreant?" asks a foggy-eyed Kayla.

Eli answers her before I can. "Context, girl, context."

But it's obvious that stumps her, too. "Delinquent," I supply before changing the subject completely. "Is your father home yet?"

"Nope," says Eli. "He called and said he had to run an errand after work, but he'd bring takeout for dinner. Nice homecoming, yeah?"

My thought exactly.

"He was out kind of late last night, too," he adds.

"Is that so?"

"Yeah," Kayla adds, giggling. "While the cat's away or whatever."

Again?

"Well, if you'll excuse me, I need to unpack."

I turn, and as I walk back to my car, Eli comes up behind me. "Let me get your suitcase for you."

Wonder if Kayla can see how the front of his jeans actually touches the back of mine, encouraging little rushes I must learn to ignore. Despite their being kind of nice, they are madly improper, and I nudge forward. "Thanks, Eli, that's nice of you."

"No problem."

He extracts my bag from the trunk and carries it inside. I follow, and when I pass Kayla, still sitting on the step, she says, "Wonder where Uncle Cavin went, don't you?"

I ignore her question, though I very much do want to know what my husband was up to last night.

Eli lugs the suitcase back into my bedroom, puts it on the bed, then turns, inching closer. "Anything else I can do for you? Drink? Snack?"

A cloud of his scent settles around me. It's an oddly enticing potpourri — marijuana, Ivory soap, Old Spice, and a hint of whatever perfume Kayla wears — and the overarching theme is primal male.

My breath catches, but I manage a hoarse reply. "I'll take it from here, thank you. I'm feeling a little drained, so I'll probably lie down for a while."

"Gotcha." He reaches toward me, rests

two fingers lightly against my cheek. "Burying someone must take a lot out of a person."

His touch is tender, something I've rarely experienced in four-plus decades on this planet. I close my eyes, swaying slightly at the energy exchange. When I open them again, he is kissing distance and I fight an overwhelming desire to see how that feels.

Wrong time. Wrong place. Wrong person.

I take a step back and his hand drops. "Actually, a backhoe did most of the work. That ground's too hard for a shovel. I just didn't sleep very well. My sister snores."

He grins. "So does her daughter, who's probably pissed that I'm taking so long. In fact, I'm surprised she hasn't come looking for me."

Me, too.

Eli turns on one foot and disappears down the hall. The room cools with his departure.

I open my suitcase and unpack it, putting everything away. Can't stand living out of luggage, and no way will I do so at home. Jordan used to make fun of me for that. We traveled a lot, and he was obnoxious about leaving his bag unsorted once we returned. I hated doing it for him, but most often did, rather than leave it for him to get around to, and then have to field his complaints about wrinkled suits and ties.

As I work, I can't stop thinking about what just transpired between my stepson and me. The attraction is undeniable, but I don't understand it. Even when I was a teenager, boys that age did nothing for me. Well, except for one.

Lucas Turner was a designated high school heartthrob. He came from a well-to-do family, drove a decent car, played sports, and ran track. His interest in me was purely physical, but I was barely sixteen and still naive enough to believe teen-boy bullshit. He swore he'd never met a girl like me, that I was beautiful and smart, maybe even too smart to be his girlfriend. Too bad that didn't prove to be the case, though he definitely taught me a lesson, one that sparked my better-educated dating philosophy going forward.

Lots of boys came on to me, but in overtly sexual ways that reminded me of my mom's men. I valued myself more than that. I would not be my mother. I was a "woman" with taste. And Lucas seemed to fit the bill. He took me to the movies, to the arcade, to UNLV games, not that I cared about football or basketball. But I was with Lucas, who claimed to love me, and at first everything was fun.

Well, everything except for the sex, which was expected in return for the actual fun. I didn't mind so much, though it was all about him getting off. I'm not even sure he understood that I was supposed to enjoy it, too. I didn't.

He grew possessive. Obsessive. Demanded to know where I was every moment of every day. If other boys so much as looked at me, he'd go off. At them. At me. More than once he grabbed me hard enough to leave a bruise. I'd suffered enough brutality at my mom's hands. I was not about to put up with it from a guy. I wasn't sure what love was, but I knew it didn't look like that.

When I broke up with Lucas, he cried. Actually cried. When that didn't work, he threatened suicide, but I knew he meant too much to himself to follow through. In fact, when I wouldn't change my mind, he didn't choose the noose. He chose to come after me.

I should've known, or suspected, at least. Enough to be cautious, and I wasn't.

I'd just gotten off work at my crappy fast food job, the one that I did my best to keep despite having to squeeze in hours around school. It was a fifteen-minute bus ride, plus an eight-minute walk to our house. I was waiting at the bus stop when Lucas pulled up at the curb.

"Get in. I'll give you a ride home."

I hesitated. "That's okay. Wouldn't want to put you out."

"Please? I just want to talk to you."

Whether out of naivete or sheer exhaustion, I let down my guard and got in the car, and immediately he hit the gas. "Hey, slow down."

"Why? You like speed, don't you?"

He accelerated, diving in between cars and trucks and bicycles, and didn't even try to brake when he passed the turn to my house. "What are you doing?"

"Taking you somewhere private."

That was the first real clue that I might be in some kind of trouble. "Lucas, please."

"Please? Yes, I like that. Say it again."

When I wouldn't he drove even faster, away from the city, up into the hills, to an isolated spot he was obviously familiar with. As soon as he stopped, I jumped out of the car and started to run. But he was faster. Stronger. He caught me, threw me to the glass-littered ground, pinned me down, and raped me.

It was a vicious assault, and he alternated between laughter and foul vitriol. I fought back as best I could, but he completed the deed and left me lying there, bloodied and oozing evidence. As he fishtailed away, spraying gravel and dust, I picked myself up, straightened my ruined clothes, and picked debris from my tangled hair. Then I limped back toward the city until a nice woman stopped and offered to take me home.

I filed a police report. Even turned over my semen-soaked panties. But when the cops questioned Lucas, he agreed the encounter was rough but swore it was consensual. Enough of our schoolmates knew we'd been dating to make it a tough call. His word versus mine, the charges were dropped.

I was force-fed a couple of valuable lessons. One: travel through life with the blinders removed. And, two: sometimes victory lies in retribution.

This is a memory best left behind, and to escape it I go into the bathroom and reach for opiated relief, knowing it will lower me into sleep. I glance at the clock as I lie down. Four twenty. By dinner all will be well. As the curtain lowers, I allow myself the pleasure of reliving the revenge.

Lucas had taken to coming into my work and sitting where he could try and intimidate me while wolfing a taco or two and chugging an extra-large Coke. It wasn't every day, but it was often enough, and I could afford patience.

My mom's medicine cabinet was over-stocked with prescriptions designed to mitigate her depression, obsessions, etc. It was easy enough to pilfer one here and one there until I collected six with the highest dosage per. I figured any more than that and Coke would not disguise the taste.

Turned out that was not a problem. He gulped down the whole, spiked thing. Not only did he OD but he passed out behind the wheel. Somehow the other cars managed to miss him as he crossed over the oncoming lane, ran up over the sidewalk, and crashed into a building.

He survived, but barely.

Sports were no longer an option.

I didn't care at all because he never bothered me again. . . .

A growl wakes me.

Growl?

Yes. My stomach, I think.

Some alarm.

I'm hungry.

Annoyingly so.

Watery light illuminates the bedroom window. Evening? No, morning, I think.

"Cavin?"

No answer.

No movement.

No noise in the house I can decipher.

My mouth tastes like I've been chewing cotton, and I think someone's mixing cement inside my head. Oh, yes. I resorted to Vicoprofen, something I've steadfastly refused for a while. Why did I cave again?

A tsunami of recollection flushes me out of bed. But I won't swim against that tide again. Not now. Not ever.

As I tidy my half of the covers, I notice Cavin's side is untouched, so maybe it's evening after all. I slip on a robe, go to the kitchen. Padding through the living room, I find my husband snoring lightly on the sofa and jiggle him awake. "Cavin?"

His eyes flutter open, catch sight of me, and he smiles. "Morning. What time is it?"

"Not sure. In fact, I wasn't certain it was morning, but since it seems to be, that means I slept for, what, thirteen hours?"

"You were definitely dead to the world when I got home." He sits up, still wearing what must have been yesterday's clothes, and his hair is in complete disarray.

"Why didn't you wake me?"

He pulls me into his lap, kisses me, too easily. "I tried, but you didn't budge. I figured if you were that deep under, you needed to sleep."

"What time was that?"

"Around six thirty. I bought Chinese, by the way. There are leftovers in the fridge."

Takeout. Right.

"Why didn't you come to bed?"

"I read for a while. Guess I fell asleep, because the next thing I knew, I was looking up at your gorgeous face. Good thing you woke me. I was having a very nice dream, and would probably still be with you in Carmel otherwise. I'm due in surgery this morning."

"Go get ready. I'll make coffee."

I've accomplished that task and am warming leftover broccoli beef when he returns. He reaches for a mug, fills it with fragrant French roast, then sits on a bar stool. "So, I was thinking about your desire for escape. I always take time off around the holidays. How about we spend Christmas in Carmel?"

"Christmas is still five months away."

"I know, but it's never too early to start planning a vacation."

"True enough, and if I can't ski, beach walking sounds divine. We'll just have to figure out what to do with Eli."

"We can always bring him with us, though it kind of defeats any notion of romance."

"Maybe we'll just kennel him instead.

Although we might have to neuter him first."

Cavin almost loses his mouthful of java. "Tara . . ."

"Of course, considering the way he pants after women, that might not be such a bad thing. I mean, Kayla. Sophia. Genev—"

My mouth snaps shut.

He reaches for my hand. "You never actually told me how you feel about Genevieve."

I've had only odd snatches of time to think about her, so the total weight of the loss has yet to solidify in my mind. "I guess, between what happened to her and burying my mom, how I'm feeling is mortal. I mean, I've already managed to spend a couple more years on this earth than Genevieve had, so maybe I should feel grateful for that. But I do hope I get more time than my mother did, especially now I've found someone I want to share a decade or four with."

"Four? Just so you know, I plan to celebrate my hundredth birthday."

"Such ambition is at once admirable and a bit disturbing."

The microwave signals my food is hot. "Chinese for breakfast?" queries Cavin.

"Absolutely. Want some?"

"No. I'll grab a couple of breakfast sandwiches and eat them on the way." He starts to get up, rethinks, sits back down. "Oh, about your revision. I asked Cory Heinlen to step in and he agreed. Pissed Roger off, but I couldn't care less. One botched procedure is one too many. Cory's looking at his schedule. We're thinking end of August, if your ROM allows."

That elicits my heavy sigh. Better come clean.

"What?"

"I want to hold off on the surgery, at least for a while. I've been walking some in addition to the stationary biking, and the knee seems to be getting stronger. At least, it doesn't hurt as much."

He is silent for a few moments. "When did you decide this?" he hisses.

I ignore the tone. "I've been mulling it over for days now. I know you believe it's the wrong decision, but ultimately it's mine to make."

I expect hot irritation. Instead, he cools off, all the way to frosty. "You're absolutely right. It's totally your decision. I hope it's the right one. Meanwhile, I'll let Cory know you've decided to wait."

"Thank you. I'd really rather avoid it if possible."

Cavin finishes his coffee. "Guess I should be off."

Once he's gone, I get dressed, then go to the office to check my e-mail. There's one from Whittell High School, reminding the parents of Eli Lattimore that the first day of school is approaching and that any student under the age of eighteen who has a driver's license must provide proof they meet minimum attendance standards to the DMV to keep said license. That's a recent Nevada law, but not sure how it will affect Eli personally, as he turns eighteen not long after school starts.

Hopefully it will get him up on time for classes for a short while, anyway. And who knows? Maybe he'll surprise me about that, too.

Next up, an e-mail from the real estate agent. *The Bairds' loan was approved. They'd like to close by September first. Is that okay?*

Other than arranging for a mover, I've closed the book on Russian Hill. I tell her it's fine and make a mental note to take care of that today, along with all the other annoying details I must attend to.

Now, from Mel: *Hey. Guess what. Ricky Martin's playing at Tahoe the Friday night after your birthday. Want to go? I mean, if we can find tickets.*

Ricky Martin is really not my thing. Still, how can I say no? Mel loves him, and it's rare that she asks to do something with me. A quick peek on StubHub reveals two front-row tickets for the early show, at an exorbitant price. I go ahead and grab them, regardless. Happy birthday to me.

It strikes me that my sister would never go to such lengths for me. I wonder if anyone would. I've been blessed — or cursed — with the role of organizer for most of my life. People expect it. Then again, I expect it of myself and generally demand to be the decision maker, something rooted in my chaotic childhood. Once I refused to submit to my mother's abuse, I was reborn.

I answer Mel: *Tickets purchased. This will be fun.*

Finally, I find an announcement from the bank where Cavin and I opened a joint account, letting me know the statement is available online. I take the time to investigate and almost wish I hadn't when I notice an unfamiliar cash withdrawal, and a large one at that. What would Cavin need $5,600 for? My alert meter jumps into the red zone.

Where's the phone? Seems like my husband forgot to share some important information. He's probably already in surgery, but I'll text him in case he's still free. *Next time you make a large withdrawal please let me know. I'd hate to overdraw our account.*

There. That's good. Not overly accusatory, but he's definitely on notice.

He'd better have a damn good excuse.

TWENTY-THREE

Apparently Cavin did have a good reason for withdrawing so much cash. The day I messaged him, mentioning it, I got a return text within a few hours: *Sorry. It was supposed to be a surprise. Please trust me.*

That was more than a week ago, and he wouldn't tell me what the surprise was, exactly. Trusting him hasn't been easy, but I've managed to stuff my inquiries and wait it out until today, which happens to be my birthday. I never mentioned that fact to Cavin. I've always preferred to cruise through the day with little fanfare. Another year slipping by like water in a stream, so what?

But this morning, he drew me from dreams, pulling me backward into the spoon of his body. "Happy birthday, beautiful lady," he whispered, lifting my hair and kissing the back of my neck. His hand crept over my side to cup my breast, and my nipples rose taut, waking before the rest of me totally did. He scissored them between two fingers with enough force to shoot sparklers, hot and just painful enough to bring me completely conscious and aware of his erection, snaking between my legs.

I rolled onto my back and he lifted above me, reaching down to reward me with passion-steeped kisses.

Forehead.

Eyes.

Mouth.

Neck.

Luscious circling of my breasts, with emphatic pauses at the tips, heightened by the roll of his tongue.

Left-right beneath them, across my rib cage, then down my stomach, stopping to rest his chin on the mound beneath my belly button. "Goddamn, I love you," he exhaled before ducking his face into the space between my knees.

Right-left up my legs, which I gratefully parted, granting access to the tunnel already sodden. His mouth settled at the entrance, tongue dancing over the desire-hardened marble before curling down inside of me. I came in twenty seconds.

"My turn," he said, moving into position and stopping, the knob of his cock tantalizing. "Say please."

"Please!"

As wet as I was, his breathtaking girth slipped in easily, and his well-practiced hips drove the length of him all the way in, up against my sweet spot. He pulled back, so slowly, an exquisite tease before rocking back into me again.

"Don't come," I begged, just as he brought me off with a huge cloudburst. "I want to watch you jack off."

"Really?"

"Really."

He pulled out of me, slick with my orgasm, and his hand closed around his cock, stroking it in a circular motion, effort on the forward direction, which surprised me. I always thought it worked the opposite way. It was a powerful turn-on, especially when he said, "If I'm doing this, so are you. Touch yourself."

I touched myself.

He stroked himself.

We traded off.

And we came together.

Afterward, he gathered me into his arms and we lay, collecting our breath and our thoughts.

Finally, I asked, "How did you know it was my birthday?"

"I have my ways." But when that didn't satisfy me, he added, "It was in Caldwell's report. I just happened to remember it."

Ah yes. Dirk Caldwell, the private investigator Cavin hired when thinking about dating me. At first that bothered me mightily, but upon reflection I could be only so angry, since it's a tool I've used myself.

"Now let me ask you something. Why the masturbation thing? You been watching porn?"

"Not in a very long time."

And only with Jordan. Raul was much too old-school. Finn was much too jealous of attributes he didn't possess. Jordan didn't care, as long as there were plenty of, as he called them, "dripping pussy shots."

I claimed I didn't know why I wanted to watch my husband pleasure himself, and I didn't at the time. But now, sitting here waiting for my very special birthday dinner at our favorite Italian bistro, I think it had everything to do with being yanked from a dream that featured Eli masturbating while I smoked weed in the hot tub. I push the thought away as our Summer Fresh Tomato Caprese arrives at the table, delivered by the irrepressible Paolo.

"I hear this is a special day," he says. "Chef Christopher has created an exceptional prix fixe menu for you, and I have personally selected the wine pairings, unless you don't trust my suggestions?"

"How can I not trust you, Paolo?" He's a master sommelier. "The only thing I'd ask for is a bottle of Cristal to go with our dessert."

"Like I could forget your appetite for this champagne? I will always remember the first night you came limping in here on Doctor Lattimore's arm. I had a feeling it was only the beginning of a long relationship."

"Really? And how could you tell?"

Paolo winks at Cavin. "I'd never seen such a glimmer in the good doctor's eyes before. Now, if you'll excuse me, I have a distinctive pinot waiting for you."

Five courses later, as I'm relishing birthday strawberry shortcake and bubbly sips of Cristal, Cavin says, "Okay. Time for your surprise."

He produces a small box, wrapped in blue foil, with a gold bow twice the size of the package itself. I tease him by turning the gift over and over in my hands. "Pretty ribbon," I comment.

"Open it!"

It's obviously jewelry, but I don't expect what I find inside. It's a stunning pendant, in the shape of a snowflake. At every point is a diamond, .10-carat weight, and in the center is an exceptional fire opal, boasting brilliant ruby-red glints that somehow remind me of the sparklers Mel and I played with as kids on the Fourth of July. It's obvious that Cavin put much thought into creating a unique piece.

So why is my first thought: *What is this an apology for?*

I sit, staring wordlessly, for a little too long.

"Don't you like it? I had it designed especially for you. There's not another like it, just like a real snowflake."

"Oh, no. I love it! I just never . . ."

"What?"

Let's give the straightforward approach, or some variation of it, a try. "Okay, this is stupid. But my first thought was what an amazing fire opal it was, and my second thought had to do with red sparks, and that brought my disturbed brain back to Independence Days in Idaho, some of which left very bad memories behind. Cavin, this is the most beautiful piece of jewelry anyone has ever given me, and the fact that you created it especially for me . . . Well, I'll cherish it forever."

His face illuminates. "I don't think your brain is disturbed at all. Okay, well, maybe a little. Here. Let's see how it looks on you."

He comes over, lifts the pendant from the box, and slips it around my neck, which he brushes with Cristal-cooled lips before retreating back across the table.

"Beautiful," he promises.

"The necklace, or me?"

"Both, and together, incomparable."

I smile. "The last time someone used that word in relationship to me was to call me an incomparable bitch."

"Jordan?"

"Finn. Right after he signed over the Russian Hill house."

"Ah. And speaking of the place, I did manage to take those days off next week."

I need someone in San Francisco to coordinate with the movers, and also to make sure Eli doesn't decide to inhabit the house when he takes Kayla over the mountain to start college. I'd do it myself, but I'm supposed to meet with Maryann Colvin and the CEO of one of the nonprofits her foundation is involved with. "Oh, excellent. I didn't really want to count on Charlie, not that he's ever totally let me down."

As boy Fridays go, Charlie was a godsend when I first ruined my knee, and I've tried to find ways to supplement his UCSF student income, even after my move to Ta-

284

hoe. But he's been awfully distracted since hooking up with Cassandra, who I've forgiven for telling him I sleep around. When I talked to her about it, she was completely contrite and chalked it up to alcohol.

"Oh, hey. Speaking of Charlie, strangely enough it seems he and Cassandra are getting serious, or at least semiserious."

"Why is that strange?" Cavin asks.

"Gee, I don't know. Um. She's almost twice his age, and her son is only a few years younger than Charlie." Taylor coincidentally being one of Eli's peers makes the entire world — or *my* entire world, anyway — feel tiny, indeed.

"I guess it's unusual but not exactly unheard of. If it makes them happy, why not?"

Good question. "You're absolutely right."

"So I'll leave for San Francisco on Sunday and drive back on Tuesday."

"And you'll make sure Kayla's all settled in before you go?"

"Absolutely. It's going to be strange with her gone, don't you think?"

"It will definitely be quieter." Her quarreling with Eli has become tiresome, and their spats have grown more and more contentious as the countdown to the start of the new semester has moved closer. "I have no real idea how the two of them feel about each other, but it doesn't seem like much love is involved, so I hope the distance gives them some clarity."

"You mean you hope they move on."

"Exactly. Truthfully, they don't have much in common, other than a bad habit or two."

"Plus a relative or two."

"Yeah. Kind of hard to get around that."

Paolo brings the bill. Cavin reaches into his pocket and extracts his wallet, and a piece of paper flutters onto the floor at my feet. I retrieve it and discover it's a receipt from the Reno jewelry store where he bought my birthday present. As Cavin hands his credit card to Paolo, I casually peruse it. One custom opal/diamond pendant: $4,967.29, minus a $1,000 down payment, left a balance of roughly four grand. And that begs the question, where did the other $1,600 go?

Cavin reads my scowl correctly. "What's wrong?"

I hand him the receipt. "I know I wasn't supposed to see this, but I did. Just wondering about where the rest of the cash from that withdrawal went."

"Oh. Of course. The Audi needed tires, and I figured while I was in Reno I might as well get them there. They're a lot more expensive up here. And truthfully, while I waited for the car, I blew a couple hundred bucks in a casino. Nothing major, but I should have mentioned it to you."

"The Audi needed tires already?" The car isn't that old.

"Yes. Apparently I somehow managed to knock it out of alignment and they wore irregularly. I was noticing it in the way it handled."

The answer came readily, but still, "So, why pay for tires with cash? Wouldn't a credit card be easier?"

"I know it's weird, but I prefer to use cash for major purchases. That way there's no chance of them earning interest. And like I said, I wanted the necklace to be a surprise and thought cash was the best way to keep it on the down low."

"Don't you worry about carrying that much money on you?"

"I didn't carry it very long."

I could argue the advisability of that or the idea of using a debit card, though our bank does have strict daily limits on those. Instead I let it rest with a simple warning. "Please keep receipts for cash purchases more carefully, or we'll have a bookkeeping nightmare come tax time."

"I know I tend to be lazy that way, but

cross my heart from here on out I will file them in better fashion. Okay? The last thing I want to do is make you question my trustworthiness, which is why I mentioned the casino."

His gambling is a bad habit but doesn't seem to be too out of hand, and I'm monitoring it cautiously. If I have to, I'll give him a monthly you-may-blow-this-much-without-penalty allowance, but I hope it doesn't come to that. I am not his mother. "I appreciate that, and so will my accountant. Our accountant, if you want him to be."

"As far as taxes, I think it makes the most sense to file jointly, but I'll leave that up to you — and our accountant. I'm not married to the one I've been using."

"Good. Brent is excellent at what he does. He did contact me about the Russian Hill sale and suggested I max contributions to the IRS to help cover the capital gains. I'll let him know we're good with that and ask his opinion on our filing status."

The tedious details of marriage.

"That's fine with me."

"Oh, and I believe you can deduct gambling losses."

"You can, but only up to the amount you win in any given year, and the IRS requires you to keep a diary documenting your losses."

Is it good or bad that he knows this?

"Do casinos report your winnings?" I ask, because it strikes me that I had a decent win at Tahoe last year and didn't claim it on my tax return. Though, considering I dropped almost the entire amount before I won it back, I pretty much broke even. I'm what you might call a casual gambler, so how would I know?

"Depends on what you're playing and how much you clear. In certain circumstances, they actually withhold twenty-five percent and make you fill out a W2g form before the payout. But not on table games, except for poker, which believe it or not has a higher threshold than slots, sports betting, or bingo before they report."

Guess I'm safe then. I was playing roulette.

"Have you had any major wins this year?" We met last December but spent a lot of time apart before we got married. I have no idea how often he frequented casinos.

"A couple, including the money I won on our honeymoon."

Yes, after dropping two grand, he managed to earn twenty-five hundred back. So, how do they look at that? Five hundred net or twenty-five gross, despite the initial investment? Considering how many years I lived in Nevada, I have no real understanding of how the system works. I rarely gambled, and always thought of it as a game.

Apparently, it's a business, as sanctioned by the Internal Revenue Service.

"So, you report all your gambling income?"

"Tara, I told you before that I once faced an audit and came away owing a substantial amount. I won't take that chance again, especially not now, with you in my life. Recklessness and partnerships are mutually exclusive."

One would hope so.

One certainly would.

TWENTY-FOUR

When Mel arrives on Friday afternoon, she breezes through the door in a formfitting leopard-print dress that is by far the shortest thing I've ever seen her in, and she looks damn good in it, too. Envy pokes at me. I'll have to pick up my workouts.

Ridiculous. Am I competing with my sister now?

Maybe she's competing with you.

I shut down the interior dialogue and ask, "Since when did you start wearing dead animals?"

"Faux dead animals, and why not? It was on sale. Don't you like it?"

"I do. It's just so . . . not what I would expect of you."

"Good. I'm tired of being predictable." She brushes past me. "So I'm here. What time are we leaving?"

"I made reservations at the Sage Room for six o'clock." It's our favored Stateline

291

restaurant and just happens to be housed in the same casino where Ricky Martin is appearing. "That should give us plenty of time. The show doesn't start until eight."

Mel gives me a glancing once-over. "You're not going like *that,* are you?"

That makes me laugh. "Uh, generally I don't go out on the town in a T-shirt and yoga pants. No, sister dearest. I'll be sure to change." I do have to wonder, though, what I can wear to put myself on par with Mel. So I guess it's a competition after all. "Make yourself at home," I tell her. "Cavin should be here soon. Eli and Kayla are downstairs if you want to say hello, but I'd be sure to knock if they're in his room. And be prepared. She's rather tenuous right now, with school just around the corner."

"Well, at least she's planning to go."

"Looks that way, but she still has time to change her mind."

"She wouldn't dare!"

"That's what I keep telling her."

Back in my room, I comb the closet for something sexy as hell, with the caveat that it has to cover my knees, one of which is still slightly swollen around small, silvering scars. I settle on a gorgeous silk sheath that falls just beneath the blemishes, unable to forget that the last time I wore it was with

Jordan. The day I married him, in fact. Some women might toss a dress with such memories attached, but all that would do is allow the offender control. I try it on and am pleased to find it still fits, if a bit more snugly than it used to.

I've gained curves.

Plus a couple of pounds.

Who asked you?

In the shower, I go ahead and shave so the skin I'm able to reveal will, at the very least, be hairless, and it strikes me that I've become less obsessive about things like perfectly smooth legs. Am I too relaxed? Too settled in a comfort zone? I've survived — and thrived — by keeping my guard up. The last thing I want is to become complacent. Complacency is a control death knell.

As I'm putting the finishing touches on my makeup, Cavin comes in to let me know he's home. I finish with the mascara, look up at him in the mirror, and he whistles. "Stunning. But you've got me wondering exactly who you're looking so gorgeous *for.* Your sister?"

"You are kid—" Okay, he is kidding, at least that's what his goofy grin indicates. "Well, if the right waiter happens along . . ."

He sidles up behind me, wraps me in his arms, and rests his chin on my shoulder.

"I'm not worried. You're not that generous of a tipper." He kisses my neck. "I'll wait up for you."

"We could be late."

"That's okay. If I'm asleep, wake me. No matter how comfortable I might appear. Deal?"

Goddamn straight. "Deal. Now I've got to get dressed. Go entertain Melody, would you, please?"

"Your wish is my command. Oh, by the way, she's looking great, don't you think? Turning forty seems to become her."

"Yeah, well, on the outside, anyway."

We leave it there. I slip into my chosen dress, which would look a lot better with heels, but I'm not going to chance them yet. It's still warm enough for sandals, so I pick a pretty pair instead. My new opal pendant is the finishing touch, drawing just the right amount of attention to the sheath's deep neckline. The mirror confirms it's a good look — enticing but classy.

As I exit my room, laughter drifts up the hallway. It's a warm blend of Cavin's and Mel's and I wonder what sparked it. Whatever it was has engaged them completely. They don't notice my approach, and as I near, I'm more than a little surprised to see how close they're sitting. Mel's bare knee, in fact, rests against Cavin's clothed one.

A jolt of jealousy momentarily stuns me. I stay frozen in place, not wanting to interrupt them. Where is this going? Anywhere at all?

Nonconfrontation? So not you.

As luck would have it, confrontation is delivered via another source. Kayla crests the stairs from the lower level. "Jesus, Mom, what are you wearing?"

Melody jerks her attention away from my husband, disengages her knee from his. "Oh, look, it's my darling daughter. Nice of you to offer me five minutes of your precious time."

"You wanted me to put on clothes, didn't you?"

Mel ignores Kayla's nasty tone. "I suppose that *was* a good thing. But why do you care what I'm wearing?"

"I don't, really. It's just your outfit is not very . . . momlike."

It certainly isn't. And her flirtation with my husband wasn't exactly sisterlike. But I can either let that bother me all evening or chalk it up to inexperience as a desirable woman. She never really learned how to play the singles game, not that she's actually single.

Yet. And neither is your husband.

I clear my throat, announcing my presence. Cavin stands, discomfort evident in his expression, and comes over to tell me, "You look beautiful. I don't believe I've ever seen that dress before."

"Well, now you have." Tepid.

He notices. "Everything okay?"

I look him straight in the eye. "As far as I know. Except we'll be late if we don't go."

Mel rises, but it's an awkward exercise in unfamiliar heels and a mini she's not used to wearing.

Cavin wisely avoids observing.

Kayla rewards the effort with a serious scowl. "So much for five minutes of my precious time. Did you have something you needed to tell me?"

Mel toddles over to give her a hug. "That's all I wanted, and it would've been awfully rude of me not to attempt communication, don't you think? I haven't seen very much of you in months now."

"Get used to it."

Wow. Kayla's all attitude considering the only possible thing saying hello to her mom could've interrupted was getting laid or getting high.

"Why don't you show your mother a little respect?" I ask.

Kayla glares. "Respect, like trust, needs to

be cultivated."

"No," I correct. "Sometimes respect is simply owed, along with thanks."

She starts to say something. Shuts her mouth. Then, "Sorry, Mom. Hope I see you before you leave tomorrow."

Mel smiles. "You're welcome, and you will. But tonight, it's all about Ricky. I can't believe I get to see him. He's hot!"

Kayla rolls her eyes. "Seriously, Mother?"

Cavin grins, amused.

I am anything but, and push my sister toward the door. "Come on."

I'm glad it's a short ten minutes to State-line. I spend the first of it silently glaring out the window, contemplating my relationships with the closest members of my extremely small family. I've always felt rather possessive of Melody — a by-product of our mother's emotional and often physical distance. But how does she feel about me?

As for Kayla, it's terribly hard to measure the depth of her feelings for anyone. Except, maybe, Eli, and she's way overboard there. What about loyalty to her parents? Her siblings? Me? Most of the time all I see is selfishness, but every now and again I get a glimpse of something deeper. A need for connection, perhaps?

Considering the only other teenager I've spent much time around is Eli, I have to wonder if egocentrism isn't the driving factor to adolescence. A way to survive those god-awful years.

It definitely was for you.

"Penny for your thoughts." Mel interrupts my reverie.

"Just considering family dynamics."

"What about them?"

I consider how to answer. "Do you think dysfunction is the new 'normal'?"

She doesn't hesitate. "I think 'normal' is a subjective word. Oh, here we are. Where should I park?"

"Valet, of course. It's the only way to go."

It's a decent hike across the casino floor to the Sage Room. We arrive five minutes past our reserved time, but the maître d' is accommodating and seats us with a respectful smile. As always, the food proves to be topflight, though we both order lighter than we have in the past. Brad, the waiter, is, in fact, rather nice to look at, and when he's totally out of earshot, I tease Mel, "He might be fun for a little fling."

"He's wearing a wedding ring."

"Is he, now? I confess I didn't notice."

"One of your very few flaws."

I'm not sure exactly how to take that, so

I'll let it go. Damn, does that mean I'm maturing? "Mel? It was just a joke, okay? I wish you didn't take everything so seriously."

She nibbles a breadstick. "That would be nice, but some habits are hard to break."

"Habits like fidelity?"

"Exactly."

"Question."

"Okay." Her tenor is noncommittal.

"Do you regret that night in Glenns Ferry? Be truthful."

"Do I regret it? No. Would I do it again? I don't think so."

"Why not?"

Her answer comes more quickly than I expect. "It made me come to grips with how much my marriage has deteriorated. I would never have done something like that in the past because I realized it would mean admitting defeat."

"Yet you're willing to give Graham another chance."

"Yes, because despite everything, I love him. If I didn't, letting go would be as simple as showing him the door. It's not. Still, I gave him an ultimatum. Either we go to counseling and make a serious effort to save what's left of our marriage or he gets the hell out for good."

"Did you ever find out where he goes when he disappears?"

"He always claims his band is playing a gig, but I can't say if that's the truth."

"Have you ever considered hiring a private investigator?"

"To follow Graham?"

Is she taking dense pills? "Uh, yeah. Wouldn't it ease your mind to know for sure what he's up to?"

"I suppose. . . ."

"If nothing else, it might help if and when you file for divorce. A little leverage can be a very good thing when it comes to alimony."

She mulls that over. "Even if I wanted to, I don't think I could afford a PI."

"You *have* been putting money away like I suggested, haven't you?"

This isn't the first time she's talked about divorce. Not sure if she's wishy-washy about it or just downright scared to try and make a life for herself and her kids without Graham in the picture.

"I try, but there isn't a lot to spare. Seems like there's always an expense I didn't expect, you know?"

They married in college. Graham has always been a part of her adulthood, so she's never had to consider a single-income existence. And he's the true breadwinner.

Successful pediatrician versus paid-per-project technical writer? No contest.

"Look. I've got a great PI who's done work for me in the past. I'll give you his name, and as a birthday present I'll cut you a check to cover his retainer."

She studies my face as if searching for ulterior motives. "That's a generous offer. I'll think about it."

All efficiency, not to mention great timing, Brad arrives tableside to inquire about dessert. We turn him down, of course, and he brings the bill. I do tip him generously. But not *that* generously.

On our way to the showroom Mel surprises me again, stopping at the Wheel of Fortune and betting dollars on the long odds.

"You, gambling?" The last time we were here I played roulette, with her bitching at me the entire time.

She shrugs. "I figured I could throw away ten dollars. I've worked for it. And what if I win?"

She doesn't. Ten dollars disappear in five spins.

"There are better games if winning is what you're after. Blackjack, for instance."

"I guess. But you have to know how to play."

That's true of any game, in- or outside of a casino. You also have to consider the odds.

As we move again toward the showroom, I'm cognizant of heads turning but have no way of knowing which one of us they're turning *for,* and that is vaguely unsettling. Mel seems blissfully unaware of the activity, or else she's playing coy, something I can't associate with my sister. It's strange.

Our seats are front row, but off to the left. That doesn't really matter as Ricky Martin masterfully plays the entire stage, which is only a couple of feet away. Every time he moves to our side, we're staring straight up at him, and more than once he sings directly to Mel and me. If I were the fan-girl type, even though this isn't my kind of music at all, I'd be swooning. Mel *is* the fan-girl type. Enough said.

Okay, the beat is infectious. And yeah, he's pretty damn hot, in a totally Latin way. So. Not. Graham.

Regardless, it's inspiring enough just to watch my little sister so enthralled in something beyond her encapsulated world. On many levels, I truly hope Graham is inspired to move on. Mel is still young enough, and now desirable enough, to immerse herself in *"la vida loca."* I've experienced "the crazy life." She should try it, too.

At least long enough to find happiness.

We are both happy enough when the encore is over, and we've made eye contact with gorgeous Ricky Martin dozens of times. As we wait for the room to clear, allowing easier access to the exit, Mel gushes about this song and that, the amazing band, and Ricky's advanced level of dance.

Finally, we turn to move toward the door, and guess who's immediately ahead of us? I can't avoid her, can't pretend not to see her or hope she won't notice me. Her dark eyes seize hold right away. "Hello, Tara. Oh, you go on, darling. I'll meet you in the foyer." Sophia sends Maury hustling off toward the restroom.

Fuck.

Though I've done nothing wrong, my face heats like it's recently been sunburned. "Sophia."

"That's me. Who's this?"

What business is it of yours? But I respond, "Oh, sorry. This is my sister, Melody."

"Of course. Nice to meet you. Cavin mentioned you'd be in town."

Don't bite. Don't bite.

How can you not bite?

"When did you talk to Cavin?"

Speaking of biting, she shows us her even, bleached teeth. "Yesterday."

Don't react. Don't react.

How can you not react?

"Yesterday?"

"Well, yes. I happened to run into him over at Starbucks. So we . . ."

I will maim her.

". . . had a cappuccino and talked for a while."

A white-hot smoke of anger billows. "He didn't mention it. It must have slipped his mind."

Maybe you should maim him instead.

She doesn't miss a beat. "Cavin can be a little scattered. Oh, but didn't you love Ricky? And what great seats you had. Bet they were pricey."

She must be clairvoyant.

I force the tremor from my voice. "They were, but we were lucky to find them."

The crowd is thinning, so we can move with less effort, something I silently urge Mel to do, and she complies, zero clairvoyance necessary. Sophia excuses herself to go meet up with Maury, and we start across the casino toward valet. About halfway there, my bladder reminds me I haven't peed since we left the house.

"I'd better use the restroom."

"I'm fine. I'll wait here."

I'm glad I chose this bathroom rather than one closer to the showroom. The line isn't too long, so it doesn't take more than a couple of minutes to get in, complete the necessary task, and get out again.

Mel's staring at something, fixated.

"What are you looking at?"

"Them." She flips her head, indicating a couple drifting toward the exit — Sophia and Maury. "Odd pair."

As we head toward the door, I explain the relationship, at least what I know of it.

"That woman is stunning. You must hate having her so close."

"Other than wanting to kill her, it doesn't bother me at all."

"It doesn't upset you that she had coffee with your husband?"

"He should have told me about it, but other than that, no."

She must know it's a lie, but she lets it go, except to say, "I'd better never catch Graham sneaking around like that."

The "or else" is heavily implied.

Yeah, but or else what?

We reach the valet and Mel takes care of sending them for the car. I reach into my purse for my wallet for a tip for the kid, and when I pull it out, my cell goes flying. "Shit." It lands on the ground with a thud, but with luck the OtterBox will keep the electronics intact.

Mel bends to retrieve it.

"Is it okay? Did the screen crack?"

She straightens slowly. "It's fine."

"What's wrong then?"

Mel hands me the phone, which is no worse for the wear. In fact, illuminated in green on the screen is the notice of a text message. From Graham. *Can we please talk?*

I have no clue why Graham suddenly wants to converse, but the idea does not sit well with my sister, who is miffed all the way home.

"Just how often do you and my husband talk?"

"Like, never."

She does not believe me. "I see. So out of the blue he asks for a dialogue?"

"Looks that way."

"What about, exactly?"

"I sincerely don't know, Mel. *He* approached *me.* Maybe he's actually worried about your marriage. Or maybe he's concerned about all these changes in you. They're huge, and they've happened so fast."

"Not really. They've happened over four

decades. He just hasn't noticed, and obviously neither have you."

That stops me. I thought I noticed everything.

Problem is you have to look.

Assumption is rarely a good thing, and I've always simply assumed I understood the framework of Mel's life. But how deeply have I ever really peered? How important is it to me now?

Does she even want me to?

TWENTY-FIVE

Saturday morning I'm making coffee when Melody appears, dressed in a sensible pair of jeans and a simple long-sleeved tee the color of cotton candy. "I've never seen you in pink before. It works."

"Thanks."

No hint of warmth.

She sits on a bar stool three feet away and the silence that builds in the space between us forms a perceivable wall.

"Coffee?"

"Black."

Also new. At least, I think so.

"No cream?"

"I gave it up for Lent three years ago and never reacquired the habit."

Lent.

Right.

Religion.

Right.

Astrology.

Right.

"Hey, Mel. What sign are you?"

This is a test.

"Libra. Why?"

"Just wondering." I hand her a mug with a smiley face, unsure where it came from. It seems out of place in these cupboards. "Are you still pissed at me?"

"Not pissed, exactly. Unhappy though. I realize good communication skills weren't a part of our programming, but I want you to know without a doubt that covert interaction with my husband is unacceptable."

Must temper my temper, which is threatening to explode. "I have not interacted with Graham, Mel. I haven't even responded to his text."

"Are you going to?"

"Yes, if for no other reason than to let him know you've commanded no interaction." After she leaves, I plan to give Graham the opportunity to bare his soul if that's what he has in mind. I do not respond well to veiled threats, and that includes from my sister, though this is the first time she has ever issued one. But I won't give that away. "Look, I'm sorry if you're upset. But I promise there isn't a problem."

"Apology accepted."

She sips her coffee.

Grimaces slightly.

Changes the subject.

And when she does, she goes straight for the jugular. "So what did Cavin have to say about Sophia?"

"I haven't discussed it with him yet. He was asleep when we got back and I didn't want to wake him."

Deal off. The last thing I needed after an argument with my sister was a confrontation with my husband. I'll see to that once Mel is on her way home. And sex will not happen until he offers a satisfactory explanation.

"You are more patient than I," comments Melody.

"Patience is something I practice." And it has generally proven wise. "Anyway, I've always thought of you as 'long-suffering,' which indicates patience to me."

"Long-suffering?" Her jaw juts forward and her shoulders stiffen. "Well, I suppose that's better than trading in husbands like used cars."

Ouch. Double ouch, in fact.

So much for apology accepted.

My patience has almost expired. "Were you referring to me?"

"Not necessarily."

Definitive.

I've never worried about how Mel — or anyone — felt about my marriages and/or their demises. But I guess I shouldn't be surprised that she has an opinion. In fact, I suppose it's strange that we've never discussed it.

We won't discuss it now, however, as Eli and Kayla come upstairs to reward Mel with a few minutes of inane conversation. I tune them out completely, thinking about my sister's recent commentary. I suppose I presumed a larger measure of respect, considering I mostly raised her, not to mention took the brunt of our mother's rage.

There you go with suppositions again.

My attention is pulled back toward the ongoing dialogue by Kayla's high-pitched whine. "No way, Mom!"

"Don't you think it makes more sense?" asks Mel.

"Maybe, but I don't care. I mean, as long as you still want to drive me, Eli?"

"Well, yeah. I mean, I planned on it," he agrees.

"Okay, fine," says Mel.

"What's fine?" Cavin shuffles into the kitchen, still wearing his pajamas and sleep-tousled hair.

"I just volunteered to take Kayla home with me now and drop her off at school next week," explains Melody. "But she'd rather ride over with Eli."

"It's our last chance to be together for a while," Kayla complains.

Eli rolls his eyes but comments, "It's my last chance to visit the city for a while. I've been stuck in the sticks too long."

Cavin pours a cup of coffee, turns. "Did you girls have fun last night?"

Mel shoots me an obvious look but exclaims, "It was amazing! What a performance!"

Now Cavin directs his words toward me. "I thought you were going to wake me when you got home."

"Slipped my mind."

There's no possible way anyone here could've missed the undercurrent, but this is not the time for the pending discussion.

Mel stands. "I should probably head home. I'm supposed to pick up Jessica around lunchtime."

"I'll walk you out," I tell her.

Her small overnight case is already by the door. She picks it up, rotates back toward the kitchen. "You're stopping by the house tomorrow, right?" she says to Kayla.

"Well, yeah. I need to get my stuff."

"And say hello to your sisters?"

"Duh, Mom."

"We'll go to the early service and be back from church by ten."

"Will Dad be there?"

"I don't know. You've got his number. Ask him."

But it's me Mel's looking at. I ignore that fact and open the door, ushering her outside. "Ricky Martin was fun. We need to do another girls' night out soon."

She nods. "Oh, hey. I forgot to ask what I owe you for the ticket."

"Don't worry about it. When you're a rich and famous author you can buy the tickets."

"Rich and . . . What are you talking about?"

"I'm talking about that novel you're writing."

No clue where that came from.

Mel laughs. "I'm not writing a novel."

"But you could. You've got the talent. Or maybe you are writing one and just don't know it yet."

"I think you're losing your mind."

"You could be right." I give her a hug. "I'm serious about seeing each other more often."

"We should. Oh, I forgot to tell you happy birthday. You look great for fifty."

"What?" I just turned forty-two.

"Joking."

"Stick to writing. Stand-up isn't your thing."

As she drives away, I realize I would like to see her more, if only to keep a better handle on the state of her life. And as I go back inside, I understand I'm not anxious to engage in the coming conflict. God, have I grown soft or what? Soft is not a good thing.

Soft is so not you. And as for your husband, lying by omission is still lying.

I pull back my shoulders, tilt my chin upward. The kids are still in the kitchen, so I start down the hallway before requesting, "Cavin, may I talk to you privately, please?"

He follows me into the office, and I shut the door behind us. Neither of us sits.

"What's up?" he asks.

"I was wondering when you last spoke with Sophia."

Boom.

His face flushes scarlet. "I . . . uh . . . Just a couple of days ago, actually. I happened to run into her at Starbucks. But then, I guess you know that."

"I do. Because Mel and I happened to run into her last night at the show and she was very happy to inform me that you two had a long conversation over cappuccinos. Was there a reason why you neglected to mention it?"

He sighs heavily. "I'm sorry, Tara, I should've told you. I just didn't want to upset you. It was a harmless cup of coffee, nothing more."

"I see. And what, exactly, did you talk about? I mean, if you think I can handle it. I'll try very hard not to get upset."

"Please don't condescend. We talked about her show. We talked about you. But the main thing we talked about was Eli. I was very clear that I'm unhappy about her inviting him into her bed."

"And . . . ?"

"And with some discussion, she admitted it was her way of getting back at me. She also said she'd recently decided it wasn't such a good idea."

"Why? Because she didn't get the reaction from you she was looking for?"

"I don't know. I didn't ask. I figured it was better to let it drop."

"Look. I understand the odds are decent that you'll run into Sophia from time to time, and I'd never ask you not to have coffee with her. However, I do have concerns about you keeping secrets from me, and that's how this feels. I'm a grown woman. I can handle you talking to your ex as long as I know about it." Now I echo the little voice inside my head. "Lying by omission is still lying. I would never lie to you."

He moves closer, takes my hand, and when he bends to kiss it, brings his eyes level with mine. "Please forgive me. I promise never to withhold information from you again, even if I think it's going to upset you. I guess I'm still working on that trust cultivation myself. How can I make it up to you? Brunch on the beach?"

I agree it's a good start, though privately I'm still irritated that this needs to be something I worry about. I'm not one to trust easily anyway. This rattled my slender faith quotient.

We manage to have an exceptionally nice day, anyway. It's an end-of-summer Saturday, so the beaches are fairly crowded, but Cavin knows a hideaway spot only a few locals are aware of. It's down a relatively steep hillside, which proves to be quite a workout for my knee, but the tentative ligaments hold. There isn't a whole lot of sand here, but giant, flat rocks surround the small stretch, and we spread a beach blanket and set up the folding chairs Cavin has transported down the hill atop one of the rocks.

He climbs back up for our simple picnic and I slather sunscreen. When he returns, we sip mimosas, nibble on strawberries,

Brie, and crackers, and mostly avoid talking by reading. But after an hour or so, Cavin asks, "Are you still angry?"

A shimmer remains, vague and watery, like a mirage lifting from August asphalt. But I say simply, "No."

"Good. Then let's get naked."

"Here?"

"We're all alone. And no one can see from the highway. Ever skinny-dipped?"

"Of course."

But not in a long, long time. And that swimming pool was a whole lot warmer than Tahoe. Even here where it's shallow and sun-kissed, the water lifts goose bumps immediately, and that's before I'm even halfway in.

"Not like that!" says Cavin. "Headfirst."

He demonstrates, comes up sputtering. Still, he takes hold of my hands and pulls, and we both go under. But not for long. His arms encircle me, and our bodies exchange a small measure of warmth before he lifts me out of the water. Then he lays me on a small cushion of sand, thighs and above on solid land, legs floating gently.

I doubt he could have accomplished an erection immersed in the frigid water, but once out it doesn't take him long. "God, you're beautiful when you're wet," he says, before proceeding to make me even wetter, and in a place the lake couldn't reach.

Warm sun on my face.

Cool breeze through liquid diamonds on my skin.

Cavin's tongue-enhanced kisses in all the right places.

It's a heady experience.

I open my legs, inviting entrance. But, most unexpectedly, he flips me onto my belly, lifts me onto my hands and knees. "Let's take a test-drive, shall we?"

It would be the first time I've attempted sex in this position since I wrecked my knee. I've been dying to do this, but I'm a little worried. "I don't know . . ."

"If it's uncomfortable, I'll stop."

I don't think he has stopping in mind.

His initial push is a long, steady climb.

Upward.

Inward.

I rock back into him until I can't go any farther, then slowly pull away. He matches my pace, opposite stroke for stroke, but finally I urge him faster as the bend of my leg begins to feel tentative. I'm glad for the deep pillow of sand, which relieves the stress enough to allow our mutual quaking orgasm.

But as soon as that's accomplished, I roll

onto my back, straightening my legs and flexing them gently again. "No damage done."

"Are you sure?"

Odd. He almost sounds disappointed.

He never even gave you a chance to decline.

"Pretty sure. Guess we'll find out when I try to make my way back up the hill. Meanwhile, is there more champagne?"

"Would I leave you high and dry?"

"Definitely not."

It's a nice afternoon, mellowed by wine, but I remind myself to quit well before I attempt the return hike to the car. That proves harder than coming down was, but I manage it with care, and feel even more hopeful that I made the right decision regarding another surgery.

We arrive home late afternoon and I don't bother to change before going to the kitchen to start dinner. That means when Kayla and Eli come in from wherever, I'm wearing a bikini beneath a short, sheer cover-up. I realize my mistake immediately.

"Wow!" exclaims Eli. "Not many guys are lucky enough to have moms who look like that! You should wear a bikini more often."

"Shut up, Eli," demands Kayla.

"First of all, I'm not your mom. And,

second, would you mind cutting up these vegetables for the grill basket? I'm going to take a shower and we'll fire up the barbecue in about an hour."

I don't wait for his answer. But I do hear Kayla complaining, "Do you always have to stare at her? It's creepy."

And I can't help but note Eli's response. "Like she said, she's not my mom, so it's not that creepy. Besides, it's damn hard not to stare at her. Too bad my dad doesn't appreciate what he's got. Hey, are you going to help me with the zucchini or what?"

Cavin is just getting out of the shower as I'm on my way in. I watch him towel off, thinking about Eli's words. It seems like my husband appreciates me. He's quick to compliment, rarely short-tempered, and seems happy enough to relinquish control. But he isn't always forthright, and that is worrisome, despite his ready excuses.

And Eli's truthful?

Now *that* is a question I'm not able to answer. My instinct insists he is, but maybe it's just that his straight-in-your-face manner belies deceit. Either way, I'm wary of trusting him too far.

"The kids are prepping vegetables for the grill," I inform Cavin. "Whenever you're ready, please go ahead and light it. I put the chicken in marinade before we left this morning, so it's ready to go. I won't be long."

"Whatever you desire, my darling. Personally, I'm starving." He winks. "All that beach action."

He goes to dress and consider the barbecue while I slip out of my skimpy clothing. I suppose I should be a bit more demure, but that is not an adjective I've ever applied to myself in the past. Postshower, with evening falling, I choose capris and a gauzy blouse, with plenty of support underneath it.

Almost demure.

Demure enough so Kayla reacts with a smug grin when I join the crew on the deck, where the barbecue is starting to smoke. "What? You've never seen capris before?"

"Not on you. They look nice, by the way."

"Not as nice as a bikini," comments Eli, souring Kayla's expression.

"I'm going in for the chicken," says Cavin. "May I pour you a glass of wine?"

"I'll do it. I need some water first."

I follow him inside, but before I reach the kitchen, the phone rings. Caller ID says it's Mel. "Hel—"

"Why? Didn't? You? Tell me?"

Each.

Word.

Is a dagger.

I'm punctured. And I have no clue why.

"Tell you what?"

Hugely pregnant pause, and Cavin's eyes cloud with concern. *What is it?* he mouths.

In answer, I just shake my head, waiting to understand.

"Why didn't you tell me you and Graham had an affair?"

"What? Who told you such an incredible lie?"

"Who do you think? Graham! And why would he lie to me about something like that?"

"I have no clue, Mel. But Graham and I never had an affair."

A one-night stand doesn't qualify as an affair.

Says who?

On the far end of the signal, my sister is breaking down. Why would Graham bring up that short encounter now? It happened twenty years ago. He came into the pawnshop several months after Raul died, looking for a set of drums. He made excuses to hang around, and I figured he was interested in seeing me. As far as I knew, he was just a cute guy, a year or two older than me, who was in med school and looking for fun. I was twenty-three, widowed, and tired of people tiptoeing around me. I was overdue for a little fun myself.

Yes, Graham was dating Melody then, but I didn't know it when I accepted his offer of a concert and dinner.

Yes, we had a great time.

Yes, sex was involved.

And the very next day, Mel introduced us at an impromptu lunch. It was one of the most surreal coincidences I've ever experienced. In fact, it threw me off balance. I never let him touch me again, only accepted one call from him afterward, and that was to ream him good for messing around on my sister. With *anyone.* We've been awkward with each other ever since.

But trying to explain any of that to Melody would be meaningless at this moment in time. Better to simply deny.

My husband stares at me, waiting to see where this goes, and I know he's more than curious. He's questioning my character.

"Melody Ann, what brought this on?" Purposely using her middle name, hoping it's evocative of our mother's favored method of demanding a response.

It works. Sort of. "Don't you *dare* talk down to me, Tara *Lynn.* It doesn't matter what brought it on. I want to know if you've ever slept with my husband."

My first thought is to go ahead and confess. Tell her the story, start to finish, exactly as it unfolded. Honesty is almost always my preferred course of action. But, all things considered, denial seems the better way to go, especially with Cavin sitting here listening in. "No."

"Really? Then how did he know about the birthmark on your lower back?"

Damn.

Straight into the middle of a shit storm. Scratch that. A regular shit tornado. Why the hell didn't I just go ahead and confess? Instead, I've become snared in the lie, and how easily I fell into that trap, which snaps shut now.

"Well?" she demands.

"One minute." I turn my back on my husband, take the phone down the hall to the office, and shut the door behind me. Safely shielded from eavesdropping ears, I confide the details, finishing with a sincere apology. "I'm so sorry, Mel. I truly had no idea it was Graham you were dating, and besides, he came on to me."

I swear I can hear my words churning in her head.

"Why didn't you tell me? Don't you think I had the right to know?"

"In retrospect, of course. But at the time

— God, I was only twenty-three — I believed slamming the door in his face was good enough. You were so happy being with him, and neither you nor I had previously enjoyed a whole lot in the way of happiness. I didn't want to take that away from you."

"What about after?"

"What do you mean?"

"I mean what about the other times?"

"Melody, I have no clue what you're talking about. We were only together once."

"Stop lying to me!"

Before I can respond, she cuts off communication. I try to call her back, but when she doesn't answer, I go to the filing cabinet, locate a business card, and text Mel: *The PI I mentioned is Blaine Pederson. It's his job to prove or disprove your suspicions have a basis in fact. Here's his number. For the love of god, please use it. . . .*

I sit in silent confusion for several minutes until, finally, there comes a small tap on the door. When I open it, Cavin hands me an extremely large glass of very purple wine.

"Want to tell me what that was all about?" he asks. "You don't have to, of course. But it would eat at me."

"Look, it happened a long time ago, and I've tried, mostly successfully, to forget about it entirely. I met Graham . . ." I relate the sordid tale. "I never mentioned it to Melody because she was completely smitten and I didn't think it was my place to burst her balloon, especially since there was no way in hell I was going to come in between them. Graham did call me afterward, and I told him if he ever cheated on my sister again I'd kick his spindly ass. As far as I knew, up until maybe a year ago, they had no marital problems other than the ordinary lust-faded-to-boredom, so it seemed the proper decision."

"Obviously he never felt the need to confess. Why would he bring it up now?"

"I wish I knew. Maybe Mel can shed some light on that, if and when she ever talks to me again."

"She'll come around."

"I hope so. Carrying grudges long-range is a family trait."

"Are you okay for now? Should I put the chicken on the grill?"

"Oh, of course. Eli and Kayla are probably hungry. I'm right behind you."

I trail him down the hall, wondering what, exactly, Graham said. Surely he didn't concoct some elaborate line of bullshit?

Or has Melody spun a big web of dishonesty inside her head?

Twenty-Six

I'm up early on Sunday to put in some time on the stationary bike before seeing Cavin and, separately, the kids off to San Francisco. Preworkout, I work out my husband in bed, since I won't see him for a couple of days. Though it produces the intended result, our lovemaking isn't exactly hot, and as always when tenderness trumps fervor, I wonder if all marriages wind up devoid of passion eventually.

Cavin decides to snooze for a while, but I roll out of bed and dutifully don a pair of shorts and a sports bra, which I cover with a tank. I grab my phone and a pair of earbuds, check messages on my way down the hall, and, of course, find none. How long before Mel deigns to speak with me again? A conversation with Graham is long overdue. But if I contact him now, Mel might believe we're conspiring some kind of cover-up. Caution is the better course of action.

For the fair days of summer, I had the men move the exercise equipment outside on the deck, where it's cool in the shade and evocative of actual forest trail cycling. I find one of my new favorite playlists, turn it on, and climb into the saddle. Theory of a Deadman fires up "Angel," and it's an excellent way to launch my cardio and, in turn, my day.

Eli, knowing my lean toward grunge, actually built some of this playlist for me, staunchly suggesting I could broaden my taste in music without losing my sensibility. He's right. Some of his selections speak to me.

Three Days Grace swears they'd rather feel pain than nothing at all, and I think I have to agree.

Evanescence requests "Bring Me to Life," and I understand what they mean.

Slipping back a little, Lenny Kravitz is covering "American Woman," and I'm pedaling inside the zone when someone taps my sweaty shoulder, startling me.

I jerk the buds out of my ears. "What?"

"Did I scare you?" It's Kayla, slurping a smoothie. "Sorry."

"Not good, sneaking up on old ladies like me."

She doesn't respond to that in the least. Instead, she says, "Can I ask you a question?"

I slow my pedaling a little. It's hard to talk while panting. "Sure."

"Why are you so obsessed with working out? You're married."

"How does one thing negate the other?"

"I don't know, only it seems like Cavin loves you just the way you are. What are you trying to prove?"

Why can't I just work out in peace? Instead, I stop exerting, allow my heart rate to lower and breathing to return to at-rest speed.

"One, I'm not trying to prove anything. Two, if I didn't burn off the calories I consume, I wouldn't be 'just the way I am.' Plus, right now it's critical for my knee to keep gaining strength so I can avoid the knife. Anyway, your mom's working out, isn't she?"

"Yeah, but she didn't get serious about it until she and Dad started fighting all the time. I kind of thought maybe the idea of divorce sparked her sudden desire to lose weight."

I'd like to argue with her, but I thought

the very same thing. "Well, I have no plans to divorce my husband. In fact, staying in shape seems like the best way to hang on to him."

Her haughty expression morphs into sheepish. "Guess you're right."

"Are you worried about your parents divorcing?"

"Kind of. Not that it really matters."

"It does if it matters to you."

"I just don't get why people fall out of love. . . ." Her eyes glitter. "Or why people cheat."

Ah yes. Whether or not she forgave Eli for his last Sophia encounter, the betrayal stung. And no matter what excuse he manufactured, her trust was fractured. "Look, Kayla. I don't want to sound harsh, but the truth is, young love rarely survives, and it isn't always distance that makes it fail. The one thing you absolutely must not do is to surrender your dreams in favor of a relationship that's tenuous at best. Your best shot with Eli, or any man, is to be successful. If you don't love yourself, and what you stand for, you can't rightly love anyone else."

"You've told me all that before."

"Yes, and I thought a reminder was in order. Keep your eye on the future, and hold tight to your aspirations. Saying good-bye won't be easy, but I don't want to see you here again until your semester break."

"But what about" — she lowers her voice — "you-know-who."

"I'm afraid I can't help you there. But think about it. How much can he love you if he's sleeping with her?"

Sheepish segues to crestfallen. I decide there's no need to mention the fact that Sophia will be living fifty miles closer than she was the last time Eli spent the night with her. Nor do I say I really hope Kayla meets one incredible guy who'll make her forget Eli altogether.

He comes clomping up the stairs, terminating the conversation, other than for her parting, "Thanks, Aunt Tara, for everything, especially for covering my tuition. I'd never have this opportunity otherwise. I promise to work hard. And I'll try not to worry about the rest."

About time she dialed back the attitude and amped up the gratitude.

"Good plan. Worry causes wrinkles, and no one's attracted to those. Now, if you'll excuse me, I still have to invest a good half hour in keeping my husband content with my body. Oh, and you're welcome."

Kayla takes her leave, most likely to make Eli breakfast. I return to my music, refocus my workout. By the time I finish and go inside, they have retreated downstairs to do whatever it is they need to do before they take off. I can only imagine.

Cavin's still asleep when I shower, but the hard splashing of water against tile wakes him soon enough, and I invite him in for some seriously sexy back (and other, more relevant, body parts) washing, careful not to forget about the risk involved with wet tile. Despite the clear — and slippery — danger, we manage second-round-in-a-single-morning orgasms, and I feel a little better about his imminent departure.

Said bon voyage doesn't happen until early afternoon. It's a lovely Sunday, and we both delay the inevitable, but finally I chase him out, a couple of hours after the kids leave. "I sent you a text with the door code. Let me know once the movers have all the furniture out and I'll change it from here, then send Carol the new one to give to the Bairds. They'll have to contact the security company going forward. Unless, of course, they trust me not to mess with them once that horrible woman redecorates my house."

"*Her* house," corrects Cavin.

"Okay, I only hate you a little for that."

"You're sure there's nothing else that you

want me to bring back?"

"Just what Charlie already boxed. It's mostly some of my favorite cookware, Riedel glasses, etc. You should have plenty of room in the back of the Escalade, but if not, let the movers take it to storage. I can go through it whenever. I figure if I haven't missed something in six or eight months, I don't really need it and I'll just send it all to Goodwill."

"I thought you had it on your mind to buy another house somewhere, and might want it for that."

"I'll cross that bridge when I arrive at the river. Besides, it would be more fun to go ahead and furnish a new house with no-memories-attached stuff." Come to think of it, that really would be better. But I've paid for storage for a year up front. I've got plenty of time to decide. "Oh. Charlie is supposed to leave the key for the storage lock on the desk in my old office. You'll have to go over and unlock it for the movers. I'll text you the address and unit number."

"I've got a feeling tomorrow's going to be a long day, and I've got quite a drive ahead of me now. I'd better hit the highway."

I hand him the keys to the Cadillac, reward him with a lingering, smoldering kiss.

"Thank you again for doing this. I'll be breathlessly awaiting your return."

He smiles. "I love it when you're breathless. And I love you, milady."

After he's gone, I spend a couple of hours researching Fresh for Families, the nonprofit I'm to meet with tomorrow. The organization delivers bimonthly bins of fresh foodstuffs to families in need, partnering with fruit and vegetable growers, as well as nearby ranchers. They also donate ugly-but-edible produce to local food pantries. Having experienced hunger myself as a child, it's a cause I can enthusiastically fund-raise for and one donors will eagerly embrace. I learn everything I can about the organization's history, its GuideStar data, board member information, etc. It's vital to know exactly who and what you're representing when you dive into a major fund-raising effort, and I want to arrive at the meeting primed.

Once my brain is stuffed, my stomach demands equal attention. I whip up a veggie-heavy stir-fry with produce purchased yesterday from the farmers' market. On the heels of my Fresh for Families research, I feel very good about what I'm consuming, even if I do chase everything with a sulfite-laden cabernet.

I eat in front of the evening news, feeling little distress over the lineup of stories: the latest crisis in the Middle East; the surge in hate group membership; a federal court overturning voter ID laws; the peppy new electric car that can travel an average of two-hundred-plus miles without recharging.

I'm still sipping my wine when the newscast gives way to an entertainment news program, tonight featuring Genevieve Lennon's funeral, one I would've avoided even if it wasn't almost five hundred miles to the south. Considering I've attended two in my lifetime, a pair in one month would be way over quota. Death celebrated? Not my cup of poison. In lieu, I lift my glass. "Here's to you, my friend."

Genevieve would doubtless not be surprised at the huge turnout — starring fashion industry gurus; movie, television, and music headliners; her regular entourage; and various others — overflowing the confines of some tony Los Angeles cathedral. Each one, at least everyone the camera lands on, is dressed to the nines, in true fashionista tribute.

I'd say all that's missing is the red carpet, but the center aisle boasts one that's the approximate color of blood. The cameraman pans to the front, where the insanely ornate casket rests, closed. Genevieve would not have wanted to be seen the way the accident left her, a fact that is deftly pointed out by the program's hostess, who would likely feel the same way if her perky, blond good looks were ruined by a two-ton truck.

I have to wonder what pertinent factors contributed to the accident. Alcohol? The evening was young, unless she'd been drinking all day. Simple speed? No one's in that big of a hurry to get to a party. Surely she wouldn't have been texting? Or did something else distract her attention?

Suddenly I remember the last time I spoke to her. "There's something you need to know. . . ." What could have been so important that she would only tell me face-to-face?

Now we leave the funeral and return to the studio, where Ms. Perky continues, "A fight is apparently brewing over the Lennon estate, which by all estimates is quite large. Though the model's will names her manager as her sole heir, her brother, a criminal attorney, has filed suit, questioning the veracity of the document. . . ."

Enough with gossip TV. Grateful I've got my own estate safely tucked away in a trust, I hit the power button, refill my wineglass, and carry it out to the hot tub to enjoy a good, long soak, one hundred percent in the nude. I flip off the lights, not because I care if anyone sees me naked, but because it's easier to see the stars, and the summer sky swarms with them tonight.

Both neighboring houses are also dark, I notice. The one to the south hasn't been occupied since we got back from our honeymoon. The other belongs to the Littlefields, who generally keep their windows lit at night as a way, Steve told Cavin, to ward off nosy bears. The big animals are famous raiders, sometimes going right through doors to get to the goodies beyond them. But Cavin claims he's seen only a couple, and they haven't stayed long in the neighborhood.

Regardless, when I get out of the tub, I circle the house, making sure every door is locked on the off chance dead bolts will deter any bears that happen by. I'm glad I check downstairs because I discover Eli neglected to secure either of the exits. Plus, he and Kayla managed to leave lots of snack trash littering both the game room and his bedroom: a pizza box, with a half a piece left; chip and candy wrappers; cans and bottles, with varying amounts of leftover sodas. Okay, this is a definite discussion when he gets home. Next thing you know we'll be invaded by rats.

Fuming, I take the time to dispose of the garbage properly and am clicking off the lights, trash bag in hand, when I hear something rustling around outside. I pause to listen. Nothing. Count to ten. Still nothing. Just my overactive imagination projecting a rodent army at the back door, or maybe a grizzly though I'm told only black bears frequent these woods.

Back upstairs, I haul the garbage on out to our bear- and ratproof trash receptacle and toss Eli and Kayla's detritus, and when I turn back toward the house, note the play of shadows where treetops shimmy beneath the moon. A warm wind has risen to rattle the boughs. That's probably what I heard before.

Inside again, I decide a small taste of tawny port is in order. I pour from a favored bottle, settle on the couch to read. After finishing the last Henry Miller, I decided to try some of the classics I avoided in college and am working on *Lady Chatterley's Lover.* The writing is lush, if a little sluggish. But tonight I've got nothing but time, and I'm not quite ready to give up on it yet.

After a while, between the wine and the book, I fall into a nice lull and am starting to doze when one of the downstairs doors shakes violently, jolting me into total awareness. The wind? No, it couldn't be. I listen intently, nerves prickling, but whatever that was seems to have vacated the stoop. Suddenly, the far door below me quakes. What the hell?

I bolt from the couch. Did I lock the front door? I reach it in record time, damn the injury, and find the dead bolt thrown, so I switch on the upper floodlights, then turn back to the slider to throw the lower-level floods. Harsh white illumination envelops the property, and as I scan the landscape, a silhouette — human, not ursine — dashes into the woods. Down the hill, a dog starts to bark.

This I can't dismiss.

TWENTY-SEVEN

"Don't panic," says the 911 dispatcher, reacting to my near-hysterical call for help. "A deputy is on the way. You're all alone there?"

I assure her that is the case. "What if this guy comes back?"

"Try to remain calm. Deputy Cross is less than ten minutes out."

More than enough time for some dedicated felon to do me a fair amount of damage. But I take a couple of deep breaths. "I'm okay." I don't mention the handy-dandy, and recently sharpened, butcher knife I've armed myself with.

"I can stay on the phone with you if you want."

Not like that would do a whole lot of good, but I keep her on the line anyway. She can listen to my dying screams as I'm murdered. "I really wish you would. Oh, hey. I think I see the deputy coming now."

I've been pacing between the sliding glass door and the front entrance, and, peering out the windows adjacent the latter, I notice the sweep of a spotlight. Soon enough, the squad car pulls up in front of the house. The brawny cop who gets out could successfully arm wrestle a bear, and his expression befits his name. He looks pissed.

Still, in his unassuming tan uniform, he plays the consummate professional, pausing to assess the house. His head swings side to side and back toward the road, and I think he must be measuring distances, as well as the building's relationship to its neighbors, and its orientation on the hillside. Now he continues to the door, which I open before he reaches it.

"Deputy Cross?"

Up come his hands, into a defensive posture. "Hey now, put down the knife. I'm not the bad guy."

I didn't even notice I'd raised it. "Sorry. I forgot I had it." I lower it to a nonthreatening position at my side.

"I sure hope you're trained in dagger wielding." His smile mitigates his consternated look. "May I come inside?"

Sure, if he can fit through the door. "Of course."

He manages the requisite squeeze and follows me into the living room, where I deposit the knife on top of *Lady Chatterley's Lover.* That does not escape the deputy's notice. "I tried to read that book once. Didn't make it very far."

"It is a bit of a slog. You just have to get to the good parts."

Discomfiture blooms in his cheeks. "Ahem. Yes, well, let's get down to business, okay? Tell me what happened."

I fill him in and about halfway through he starts nodding his head.

"We've had a string of B and Es — that's breaking and enterings — in the area. Mostly vacation cabins, but not all of them, and this house has the appearance of a place that would have good stuff to burgle."

"So, you think that's what this was?"

He shrugs. "Could be, unless you've got another reason for someone trying to get inside. You have a stalker?"

At the moment, no. "Not that I'm aware of."

"Not much of a point to stalking if the victim isn't cognizant of the activity. I mean, where's the fun in that?"

The man is blunt. I suppose that's a good thing in a cop.

"Now, do you want to show me where the break-in attempt occurred?"

"Downstairs."

He follows my deliberate descent, and I gesture to the doors on each end of the hall. Outside, the floodlights reveal footprints in the soft dirt, and traces of soil on both cement landings. Deputy Cross tracks them with his flashlight while I wait in the game room. Eventually, he returns, carrying a crime scene kit. "Looks like he came down that exterior staircase to the eastern door first, then circled the house to the back. I'll dust for prints, but odds are good I won't find any."

"Oh, you definitely will find *some*. My husband's son, Eli, lives down here, and until today, so did my niece. They both use these doors regularly."

"It would be good to have their prints for comparison, and yours and your husband's, too. Any chance of that?"

"Everyone's gone for a couple of days, I'm afraid. My husband and stepson will be home Tuesday evening. Kayla's starting college in the Bay Area so she won't be back for a while. But that's Eli's room. You could probably get whatever you need in there, including . . ." My nose wrinkles. "DNA evidence, if you get my drift."

He laughs. "I see. Well, I won't require that, so I'll leave the sheets alone. In fact,

I'll probably come back and do the finger-printing once your family gets home. It's more reliable that way. Right now I'll be tied up for maybe twenty minutes, and I'll need you to fill out a police report. You can take it upstairs, if you'll be more comfortable there." He hands me a clipboard with the required statement attached.

I can't think of a good reason to stay and watch, so I agree to meet him in the living room once he's finished. "Be sure and lock up?"

"Cross my heart."

I'm just wrapping up my statement of facts when Deputy Cross lumbers up the steps and into the room. "All done."

"Did you find anything?"

"Several partials. We'll run them through the database and see what turns up."

"Was I in danger?"

"Hard to say. Some intruders do arm themselves. It's always possible a confrontation could lead to bodily harm. And unless you're really good with that" — he points to the knife, still sitting atop the book — "I wouldn't suggest trying to use it for protection. Too many ways things could go wrong."

"What *would* you suggest?"

"Other than investing in a good alarm

system, if you were my wife, I'd make sure you had a gun and that you knew how to use it. Do you happen to own a firearm?"

"If I did, would I be running around with a butcher knife instead?"

"Good point. Are you at all familiar with guns?"

"Some. I grew up in rural Idaho, where pretty much everyone had one. My sister and I used to target shoot with one of my mother's boyfriends. Barney insisted the apocalypse was imminent, and we had better know how to aim straight."

"Have you ever owned one?"

"My first husband did." Raul collected guns, and often brought special models home when they found their way into one of the pawnshops. "Ironically, they were stolen in a break-in, not long after he died."

"You never replaced them?"

"No."

"Why not?"

"My second husband. He had a rotten temper and corrupt friends. I felt safer not having deadly weapons around."

"What was he, a career criminal?" The deputy grins.

I return his smile. "In a manner of speaking. A politician."

"Ah. Well, sounds like he's past tense.

What about now? You're not afraid of your current husband, are you?"

"Only of catching whatever germs he might bring home from the hospital. He's a doctor at Barton. But other than that, no, not at all."

"What about your son? Or your niece?"

"Eli is my stepson," I correct. "He's almost eighteen, with the commensurate lack of sound judgment. And Kayla takes medication for some mental health issues. But I've never seen either of them act out violently toward themselves or anyone else."

"Then you might take my suggestion seriously. Just be sure to acquaint yourself well with your weapon. Guns are like people. They all have their quirks. Okay, let me see that police report."

He skims it, nods. "This should do. I'll be in touch in a couple of days. Meanwhile, we'll increase patrols in the neighborhood. And don't be afraid to call if you notice anything unusual."

"Can I keep the butcher knife handy?"

"If it makes you feel better. But please leave it there until I'm gone. If there's a problem on the front step, I'll take care of it."

I walk Deputy Cross to the door, noting the size of the firearm holstered on his ample hip. I don't think I'd need something that big, but remembering how helpless I felt hobbling around after my last surgery, I am definitely considering the idea of handgun ownership. "What kind of gun would you recommend?"

He turns back to me. "Keep it simple. You want a small, reliable semiautomatic. Something you could tuck in your purse, but also something you can count on finding its target clear across a big room. Smith and Wesson has some excellent options, but personally, I prefer Glocks. There are several reputable gun shops in Reno and Carson City, but you might consider one that holds personal-protection and concealed-carry classes. They're a bit pricey but worth your time. No use carrying if you have no real idea how to use a gun when you need it, and if you want to stash the weapon in your bag you'll need the permit."

True enough, and I doubt plinking cans with a .22 rifle thirty years ago qualifies. "Thank you for your time and advice. I'll conduct some diligent research."

"No problem. I'll be in touch, or somebody from the department will."

I watch his hulking form retreat, then carefully lock the front door as he reenters his patrol car. Normally I'd flip off the floodlights, but this is a good night to keep them on. Considering the way I relied on the alarm system on Russian Hill, I'm not sure why I haven't suggested installing one here, but it's something I'll remedy first thing.

It's a little after eleven. Cavin will probably be asleep, but I dial his number anyway and am surprised when he picks up immediately. "Oh, hey. I was thinking about calling you but decided it was too late."

"Ditto. But then I thought you should hear what happened tonight."

He is silent through the storytelling. When I wrap it up, he's freaked-out. "Why are you still in the house? Get a hotel room and I'll be home as soon as I can tomorrow, unless you want me to come right now."

"Don't be silly. You can't drive home tonight, and as for a hotel room, you have noticed the tourists in town? This is high season. I doubt I could find a place to stay, and besides, I feel safe enough locked in here, butcher knife by my side. Every floodlight is on. The property is lit up like a car lot. And Deputy Cross promised extra patrols."

"Tara, I know you're fearless, but —"

"Seriously, I'll be fine. It's a very big knife."

"Very funny. I don't think you should take this too lightly."

"Really, I'm not. I'll call a security company tomorrow. In addition to an alarm system, I think motion detectors connected to the floodlights would deter both burglars and bears."

"That, my dear, is a very good plan."

Let's see what he thinks about this one. "Also, I'm looking into purchasing a protection piece."

"A what?"

"A handgun."

Silence.

"No comment?"

"That seems like a decision we should make together."

"You have a problem with owning a gun for personal safety?"

"On a purely philosophical level, no. But on a personal level, I do. You know my mother committed suicide. It was my father's gun she used. He always kept it locked up, especially once her bipolar disorder kicked into high gear. But she managed to find the key to the lockbox. It was only after she died that he finally disposed of it."

Sobering.

"I'm sorry, sweetheart. I had no idea that's

the method she chose. I believe that's unusual for a woman."

"Mom rarely did things like everyone else, and once she decided death was her best option, she wanted to be very sure not to wake up again."

Not a pretty picture. Considering Kayla's issues, and the fact that she's threatened suicide in the past, I'd have to be very careful to keep a weapon well hidden while she was visiting. But with luck, she might not be hanging around much anyway.

I think a subject change is in order. "So, what time did you get to San Francisco? Why wait so long to call?"

"Long, complicated story . . ."

Escalade got a flat going over the Sierra, out in the middle of nowhere. Waiting on AAA. A motorhome caught fire, closing I-80 outside of Fairfield. Detour was bumper-to-bumper. So was the Bay Bridge, due to a Giants game traffic complicated by a public transportation worker strike.

"I finally got to the house around nine," he continues. "Charlie was here, still packing up stuff. Didn't you say he was finished?"

"I thought he was."

"Apparently, he put it off till the last minute. I'll go through several of the boxes and bring what looks most important."

Suddenly, I wish I'd gone along. One, so I'd know everything about tomorrow's move will be copacetic. And, two, so no notion of weaponry would've ever crossed my mind.

"Oh, one more thing," says Cavin. "Eli and Kayla showed up a little while ago, wanting to spend the night. I said okay. It was that or get them a hotel room. Tomorrow, after Eli drops Kayla off at school, I'll set him up at the Fairmont. He wants to hang out in the city for a couple of days. The original plan was for me to spend two nights there with him, but once the movers are finished here I can leave."

"No. Enjoy the extra time in the city."

"You sure?"

"Positive. You'll be home on Wednesday though?"

"I have to be. I've got a surgery Thursday morning."

"Okay, I'll say good night, then."

I go on to bed, thinking about Cavin and Eli, who always seem to be at odds here at home. Interesting that they planned to spend time together in San Francisco. Are they seeking common ground? Can they reach it in neutral territory?

Eyes closed against the harsh shadows thrown by floodlight glare sneaking in through the blinds, it's a toss-and-turn night. I'm sleeping on porcupine quills. Every nerve quivers, spectacularly on edge. The forest is alive with nighttime noises I usually don't hear.

It's the wind, my brain understands, knocking on glass and wood.

It's human, my heart insists.

He wants in.

Where's the knife?

He wants you.

Where's my gun?

Toss right.

Turn left.

Glance at the clock.

12:18

12:46

1:07

1:39

Finally, I get out of bed, go into the bathroom, and gulp a single Vicoprofen, washing it down with long swallows of water. It'll make me groggy in the morning, but at least I should get a few hours of decent sleep. If my head is too thick, I'll reschedule my meeting, but I hate to look like a flake on day one of any new business relationship. Accordingly, I set my alarm for eight a.m., the latest I can possibly sleep and still have a chance of arriving on time.

One thing I refuse to do is be tardy.

Back beneath the covers, I take deep breaths and convince my body to succumb to the lure of the poppy. Rather than deny their existence, I watch silhouettes dance outside the window, knowing they belong to treetops. No corporeal being could meander there, two stories above the ground, and I'm not afraid of ghosts.

Not really.

Which sort of begs the question: What *am* I afraid of?

Intruders? After tonight, there might be a sense of trepidation. But despite Cavin's concern, I've decided to make that gun purchase. I'm determined not to live in fear of random encounters. Which leads me to strangers. One-night stands are lost to me now, and I'm fine with that. And since I'm careful about the places I frequent, the odds of that one determined creep targeting me are exceptionally low.

Relationships? As for ex-husbands, one's dead; one's in prison; and the third is now free of any financial responsibility toward me. As for uncommitted partners, I've freed myself of worry. It's been nine months since the last one, with no repercussions. As for my current partner, no, which could be a problem. But I haven't turned off my spousal radar completely.

Aging? Like most women, of course, but I've got the financial resources to slow the process and the internal drive to keep in shape, and my health is stellar. I'm never sick and rarely clumsy enough to damage myself. Prior to taking that fall at Heavenly, my only hospital experiences were a couple of ER visits for mango attacks.

Each checkmark on that list earns a bit more relaxation. But now I start thinking about the things that *do* scare me, at least a little.

Family. This one is weird because not so very long ago I thought I knew exactly where I stood at the fringes of the fold. Mom never mattered, and I totally lost my fear of her violent outbursts after the day I fought back and won. But I've always thought I understood my sister inside out, and her recent evolution is unnerving. Ditto the change in her husband. Maybe not fear inducing but definitely worth keeping an eye on.

Parenting? Um, yeah, though what I've been doing could more reasonably be termed "pseudo-parenting." I'm a total fraud when it comes to guidance, gentle or otherwise. I've got so little experience that some of the kids' actions surprise me. Sex and drugs right out in the open, no real concern about who might happen by? No filters. No discernible morals. Is it all modern teens or only those recently dropped into my lap?

I've known Kayla since she was a baby. Watched her grow, though from a distance. Photos and e-mail updates can't totally inform a relationship like that, and the longer she was under my roof, the more I realized that I have no clear idea what kind of person she is. Most of the time she seems docile enough, but every now and then I see hints of the instability mostly mitigated by her meds.

And Eli, well, if anything scares me, he does. He's brash. Unpredictable. Determined. Demanding. For an overprotected boy, not quite eighteen, he's way too mature and wears his manhood proudly. Arrogantly, in fact. Why the hell do I find that so damn attractive?

Maybe it's me I'm really afraid of.

My limbs feel weighted, and I know I'll tumble toward sleep very soon. I close my eyes against the spectral waving outside the window, listen to the chant of the wind. It's got rhythm . . . soul . . .

Twenty-Eight

An insistent chime drags me into the light of morning. I curse but open my eyes. Eight a.m. and I've got somewhere to be.

Hopefully the sting of a cool shower will thin the porridge inside my skull. I start the water hot, the correct temperature to shampoo with. After I rinse conditioner from my hair, I gradually turn the faucet toward cold and, once my skin is covered with goose bumps, assess. I'm totally awake, mostly aware. Hopefully caffeine will finish the job.

Naked, hair dripping, I hit the kitchen and start the coffeepot, then remember the floods, needlessly lit in the daylight. I go to the front door first, flip off the upper lights, then make an about-face toward the sliding glass door. As I reach for the switch, movement just beyond the tree line catches my eye.

I stomp out onto the deck and loudly demand, "Who's there?"

The sound of my voice shocks the interloper into action. The boy, who's maybe ten, moves into the open. "Sorry. I, um . . . We are staying over there. . . ." He points down the hill. "Our dog got off the leash and I was trying to catch him, but he started chasing a squirrel and he ran up here and wouldn't come back and . . ."

The kid is nervous.

Uh, as well he should be, considering I'm standing here in the buff, something I might not have noticed except the chill morning air has sharpened my nipples into taut peaks. Still, no use making him think the female form is anything less than art. I make no move to cover up. "It's okay. Don't worry. I'm sure your pup will come back to you. Meanwhile, my woods are your woods."

I turn away, pausing long enough to reward him with a decent rear end snapshot and wishing it were possible for us to fence our perimeter. But the Glenbrook Design Review Committee has definite rules about fences, walls, and hedges not delineating property lines or blocking the neighbors' views. Wonder how they'd feel about random vacationers reviewing my design.

Inside, I pour coffee and take it back to my bedroom, where I dress to impress in a turquoise silk suit. Unfortunately, I'll have to skip the pumps I prefer to wear with this outfit. Five-inch heels and knee injuries are mutually exclusive, as are business meetings and excessive makeup. Don't want to look sexy, just terribly attractive. Despite the relative lack of sleep, with hints of foundation, blush, and mascara, I think I manage to accomplish that.

Three cups of joe and two scrambled eggs, no toast, chase away most of the cobwebs, so I'm raring to go. I've come up with what I believe will be a brilliant late-spring fundraiser, and I'm anxious for feedback. In fact, other than my honeymoon, I haven't looked forward to anything quite this much in a long time.

I arrive at the Parasol Foundation at ten before the appointed hour, which gives me plenty of time to run a brush through my hair, apply a pale sheen of lip gloss, and swallow an ibuprofen to ward off the vague headache threat I'm suddenly feeling.

Maryann greets me at the door and ushers me back to a sedate boardroom, where one seat at the long table is already occupied.

The man who stands is in his early fifties and not a whole lot taller than I am. His casual dress and collar-length silvering hair belie his CEO title but are admirable. This is a man who's comfortable with himself and the job he does, and that in itself is remarkably attractive.

Maryann makes the introduction. "Tara Lattimore, meet Jason Cunningham. I've filled him in on your background and forwarded the references you provided."

"Very happy to meet you, Mr. Cunningham."

"It's Jason, and I hope it's okay if I call you Tara. Too much formality gives me hives."

I smile, at ease already. "Mangoes top my list of hive givers, but formality runs a close second."

"You're in luck. Mangoes can't be produced locally, so we don't deal with them at all. Shall we sit?"

He and I do. Maryann excuses herself. "Let me know if you need something. I'm just next door."

"How familiar are you with Fresh for Families?" Jason asks before our butts are fully planted.

"I did a little research. . . ." I outline what I gathered in two hours.

"I'm impressed."

"And so am I, with the organization. It's a cause I can happily support, both financially and with whatever fund-raising help you'll allow me to do. I still maintain an extensive list of past supporters, many of whom I have no doubt will embrace Fresh for Families, and of course I would need access to your own donor rolls."

"Sounds like you've given this a lot of thought."

"I have. In fact, I had an idea for a fund-raiser. . . ."

I outline my plan to invite potential donors to tour the properties of a couple of his growers. "I was thinking Apple Hill, since it's close and will be producing fruit by then. That has a two-pronged advantage — one for Fresh for Families, and one for your growers. We could create a short video showing the grower-to-you process, followed by the FFF distribution process, and finish with some testimonials."

I let that much sink in.

"Ambitious."

"Wait. There's more. After the tour, we finish with dinner at one of the nearby El Dorado County wineries. There are several with plenty of space for the size group I'm sure will want to participate. Again, it's win-win, and the winery can write off their costs as an in-kind donation. I'm also thinking we could entice a B and B to donate a room for a night or two as an incentive for larger donations. Other than producing the video, which should be done right, I don't foresee major out-of-pocket expenses for FFF at all. And you can use the video for any promotional purposes."

He sits considering for several long seconds. "How long have you had to think about this?"

I laugh. "A couple of days. Okay, a day, and a busy one at that."

"Where did you come from?"

"San Francisco, though not originally."

"That's not what I meant. I mean, how did this connection happen? Fresh for Families needs someone like you. We could make it a paid position."

I start to say no. But I don't want him to think I'm completely altruistic, and yet don't want him to know the extent of my financial circumstances. "Tell you what. This one's on me, and if I perform as expected, we can talk about future compensation."

"Sounds good, except for one thing. I'd like to do it earlier. Can you pull it together by late October?"

I experience an unexpected rush of nerves. Two months, give or take? "If I go to work on it right away, I think I can. We'll need to secure the venue immediately. And you'll need to compile a list of former and pro-spective donors."

"The donor list is no problem. Oh, and as for the venue, I love the winery element. As you probably know, the area is beautiful in the fall. Are you a fan?"

"Of El Dorado wineries? Truthfully, I've never investigated them. My real love of wine came at the behest of an ex who was a Napa aficionado. But I'm more than willing to explore."

"You should, and Amador and Calaveras Counties as well. They're connected, and each has its standout vintages. Not as famous as Napa or Sonoma or California regions to the south, which means they're not as crowded, despite the fact they've been planting vineyards since the Gold Rush days."

Ah, good. We have something in common, an excellent way to start any game. "That's right. John Sutter himself planted grapes, yes? In Coloma?"

"Actually, I believe you're thinking of James Marshall, who first discovered gold in Coloma at Sutter's Fort. He never found the mother lode and after a while decided growing wine for thirsty forty-niners was a more lucrative option. The Sutter reference is valid, in a way, however. It was his daughter who founded the Sutter Home Winery in St. Helena."

"You know your history."

"California history, anyway. And I'm something of an oenophile myself."

"With your permission, I'll start laying some groundwork for the fund-raiser. I've used a video production company in the past, if that's something you want me to do for you. Or if you have another one in mind, I'm happy to give them my ideas and let you iron out the details. But that's probably where we should start. It could take a while to produce what we need. Meanwhile, you might contact some of your growers. I'd like to tour a few farms and talk to their owners if possible."

His grin is charming. "You are quite the dynamo. I believe I'll leave as much as possible in your capable hands. You let me know what you need from me. I think we should come up with a title for you, don't you?"

"It's good to have, yes. Makes me sound official."

Jason mulls it over. Finally, he suggests, "How about director of philanthropy? That sounds not only official but also quite important."

It has a nice ring. "I like it. So then, it's

okay if I get started?"

"Absolutely. Here's my card. Feel free to call, text, or e-mail me anytime."

"Thank you, Jason. I'm excited to work with you." As soon as the words leave my mouth, I realize how true they are.

A warm handshake seals the deal, and on my way out I stop by Maryann's office.

She's on the phone but waves me in the door and wraps up her call. "How'd it go?"

"Great. We're off and running, in fact. I just wanted to stop by and thank you for the connection. Jason will be fun to collaborate with."

"He genuinely cares about his programs and the people they serve. You'll find he's built a lot of goodwill, but a nonprofit can never have enough of that."

"I understand completely. On another note, I just wanted to mention Genevieve and how awful it was the way the accident happened."

"Sobering. I drive that stretch of highway several times a month. I've definitely slowed down through there. And I have to say I do feel a little guilty about it."

"Oh, but you shouldn't. Not your fault that truck pulled out in front of her or that she was going so fast."

"I know it's not my fault. In fact, I just

read that the autopsy report showed prescription painkillers, plus a blood alcohol level of point nine. Still, as far as I know she was coming to my party."

"Sounds like a series of poor decisions on Genevieve's part."

I wish I could muster more sympathy. But really, she was as much to blame for the accident as the truck driver was. Not that she deserved to die.

You understand the term "oxymoronic"?

I think about that all the way home, at least until I turn into our neighborhood and come around the corner to find a fleet of fire trucks obstructing the access to my house. I pull up across the street, and when I open the door the first thing that hits me is the stench of smoke and wet, scorched earth. I can't see what burned, but it must have been major.

I hurry to cross the street, maneuver between vehicles, and find myself staring at the northern face of our house. The siding is scorched, ground to second-story eaves, and the land between our neighbors and us has been flame-cleared of pine needles and other vegetation, all the way to the woods behind, where several trees wear blackened bark. Small puffs of vapor lift like fog from the soaked dirt.

Several men wearing yellow coats and helmets are winding hoses and assuring themselves that the fire is indeed out. One stands off to the right with our next-door neighbors, Steve and Bethany Littlefield. When he sees me, Steve waves me over.

"This is Tara Lattimore," he tells the man, who turns out to be the fire chief. "She and her husband own the house."

"What happened?" I ask, mystified.

Chief Paulson shrugs. "Probably a careless match. We couldn't find evidence of anything else. You were lucky your neighbors turned up when they did, or it might have been a whole lot worse."

"It was burning pretty good when we got here," says Bethany. "Steve grabbed a garden hose and did his best to wet down what he could while I called 911. Fortunately the station isn't too far away."

"I don't understand. Everyone else is out of town, and there was nothing amiss when I left this morning."

"Looks like it started at the edge of the trees," explains Chief Paulson. "It's possible that whatever spark initiated the blaze smoldered in those needles for hours, maybe even longer. They were pretty thick. We always recommend home owners keep them cleared."

"I . . . I didn't realize. . . . From now on we'll do better."

Steve grins. "Not much left to do for a while, though you'll want to have all that burned stuff raked up and removed, or we'll both be choking on the stink."

It isn't impossible that Steve or Bethany might be responsible, I suppose, but the thought that keeps running through my mind is Eli and Kayla and their lax smoking habits. They've been gone since yesterday, but according to the chief, that doesn't necessarily deny culpability.

"Yes, and I have someone in mind to do the raking, though he isn't due home for a couple of days." I take another look at the charred siding and notice one of the downstairs doors that were tested so rudely last night. "Hey. Wait." I relate the details of the attempted break-in. "You don't suppose the burglar could've done this, do you?"

Chief Paulson shrugs. "It's possible, though probably not purposely. There are better ways to break into houses than starting them on fire. You might just torch what you're looking to steal, not to mention yourself. Besides, flames kind of defeat the stealth factor."

Excellent points.

"You've put my mind mostly at ease. By

the way, Steve and Bethany, the cop said this guy has been marauding homes in the neighborhood. I recommend vigilance."

Bethany nods. "Thanks for the heads-up."

"He tries breaking into our house, he's in for a nasty surprise." Steve winks. "We both have concealed-carry permits."

Validation.

"I suppose I should go call our insurance company." I thank everyone again for the help.

The Littlefields turn toward their driveway, and Steve calls over his shoulder, "Let me know if you need anything. We're here through next week."

"I will. Appreciate it."

The first thing I do when I go inside is call Cavin, whose phone goes to voice mail. "Hi, honey. We had a little problem today. Okay, a fairly large problem. The good news is the house didn't burn all the way down. The bad news is there's extensive damage to the siding on the north side. I'll call the insurance company and have them send an adjustor."

Next I call Eli, who does answer. "Hey, Mama. What's up?"

"Don't call me Mama. Just thought you'd like to know about a fire here today."

"What? Is everything okay?"

368

"Not exactly, but it could've been worse. Just FYI, when you get home you can rake up the burned pine needles."

"Why me?"

I can picture his face, scarlet anger rising.

"Guess you'll have to be a little more careful with your incendiary devices."

"What are you talking about? I wasn't even there when it started."

"Sometimes sparks smolder. You could have thrown a match or a marijuana butt down anytime."

"Marijuana butt? The least you could do is use the correct terminology. A roach doesn't stay lit very long. Besides, I never toss them. Why waste perfectly good weed? And I don't use matches."

I expected denial. What I did not expect were logical talking points. But now he asks something totally out of left field. "What if it was Dad?"

"What do you mean?"

"What if he's responsible for the fire?"

"Don't be ridiculous, Eli, he wasn't even h—"

"Yeah, well, neither was I."

I don't want to argue. Eli and Kayla smoke outside. Cavin doesn't smoke at all, and I've never witnessed him holding a match, only butane lighters to start the fireplace or barbecue. So how would carelessness even be possible . . . ? Wait.

"You're not suggesting arson, are you?"

"Stranger things have happened."

"Why would your father want to burn down the house?"

He pauses. "Insurance, maybe? Just a thought. I wouldn't lose sleep over it."

Eli, the inciter.

It's a very long day, the successful morning unfortunately eclipsed. The insurance adjustor will be here bright and early tomorrow, followed by the owner of a local siding company, who'll give us an estimate. I also contact three yard services about removing the burned vegetation. All claim heavy workloads. One says maybe next week; the other two the week after.

As a last resort, I scour work-wanted ads on Craigslist and find a guy who says he's licensed and insured to do hauling and handyman work.

"How much would it take for you to bring a couple of guys and get out here ASAP?" I don't even ask for references. How complicated can raking and bagging be?

Handy Al bites. The cost is premium, but it will be worth it to alleviate the smoke smell permeating everything. He promises to get the job done tomorrow. I love how money talks. Wish more people were as eloquent.

Cavin is matter-of-fact when he calls, late afternoon. After I recount the facts, he comments simply, "Well, at least no one was hurt, and like you said, it could've been worse. We should probably pick up a nice bottle of something for the Littlefields, don't you think?"

That's it? I'd have thought he'd be more upset.

"I do, and I will," I agree. "But aren't you curious about how the fire started?"

"Sounds like some kid playing with matches."

I almost bring up Eli and Kayla, but then I remember the boy looking for his dog. He could have been the culprit, or any one of our neighbors who sometimes cut through the unfenced property.

"Oh, I spoke with the insurance company. The adjustor will be out tomorrow, but there's a decent chance they'll only cover the side of the house that burned, including any structural damage. And the siding company says it will probably be impossible to match the old cedar siding with new, so we'll want to consider replacing it all."

"Sounds expensive."

"Depends on what we replace it with, but

the range who took it upon himself to initi-
ate a conversation with me. His motivation,
I'm sure, wasn't purely firearm-related.
Nevertheless, he was a font of information,
and I'm happy to use some of it now. Once
I've removed the firing debris, all the dirty
paper towels, swabs, and rags are neatly
disposed of by turning the plastic bag inside
out, locking it within. Then I lube 'er up,
holster the gun without strapping it on, and
tuck it away in the prescribed location.

As I work, I watch Handy Al and his guys
finish the yard cleanup. It was a huge job,
and I'm surprised they're almost done,
although they did arrive at seven a.m. I was
still in my short pajamas, which covered
enough to allow me to direct the trio, none
of whom tried very hard not to stare at the
braless assets beneath my tank top. No
problem. Turnabout's fair play, and the
three, who obviously labor for their wages,
are built. I allow myself a pleasant glimpse
of eye candy.

Once the gun detail is accomplished, I do
my time on the stationary bike, not that I
really feel like it. But it's vital to both my
physical and mental fitness. When I finish
the hour and shower off the sweat I earned,
it's dinnertime. Considering I skipped
lunch, I'm damn sure going to enjoy it. I'm

on my way to the kitchen when the doorbell rings. A peek through the viewfinder tells me it's Deputy Cross.

"Evening. Just stopped by to let you know we picked up the guy who we believe is responsible for the burglaries in the area. I don't think you'll have any more problems, at least not with him. Since we'll compare his prints with the ones I got here, we shouldn't have to bother your family for theirs after all."

"What great news! Oh, I did take your advice."

"Advice?"

"Yes. I bought a protection piece and spent quite a bit of time today learning to use it."

"That was fast, but good for you. What did you decide on?"

"A Glock 19, Gen4."

"Excellent choice. I hope you never have to use it, but better safe than sorry."

"I agree wholeheartedly. Thanks again, for everything."

He ambles off, his bulk no less formidable in the failing light than it was in the middle of the night. I'd hate to be on the wrong side of that man. If it came down to pursuit, I doubt he could run very fast, but if he managed to catch you, he could do some major damage.

Feeling just a bit smug about how much I managed to accomplish today, I reward myself with a nice New York strip and Caesar salad, light on the dressing. Tonight, I shun the TV and take my dinner out onto the deck to enjoy the quiet summer evening, the last I'll have to myself for a while. I like the solitude, really. Before I met Cavin, I'd grown used to living alone, and while I prefer being partnered, I never before had to deal with the added baggage of children. Sometimes my new home feels terribly crowded.

There is movement in the trees, but it's slight. A deer, perhaps, or something even smaller, not really wanting to draw attention to itself. I wait, hoping to catch a glimpse, but it never materializes. Somewhere in the neighborhood, someone is barbecuing, and elsewhere children are outside playing. A dog barks; another responds. It's all quite normal.

Just as that thought coalesces, it strikes me how much my definition of "normal" has changed, and in only a few months. Not so long ago, it meant jet-setting and rubbing elbows with politicians and celebrities like Genevieve Lennon. Now it apparently means a good steak and better glass of wine, at home in the woods, sans bear or burglar activity. The question becomes: Is this life-style enough to satisfy me long-term?

Short-term, I clean up after myself, pour a big glass of one of my favorite reds, and go find my phone. I need to talk to Cavin, see how things went today. In fact, I'm a little surprised I haven't heard from him yet. But there is no message or voice mail, and when I call him, he doesn't answer, so I leave my own recorded request: "Touching base. How'd everything go? Call me when you get this message."

An hour passes, invested in my book, and when I don't hear back, I decide to try Eli, who answers immediately. He always does. "Hey, Mom, what's up?"

I grit my teeth at the name. "Nothing important. Just trying to get hold of your father, and he hasn't responded. Did you get moved into the hotel okay?"

"Oh, yeah. I'm ingesting room service as we speak."

"I see. And where is Cavin?"

"You don't know?"

"Eli, if I knew I wouldn't have asked."

"Ha. Right. Well, he went out to dinner with your sister."

"Mel?"

Stupid question, and he pounces. "You

384

have more than one?"

"Not that I'm aware of."

"That's what I thought. Yes, with Melody. She drove over to help Kayla settle in. I bumped into her and mentioned we were staying at the Fairmont tonight, so she got a room here, too."

That much makes sense. "I see. Did your father say when he'd be back?"

"Nope. Hey, Dad said someone tried to break in?"

"Seems that way. Apparently he'd burgled several nearby homes. But the cops think they got him."

"Already?" He sounds disappointed.

"That's a bad thing?"

"I was kind of hoping to kick his ass."

Perfect. "That won't be necessary. And it's probably a good thing for you they arrested him. They wanted to take your fingerprints to compare with the ones they lifted from the downstairs doors."

"Why would that be good for me?"

"I don't know. In case you're ever involved in something you shouldn't be?"

He laughs. "No worries. If that ever happens, which of course it won't, I won't get caught. I grew up on a steady diet of *Law and Order*."

Wonder how many incarcerated people

said the same thing preincarceration.

"Do me one favor, please? When your dad gets back, please have him call me. It's okay if it's late. I'll be waiting to hear from him."

"Will do. Oh, by the way, the new owner stopped by your house while we were there. She had some interior designer with her. I don't think you'd like what she has in mind."

Thanks, Eli.

Yeah, thanks a lot.

"Guess it's a good thing I wasn't around, huh?"

"Oh, I don't know. I'm sure it would've been entertaining. I'm sorry you let the house go, by the way. It's awesome."

Yeah. What were you thinking?

"What's done is done." And I'm done with this conversation. "Don't forget to have your dad call me."

"Will do."

After he hangs up, the place feels empty, so I resort to television. Luckily, I find an old Woody Allen movie I never watched before. I'm not a huge fan of his, but *Manhattan* proves to be worth viewing. I settle back on the big pillows, turn down the interior lights, and thoroughly enjoy my girls' night in with myself.

When the credits roll, I turn off the TV

and close my eyes, listening to the rising wind through the treetops. Falling. Falling. Falling.

What's that noise? The annoying chiming tugs me out of a very nice dream, up into semidarkness. Oh. My phone, and the ringtone informs me it's Cavin. My hand shoots out, almost knocking it off the coffee table, but I manage to hang on to it and answer right before it goes to voice mail. "H-hello?"

"It's me, honey."

"I know. What time is it?"

"Late. A little after twelve. But Eli said you wanted me to call whatever time I got in."

Everything falls into place, slow-motion. "Wait. You were out with Mel until midnight?"

"Well, we had dinner and then we came back to the hotel for a nightcap and ended up having more than one."

"You got drunk with my sister?"

"She got drunk and I watched, actually. I don't think she's used to hard liquor, and she was tossing back chocolate martinis like they didn't contain vodka."

"Is she okay?"

"I made sure she got to her room safely, but she's not going to feel great in the morning."

"That's not what I mean. What's going on with her?"

He takes a deep breath. "Basically, she really believes you and Graham had some grand affair. In fact, she's not sure it's over, even now. I did everything I could to convince her otherwise. Toward the end of the evening, either I was swaying her or she just stopped listening. At least she quit arguing."

"I don't get it. Graham and I have barely spoken to each other throughout the twenty years they've been together. We'd have to be brilliant actors. And beyond that, Mel should know me better."

"I said as much, sweetheart. I'm not even sure why she decided to open up to me — whether she was looking for information or trying to make me jealous or what. It was a very strange night."

Strange, indeed.

"Jealous?"

"Maybe 'suspicious' is a better word. She strongly suggested I keep you close to home and maybe even put our favorite private investigator to work."

"Following me?"

"Yep."

"Believe it or not, I haven't even looked at

another man since I met you." Okay, that's a slight exaggeration, but I haven't looked at one lustfully. "In fact . . ."

I come very close to telling him about Mel's little indiscretion while we were in Idaho but change my mind. I promised her I'd keep her secret.

But would she do the same for you?

"What?" he asks, curiosity piqued.

"In fact, the best-looking, most endowed man in the universe could dance naked across our deck and I'd close my eyes."

"Hey. I thought *I* was the best-looking, most endowed man in the universe."

"Okay, the runner-up could perform *Swan Lake* in the nude and I'd close my eyes the entire time."

He laughs warmly, and suddenly I miss him. Despite enjoying my envelope of seclusion, I'll be happy to have him home. And tomorrow night, we'll have mad, unfettered sex. Not that I have anything to prove, but I don't want the thought to even cross his mind that I might be interested in anyone on the side. Especially Graham.

For now I change the subject, quizzing him briefly about the movers. All seems to have gone well on that account. My beautiful furniture has now been transferred into climate-controlled storage, where it will stay until I figure out what I want to do with it.

"It's late, so I'll let you go to bed. Will you do me a favor before you leave the city tomorrow and stop by Boudin's?" It's my favorite San Francisco bakery. "I've got a sudden urge for fresh sourdough French bread. Pick up a loaf for dinner and a couple extra to put in the freezer."

"Anything for you, milady. I'll be home before supper. Sleep well."

I try, but between the catnap and Cavin's information about my sister, I spend too much time lost in thought. I wish I knew how best to deal with Melody's idiotic notion. Keep quiet? Confront her? Confront Graham in front of her? Anyone but my sister would simply be excised from my life. But the one person I've ever been able to count on absolutely is Mel. And while I can, and absolutely will if I must, survive without her presence, it would chisel a crack that might well become a chasm.

Goddamn it, Graham, what have you done?

Fuck Graham. What's Melody done?

THIRTY

I wake to slight movement in my bed. I've slept alone for months now and the smell of last night's sex disorients me at first. But now I remember. The man is a stranger, one I only just met a few days ago. I liked his smile then, liked even more our mutual interest in poetry and music. I liked that he took an immediate interest in me.

It's early.

Still dark outside.

In here, the candle mosaic hanging on the far wall provides just enough light to cast a faint shadow when I slip out from beneath the covers and go into the bathroom. I enjoyed the encounter. He was a decent lover, eager enough to give as well as receive. But I'm not in the mood for an encore this morning, and I want a shower.

Hot water cascades through my hair and down over my back, and the scent it carries is gardenia.

Familiar.

Past tense.

I haven't used that shampoo in years.

I turn off the tap. Pad across the tile, trying not to slip. Wrap a towel around myself. As I approach the door, there's a bloom of noise on the far side. Voices. Laughter. Dishes.

Dishes?

Gardenia-scented hair still dripping, towel slipping slightly, I fling open the door and find myself entering El Caballero, my favorite Mexican restaurant. At least, it was twenty years ago. At a central table, Melody looks up, smiles, and waves at me. The man who's sitting across from her stands. Turns. No.

It can't be the stranger who loves beat poetry.

Grunge music.

Fucking me.

"Graham."

I throw myself out of the dream, out of bed. God, I was right back there in Las Vegas, twenty-three years old. It was completely real, up until I walked into the restaurant wearing only a towel. Two decades ago I wore actual clothes. Well, except for those hours in bed.

Hours with Graham.

I've tried very hard to forget our one-night stand. But the details that were just exhumed from buried memories resurrect it quite clearly. He is not the man my husband is, but, at least back then, he was intelligent, well-spoken, and generous when it came to sex. Had he not been involved with my sister, there probably would have been other nights together. Maybe a few afternoons, too.

But he'd been dating Mel for a while. Walking into that restaurant, discovering it was he she was so smitten by, was a complete shock and surreal coincidence. I made it very clear to him afterward that I had no interest in pursuing a relationship. Melody never found out about that night.

Until now.

Yes, until now.

I accomplish my workout prebreakfast and after a short burst of sustenance decide to start work on the Fresh for Families project. I'll need to scout locations for the video shoots ASAP. I e-mail Jason:

Morning. I want to interview some of your growers, preferably at their properties, so we can decide where to shoot video. Can you set that up right away? I'm willing to work over the weekend if necessary. Touring the locations is vital, and sooner rather than later is always best. Also, I've decided it might be better to use a production company closer to home, which will save travel costs. With your permission, I'll investigate several.

I could just call him, of course, but I've found paper trails useful in the past. They keep everyone on board, and there's a record of communication chains. Apparently it was a good decision, because I'm still at my desk when he responds.

Love your enthusiasm. I'll make some inquiries and get right back to you. As for the production company, I'll trust you to choose the right one.

I spend some time looking at websites, some in Reno and others in Sacramento, and ultimately decide to talk to five in the Sac area, as most of Jason's growers are on the western side of the Sierra. I invest thirty minutes in discussion with each, outlining our vision for the video, as well as reminding them about the nonprofit's mission. I'm not necessarily looking for a discount but would like to hear sympathy for our cause reflected in the voice on the far side of the conversation.

Eventually, I weed them to three and request links to videos they've produced that reflect similar goals, plus a budget and short outline for the projects they'll propose, and I give them three days to accomplish that. Hopefully we can start filming within the next couple of weeks.

The process takes several hours, and by the time I've completed it, I get an e-mail back from Jason.

Everyone I've talked to is excited to be included. If you can go Friday, I'll pick you up and we can drive over the mountain. We should leave by nine, if that's okay, so we won't have to hurry. We can visit the Fallon farms another day, but probably should include them in the video as we won't use them for the fund-raiser.

Good point.
I reply:

Friday is fine. I'll be ready by nine. But I'd like to get out to Fallon tomorrow. I can drive myself if you send addresses and let them know I'll be coming. Oh, and I've got three Sacramento-area production companies sending proposals by the end of the week. We have a great start.

He's obviously still at his computer, because his response takes only a few minutes.

Like I said, I love your enthusiasm. I'll get in touch with Fallon.

That was an excellent half day's work. Satisfied, I start toward the kitchen to consider what to make for dinner, and when I'm halfway there, the doorbell rings. It's the crew leader of the company that's scheduled to replace the siding.

"Kind of late in the day, isn't it?" I ask the foreman, whose name is Hector.

"Yeah," he acknowledges. "Sorry. Two of the guys called in sick, so I had to pull these dudes off another job. Today's all demolition anyway. Okay if we get started?"

I agree it's fine but soon wish I didn't. The noise reverberating off the side of the house is going to drive me insane. Glad they'll be here only a short while this afternoon and that I'll be away for the next couple of days.

We are blessed at the lake with several fine farmers' markets, so there are lots of fresh veggies and herbs in the fridge. I decide on a nice minestrone. The food prep doesn't take much concentration, though it is time consuming. Wash. Stem. Chop. Dice. Mince. Sauté. Brown. Season. Add liquid. Bring to a slow boil. Reduce heat. Cover. Simmer low until dinnertime.

When that's finished I make my way downstairs to check on the progress outside.

Surprisingly, the three men have managed to remove the entire upper half already. Considering the height of the house, I'm impressed. "Wow," I tell Hector. "You guys are fast."

"Faster taking it down than putting it up. But we've had lots of practice at both. We'll be finished with the demo by tomorrow morning, and then comes the hard part."

"Have you found any damage under the siding? The adjustor said you might."

"Nope. Not so far, anyway. Look for yourself. The siding's more burned down low, though, so we'll see *mañana*. We're gonna wrap it up for the day pretty soon."

I take my leave, and as I turn in the direction of the door, an object in the dirt by the step catches my eye. Anger erupts when I recognize what it is. I reach down, pick it up, and spin back toward the workers, luckily using my left leg as the pivot. That could have set my rehab back weeks.

"Who did this?" I demand, catching the men off guard.

Hector speaks for the crew. "Did what?"

"Who tossed their cigarette out here?" I extend my hand, showing him the offending butt.

His head shakes without hesitation. "None of us, lady. It's a company rule. No smoking except in our trucks."

If disbelieving looks were bullets, I just shot him dead.

"No, really. We would never smoke on a job, and anyone who tosses a butt in a client's yard is an ass. I can vouch for these guys. Not asses."

The not-asses in question keep working without comment.

He's convincing. "Well, okay then. It's just . . . I can't think of anyone else who might have done this."

"You got kids?"

It's a fair question, but one I don't answer. Instead, I retreat, stewing. Who could have done this? Handy Al et al raked every inch of this area, and the resulting debris was bagged and hauled away. Is it possible they missed this? Or has someone been out here since? If that's the case, who?

Of course, it could be random. It could have blown in from the street or from the house next door. I'm just about ready to chalk it up to that when I notice, several steps toward the trees, what looks to be a second butt. I move closer. Bend to pick it up. It is, and it's the same brand — Newport. Okay, logically they could have come from an ashtray dumped on the road and picked up by the wind.

But instinct warns someone's been smoking out here, and recently, like within the last couple of days.

Definitely time for camera surveillance.

Which reminds me I forgot to call a security company this morning. I go inside to remedy that and wait for Cavin to get home, very careful to lock the doors behind me. I'm reading when I hear a key turn in the lock, and when I look up from my book, I'm surprised to see it's Eli.

"I thought you weren't coming home until tomorrow."

He shrugs. "Yeah, that's what I originally said, but I knew how much you were missing me."

Funny kid. Glad I made a big pot of soup for dinner. "I expected your father sooner. Have any idea where he got waylaid?"

"Beats me. Anyway, waylaid is better than just plain laid, right?"

I suppose he's got a point, not that I'll give him the satisfaction of saying so.

"Everything okay with Kayla?"

He puts down his backpack, tosses his keys on the counter, comes into the living room, and flops in the chair adjacent the couch. "She did get a little emotional but held it together pretty well. Probably a good thing her mom was there. That's a nice school, by the way."

"Very. I hope she does well. A girl needs solid footing in a world dominated by men."

Eli grins. "In my admittedly shortsighted view, women hold the power, if not the wealth. You, of course, enjoy both."

Eli, the man.

"I won't apologize. I've worked hard for both. Oh, speaking of work, I've got a new project I'll be very busy with for several weeks." I give him a thumbnail sketch. "I'm driving over to Fallon tomorrow. Have you ever been there?"

"Bumfuck, Egypt? Nope."

Eli, the boy.

"Any desire to ride along?" Did I really just invite his company?

He looks me straight in the eye. "If you think I can be useful. In fact, if there's anything I can do to help with your project, I'd be happy to."

Eli, the man.

"Thanks for the offer. There's plenty to do, and not a whole lot of time to do it.

Maybe you could suggest ideas for the menu." Might as well give him something to invest a bit of energy in.

"Hot dogs and Cheetos?"

Eli, the boy.

Which do you prefer?

Eli glances at the book sitting beside me on the couch. "*Lady Chatterley's Lover.* Interesting choice."

"You've read it?"

"Of course. We had to choose classics at the Athenian, and the ones with illicit sexual encounters tended to draw me in better than those featuring whale hunts."

"Somehow that doesn't surprise me."

"Does anything I do surprise you?"

"Not really. Not anymore."

He leans in toward me, plants his face close enough to mine so there's no way not to look into his eyes without appearing to be a coward. "How can I change that?"

Before I can answer, the front doorknob rattles as Cavin finally makes an appearance. Eli retreats, but slowly, something his father overlooks entirely.

"Sorry I'm a little late. I didn't miss dinner, did I?"

I clear my throat, find my voice. "No, but it's ready. I expected you sooner. Did something happen?"

He shakes his head. "I decided to stop by my office and go over the films for tomorrow's surgeries so I wouldn't have to leave too early in the morning. Then I just kind of got caught up in paperwork. But look, I remembered your French bread."

"Our French bread," I correct. "Why don't you two go wash up and I'll put dinner on?"

Cavin heads back to our bedroom with his overnight bag, but Eli wanders into the kitchen and uses the sink there.

"I'll set the table," he offers.

"We'll just need butter knives and soup spoons."

As he removes the requisite items from the silverware drawer, I reach over him into the cupboard above for bowls and plates. When we're mere inches apart, he lowers his voice. "Strange Dad didn't call to let you know not to worry, huh?"

"Men can be thoughtless sometimes. It's not a big deal."

He straightens. "And some women are naive. I just wouldn't have expected you to be one of them."

Eli, the man, is maddening.

THIRTY-ONE

The next week will definitely keep me busy. With the siding company promising at least two more days of noise pollution, I'm happy to invest the first one into driving east to Fallon, Nevada. Its high desert landscape belies the fact that the Naval Air Station Fallon is the area's largest employer and home to the real-life Top Gun training academy. Farming the arid but rich land was made possible at the turn of the twentieth century by Francis Newlands, whose vision encompassed a huge series of irrigation canals throughout the region.

Fresh for Families partners with three Fallon produce farmers, two ranchers, and a dairy farmer. Together they provide lettuce, corn, onions, melons, beef, lamb, and, of course, dairy products, supplementing the diets of families in need. The day I visit is oppressively hot, as Eli, who decided to come after all, keeps reminding me on the drive between properties.

"It's hot as literal hell out here. Who would want to live in this godforsaken part of the country?"

"I've spent some hot-as-hell days in Sacramento. You lived there."

"Not by choice. Anyway, at least there's shit to do in Sac."

"I'm sure there's plenty to do in Fallon, Eli." Not that I can actually discern much, but the town itself is rather charming, at least the historical Main Street section.

"You mean like hunt and fish and watch corn grow. Maybe catch sight of a jet or two."

The words are barely out of his mouth when a fighter pops up above the scrub brush, roaring into the sky. "You have to admit that's pretty cool."

"Cool. Right. Unlike the temperature."

"Quit griping. You were the one who wanted to come." Which surprised me, considering he generally prefers to sleep in, and I was adamant about being on the road by eight thirty. In fact, he snoozed most of the way down the mountain and became communicative only when we stopped for gas.

"I figured the drive would let us talk."

"About what?"

"To start with, school. I'll have enough credits to graduate at the semester break. Then I thought I might take the spring semester off and start SNC the following fall."

"I guess that's up to you. Why talk to me about it?"

"I need you to run interference with Dad."

"You mean he's not supportive of your plan?"

"I haven't even discussed it with him."

Sounds like an end around. "First of all, I'm not sure what you're worried about. And secondly, what exactly are you planning to do between January and August?"

"Ski bum while there's snow, and beach bum after. I'm hoping you guys will let me chill in the Carmel house for a couple of months."

"Alone?"

He answers with a shrug.

"Eli, you'll barely be eighteen. I'm not sure . . ." It strikes me that, strangely enough, I'm not sure I want to have him gone. Which makes zero sense at all, considering how little I wanted him with us when he first moved in.

"You could always come supervise," he coaxes.

"Sounds dangerous."

"I thought you thrived on danger."

Before I can respond, my GPS beeps. *"You have reached your destination on the left."* It's a welcome interruption.

We spend several hours perusing cantaloupes and cornfields and talking with owners about their operations. We learn that farmers routinely grow more than they can sell to their primary markets. Sometimes as much as fifty percent of their produce gets turned back under, which is more efficient than it might seem. But for some the waste is unacceptable. Fresh for Families sends volunteers out to collect and distribute excess crops, making it a win-win situation, especially with the write-offs available to the farmers.

Our final stop is a dairy farm. "Holy shit," exclaims Eli when he opens the passenger door. Let's just say bovine excrement carries a very unpleasant smell when the temperature hovers close to one hundred degrees. We'll have to arrange the video shoot for a cooler day if possible.

Despite the odor, the property is beautiful, especially the pasture where at least some of the black-and-white cattle graze. Plenty of fodder for a camera crew. It's a medium-size operation, we're told, with 125 cows each producing an average of seven gallons of milk per day, so many are in the barn, giving to the cause.

Troy, whose father established the place twenty-eight years ago, explains, "There isn't a lot of money in dairy farming, unless you're a huge operation. We treat our animals humanely and can rightly stamp our milk 'organic.' And that cuts into the bottom line. All we can afford to donate to the program is fifty gallons a week."

"So, why do you do it, then?" asks Eli.

"I do my best to live a God-fearing life, and if I can fill a few kids' bellies, I figure when my time comes I've got nothing to worry about."

Eli and I are back in the car before I comment, "Altruism. Imagine that. It's a rare concept these days."

"Are you altruistic or are you getting compensated for this work?"

"Not for this project, but if I decide I want a paid position, one's been offered."

"Really? You can make money in fundraising? Because I might be good at it."

My first reaction is *no damn way,* but on second thought, it just might be something he could do. God knows he has a knack for persuasion. "Maybe so."

"But if you're not getting paid, what's in it for you?"

"It's a game."

"How do you win?"

"By convincing people to open their —"

"Don't tell me. Hearts?"

"No, their checkbooks. The bigger the check, the bigger the win."

He considers. Grins. "Sounds like fun."

Exactly.

Armed with lots of ideas for whichever production company I choose, we embark on our journey home and are almost to Carson City when Eli drops a bomb. "So I hear you're sleeping with Kayla's dad."

"I most certainly am not!"

"But you did."

Okay, this is so none of his business.

But someone has managed to make it that.

How do I respond?

In this case, since he just might be reporting back to that someone, the truth is probably my best choice. "Eli, I don't need to defend myself to you, but since you've somehow become involved in this discussion, I will tell you the same thing I told Melody, and your father is privy to it as well. I met Graham twenty years ago while he was still in med school. We went to dinner and a concert and, yes, we slept together exactly one time. I had no idea he was dating my sister, but as soon as I discovered that, there was no more 'Graham and me.' End of story."

"I believe you. And just so you know, I told Kayla I totally doubted you were having an affair with her dad."

"Wait. How does Kayla know?"

"I guess I told her. I figured if your sister was crying to Dad about it, it wasn't exactly a secret, and I wanted her to understand I think it's bullshit."

I really have to deal with this, don't I?

Yes, and very soon.

But for now, let's divert the conversation. "Speaking of Kayla, I haven't had a chance to ask how you feel about her being gone. Will you miss having her around?"

"Some. It's nice to have sex readily available, you know? Especially when you don't have to be married to get it when you want it."

"Easy sex is the only reason you'll miss her?"

"Look, I'm not in love with her. You know that, and she does, too. Or at least she ought to. And honestly, there were times when she made me feel . . . I don't know. Uncomfortable?"

"Really? Like how?"

"I said she was dependent. A better word might be 'possessive.' Most of the time I could deal with it, but sometimes — maybe she was off her meds or whatever — she kind of went ape shit over little stuff like my checking out girls at the beach. I mean, I'm not blind."

He's not exactly subtle, either.

"You don't think maybe finding out about you sleeping with Sophia while she was in California had something to do with her mistrusting you?"

"I guess. But you know what she said? That if she ever caught Sophia and me together, she'd make damn sure it would never happen again. And the way she said it creeped me out. Once in a while, she's scary, man."

"Oh, come on. You're exaggerating."

He says nothing, but out of the corner of my eye, I can see his head swivel slowly, left-right-left.

"If you felt that way, why didn't you just break up with her?"

"Scary chicks are great in the sack."

"Eli . . ." I warn.

"No, look. First, there's the you-and-Kayla connection. I didn't want to take a chance on pissing you off. Plus, I really wasn't sure what she might do, to me or to herself, if she went all the way off the deep end. Anyway, I knew you'd make damn sure she'd start college, so I figured I could just wait her out."

"Are you telling me you're actually afraid of her?"

"Let's just say she probably shouldn't be allowed too close to a loaded gun."

Boom.

Figuratively thinking, that is.

But I'm having a hard time wrapping my brain around this. I've known Kayla her entire life and never intuited anything menacing about her.

Then again, other than the short time she spent living under my roof, I've probably been around her on only a dozen occasions. How well can you reasonably "know" someone in those circumstances? I was surprised at her total disdain for her parents' concerns about her boyfriends, especially considering she actually disappeared for a couple of days, not a word to let anyone know she was safely shacking up with some sleaze. She drinks, smokes weed, and she could very well be experimenting with harder drugs. All that self-medication could contribute to the suicide threats Mel mentioned, as could forgetting her prescribed meds.

Do suicidal tendencies go hand in hand with homicidal propensities?

411

"Anyway . . ." Eli interrupts that very long stream of negative thoughts. "I wanted to thank you for not telling Kayla about Sophia moving to the lake. It would've pissed her off majorly."

"I decided it was not my place to tell her, Eli, though I do think she has the right to know. Unless you officially sunder your relationship. Besides, I wasn't one hundred percent positive Sophia would actually make the move. There's always the possibility she'll change her mind."

"Nope. She's already there."

"Are you sure? How do you know?"

"I talked to her. She's living in a condo up on Kingsbury Grade, right next to Heavenly."

The boy is a wellspring of information.

"When did you talk to her?"

"On the way back from San Francisco last night."

"What?"

He lifts his hands in the air, wiggles his fingers. "No worries. Hands-free technology."

"That's not what I mean. Did you call her or vice versa?"

"Does it really matter?"

"Yes!"

"Okay, okay. I called her, just to see how

she's doing. She was all wound up about her new show and living at Tahoe. Her condo's ski in, ski out, and —"

"I don't care."

"I'm sorry?"

"Eli, why would I care about what Sophia's wound up about? I don't care about her at all."

"Oh yeah, I forgot you were jealous."

"I'm not jealous. I'd just prefer she stay off my radar." Weak. "Not to mention off my property."

"You including Dad as your 'property'?"

Sometimes I really want to smack him. I reel that thought in and answer, "I trust your father, Eli."

"Up to you, I guess. And what about me?"

"Do I trust you? No, but I don't have to, do I?"

He feigns grabbing his heart. "Shot through. But I'll survive."

Now he turns up the volume on the radio. Guess that means we're finished conversing. I satisfy myself with listening to him sing along with some of my grunge favorites, and truly showing off his vocal ability by nailing Alice in Chains' "Rooster."

I wait until he's finished to ask, "How do you know this music, anyway?" He didn't miss a lyric.

"You and my mom have something in common. Besides my dad and me, that is."

Good enough.

We're almost home before I remember to ask, "Neither you nor Kayla smoke, do you? Cigarettes, I mean."

"Nope. One habit I never picked up. And I've never seen her smoke, either."

That's what I thought.

When he inquires why I asked, it's a fair question.

One I'm not willing to answer.

Four decades of play have taught me to hold some cards close to my chest.

THIRTY-TWO

The day I spend with Jason, traipsing through fields and orchards, is pleasant enough, though by the end of it my knee feels like it's experienced far too much weight-bearing activity. Happily, at least, much of it is at altitude, which mitigates the heat to a great degree.

We also tour a couple of elevated wineries — some of Jason's favorites — and one stands out to me as perfect for what I have in mind. They do weddings here, overlooking the American River Valley, and there's plenty of space both outside and in the building itself to accommodate whatever the capricious weather gods might throw our way in early October.

The owner himself is in the tasting room, and Logan has heard of the FFF programs through one of the local growers he knows, so he's immediately open to my idea. "Tasting closes at five on weekends," he tells us, "so an evening event isn't impossible. We'll have to look at dates, as we do have a couple of weddings scheduled for October."

"We are a nonprofit," I remind him, "so our budget is limited. Not sure we could pay as much for the facility as a bride might be willing to. But of course, you could write off any in-kind donation on your taxes."

I give him my best temptress imitation, and apparently I'm not too out of practice because he rewards me with a smile, which says he wants to work with us. Or me.

"I don't suppose it would work on a weekday?"

"Unfortunately, no. The idea is to show donors around a couple of the Apple Hill orchards that we work with, hopefully boosting business for them as well. But if you think about it, we'll be pulling in people from points distant who might not otherwise discover your wonderful wines, so that's a plus for you, too."

He thinks for a minute. "Let me go consult the calendar, not to mention my wife. I'd love to work out something with you."

"Please discuss a bottom-line price so we can decide if our budget can accommodate it. And while we're here, I'd like to taste a couple of your big-bodied reds. My cellar's in need of replenishment."

"Cellar, eh?"

"Yes. I had quite the vault in the Russian Hill house I just sold. Moving those bottles to Tahoe was a serious accomplishment. Now I need to have something substantial built there, so if you can recommend a good storage system, I'd be grateful."

"Here. Start with this 2013 Syrah and I'll be right back." Logan pours two samples, then disappears.

Jason lifts his glass in a small toast. "To October fund-raisers."

I take a sip of a fine syrah. "To excellent vintages and generous winemakers."

When Logan returns, he has a possible date. "Looks like the last Saturday will work. Is that good for you?"

Exactly what I was hoping for. "It's perfect. Thank you."

We talk wine and racking for fifteen or twenty minutes. Every now and again I glance at Jason, who is watching with amusement. I ask to try something else and steer our dialogue toward the accomplishments of Fresh for Families, a bit about my previous fund-raisers, and the upscale clientele likely to be attracted to well-publicized goodwill.

I taste a petite sirah, two cabernets, a zinfandel, and a fabulous Barbera, and am glad

Jason declined a sip of anything but the syrah. He's driving, and it would be impossible for me to take the wheel, at least without napping for a while.

But the tactic definitely worked. I go home with three cases of decent red wine and Logan's commitment to let us use his winery for our event for the cost of staffing it. He even offers to fire up the barbecue, don his chef hat, and cook for our crowd.

Voilà!

"Date and location locked in," I tell Jason on the way home.

"Seems so," he agrees. "Impressive."

"I hope everything falls into place as easily. This is a big undertaking, and I foresee it growing into quite an event."

"I don't doubt that at all. You are genuinely persuasive."

"Only one of my many talents, and thank you. Now that we know the 'when,' we'll need to coordinate with the growers as far as touring their properties, plus figure out the details of the video shoots. I'll get straight on that tomorrow."

It's early evening by the time Jason drops me off at home. "May I help you carry in your wine?" he volunteers.

"Of course. You can meet my husband."

We each grab a case to take inside. Cavin's

in the kitchen. "Good. You're home. Perfect timing. Dinner will be ready in thirty minutes." He comes over to relieve me of the carton in my arms, but first extends a hand, forcing Jason to set down his own box and shake. "I'm Cavin. You must be Jason. It's good to meet you."

"You as well. Your wife is a live wire, in case you don't know."

Live wire. I like it.

"Believe me, I knew it from the minute I met her, even if she was strapped down to a gurney."

"Honey," I interrupt, "there's another case of wine in the back of Jason's SUV. Would you mind?"

"Three?"

"I think she mostly bought them as a bribe," Jason says.

"Did it work?"

"Do you really need to ask?"

The two men laugh and Cavin follows Jason out to his vehicle.

"Bye," I call, before collapsing on the couch.

Cavin soon returns with the last of the wine. He sets down the box, then takes an assessing look at me. "You okay?"

"Tired and a little headachy. Would you mind bringing me a couple of ibuprofen and some water?"

He delivers the requested items, kisses me gently, then looks me square in the eye. "Two long days in a row, with a lot of time on your feet. You should rest up tomorrow."

I swallow the pills. "The security company is supposed to come in the morning. I'll follow them around, then do my best to sit out the afternoon. I'll have a lot of telephoning to do, but I can accomplish that butt in chair."

"Promise?"

"Absolutely."

He straightens. "Good. Jason seems like a nice guy. I take it your day was successful."

"Yes, we accomplished a lot today." I give him the overview as he goes to start the vegetables.

He opens the fridge. "Asparagus okay, or would you rather have spinach? I can sauté it with garlic and olive oil."

"Choices, choices. Either's fine by me. Maybe you should ask Eli."

"Oh, he won't be home for dinner."

"Really? Where is he?"

"I'm not sure. I just got a text that said not to expect him, and he'd be back late."

I've got a pretty good idea where he went. "Did you know Sophia's living in Stateline now?"

"No. I haven't seen her since Starbucks. How do you know?"

"Guess."

"Oh. You think that's where he is?"

"Where else?"

Rather than respond to that, he redirects: "Did you decide on the vegetable?"

"Spinach."

"Good decision."

"Want help?"

"Nope. I've got this."

The ibuprofen has worked its magic; the pain has receded. I move to a kitchen bar stool, where conversation will be easier. Besides, "I like watching you work. At least, I like watching you cook. I wish I could mince garlic as fastidiously. I always end up with pieces on the floor."

"That would be me and bone spurs."

"What?" His words finally sink in. "Oh. You mean on the operating room floor. That's rather disgusting. I wouldn't make a good nurse."

"That's all right. You're good at just about everything else."

Once the spinach is safely in the pan, I ask, "So has Eli mentioned his plans for this year to you?"

"Plans?"

I repeat Eli's list of goals and desires.

"He thinks I'm going to finance his bumming around for six months? Not to mention allow him to stay in the Carmel house? What planet does the boy live on?"

Planet Sophia, obviously.

"I thought I should let you know."

"Why would he come to you first?" He's fuming.

"No clue. He also asked me to run interference."

The oven buzzer sounds, signaling the chicken has finished roasting. Cavin turns down the heat on the spinach, removes the bird from the oven. And wow, does the sizzling fat in the pan release an amazing scent. Coupled with the sautéed garlic, it's olfactory paradise. Now I'm really glad I chose the spinach.

"Oh my God!" I exhale. "I'm pretty sure I'm starving. In fact . . ." I run down the day's activities in my head. "I haven't eaten since breakfast." Which explains why the wine tasting threatened head hammering.

But Cavin's thoughts are elsewhere. "You know, I get that Melissa spoiled Eli all the way to rotten. But I really can't quite comprehend how his brain works. Is it too late for him to mature into an actual thinking human being?"

"Highly doubtful. But stranger things have

happened, and I don't believe as his father you're allowed to give up on him just yet."

"Okay, fine," he says, all pouty, and that's really rather charming. "But sounds like he and I are way overdue for a very long talk."

"Indeed. But since he's not here, and that chicken is, could we please eat? If my mouth waters any harder, it's going to be decidedly unattractive."

"I kind of like your mouth wet," he teases, reaching for a knife to carve the chicken. "At least, some of my body parts do."

"Tell you what. You give me one of those breasts and I'll see what my wet mouth can do for you later."

He loads up a plate with sautéed spinach and white meat, slides it across the bar in front of me. But before he fixes his own, he comes around and slips a hand inside my blouse. "Tell *you* what. You give me one of these breasts and I'll guarantee what my wet mouth will do for you later."

"You've got a deal, mister."

After dinner, with Eli gone and the neighboring houses empty, I suggest we take our just-purchased-today, Double Gold Award–winning cabernet out to the hot tub, where we sit and soak in the buff, listening to irresistible alternative music. By mutual silent agreement, we don't talk about work or crazy relatives or try to make plans for the weekend.

The water's heat erases any vestige of pain and makes my muscles pliable. When we've emptied our glasses, I put them aside and scoot sideways into Cavin's lap, and all it takes is a demanding kiss to bring him rigid between my legs. It would be easy enough to allow him entry right here, right now. But that would deny all the earlier talk of wet mouths.

"Sit up on the edge," I tell him.

I am able to kneel on my left knee and extend my right leg to the side. It's awkward, but it doesn't hurt and allows me to go down on him without much of a problem. Some women, I've heard, don't enjoy giving head, but it's almost as much a turn-on for me as receiving it is, even though it's something of a feat with Cavin because of his size.

But I enjoy a challenge, especially this one, and at this angle I can bring him over my tongue and into my throat on entry, then slowly lift my face, applying enough suction to make him moan his pleasure. At one point I pause long enough to ask, "Is my mouth wet enough for you?"

"Perfect," he manages, asking for more with the plea of his hands.

I make him as slick as I can, then fold my breasts around him, sandwiching his pulsing shaft. Up. Down. Up. Down. Sensuous rise and fall. His hands enfold mine and he quickens the tempo, grasping my nipples in the Vs of his fingers and vising them to the point of just-pain. Together, we bring him very close to climax, something he refuses.

"Get out," he says, and when I do he lifts me off my feet and lays me gently on a big beach towel spread over a lounge chair. "I believe I gave you a guarantee. Close your eyes."

To the tune of R.E.M.'s "The One I Love" and the forest's own night music, I give myself completely to the demands of my husband's mouth and tongue, and he makes good on his promise, rewarding me with a great silken wave of pleasure.

Rather than chance the chair's flimsy nature, he tugs the towel, with me still on it, to the relative stability of the deck itself. Quickly, he's inside me, brimming me with every thrust, and oh, how I wish I could lock both legs around his waist. I make do with one, lifting my hips as best I can to meet the drive of his body.

What's that noise?

It's a low, primal growl, and I realize suddenly it's emanating from me.

425

And what it means is I'm coming now.

No, more than that.

My orgasm escapes in a superheated geyser.

"Holy hell!" exclaims Cavin.

One strong arm lifts me gently, turning me onto my side, and he enters me from behind. Five long, hard strokes, and he shudders, exhaling, "God, I love you," into my hair as he comes. My husband is sexy as hell.

He gathers me into the cup of his body, smooths my messy tresses, calms my stuttering heart, running his fingertips softly along my moonlight-bathed skin. It's lovely, and not the kind of gift one could expect after sex with a stranger.

But drifting here in the afterglow, I'm almost certain I detect a hint of lit tobacco. "Do you smell that?"

"What?"

"A cigarette." I sit up and reach for the clothes I shed beside the hot tub.

"I don't smell anything. But relax. I'll take a look." He slips into his boxers, goes to the railing and investigates the perimeter of the deck. "Nothing. Your paranoia is showing."

No, it's not. Not even close.

THIRTY-THREE

The siding company has finished the job. The security company will start installing cameras, motion detectors, alarms, and a couple of extra protocols on Tuesday. Cavin and I spend a quiet weekend catching up on work-related loose ends and enjoying a Sunday brunch on the lake at Camp Richardson's Beacon Bar & Grill.

With summer winding down, it isn't as crowded as I expected, and the bike rental place looks lonely, so we pick up a couple and cruise the gentle cycling path through the old growth forest. Playing tourist on home turf feels a little strange, but we have a great time doing it and it's nice for all that pedaling to actually move me from point to point. Stationary biking has definitely grown old.

Eli spent most of the weekend away from the house. When he finally stumbles in Sunday evening, red-eyed and slurring slightly, I quiz him about where he's been, and he answers with a noncommittal, "Better you don't know. You wouldn't be pleased."

Rather than have him confirm what I suspect, I shift gears. "Once school starts I hope you'll have sense enough to stay away from known drug users and concentrate on your studies."

"You don't have to worry. I'm not into anything heavy. Weed is one thing. Addiction is another, and not something I'm willing to take a chance on. I do have priorities, believe it or not, and brain damage isn't one of them."

Some soliloquy.

"I'm no expert," I continue, "but I've heard that cocaine attracts some pretty bad people. You can't know who you might run into at her place."

He falls silent for a couple of seconds but at last says, "So you know, she's not into coke anymore. The only thing I saw her using was prescription drugs, and downers at that. And I'm not afraid of her dealer."

Cavin happens upon the conversation, and the mood quickly takes a tumble. "I assume you're referring to Sophia. Why don't you do all of us a favor and steer clear of her? None of us needs her presence in our lives, and that includes you."

"Yeah, you'd like that, wouldn't you? Jealousy doesn't become you, you know."

"Jealousy? Are you implying I'm jealous of you, you little shit? Because that is preposterous."

"Preposterous. Ooh, big word, Dad. I'm impressed. Look, I understand why you'd be nervous about me hanging out with Sophia. But don't worry. Your secret is safe with me."

Cavin and I both react at the exact same time, with the exact same question: "What secret?"

"If I told, it wouldn't be a secret anymore, would it? Actually, I'd love to confess, but I promised Sophia I'd keep quiet, and, unlike some people's, my word means something."

Eli glares at Cavin, who returns his angry stare. My eyes stray between their two faces, trying to discern the silent communication. But all I keep coming up with is how much their resemblance is growing, especially with Eli's refusal to shave lately. The thought allows me to interrupt the ugly posturing.

"You are going to remove that facial hair before tomorrow morning, aren't you, Eli?"

He actually smiles at Cavin in a sinister way before turning his attention back toward me. "What? You don't like my stubble?"

"I don't think your school will appreciate it. My opinion is irrelevant."

"Not to me, and that's fine. I'll shave. In fact, I'll go do it now. Seven a.m. is going to roll around awfully early."

"Don't you have to be at school by, like, seven thirty?" I ask.

"Yep. It's only ten minutes though. Hop out of bed. Put on jeans. Brush my teeth. Plenty of time."

"What about breakfast?" Is this mom-sounding person me?

"Lunch is early. I'll be fine."

"He's a *grown-up,* Tara. Leave him alone. If he gets hungry, he'll get up earlier on Tuesday."

"Whatever you say." At least he won't have time to smoke dope before his classes. Off he goes to shave or whatever. I wait till he's out of sight before querying, "What exactly was that all about?"

"The 'secret' thing? Or the 'jealous' thing? Because either way, I have no clue. Just stirring up sewer sludge is my guess, or trying to distract us from whatever it is he's been up to. 'Baffling us with bullshit,' as my dad used to say."

"Quintessential Eli."

"Yep." Cavin comes over and takes my hands, interweaves his fingers with mine. "I've said it before, and I'll repeat it as many times as I must — I don't keep secrets from you. And as for my son having sex with Sophia, I only care because, one, it bothers you immensely and, two, I know he's going to get hurt. He wouldn't keep going back if he didn't have feelings for her, and she is a coldhearted bitch. On one hand, he deserves it. On the other, I wish I could help him avoid it. But he's not going to listen to me."

"Not sure he's ever listened to anyone."

"Believe it or not, I think he listens to you."

I consider that. "Maybe a little." And only with an ulterior motive firmly in place. Still, it is strange that I've become his confessor.

"Come on, let's go sit." Cavin coaxes me over to the couch. "I've been thinking. If Eli manages to pull off graduating early, rather than allow him to trash the Carmel house, what about packing him off to Europe or Australia for a couple of months?"

"Alone?"

"Why not? He's totally independent, and lots of kids take time off to travel before starting college. He can get it out of his system."

Plus, he'd have to vacate Planet Sophia.

"Have you discussed it with Eli?"

"Not yet. I wanted to get your take on it first."

"I think it's a great idea, if he'll go for it. You should probably talk to Melissa, too."

"We've got plenty of time to work on both of them. At the very least, it will jump-start the discussion."

We indulge in a nightcap, but before bed, I excuse myself to check e-mail and messages. Two of the three video companies have sent proposals, which I'll peruse in the morning. There's an e-mail from Jason, too.

Hope you managed to relax a little this weekend. When you get a chance, you should follow our Facebook page. I'll make you an admin so you can post there. Here's the link . . .

Working weekends. Not a bad thing to do. I'll investigate the page tomorrow and see about other social networking sites that might be a good fit for FFF as well. It's been a while since I've plugged into them, so I'm sure there's something new.

Several junk e-mails. Delete. Delete. Delete. And a "Welcome to the New Year" e-mail from Eli's high school. Oh, look. Enrollment is up this year, to 252. Well, at least he'll get personalized attention.

Next I check texts and am surprised to find one from Melody. And more surprised to read it. *Have you seen Graham?*

I start to text her back. Instead, I call and hope she chooses to answer.

She does. "Hello?" Her voice is sour.

"Um, hi. Wondering about your message. Why would you think I'd have seen Graham?"

"I don't know. Because I haven't?"

"Mel, start to finish, I've spent every minute of the weekend with Cavin. I'm happy to put him on to confirm that for you if you don't believe me."

She sighs and I know she's softened. "No, that's okay. Sorry."

"When did you last see him?"

"Right after I got back from San Francisco on Friday. As soon as he knew I was here to take care of the girls, he was gone."

"He said nothing before he left?"

"No. I went to pee and that's how long it took for him to vanish."

"You didn't really think he'd come up here to be with me, did you? Doesn't he have patients he has to see tomorrow?"

"I assume so, but he hasn't discussed work nor extracurricular activities with me."

"Mel, I'm sorry things are falling apart

433

there, but I am not to blame. What I told you about Graham and me is completely true. I would never lie to you."

"That's what I've heard."

I struggle to think of a new approach.

But Mel beats me to it. "Remember when you offered to cover the private investigator's retainer? Are you still willing to do that?"

So she called him.

"Of course. How much does he want?"

"Fifteen hundred."

"No problem. I'll send you a check."

"Not to me. Please send it directly to him so he can get started right away."

"I'll put it in the mail first thing."

It will be worth every penny to eliminate myself from her suspect list. Okay, end of *that* conversation. Let's try a whole new direction. "Hey, Mel. Are you still planning on hiking Half Dome for your birthday?"

"Not this year. A big rock slide took out half the face. So, no Yosemite for me."

Perfect.

"Listen. I'm working on a huge fundraiser. The event happens to be the day before your birthday, at one of the Apple Hill wineries. Great food. Good wine. Dancing. I'd love for you to come. In fact, why don't you plan to spend the weekend? We'll

434

have an intimate celebration the day after the big event. Bring your family and let's do it right."

She is quiet for several long seconds. "Thanks for the invitation. I'll think about it."

I shouldn't have to convince her, but if it helps smooth things over . . . "Please. I really want you there. And it's your fortieth. It should be special."

"Tara, I really will think about it."

"Let me know soon. I'd like to make plans."

I hang up, and since my phone is still in my hand, I take a minute to call Kayla, who also picks up right away. "Hi, Aunt Tara."

"Just checking in. How'd your orientation week go?"

"Awesome! I've got a cool roomie, and my teachers are great . . ." Her ten-minute monologue makes me hopeful that she'll take school seriously. As mood swings go, she's definitely up. At least, until she says, "Of course, I miss you and Uncle Cavin and . . ." And now she's sniveling.

"Hey. Let's go back to awesome, okay? Eli starts school tomorrow, and as near as I can tell, he's got like thirty classmates, so not a whole lot of competition there. Pretty sure you're safe."

Minus Planet Sophia.

But her obvious emotional flip within such a short time makes me ask, "Are you solid? I mean, are you conscientiously taking your meds?"

"Mostly. Sometimes I forget when I'm busy or whatever. Then I usually catch up later."

"Kayla, I'm not a doctor, but I happen to be married to one, and your father is one as well. Talk to him or to Cavin. There's a reason why prescription labels tell you how much medication to take, and when. I don't think you can 'catch up later.' "

"Okay. I'll try to do better."

"Don't try. Just do."

"Gotcha."

I believe I've been dismissed. Except, "Listen. I've got a big fund-raiser the weekend of your mom's birthday. I'm trying to convince her to come up to the lake. You're more than welcome to join us. In fact, I think you should."

"Will Eli be there?"

"He's helping me with it, so he'd better not miss it."

"I'd love to come. But what about transportation?"

"We'll figure that out as we get closer. Meanwhile, work hard and succeed. Success is a woman's most dangerous weapon in a world run mostly by men. Autonomy. That's what you're after. Once you've achieved that, you'll be irresistible."

"If you say so."

"I do. Oh, hey. You haven't heard from your dad, have you? Your mom hasn't seen him in a couple of days, and she's worried."

She takes two beats. "Worried that he's spending the weekend with you?"

Goddamn it, Eli. Now I have to go there. "That was her concern, yes, but I have no idea why. She seems to have forgotten I have a husband who I love very much, and zero desire for anyone on the side, especially not your father. That's not how I operate."

"That's what I've heard."

Déjà vu.

"I did talk to Dad, actually. He called to check up on me, see how I like school so far."

Wow. I guess I didn't realize he was concerned about her. Mel has always claimed he's indifferent. "Really. So, where has he been?"

"His band had a gig in Napa. I'm surprised Mom didn't know about it. Those two should try *communication*."

"I agree."

They should indeed.

437

As long as you're not the main topic of conversation.

I sign off with Kayla, and as I disconnect, an idea strikes. We need a band for the fund-raiser, and Graham happens to drum for one. I text him. *Call when you get this, please. It's important.*

THIRTY-FOUR

With just a couple of weeks until the Fresh for Families Fall Fun-raiser, I've got things pretty well set. The video is in the final editing stage, and I'm pleased with the footage. Evergreen Productions has been easy to work with and totally professional, completing every step of the process on time. I'd use them again in a heartbeat.

Jason and I chose three farms and an orchard for the tour. Narrowing down the list was difficult, but we relied on both scenic quality and proximity to each other, not to mention the winery. We've hired a couple of mini-coach buses to accommodate the sixty-eight people who've committed to take the tour. We expect another seventy-five to attend the evening's activities, which will include screenings of the video, a silent auction, sensational food, and music.

Providing said music will be Graham's

band, Underground Parking. I was a little surprised when he called me back. I figured I'd have to track him down, but I guess he thought he owed me an explanation about what he told Mel. He did, of course, and we got to it eventually. First, however, I mentioned the October event.

"We're always looking for gigs, but don't you want to hear us play first? So happens we'll be performing in Truckee over Labor Day weekend."

Cavin and I made plans to go have a listen that Friday night. Unfortunately, he was called in for an emergency surgery last minute, so I drove over to Truckee by myself. The band was playing at a local pub, which was crowded due to the holiday, but Graham had managed to reserve a small table right next to the stage. I allowed myself a single glass of wine and enjoyed the music immensely.

As I watched Graham wield his drum-sticks, I couldn't help but be impressed, and it hit me that after twenty years I'd finally accepted his invitation to listen to him play. Those two decades brought many changes to me, but his life has remained very much the same, at least until now.

When the band took a break, Graham and I wandered outside, where he shocked me by lighting a cigarette. Marlboro, not Newport.

"Since when do you smoke?" I asked.

"I've carried the habit for years, though I usually only indulge it when I'm pretending to be a rock star."

"You realize it's bad for your health, doctor?"

"Yeah. What I didn't realize was that you cared."

I was glad the alley behind the bar was gently lit so he couldn't see the way my face flared. I shrugged. "It's your life, but I'd rather you didn't widow my sister unless you've got your will in order."

He inhaled deeply, exhaled away from me. "No worries there. If I die, Melody will be well provided for. Probably even better than with me still kicking, but please don't tell her that."

"I think you're safe. She's not the homicidal maniac type."

He took another long, slow drag. "I hope you're right."

I laughed, but then it struck me that he might not have been kidding. "Look, Graham, I realize, as you recently said, that we've spent a good number of years mutually distrusting each other. But I'd appreciate any insight you can offer. What's going

441

on with Mel?"

"You tell me. She's been pulling away for a while now. She's distant. Cold. Secretive, even."

"Huh."

"What?" He exhales a slow stream of nicotine.

"That's what she's been saying about you."

"Me? Secretive?"

"Well, yeah. That you spend weekends away. Took off for a week in Las Vegas a few months ago. Stuff like that."

"Tara, that week in Vegas was a conference. She knew all about it. I even asked if she wanted to come along, though I wouldn't have had a lot of time to spend with her. And as for weekends away, they're all about the music. About the worst thing I do is feed a mediocre nicotine habit and chase it with alcohol."

"No women on the side?"

"Would you believe me if I said no?"

The strange thing was, I might have believed him, except he didn't actually say no. Still, I wasn't quite finished.

"It doesn't matter what I think, does it? Mel's positive you're sleeping around, and now she thinks you're sleeping with me. Why did you tell her about that night you and I were together? It was such a long time ago."

He finished his cigarette before answering, stubbed it out on the cement with his foot. "I don't know. After she got back from Idaho, she was just such a bitch. All she wanted to do was fight, and she kept holding you up as this shining example of fidelity. And then, when she came home after Ricky Martin, she went on the offensive over that stupid text message. I guess I was a little drunk and desperate to hurt her, and . . . God, I'm sorry, Tara. She was so smug and cocksure. I wanted her to question everything she clings so tightly to. Including you."

His explanation was weak but sincere. I told him I forgave him, though I still don't trust him, and realize winning back my sister's trust will take prolonged persuasion. So I was a little surprised when she called to let me know she would spend her birthday weekend at the lake, and her husband would, too. The plan is for her to come over alone on Friday so she and I can enjoy a quiet night together before Graham brings the girls up the following day.

Kayla will be here on Saturday as well, shuttled by Charlie and Cassandra, who I talked into bringing her checkbook. She agreed as long as Taylor could come, too. She doesn't want to leave her son home alone, and I don't blame her. What that means is a houseful of people, and what *that* means is Mel and Graham will share one guestroom, Charlie and Cassandra the other. The younger girls will camp out on the floor of the game room, and no doubt spend all their time giggling about the older teenage boys, one of whom (and hopefully *only* one) will be sleeping with their sister.

It's going to be a crazy weekend, so I'm making sure everything is in control now, or at least as much in control as possible. Cavin isn't very much help, but Eli has been more supportive than I would've thought possible. Working around his school responsibilities, he helped decide the menu and is coordinating with the caterer. And, under Jason's direction, he's spent hours facilitating the silent auction donations, which has saved me much time and energy. Not only that but he will be shepherding one of the buses touring the farms.

Eli, the man.

That's official as of today, his eighteenth birthday, though I can't say the legal designation has changed much of anything. He still looks the same. The unusual helpfulness is the product of something else. Don't ask me what.

Tonight he asked to go out to his favorite Thai restaurant on the south shore. He has no idea that his birthday present is a round-trip ticket to Sydney, plus a bed-and-breakfast stay, to be used postgraduation. Cavin was supposed to pick up the vouchers yesterday, but he didn't mention having done so last night. But since I've got a follow-up appointment with Dr. Stanley, I purposely arrive early so I can stop by Cavin's office to see.

Cavin's receptionist looks up when I enter. "Oh. How are you?" As usual, her tepid voice and casual demeanor irritate me immensely.

"I'm doing well, Rebecca, thanks. Is Cavin around?"

"He's with a patient but shouldn't be much longer."

"I'll wait. I need to talk to him."

It's ten minutes, with a pair of *Sports Illustrated* magazines and a four-month-old copy of *Time,* before I hear noise in the hallway, indicating Cavin has finished with his patient. My face is still burrowed in the *Time* when a somehow familiar voice asks Rebecca for an appointment in a week.

I drop the magazine and confirm it's Sophia, dressed in thigh-high shorts and a

445

tight, boob-deep tank top.

Her back is still to me when I ask, over her shoulder, "What are *you* doing here?"

When she turns and sees who's asking, she smiles. And behind her, Rebecca offers a smarmy grin, too. I'll have a word with her later.

"I seem to have injured my rotator cuff," Sophia answers reasonably. "I don't even have a GP here, so I figured I'd go to the only doctor I know, who just happens to be a rotator cuff expert. Lucky me, huh?"

"Quite the coincidence. I'm surprised you got in to see him so quickly."

"We had a cancellation," Rebecca scrambles to say. "And I remembered she and Dr. Lattimore were, uh . . ."

"Friends," supplies Sophia.

Interesting synonym for "fuck buddies," although they both might argue that's not what they were. But since I can't stand thinking about how close they used to be, it's how I have to look at their past relationship.

It is past, isn't it?

Take the high road. Take the high road. Tough, when what I really want to do is stomp Sophia into the tile. "If you ladies will excuse me, I've got important business to discuss with my husband. I hope your

446

shoulder improves."

I find Cavin in his office and my fangs must be showing because his face loses most of its color. "Uh . . . Guess you saw Sophia, huh?"

I have to work very hard to keep my voice steady. "I did. It was an unpleasant surprise. You might have mentioned she had an appointment with you."

"Tara, other than surgeries, I rarely know ahead of time what patients I'm seeing on any given day. I had no idea she'd be here until I saw her name on the chart hanging outside the exam room door."

"I'm sure you understand how uncomfortable it makes me, and I heard her ask for a follow-up appointment."

"Yes. Her shoulder is so swollen I can't even order an MRI to see what the problem is. I told her to alternate heat and ice for a week and come back."

"Standard operating procedure."

"Yep, which is why I don't think I just violated doctor/patient privilege by sharing that information."

"Well, I'm sure you know I'd rather there was no Cavin/Sophia privilege to violate. Any chance you'd consider referring her elsewhere?"

"If it turns out it's more than a muscle

pull, of course. Treating her feels kind of icky anyway."

"Icky? Is that an official medical idiom?"

He nods sagely. "Preferred terminology for conditions like ingrown toenails, pink eye, and exes."

I can't help but laugh, despite the fact that I hate the way this is going. I'd prefer to stay angry right now. "Anyway, I didn't drop in on the off chance I'd catch you with an old girlfriend. I was wondering if you had the chance to stop by the travel agent's, or if you need me to do it on my way home."

"We don't have to give him the actual vouchers tonight, you know. We could just tell him about the trip."

That is so not my style. I pout displeasure. "I want it to be a nice surprise, so they need to come gift wrapped. I don't mind stopping. I just wish you would've —"

"I didn't say I don't have them."

Now I notice the idiotic grin on his face. "You are evil. Okay, then, I'd better run or I'll be late for my appointment."

"I've got a ton of paperwork to finish up before I leave, so I'll meet you at the restaurant, if that's okay."

"You going to gift wrap the vouchers?"

"I'll leave that to you. They're in my car. You know where I park, right?"

"I do."

I make it my business to know everything about my husband.

Everything?

This interior dialogue isn't totally new, but the dueling voice has become louder, it seems. I fret about that on the way to Dr. Stanley's, where his receptionist informs me, "The doctor was called out of town on a family emergency. You'll see Dr. Heinlen today. He's familiar with your history."

The office is busy, but I don't have to wait too long before a stout nurse calls me back to an exam room. Paula is the picture of efficiency, taking my vitals without excess verbiage. In fact, she mostly grunts, which I find alternately disgusting and amusing.

"What do you think, Paula? Am I going to live?"

"Looks like you're good. For now." And off she goes.

In short order, Dr. Heinlen arrives. My first impression is "straight out of med school," though he's probably older than he looks. Cavin has a lot of respect for his surgical expertise, which is why he chose him to do the revision I decided against. I can't comment on that, but I can say his professionalism is impressive.

He reaches for my hand. "Tara. I'm Cory

Heinlen. So happy to finally meet you. Cavin raves about you, and I can see why."

Hard not to like the man. Either man, in fact.

"Thank you. Sorry — at least that's probably what I should say — that I didn't invite you to dig around inside my knee. But I think it was the right decision."

"If you give me a minute, I'll offer my opinion. I did go over your last test results, so I've got a decent idea what we're dealing with."

He manipulates the leg carefully, checking for extension and flexion. "Any pain?"

"Not really. A little after exercise sometimes, and if I weight bear too long it tires."

"And the training? All good there?"

Dr. Stanley recommended my first-ever female personal trainer.

I've been seeing Kami, though not as often as I might, and not because she's a woman. I've got a lot going on lately and feel like I've got a handle on my personal training. However, she does push me, so I try to make time.

"Oh, yes. We've been concentrating on core strength and gait training — I still walk with a slight limp. However, my proprioceptors seem to be in good working order."

"Proprioceptors, huh? Sounds like you

enjoy research."

"I like understanding what's in play and what's at stake."

"Wish I had more patients like you."

"I'm good with referrals. In fact, I can think of someone who just might be a good fit for you."

If, as it turns out, the bitch needs rotator cuff surgery.

"You'd refer this person to me, rather than your husband?"

"Uh-huh. For personal reasons."

He can't help but read between those two short lines. "I see. Well, happy to treat your friend, for whatever reasons. My caseload is fairly heavy at the moment, too, but if she says you sent her, I'll work her in."

He finishes the short exam. "Tell your trainer I don't recommend jogging yet, but you might try an elliptical. Gently. Overall, I'd say keep doing what you're doing. Cavin was sure a revision was necessary, but I think you made the right call."

Validation.

"Any other questions for me?"

"Are you married?"

"What? No. Why?"

I shrug. "In case I've got a referral?"

At least I leave him laughing.

Before I go to my car, I circle around to

where Cavin parks to get the travel certificates out of his Audi. It takes a minute to locate them, stashed out of view in the center console, sandwiched between a prescription pad and an ATM receipt from Harrah's casino. Twenty-five hundred dollars, withdrawn three days ago.

Disturbing.

I grab the vouchers, and as I cut across the parking lot to my Beamer, I try to remember if Cavin was late that day. I've been so caught up in fund-raiser planning, I can't really say for sure. But I'm positive he never mentioned a gambling stop — win, lose, or break even.

Something else is nibbling at me, but I can't quite discern what it is. Something Cavin said in his office —

A horn honks suddenly, loudly, immediately behind me. I turn to find I've wandered out in front of a delivery truck. I duck to the left and offer the driver a small, embarrassed wave, which is met with a flip of his middle finger before he accelerates past me. I accept it as a deserved rebuke and chastise myself severely. I do not want to be a speed bump.

When I get home, I grab the mail, take it inside, and toss it on the counter. One envelope draws my attention. The return address is from Blaine Pederson, the private investigator I referred Mel to. It's a bill for expenses and hours invested beyond what the initial retainer covered. He's already put in quite an extensive amount of time, and his fuel expense indicates he's done a fair amount of travel. What exactly has Graham been up to?

The added three-hundred-dollar tab doesn't surprise me, nor does the fact that Pederson sent the bill here, as I paid the retainer directly. What's odd is the notation at the top that says *File of Tara Lattimore.* Shouldn't it be *File of Melody Schumacher?*

That triggers the early warning part of my brain, and when that kicks into gear, I know what it is that bothered me earlier in the parking lot. Cavin said Sophia's shoulder was so swollen he couldn't order an MRI. But I'd just seen her a couple of minutes before that. Wearing short shorts and a revealing tank top that invited inspection of her obvious assets. Surely I would've noticed one shoulder bloated larger than the other.

I didn't.

THIRTY-FIVE

Eli's birthday provided little fanfare but plenty of fireworks. Over big bowls of delectable green curry, I handed him the beautifully wrapped box containing his travel vouchers.

He shook it gingerly. "Awfully light. Don't tell me. It's a gift card."

"In a manner of speaking," Cavin said.

"Only much more creative, at least I think so," I added.

I watched his face as he opened the package and discovered what was inside. "Australia? Trying to get rid of me?" But he smiled.

"Not until after you graduate," I told him. "But then, absolutely."

We talked a little about the trip, and he seemed excited by the prospect, though it can be hard to measure Eli's enthusiasm accurately.

After dessert (mango sticky rice, which I

watched the men ingest from a safe distance), Eli took off to do some celebrating on his own, and that's where the fireworks came in. Turned out he'd gone to Sophia, who wished him a happy birthday and sent him on his way. He blew in through the door like a cyclone.

"Fuck that motherfucking bitch. Goddamn whore."

Cavin had gone to the bathroom, but I was sitting in the living room. "Sounds like that went well."

"She told me she didn't want to see me anymore. That if her investors found out, it wouldn't look good."

"Sophia?"

"Who the fuck else?" He was still yelling.

"She probably has a point."

He lowered his voice a little there. "She probably has other reasons."

"Like what?"

"Like . . . Dad."

"You mean because he told her he didn't appreciate her sleeping with you?"

He rolled his eyes. "I didn't know he talked to her about me, but hey, no big surprise. And no, that's not what I meant."

The look I shot him was a silent "What the hell are you talking about?"

"God, you really are dense, aren't you?"

"That isn't very nice." Cavin returned at that point. I have no idea how long he'd been listening.

"Yeah, well, neither are you," snapped Eli. "And you really ought to come clean to your wife."

"About what?"

"You and Sophia."

"Not this again. What am I supposed to have done now?" Cavin moved in between Eli and me, so I couldn't see his face.

But whatever Eli saw caused him to back up a couple of steps. "Fuck it. Tara wouldn't believe me anyway. I'm out of here. There's a big fat bud with my name on it."

He disappeared downstairs.

I queried Cavin about Eli's remark.

Cavin denied any knowledge.

I let it drop.

Again.

Later, however, Eli cornered me at the sink as I poured a glass of water. Cavin had already gone to bed, but the earlier interaction had wrested me from dreams, and what happened next denied me sleep for most of the night.

Shirtless, Eli slithered up behind me, left no air between his flannel pants and the silk of my thigh-length robe. He slipped his arms around me, dropped his lips to the pulse behind my ear. "You should know Dad and Sophia have an arrangement."

His breath was a summer zephyr, hot through the thin fabric covering my shoulder. Other than for a slight sway, I didn't move. "What kind of an arrangement?"

"I wish I could tell you for sure. All I know is, I happened to see her phone, and up on the screen was a message from Dad. It said, *See you then.*"

"You're certain it was from him?"

"Positive."

"Why tell me now?"

"I don't want you to be blindsided."

If I doubted that at all, the way he lifted my hair and circled my neck with tentative lips persuaded me that he believed every word. Every ounce of his youthful awkwardness vanished in a gust of passion that almost knocked me off my feet, though Eli was right there to catch me. In that moment, had he picked me up and carried me into his bed, I would've forgotten his father, sleeping just down the hall.

But he hesitated long enough for me to remember the stakes and how easy it would be to lose the game completely. I lifted my glass, took a deep swallow. "Thank you for the information." I turned, gave a little shove that made him take a step backward, and peered up into his eyes, seeking some sign of deception. Finding none, I wet my lips with a sweep of my tongue and rewarded him with one lingering kiss before pushing past him to return to my own sleeping quarters. "Happy birthday."

The close encounter left me trembling. What had just happened? What had almost happened? And what was happening with my husband? If I dozed after that, it was amid a whirlwind of questions.

Was Eli right?

He seemed sure.

But was he truthful?

Why would he lie?

He lies all the time.

Says who?

Cavin.

Cavin doesn't lie?

I ruminate on that as I down a power shake in preparation for a session with my trainer. But I tuck it all back away when my husband joins me in the kitchen, wearing khaki shorts and a bright chartreuse shirt I've never seen before.

"You trying to blind the other golfers or what?" I ask.

That elicits a wide grin. "Considering how rarely I play the game, I need every advantage I can get." He's taking part in a fund-raising event benefitting the Barton Foundation, the hospital's charitable giving arm.

"How late do you think you'll be?"

"We'll probably knock back a couple after we finish, but I'll be home in time for dinner. You sure you don't want to come along?"

"No thanks. I have no desire to play golf, and observing it is the approximate equivalent of watching grass grow. Anyway, I've got an appointment with Kami."

"Moderation, okay? I know Cory says everything's looking good, but pushing too hard now could be counterproductive. Don't make your body rebel any more than it already has. You aren't getting any younger, you know."

Ka-boom.

"I do hope that was just a tasteless joke."

"Sorry. Didn't mean to offend you. I only meant your age will affect the speed of your recovery, even without injuring yourself in a careless fall or thoughtless over-rotation. I know you hate the brace, but I highly recommend you utilize it to eliminate any chance of a twist."

"Would you quit talking as if I'm geriatric, feeble-minded, or both? Thanks for the advice, and please run along now. I'll be fine and dandy."

He considers a retort.

Changes his mind.

And that is a very good plan.

Once he vacates the house, I pack my gym bag, purposely leaving the brace behind. Age? Fuck him. Age is a state of mind, and a body trained to ignore chronology.

Sounds like something you'd read in an AARP bulletin.

Good point.

I go into the bathroom, take a long hard look in the mirror. It's been a while since I've had my hair done. At the part, a sprinkling of white undeniably blends with the red. I'll fix that next week. I make a mental note to call my new hairdresser, Jayne. Maybe we'll have to discuss an updated cut, too, though I've worn my hair this way forever. Something shorter. More stylish.

Younger.

Over the years, I've spent a small fortune on skin-care products, with the occasional laser peel and semiregular Restylane injections to deny time's incessant whittling. I've managed to keep the crow's-feet mostly at bay but today find hints of four-plus decades of living. My regular plastic surgeon, who I trust completely, is in San Francisco, so I'll either have to drive over or find someone here. Either way, it should be soon.

My body has been firmer. The relaxed workouts have taken a small toll, but nothing that can't be fixed as my rehab progresses. Having never borne children, I have a tauter stomach and breasts than those of most women my age. The rest I'll rebuild quadrant by quadrant.

A disturbing question surfaces: Is that what Cavin wants?

Why wouldn't he?

I don't know. But why would he encourage me to slow my training schedule?

So you don't screw up your knee forever?

Okay, fine. Maybe he doesn't want me helpless.

Or fat. Probably not fat, in fact.

God, I'm sick of arguing with myself.

Fact is, I'm a born cynic. Trust will never come easily, if it ever comes at all, and that has mostly served me well. But while I take great pride in the fact that it's hard to put one over on me, the constant surveillance wears on a person after a while. Processing recent revelations has been a struggle.

Cavin and I have been married a little more than three months, which is one-third the total amount of time we've known each other. That's long enough to have discovered dents in my prince's shining armor. He isn't particularly savvy when it comes to financial

461

concerns, and his propensity for withdrawing large amounts of cash to carry in his wallet, not to mention devote to games of chance, is worrisome. He works hard but likes to play, and now I have to wonder where, and with whom.

On the plus side, he is respectful and kind, two traits many men largely lack. He is supportive of my ambitions, and that is no small thing. The extra hours he's been putting in at the hospital seem to be paying off. At least our joint bank account reflects a decent balance, one that I haven't had to augment this month.

I could if I needed to, without touching my investment accounts. The check for the Russian Hill house arrived last week. I thought long and hard about where to put that $1.6 million and decided to leave it in my personal money market for now. At some point I'll invest in another property. I just don't know where yet.

I finish dressing, gather my things, and head to the gym, where I ask Kami to challenge me. We remain conscious of the offending knee but work everything else to a demanding degree. I finish up, tired, sweaty, a little sore (muscles, not joints), and satisfied. Anything but old.

On the return trip home, I find myself

mired in a line of slow-moving traffic due to some sort of incident ahead. Roadwork or accident, we creep along at ten miles an hour. Rather than fret, I turn up the radio and fall into a grunge-inspired reverie, driven by a heavy beat.

The percussion carries me back to a place I haven't remembered in thirty-odd years. I came home from school and, as often enough was the case, the noises drifting toward the front door told me Mom was entertaining some man not far beyond. I didn't have to go looking to stumble upon them, rutting in the kitchen of all places. He had her bent over the beer-bottle-strewn counter, driving into her from behind.

I gasped at the sight of his pimpled white ass, and they both turned enough to see who made the noise. His face was nondescript — just another truck stop conquest. But I'll never forget my initial impression of the woman who couldn't have been much older than twenty-eight or -nine. A single word surfaced in my mind.

Crone.

Season of the Crone

Splintered knuckles tap
against the window, leave
warnings, etched in silver,
upon the panes of glass.

The crone, again, has come to call.

She drops embroidered skirts
in a flounce of snowflakes,
abandons them, draped across
westward hills.

In a caravan of clouds, she journeys east.

Naked, she lights on your doorstep.
Can you hear her, chanting
morning mantra? Listen
to her, ranting at the night.

Hers is the voice of the siren.

Throw wide your windows,
invite the witch inside,
part your lips and accept
her bitter kiss.

You cannot fight her frozen spell.

Feel her toothless gnaw against
the protest of your flesh, hunger
unencumbered by wool or fire.
In this season of the crone,

only the foolish believe they can prevail.

THIRTY-SIX

Tomorrow is the Fresh for Families fund-raiser, and the culmination of weeks of work. Everything is in perfect order. At least, I'm pretty sure it is. There's always the slight possibility that I missed some detail. But I really don't think so, and anything that might go wrong is not within my realm of control.

The buses are waiting at the winery. The caterer has been vetted and comes highly recommended. It was Eli's idea to use food provided by the farms that donate to the cause, and those fresh-from-the-fields ingredients will be delivered this afternoon and held in cold storage in the winery cellar. Jason has rounded up a crew of volunteers who will set up the tables and chairs, add centerpieces and silverware.

On a personal note, both the color and style of my hair have been revamped. I couldn't bring myself to cut it really short, but Jayne trimmed it shoulder-length and added lots of layers, highlighting a few. The new dress I chose is pale aquamarine, and although I'm cautious of UV, I've allowed myself a sunscreened tan, one I'm settling down on the deck to deepen slightly this afternoon.

Cavin's at work. Eli's at school. None of the neighbors are currently home. So it feels private enough out on the deck to sunbathe in the nude. I can't stand tan lines. I turn up the music, settle on a heavy beach towel draping the chaise lounge. When I close my eyes, Nirvana's "In Bloom" launches, transporting me back to a day in Las Vegas.

I was seventeen, and I'd spent the afternoon ditching school in favor of unspectacular sex with Barry Lewinski. As I chased him out the door, my sister came home, passing him on the step. She wrinkled her nose at the stink of sweaty sex clinging to his body.

She went to do her homework while I showered away my own telltale scent, and as I fixed us dinner, she put on Nirvana's *Nevermind,* which was our favorite album at that time. We knew every word by heart.

Growing up, Mel and I shared a passion for music and poetry. We escaped into a sea of words whenever things got rough, and that was often.

That day, as I put water on to boil for Kraft mac and cheese, she asked, "Do you love Barry?"

"Love? No way."

"So why do you . . . you know?"

"You don't have to be in love to have sex. Look at Mom. Do you think she loves the jerks she sleeps with?"

She thought a second. "Probably not."

"Well, then, I rest my case."

As I dropped the macaroni into the water, she stumped me. "I thought you were better than Mom."

Melody at fifteen. Rarely did she question me, but when she did, it was with a sharp tongue, one that sliced right to the bone. So I guess maybe there were hints of Melody at forty even then.

So much for relaxing. I straighten in the chair, and when my line of sight clears the deck railing, my eyes discern swift motion in the shadows of the trees. I don my robe before I stand, go to the railing to peer deeper. "Who's there?" I call.

But the only response is rustling behind a small copse the burn ignored.

"Hello?"

No answer but a crackling of twigs in the forest depths, suggesting someone striding quickly away. My stomach knots unease, though I can't detect an outline of any living thing.

Suddenly I realize I have a way of investigating, via the camera system we so recently had installed. Sticky with coconut-scented sunscreen, I go inside, locking the door behind me and praying Eli had the sense to secure the downstairs doors, too.

Apprehension glitters, though I'm not sure why. It was probably nothing but my overactive imagination, or maybe Mom's ghost, escaping memory to haunt my afternoon. Why am I so paranoid, anyway? We haven't had a problem since they locked up the neighborhood burglar.

Maybe he got out.

Why would he come back here?

Maybe it was the kid, wanting another peek.

Vacationers don't rent for multiple weeks.

Maybe it was a bear. A raccoon. A deer.

Or something completely invented.

I ponder these things on my way up the hall to check the security camera view. The system is designed to start recording whenever unique movements trigger it, or you can turn it on remotely any time you like to have a look around the property.

The office door is ajar.

A sudden surge of nerves sparks a break-out of goose bumps over my entire body, teases the hair at the nape of my neck, and sharpens my nipples into hard points. Retreat or investigate? I listen carefully but discern no distinctive noises, so I tiptoe forward and nudge the door open.

"Eli!"

He's sitting behind the desk, studying the monitor. "Did you know the camera on the corner of the house looks straight down onto the deck? Check out the great view." The chaise I recently employed is prominently featured.

"I didn't realize you were home."

He shrugs. "I'm stealthy like that."

"So you decided to spy on me?"

"Some temptations are hard to ignore."

"Why didn't you just come out on the deck?"

He stands, moves around in front of the desk, but stops short. "Because then you would've covered up."

For all his apparent worldliness, there is vulnerability on display here, too. I had no idea it could be so alluring. I loosen the sash on my robe. "Are you sure?"

His eyes grow wide, but he doesn't move. "Very funny."

I untie the sash completely, revealing a

long strip of flesh. "Not kidding."

He crosses the space between us in a single long stride, but again his confidence falters before he dares to touch me. "I . . . I . . ."

My robe falls all the way open. "Go ahead."

Still, he hesitates, so I lift his hands to my breasts. He closes his eyes. "Oh my God. I never expected . . ." He begins a slow, sweet exploration, made easy by the coconut oil still clinging to my body. His left hand traces the upper contours, a single finger trailing back and forth between the risen peaks of my nipples. His right walks down my belly, through the soft forest of hair, to the valley beneath, slips inside.

His lips touch mine, whisper upon them, "Beautiful."

But that's as close as we come to kissing, as if that act would join us too intimately. Make this wrong.

There can be no right or wrong. Only what is in this moment.

I reach for his shirt. Fumble the buttons. Who's the clumsy one now?

"I'll help you," he says, but just as the words leave his mouth the doorbell rings.

We pull away like we bit each other, and I scramble to cover up again, though whoever it is can't possibly see us in here.

"Shit," says Eli.

"Double shit," I add.

Eli laughs, and that makes me laugh, too.

"Should I answer the door?" he asks. "Or do you think they'll go away?"

"It's probably Mel."

"Then I'll get it. But first . . ." He licks his fingers. "Yum."

Matter-of-fact. No discussion. End of scene. Lights down.

Exiting the office, I turn left to my bedroom. "I'll take a shower."

Eli turns right toward the door. "I'll entertain your sister."

Hopefully not like he just entertained me.

I run the water steaming hot, stand beneath it until it fades to lukewarm, a series of words cycling through my deviant mind. Temptation. Imprudence. Distraction.

Indiscretion. Reaction. Impulsiveness. Rebellion. Recklessness.

Revenge.

I shove all of that out of my head as I dress in a comfy jogging suit that covers almost every inch of skin. Then I go to find Mel, who's in the kitchen watching Eli work on dinner. The two chatter contentedly and the blissful domestic picture makes me cringe. It looks like it should be viewed in black and white on an ancient tube television. Except, if it were one of those old TV shows, my sister would come over for a hug. All she offers is a lukewarm wave.

Eli pretends total indifference.

Admirable.

Okay, keep this thing together. I plaster on a smile. "Glad you made it. How was the drive?"

"Some road construction, but what else is new?"

Hurray for small talk.

"What's on the menu tonight, Eli?" I ask.

"Halibut. I'm fixing the marinade now."

"You don't mind if Mel and I retire to the deck, do you?"

"Nope." He turns and winks at me. "Just remember you're not alone."

Melody looks confused but doesn't ask for clarification.

"Should we take some wine with us?"

"Sounds good," she agrees.

Before I can accommodate, Cavin comes in the front door. "What a day. What a week. Thank God it's Friday." He comes straight into the kitchen, kisses me on the mouth and Mel on the cheek.

"Where's mine?" Eli asks congenially.

"Very funny."

The echo of Eli's earlier remark is slightly

unnerving. I double-check my zipper. "Mel and I were just about to take some wine outside. Join us?"

Cavin shakes his head. "I'll pour for you ladies, and then I have to change. I'm supposed to meet Ben for a couple of beers."

"Who's Ben?" asks Eli in a sneak attack.

"I don't believe you know him," answers Cavin, investigating the small countertop wine rack we purchased to use until we build a proper cellar. "There's a pinot open. That okay? Hey. What's this?" He leans over the granite for a closer view.

"Oh," says Mel. "It's strudel. Suzette wanted to show off her culinary expertise."

"Well, it looks delicious. Save me some." He fills two glasses with the amethyst-colored pinot, hands one to Mel. "Enjoy."

"What about me?" Eli asks. "Can I have some?"

Cavin rolls his eyes. "First off, it's 'may' I? And I don't think so." He offers me the second glass, turns and heads toward the bedroom.

Eli waits till he's out of sight and pours himself some anyway. Mel and I share incredulous glances, which he masterfully deflects. "What? Dad said he didn't think so, not that I couldn't."

"That's between you and him."

Mel follows me outside. I take the Adirondack and she sits at the picnic table, sniffing the air. "Still smells a little like smoke out here."

"Does it? Guess I'm used to it. Most everything's cleaned up, but those trees at the front of the stand are charred. They should survive, though. At least, that's what we've been told."

"You were lucky."

"We've been told that, too, as well as being lectured about defensible space. Who knew? Not like it's something you have to worry about on Russian Hill."

She looks up at the camera, which stares back. "Any more trouble with burglars?"

Strange question. "Not since the cops arrested the guy. But how did you hear about that?" I haven't discussed it with her.

"Cavin mentioned it at dinner in San Francisco."

Right. That was the night after the excitement. And she quizzed him about Graham and me. "I do hope he managed to convince you that all is right in our marriage."

She's quiet for a moment. "He did his best."

Not a real answer, and I'd prod more, but Eli interrupts us. "If you don't mind, I'll start the grill."

He's busy doing that when Cavin comes out to say good-bye. "I might toss a few bucks onto a blackjack table, so don't worry if I'm out late. I promise not to drink too much. But should I happen to break that promise, I promise to take a cab home."

"Promise you won't break *that* promise."

"Promise."

"Shut up already," demands Eli, defying his father by taking an obvious sip of pinot.

Cavin ignores him. "See you girls later."

"Have fun, but not too much fun," quips Eli, putting wood chips into a metal box that he places on one side of the grill. He turns on all three burners so the heat will rise quickly. Then he goes back in the house to season the halibut.

It doesn't take long to cook, and whatever he put on it is perfect — sweet and spicy and garlicky. The earlier discomfort with Mel fades into our full bellies, aided by two bottles of wine. Once the sun is all the way down, the air turns nippy, so we move inside to try some of Suzette's strudel. I'd leave it alone and save the calories, but Melody insists it would hurt the girl's feelings.

Eli cuts three way-too-big pieces. "Ice cream?"

"Not for me," I say, but Mel agrees a little vanilla would go well and Eli delivers our plates, sofa-side.

I treat myself to a huge ice-cream-free bite. "Wow. This is great. The pastry is flaky and the filling . . . Is it peach?" I enjoy another forkful. With the third, the roof of my mouth erupts furious bumps and a vicious itching follows them down my throat. My tongue balloons, but I manage to say, "EpiPen!"

"Oh, shit," exclaims Eli. "Mango."

Melody jumps up. "Where is it?"

I look around for my purse. There. Kitchen counter. I point. She dives for it, searches diligently inside. Shakes her head. "Not here."

Throat is closing.

Sinuses, too.

Cheeks puff.

Eyes sink into the bloat.

"Old purse. Coat closet."

Eli is on his feet, moving toward the front door. He yanks open the closet, finds the handbag, comes running, and dumps it on the table. There's a loud clunk as the Glock hits wood, but it's the EpiPen he grabs hold of. Ignoring the gun, he pops the injector out of its plastic tube and thrusts it in my direction, and I jab it into my thigh.

Mel shrinks back against the wall, stuttering, "I didn't know. Sorry. I didn't know."

So why is she smiling?

Immediately, the swelling begins to recede and the hives shrink. "Okay. Better."

Now, confident I'm not dying, Eli picks up the Glock, takes it out of the holster. "I didn't know you had a gun."

"Put that down." The words scratch my throat.

Curiosity apparently satisfied, Eli holsters the gun, sets it on the counter. "What is it?"

"Glock 19, Gen4."

"Do you know how to use it?"

I nod. Shit. He was never supposed to know it existed. Suddenly, my stomach knots. Releases. Knots harder. God, I hope nausea is the worst of this.

"Leave the gun alone. I'll be back as soon as I can."

I'm not able to make it to the bathroom, so I opt for outside, which is only four long steps away. I reach the railing and puke over it, onto the dirt below.

Wine.

Fish.

Lettuce.

Three big bites of mango-laced strudel.

Finally, emptied, I turn back toward the house. The gun is no longer on the table. But it isn't Eli who's studying it. In fact,

almost caressing it.
It's Melody.

THIRTY-SEVEN

Once again I dismiss the need for ER care, despite feeling quivery and disoriented. The allergic reaction was as bad as the last, or worse, and I know another would be worse still.

I sink into the comfort of the big armchair. "Eli, would you please bring me a glass of water?"

"Sure thing."

"Are you finished looking at that?" I ask Mel, suddenly nervous about her handling it, and she gingerly surrenders the Glock.

"Is it loaded?"

Some afterthought.

"Wouldn't be much good for protection otherwise."

"I didn't realize you were that scared," opines Eli, returning with my water. "All because there might or might not have been someone trying to break in?"

I indulge in three long, cleansing, cooling

liquid swallows. "Eli, not only am I positive someone was determined to get inside but Detective Cross thought so, too. In fact, it was his idea for me to purchase a weapon that would work more efficiently, and at greater distance, than a butcher knife. I hope I never have to use it, and I never meant for you to see it."

"I probably wouldn't have, either," he says. "Not like I regularly go digging through your old purses."

I note he didn't mention my underwear drawer.

"I would certainly hope not. I don't suppose I could talk you into not telling your father about it. He was fairly adamant that I not have a gun in the house."

"Because of me? Guess he thinks crazy begets crazy, huh?"

"Not necessarily. It had more to do with your grandmother's suicide."

Eli can't hide his surprise. "That's how she did it? I always figured it was pills or something."

"It is unusual for a woman to use a gun. But if you're serious about an attempt, it's got to be the most sure way to accomplish the deed." Marginally less shaky, I stash the Glock back in the handbag. I'll have to remember to move it later. "Would you please put this back in the closet and try to forget it's there?"

"Okay. Then, if it's cool and you don't need me for anything else right now, there's an on-demand movie I want to see. I'd offer to watch it with you, but I wouldn't want to offend anyone." He winks. "And don't worry. I won't tell Dad about the gun."

"Thank you, Eli. In fact, thanks for everything you did for me today."

"Aw, shucks, Mom. It was nothing. Next time, happy to do a lot more."

He smiles in nondescript fashion, replaces the Glock-heavy purse in the closet, and heads downstairs.

When he's out of sight, Mel asks, "Where did you buy the gun?"

Strange question. "From a door-to-door salesman."

"Really?"

"No, Mel. I bought it at a gun store in Reno. All legal and everything. Why?"

"I've been thinking about getting one, but I had concerns about Kayla. Now that she's out of the house . . ."

"You? You think you need protection?"

"Sacramento is a rough city and I don't always feel safe when Graham's not around. If he decides to move out of the house, I'd like to know I can take care of myself and the girls if need be."

"He's leaving?"

"It's possible."

Sure didn't sound that way when I last talked to him. But I don't dare mention he and I have spoken recently.

"What about the PI? Has he come up with anything?"

"Nothing concrete, it seems. Not yet. And I'm afraid he's eating up the retainer."

"He already has."

"What do you mean?"

"I just got a balance-due statement from Pederson —"

"Oh. I'm sorry. Guess it was more complicated than he thought. I'll try to pay you back."

"I'm not worried about the money. It's only three hundred dollars. But I was wondering if you used my name when you hired him."

"Um . . ." Extended pause. "I did, actually. He already knew you and was billing you, so I thought it made the most sense. Plus I didn't want Graham to find out."

"May I ask what the PI *has* found?" Must be something there, after putting in all those hours.

"It's personal."

Fair enough. "But he didn't follow Graham here, did he?"

"No."

At least there's that. No need to gloat. "I do hope that quelled your suspicions."

She doesn't respond, except to say, "I really wish I didn't have to ask you to cover his bill."

Conversation brakes to a sudden halt right there. So I ask, "Want to watch TV?"

I let her pick the shows, and after a couple that I try to follow with her backstory prompts, she wanders off to bed in the downstairs guestroom. She knows the way, which is good, because I don't have the desire to guide her. Despite her making the effort to visit, the rift is clear.

I try calling Cavin, but if he's in a casino, he likely won't notice his phone, which seems to be the case. Rather than return to television, I switch on some low-volume music and pick up my current reading material: *Flowers for Algernon.* The book is about two mentally handicapped individuals — one human, one mouse — who gain superior intelligence with the aid of experimental technology. For a while, I assume, as I haven't finished it yet. But it seems that Charlie, whose original IQ of 68 bloomed into an all-time high of 185, now sees his world through very different, comprehending eyes.

His mother wanted him institutionalized.

His sister hated him for his disability.

Coworkers he believed were his friends actually mocked him, and later resented him enough to get him fired.

The woman he fell in love with could never be his soul mate.

Was his previous ignorance, in fact, bliss?

I've just reached the part where smart Charlie's research finds a flaw in the scientific theory behind the intelligence-augmenting procedures he and mouse Algernon were subjected to.

Having understood the world on different terms, what would it mean to revert?

How can so few pages contain such immense questions?

I read until exhaustion finally overtakes me. Cavin still isn't home when I give in to the lure of couch cushions and a luxurious velour throw. Sinking into their comfort, I can't help but conjure a slow-motion video of my earlier cat-and-mouse game in the office. If mature men are easy, inexperienced men are more so. Even boys as bright as Eli are rocket fueled by libido.

But it was really rather nice, and my own libido rises as I replay the short encounter. I close my eyes, allow my own hands to play the role of young lover. Self-pleasuring can never match the energy of the real thing, but it does take the edge off enough to allow a slow drift toward slumber.

When my bladder rouses me, I wake to an unlit house. I use the hall bathroom and travel as quietly as I can toward our silent bedroom, where my husband snores softly on his side of the mattress. The nightstand clock informs me it's four o'clock in the dark of morning.

I wiggle out of my clothes, and when I lift the sheets, I'm greeted by the smell of fresh soap and shampoo wafting off Cavin's blanket-warmed skin. A veil of suspicion envelops me. He showered when he got home, that's abundantly clear. The pertinent question is, why?

Regardless, desire erupts like the recent mango-fueled hives — fast, hot, insistent. I reach for my man, certain my touch will disturb his dreams, coax him into consciousness, as it always has in the past.

He stirs.

Nothing more.

I soothe two fingers along the contours of his side, down his leg.

Lost in sleep, he sighs.

Fully conscious of my own limitations, I turn into his heat. Kiss his mouth. His neck.

Pause my lips at the beat of his heart.

Steady.

Slow.

Not so much as a hopeful flutter.

My hand explores the few curls on his chest. Belly. Drops to caress the muscles of his thighs, and turns so my fingertips brush his cock, which at last promises to consider my inspired invitation.

It rouses.

Writhes.

At last refuses.

Still submerged in slumber, Cavin moans. Turns over.

I shrink back into my pillow, a barrage of what-ifs volleying against the inner walls of my skull. I won't sleep now, so I get up and dress in flannel to ward off the cool of not quite dawn. I return to the couch and my book, where Charlie struggles with the meaning of his sexual being.

Him and me, both.

THIRTY-EIGHT

Saturday morning, huge day ahead, I'm up just a couple of hours beyond the time I went to bed. The rest of the house is asleep. Cavin is the first to make an appearance, and I'm glad for that. I've got questions the others don't need to hear voiced.

Hair tousled, eyes holding fast to the remnants of dreams, he smiles. "Morning, milady. How was your evening?"

Ignoring the pointless question, I gesture toward the kitchen counter. "There's coffee."

"I know. I can smell it, and you've got a cup in your hand." He goes to pour one for himself. "Something wrong?"

"You got in late."

"I told you that was possible. You're not angry about that, are you?"

"Depends."

"On . . . ?"

I consider my words carefully. "Why

didn't you wake me up when you got home?"

He sips his coffee and scans my face, trying to read my expression. "I tried, actually. You were too far gone. I figured maybe you and Melody tied one on."

"No, it was actually epinephrine and me, and it wasn't a pleasant experience."

"What?"

"The strudel had mango in it. Apparently, Suzette wasn't aware of my allergy."

He sets down his cup, comes over, puts one hand on each cheek, and dips his face to look into my eyes. "Why didn't you call me?"

I back away and his hands drop. "I did. No response. Don't get me wrong. I knew it was a long shot that you'd notice the call. Besides, I didn't want to disturb your . . ."

"My what?"

"Fun."

He grins. Straightens. "It wasn't that fun."

"Good to know."

"You are mad."

"Not really."

"What about?"

"You showered when you got home."

He should be used to my forthrightness by now, so I'm a little surprised when he takes a step back and cocks his head. "Uh,

490

yeah. I spent four hours in a casino and came home permeated with cigarette smoke. Why would you think I'd do something as crazy as soap and water otherwise? Scrubbing away evidence of sex?"

All I can do is shrug.

"Seriously, Tara? Misplaced jealousy does not become you. Is this because your sister's here?"

Odd question.

"Is what because I'm here?"

We both start at the sound of Mel's voice, preceding her up the stairs. At least she gave fair warning.

"Nothing," I say.

But Cavin takes the direct approach. "Tara seems to have it in her head that I got laid while I was out last night."

"Oh," says Mel, quite obviously doing her best not to react. "Um, I'll go on outside and let you, uh, discuss. Mind if I grab some coffee first?"

"Help yourself," huffs Cavin, moving out of her way.

The three of us look in different directions, as if giving each other access to our thought-processing rituals might make them moot.

At this point, I couldn't care less about what Mel thinks. Her brain is askew anyway.

As for Cavin, the worst thing about his assertion is I can't find a reasonable way to deny it. Not that I'd even try with Melody as a witness. The last thing I'd want is her testimony. Besides, it's her birthday. Not her zoo, not her orangutans, bring the lady a cupcake.

That reminds me. "Happy birthday, by the way," I say when she walks past, mug in hand.

"It's tomorrow, remember? But thank you. Now, if you'll excuse me . . ." Rather than choose the deck, where she's bound to overhear something she shouldn't, she opts for the front door.

I don't see Cavin angry very often, but he's definitely pissed now, which makes my own anger retreat like a spider into a corner. I lower my voice. "I'm sorry. I don't mean to be paranoid, but the thing is, when I came to bed last night, I wanted sex. I tried very hard to rouse you, or at least your penis, but no go. I guess that made me a little hurt and a lot suspicious."

"Okay. So, why didn't you just wait a little and try again?"

"Fair question. I guess I just don't feel very confident lately. In fact, I feel like a big, bloated slug. I can't work out like I want to, and I have no reason to put on makeup or dress in something pretty. You deserve better."

His whole frame softens. "Tara, I don't care about any of that. While I might have initially been attracted to the package, I fell in love with the woman beneath the wrapping."

I drop the tense demeanor. "Easy to say. Harder to believe. I'll work on it, though."

"So, all is well?"

"Depends."

"On what?"

"Did you win or lose last night? At the tables, I mean."

"May I pour you another cup of coffee?"

Uh-oh. "Are you changing the subject?"

"I suppose I was trying. Fact is, I was up quite a bit for a while, but in the end I lost a bill."

"A bill? Like a hundred?"

He clenches his jaw. "Like a thousand."

That is not what I wanted to hear. "I see."

"But don't worry. I keep a special gaming account. My winnings always go in there, and it's still very much in the black."

The more you learn. I wish I would've taken a better look at that ATM withdrawal receipt in his car. I never thought to check account numbers. I'll have to be smarter going forward. "It's hard not to worry about it, Cavin."

"I know. I'll try to do better myself."

"Better as in don't gamble as much, or better as in win more often than you lose?"

"Both."

One is in his control, the other not. Still, I make an effort to lighten the conversation. "Well, there goes that Hawaiian vacation."

"Don't say that. I'll set up a lemonade stand to make up for it."

We both fake laugh, and I guess that's that for the moment because I really have to concentrate on what lies ahead today. "I should probably leave here around noon. It's an hour to the winery, and the tour begins at two. That should give me plenty of time to iron out any bugs."

"Is Eli riding with you?"

"Yes, and Melody, too. Eli wanted to bring his own car, but parking will be limited. I told him he could drive the Escalade home if he wants to leave early, and I'll hitch a ride with you. We can figure that out on the far end."

"You trust Eli with your car?" He sounds incredulous.

I smile. "He's borrowed it before and always returned it without a scratch. In fact, I think that new little ding in the door happened under your watch."

Cavin's cheeks flare. "Runaway shopping cart, and it wasn't mine. Sorry. I kind of hoped you wouldn't notice."

"How well do you know me, my darling? I notice everything, at least about things that matter to me."

An odd look crosses his face, one I can't decipher. "I can talk to a body shop, get an estimate."

"I'm sure the repair would cost a lot more than a small annoyance is worth."

"You're probably right. So . . ." Abrupt subject change. "About tonight. What time should I get there?"

"Five thirty-ish. The buses will return around then, and the bar will be open. Dinner's at six, and Graham's band will fire up for dancing at seven."

"You don't need help with anything before that?"

"I believe we've got everything covered. Just show up on time, looking like the debonair doctor you are."

"I will arrive promptly, dressed to the nines in tails and stethoscope."

"A regular tux will do, and please make sure the stethoscope matches your cummerbund. Oh. You *could* do me a favor. Mel's girls are bringing sleeping bags, but apparently Cassandra's son doesn't possess such a thing. Could you please locate one for Taylor and put it in the game room? Everyone not claiming a spot on a bed will sleep on the floor in there."

"Sounds like a recipe for teenage foul play."

"If kids want to play, they'll find a way. Not my job to worry about it."

"I suppose that's true. So the plan is for everyone to meet up at the winery, right? No one's coming by here first?"

We've been over this. Did he forget? "The house will remain guest free until after the event. Then tomorrow we'll celebrate Mel's birthday with a lake cruise on the MS *Dixie II.*"

"You are quite the planner."

"It *is* a strong suit. Now if you'll excuse me, I need to get beautiful."

I send Cavin downstairs to remind Eli he needs to be ready by noon, then sequester myself in the master bath, where I spend way too much time perfecting my makeup and hair. By the time I withdraw from our bedroom, new dress revealing a fair amount of sun-kissed skin, it is almost time to go. Luckily, Melody is waiting, and so is Eli.

When he sees me, he actually wolf whistles. "Wow, Mom, if that dress doesn't net you some large donations, I don't know what would." At my cross look, he adds, "I know, I know. Don't call you Mom."

Melody, whose pink sundress exposes even more skin than mine, says, "I think it's kind of cute when you call her Mom."

At least she found some semblance of a sense of humor.

THIRTY-NINE

The tour of the Fresh for Families farms goes off without a hitch. I serve as escort for one bus, and Jason takes charge of the second. Eli and Melody volunteer to stay behind to help with the food and set up the silent auction.

Before we leave, Mel pulls me aside. "Your Jason is kind of cute. Is he attached?"

"First of all, he's not 'mine,' and no, he isn't attached, at least not that I'm aware of. I'm surprised you're interested, though. I thought you were trying to work on your marriage."

She shrugs. "Doesn't hurt to have options."

It's a valid opinion.

Eli is all business, effortlessly coordinating caterers, winery workers, and volunteers. He's mature way beyond his years. I'm glad I decided to trust him. And who knows? Maybe he does have a future in fund-raising, or at least event planning.

The coaches are comfortable, and the farmers are accommodating, graciously answering every question while guiding us around their properties, some of which are already dormant beneath the early autumn sun. It's a gorgeous afternoon, with only a small breeze carrying the perfumes of soil and toasted cornstalks, the vague scent of manure.

We pull back into the winery parking lot at 5:28, right on time. I'm proud of that, too. I *am* quite the planner. Destined donors exit the buses and head straight to the bar or to the patio, where hors d'oeuvres await and barbecue smoke trails into the darkening sky.

I'm gratified to see the seamless motion.

Outside, where big warming trays hold a fragrant array of foods, Eli converses with the head caterer, perhaps about a career in the business. Who knows? I circle the long tables, nod approvingly, and give Eli an awkward hug.

"Everything looks wonderful. Thank you."

"No problem, Mom."

For once that doesn't bother me.

Inside, on the far end of the large tasting room, Graham and his guys are setting up instruments and amplifiers. When he sees me, Graham offers a vague smile and gives a small wave. I circle the room to ask, "Anything you need?"

"A happier wife?"

We both glance toward Melody, who's pretending to watch Suzette and Jessica put pencils next to the silent auction sheets. But we know her sour scowl means she's been monitoring our innocent exchange.

All I can do is sigh.

"Be sure to grab something to eat before you start to play. Logan is barbecuing tri tip. He insisted on providing the meat, says it's his specialty."

"As soon as we finish here," agrees Graham.

Cars keep arriving, spilling people happy to celebrate FFF's accomplishments. Jason and his volunteers direct them to the bar and food, and the evening is off to a splendid start.

Cavin has yet to make an appearance.

I'm only slightly annoyed. Well, slightly more than slightly.

Regardless, I have work to do. I circulate, inviting our guests to please detour into a back room where the expertly crafted video plays in an endless loop, reminding them of the wide network of growers committed to helping families in need and how their donations, large or small, can help them, too.

I'm outside, talking wine with Logan and his wife, when a familiar squeal slices through the laughter and chatter. "Eli!"

Kayla rushes over to him, jumps up and puts her arms around his neck, then kisses him long and hard. Inappropriate for this setting. Even Eli looks embarrassed, and nothing fazes that kid. Luckily, Taylor joins them, giving Eli the excuse to pull slightly away, though Kayla keeps a tight hold on his hand.

"Hey, girl. You look amazing." It's Cassandra, with Charlie close behind, and I realize I've missed her. It's good to see her face. She's the closest thing to a motiveless friend I've ever had, and while our conversations rarely ran very deep, at least we talked.

"So happy you made it." I reach for a quick hug. "You, too, Charlie. Thanks so much for coming and for bringing Kayla along."

"No problem," he says. "She added entertainment value."

"Really?"

"Yeah. She and Taylor explored a laundry list of conspiracy theories. Did you know that 9/11 was part of a government plot to invade Iraq in a quest for oil?"

I grin. "I've heard that theory advanced, yes. Sounds reasonable to me. But then, I still believe in unicorns."

"Oh my God," he says. "You, too?"

"The two of you can discuss that later," interrupts Cassandra, "along with Bigfoot and Tahoe Tessie. But where's that gorgeous doctor of yours?"

"Making house calls, apparently. I haven't seen him."

"He's right there," insists Charlie, pointing behind me.

I turn and there he, in fact, is, with Melody at his side. When they get closer, they split.

Drink in hand, Mel goes to talk to Kayla, who must've ignored saying hello in her effort to glom onto Eli. Cavin comes over to me, looking elegant in a tail-less, stethoscope-free tux. "Sorry I'm late," he says. "An accident on fifty had the highway backed up for miles." He's never without a logical excuse, and he isn't all that late, anyway. He turns his attention to Cassandra and Charlie. "So good to see you again. Quite the shindig my wife has created, isn't it?"

They agree that it is, and I encourage them to get some food before the music begins. "I expect a dance or two," I tell Cavin.

"Can I bring you a glass of wine first?" he asks.

"Later. I want to stay clear-headed for a while."

"You know, I don't believe I've ever seen you otherwise," he says.

"I have!" chimes Cassandra.

Wisely, Charlie remains silent about the time he and I tied one on in San Francisco, not that anything untoward happened because of it, despite his overt invitation. Neither Cassandra nor Cavin needs to be privy to that.

Charlie does say, "Well, I could use a glass of wine. Cass?"

I flinch at the nickname, but she doesn't at all. "Please. I'll hold us a place in the food line."

"I'll go with you, Charlie," says Cavin.

And suddenly I'm standing alone.

I survey the milling guests. Everyone wears a smile. Almost everyone, that is. Mel can't quite seem to find one. She hovers off to one side, sipping a glass of what's definitely not wine and absentmindedly tugging at the hem of her short skirt. Despite her newly sculpted body and youthful hair, the anxiety creasing her face makes her look older than her forty years.

I make my way over to her through the thickening crowd. "Everything okay?"

She meets my eyes. "Sure. Why?"

"You look unhappy."

"I'm not happy, Tara. I thought you knew that."

"What can I do to help?"

She snorts. "Get me another drink?" She tosses back what's left of the current one. "Never mind. I'll get it."

Off she goes, and now I'm confused. She seemed fine on the ride over. What happened between then and now? Maybe Eli knows something? I scan the patio, but he, Kayla, and Taylor are nowhere in sight. I can only guess what they're up to. I wander toward the tasting room, stopped every few feet by queries I must take the time to answer. When I finally manage to reach the door, I'm stunned to find my husband chatting cordially with Sophia.

She was not on the guest list.

Maybe you need a glass of wine after all.

I choose to abstain. For the moment.

The guitar player strums his instrument, signaling the start of the band's first set. I wave a thumbs-up sign at Graham, and when I turn around, I see Austin and Mary-ann Colvin exiting the room where the video's playing. Ah. That's how Sophia knew about tonight. They must have encouraged her to come. They join her and Cavin now, and I guess I probably should, too.

I cross the room in three long, confident strides, and at my approach Cavin moves a few inches away from Sophia, who smiles in a way I really don't care for. I refuse to reward her with the reaction she so obviously wants. In fact, I ignore her completely and instead extend my hand toward the Colvins.

"Good evening, Maryann. Austin. Thanks so much for coming."

"But of course," says Maryann. "We wouldn't have missed it for the world."

Austin gestures in a semicircular motion. "Great job. You've accomplished a lot in such a short amount of time."

"She's a wonder," observes Cavin.

"Yes," hisses Sophia. "A wonder."

I offer her a calculated grimace. "I hope you brought your checkbook. Fresh for Families can use your support. Please take a few minutes to view the video and open your . . . heart. Cavin, darling, I'd like that glass of wine now. Would you mind?"

"Not at all. If you'll excuse me."

Sophia watches him go. "What is it about

a man in a tux that brings out my inner deviant?"

"Inner? You have more than one?" Slip of the tongue, and I'm not even drunk. I remind myself to take it easy.

Maryann gasps, but Austin chuckles and saves me. "Wish there were more deviant women in the world. They make life so interesting. Let's get something to eat, shall we, my dear?"

He leads his wife away, and once they're out of earshot I pointedly tell Sophia, "You do not belong here."

She takes it in perfect stride. "Oh, but I do. I'd worry about that if I were you. Meanwhile, I did bring my checkbook."

Sophia pushes past me and a familiar voice, steeped in alcohol, falls over my shoulder. "That woman is a serious bitch."

"I know, Mel, I know."

I'm uncomfortable with the whole situation, so I'm happy when Cavin rescues me with a big glass of syrah. "Sorry it took so long. The place is packed. Well done."

"I could do with one fewer person."

"I had no idea she'd be here."

I really hope that's the truth.

"I know."

"Why don't the two of you dance?" I suggest to Mel and my husband. "Maybe that would encourage people out on the floor. No use letting good music go to waste."

"I haven't danced in years," says Mel. "I don't think I remember how."

"It's like riding a bike. Your body will remember how." I take her glass. "Go on. Let your hair down."

She looks doubtful but follows Cavin, and while she isn't exactly relaxed at first, after a minute or two she's actually moving to the beat. Before long, others join them, including the Colvins. Austin has pretty good moves.

I travel the far wall, where the silent auction items are drawing attention, the bids increasing to a satisfying degree. I even bid on a couple myself — a new pair of skis, and a weekend stay at a spa in historic Genoa, Nevada. Then I allow myself the luxury of a bathroom break. It's been hours since I peed, I realize.

I have to wait for whoever's inside the restroom marked with a skirted stick figure, and have almost decided to use the men's room when the door unlocks. Just beyond is Kayla, whose eyes are shot through with crimson streaks. Not to mention, she reeks of liquor.

"Having a good time?" I ask.

"Uh . . . yeah."

"Maybe a little too good?"

"No sush thing," she slurs.

"You'd better quit now, and if Eli is anywhere close to the state you're in, you might encourage him to quit, too. How exactly did you score the booze?"

She grins. "Wouldn' you like to know?"

"Actually, yes, I would."

"I'm jus' relaxing, Aun' Tara. Been working hard, like you wanted. I deserve a li'l fun."

"Keep it in check. Hangovers aren't so fun."

I use the bathroom before someone else wants it and am washing my hands when all hell breaks loose.

"You leave him the fuck alone!"

The music stops and footsteps pound as I rush out the door, into the tasting room, where Taylor and Cavin are pulling my niece up and off a woman splayed on the floor at Eli's feet. I'm half gratified, half mortified to discover it's Sophia. Witnessing the scene are most of our guests, including Cassandra, Charlie, and Melody, in whose embrace Kayla is sobbing.

Eli helps Sophia off the floor.

"Don't touch her!" screams Kayla, completely unhinged.

"That's enough!" orders Cavin, taking

charge. He puts an arm around Melody's shoulders and steers her toward the patio, obliging Kayla to go, too.

Eli looks at Sophia, as if asking for her permission to leave. In answer, she shrugs, and he reluctantly trails the others outside.

"Okay, everyone," announces Jason. "Looks like someone maybe had a little too much to drink tonight, but everything's under control. The night is young. Let's get back to why we're here. Music, please!"

Sophia and the Colvins are huddled in a tight knot. I go over to them. "What happened?" Stupid question. I've got the gist of the answer, if not the details.

"I was dancing with Eli," answers Sophia, "and that . . . that . . . person came barreling into me."

"Are you okay?"

"My ass will be bruised, and my scalp is sore where she yanked on my hair, but other than that, I guess I'm fine."

Pretty sure her ego is black-and-blue, too. *Go ahead and smile.*

"Do you know that little monster?" asks Sophia.

The answer is obvious. "I do."

"I don't think she belongs here," she mocks. "Did she bring her checkbook?"

I hook Sophia's elbow with mine. "Let's

talk." I walk her toward the front door and, when we're outside, drop her arm. "Kayla is Eli's girlfriend. She's been away at college and was anxious to see him. I'm sure it was something of a shock to find him dancing with you."

"She's drunk."

"I realize that, and of course her overreaction hinged on that. I, however, am sober, and I want you to leave."

In the yellow glare of the porch light, I can see the knot-unknot of her fingers and the tense rise of her shoulders. I expect a jab. Instead, she parries, "Fine. If I manage a winning silent-auction bid, Cavin can let me know."

She rotates on one heel, and as she goes in search of her car I say out loud, "Over my dead body." Two beats. "Or yours."

When I turn, Cassandra is standing right behind me. "What was that all about?" she asks.

"Just removing a thorn from my side. I'll give you the lowdown later."

We go back inside, where all seems to be well. The first thing I do is go over to the silent-auction table and find Sophia's bids.

And raise them.

FORTY

Despite Kayla's melodrama, the Fresh for Families fundraiser was, by everyone's assessment, a huge success. The ultimate tally won't be known until all donations are accounted for, and several people will mail them or send them online. But what came in last night alone, including the silent auction, was close to sixty thousand.

My bids netted the skis and two tickets anywhere Southwest Airlines flies. I despise Southwest, with its unassigned seats and peanuts for food, but I had to outbid Sophia. Wonder where she wanted to go.

And with whom.

I had to stay late to help with the bookkeeping and oversee the cleanup, so I sent everyone home ahead of me except Graham, who needed to break down his equipment anyway and offered me a ride. That was good, because I wasn't about to let either Eli or Mel drive the Escalade. Instead,

I gave the keys to Charlie, after a heavy assessment.

"I'm in fine shape," he claimed.

"Prove it."

He recited the alphabet backward without a stumble. Good enough.

Eli, who was still fuming, went with Cavin, leaving Taylor and Kayla to go with Cassandra. Charlie carted Melody and the younger girls. Mel wanted to stay and supervise her husband and me, though that isn't the way she put it. But by ten, she was almost asleep, drugged into oblivion by one too many Scotches on the rocks. I refused to take no for an answer.

Graham and I packed it in around eleven fifteen, both of us tired but content. Rather than sit in total silence, I used the time to ask, "Any idea what got into Mel today? By the time we got back from the tour, she was already on edge and drinking."

"I guess she and Suzette got into it earlier. Suz wants to spend next year as a foreign exchange student and put in an application. Melody said okay, thinking she would never be accepted. She was, and she got her country of choice — Austria. You know how much she loves her snowboarding. But now Mel wants her to back out."

"I don't get it. Sounds like a great opportunity."

"It totally is. Honestly, I have no clue what Mel's objection is."

I thought for a minute. "Maybe with you leaving, she's afraid to let go of someone else."

"What do you mean, leaving? I'm not going anywhere."

"Oh. Good. I'm relieved to hear it."

The conversation ended there because a raccoon wandered out into the highway in front of us. Graham expertly steered around the creature, who was, I'm sure, even happier about that than I was. Graham slowed down, worried about other nocturnal adventurers, and we arrived, safe and sound, at home a little before one.

I did not check up on the sleeping arrangements. I figured the adults in charge could handle it, and if they couldn't it wasn't my job anyway. Besides, the atmosphere downstairs could only have been strained at best. Pretty sure I heard muted arguing, but I can't say who it was.

Due to alcohol or sheer exhaustion, everyone sleeps in late the next morning, emerging from their personal cocoons disheveled and/or fighting hangovers. With a couple of exceptions, they ask for ibuprofen, antacids, Pepto-Bismol, water, or coffee. No hair of the dog.

So I guess it isn't surprising that our *Dixie* cruise feels more subdued than celebratory, especially when the Tahoe wind rises, as it often does in the afternoon, causing an up-and-down, side-to-side motion. No one eats, and only Cassandra, Charlie, and I sip the champagne I bought to toast Mel's fortieth birthday.

The unusual dynamics must be obvious, even to strangers.

Eli has taken the two younger girls under his arm. I'd worry about him putting the moves on Suzette, but I'm more concerned about older women.

He's definitely not talking to Kayla, who flirts unmercifully with Taylor. The boy eats it up. It's not like he cares what Eli thinks. They're acquaintances, not close friends.

Cavin and Graham are talking. About what, I have no clue, but they do not include Mel in their conversation.

Melody acts the strangest of all. It's like she's barely here with us in the land of the living. "I'm not feeling well," is her excuse for sitting off by herself, eyes closed, one leg twitching.

"Some party," observes Charlie.

"I was thinking the same thing," I agree.

"We'll just have to consider last night the

party," says Cassandra.

Charlie nods. "Yeah. And today is the aftermath."

"We can enjoy it, anyway." I tip my glass toward my sister, who's too lost inside herself to notice. "Happy birthday, Mel! And many more."

As if in answer, she jumps to her feet and leans over the railing, spilling whatever her stomach was holding into the azure Tahoe water.

"Ahem," says Charlie. "I think I'll go hang out with the guys."

Mel stumbles back into her seat, nodding her head and closing her eyes, a clear statement to leave her alone. Cassandra and I spend the rest of the cruise discussing San Francisco. Tahoe. Charlie. Cavin. Off-Broadway. Shakespeare at Sand Harbor. Genevieve Lennon. Nick, the personal trainer I had back in the city. The one I made the mistake of sleeping with. The one who changed gyms when my complaint made him lose his job, and ended up working at Cassandra's gym.

"He got fired from there, too, you know," she tells me.

"Really?"

"Yeah. I guess he slept with the owner's wife."

"Some people never change."

I consider that carefully. Some people never change. Prince or troll, they hang on tight to the truth of themselves and feel no need to trade places. Others work very hard to transform themselves, and not always in positive ways. I fought my way out of "Idaho," and through three marriages to men not suited for me. How this one will end is anyone's guess. Divorce? Death? It can only be one or the other.

Back at the marina, Cassandra herds Kayla and Taylor into her car. She and Charlie packed up for the return trip before we left home so they could head straight back to San Francisco. Kayla glances at Eli, but whatever she sees convinces her there's no need for a good-bye. So maybe last night drove the final wedge between them, which in my opinion is for the best.

The Sacramento returnees left their stuff at our house, which is on the way. The kids ride with Cavin and Graham. Mel joins me in the Beamer. The others take off, but I pause long enough to inquire, "Are you okay?"

When Mel looks at me, her eyes seem unable to focus. "I will be once I swallow a Xanax. I left them in my overnight case."

"I didn't know you were taking meds."

"I needed something to combat my anxiety."

"Be careful. Xanax can be habit-forming, and it isn't without side effects."

"Thanks for your concern, doctor, but I've got it under control."

I don't quiz her more and when we get home she disappears, I presume to go pop a pill to do battle with her nerves.

Cavin's in the kitchen, fixing sandwiches.

"Finally hungry?" I ask.

He shrugs. "I figured the kids, at least, might want something to nibble on in the car. I'm surprised the girls haven't asked for food. They weren't drinking last night. At least, I'm pretty sure they weren't."

The young women in question are out on the deck with Eli, who looks vaguely amused by their cheerful chatter. "It was nice of you to think of it. Here, let me help."

We are wrapping the sandwiches for travel when Graham crests the stairs and comes into the kitchen. He glances around. "Where's Melody?"

"Did you check the downstairs bathroom?"

"Uh, yeah. I just used it."

Odd.

I call to the girls, "Have you seen your mom?"

Negative.

Graham goes to the front door, peeks outside. "Her car is gone."

"That can't be." I stomp up the hallway, take a look for myself. He's right. She's gone. "Why wouldn't she say good-bye?"

"No clue."

I gesture for us to step out front, closing the door behind us. "Did you know Mel's taking Xanax?"

"What? No. She never discussed it with me."

"Could that be responsible for her unusual behavior of late?"

He nods. "It could, actually. It could explain a lot."

Graham's compelled to leave immediately. He calls to the girls to get their stuff, and they retreat to do exactly that. While they're gathering their essentials, I try calling Mel, not that I expect her to answer, and she doesn't. I leave her a voice mail. "Where did you go in such a hurry? It would've been nice to say good-bye."

Eli carries the girls' stuff out to Graham's car, and Cavin hands over the sandwiches. As Graham starts the engine, I urge, "Please let me know you made it home safely. Mel, too."

He promises he will, and as his taillights

disappear my concern dissolves immediately. Mel's circus. Mel's orangutans.

What's left of the afternoon dissolves into evening. Our appetites return with a vengeance, and we are at the dinner table enjoying pizza and salad. Cavin turns on a local newscast at the top of the hour. All three of us almost choke on the lead story.

"Douglas County Sheriff's deputies are on the scene of an apparent murder on Kingsbury Grade," intones the anchor. "Details are sketchy, but the department confirms the victim, Sophia Garibaldi, died of a gunshot wound to the chest. . . ."

"Holy fucking shit!" exclaims Eli.

"No." Cavin's face drains of every molecule of pigment.

"Oh my God." Those words are mine.

The studio cameras give way to a live shot with a young reporter who looks green, and not because of the lighting. She's standing in front of an upscale condominium complex with, of all people, Deputy Cross. "Can you tell us what happened?"

"It's an ongoing investigation, and we don't know a lot yet. What we do know is that she was scheduled to meet with a friend and when he was unable to contact her, he called us. We found her on the living room floor, unresponsive, with a bullet wound to the chest. The state of her body confirms she died sometime last night. The television was on, with the volume extremely loud, which might explain why no neighbors heard the gunshot. . . ."

We sit in stunned silence, which Eli finally breaks. "Who the fuck would do that? I mean, she was a bitch and all, but . . ."

"Maury, maybe?" I guess.

"He's an old dude, and probably in love with her," says Eli. "Why would he kill her?"

"Scorned love often leads to crimes of passion," I reply. "He wasn't with her last night."

"Oh shit. You don't think she was sleeping with him, do you? Because that would be sick."

"Frankly, Eli, I don't think she cared about who she slept with, as long as it got her what she wanted. In fact, wasn't it you who once said something like that to me?"

Cavin remains silent. I can almost see the jumbled emotions pinwheeling inside his head. Whatever their relationship had become, he still cared about Sophia, that much is obvious. Finally, he manages, "How could this happen? I just saw her."

The remark stokes small embers of jealousy. And satisfaction. "We all did. She always made a point of being seen."

"I just danced with her," adds Eli, as if we need the reminder. "It was probably her last dance."

I'm guessing he's right. And it reminds me how intimately Sophia was connected to this family, which means we can probably expect a visit from law enforcement.

It only takes two days.

FORTY-ONE

Cavin's in surgery.

Eli's in school.

I'm loading the dishwasher when the doorbell, expected, rings.

Detective Martina Lopez introduces herself. "May I come in?"

"This is in regards to . . . ?" I don't even sound like I have no clue.

"Sophia Garibaldi. You're familiar?"

"Of course. Do come in." I lead the way inside. "Can I get you something? Coffee? Water?"

"No thank you."

I gesture toward the armchair. "Please sit."

"Thank you."

All this politeness is irritating. "What can I do for you?"

"I'm sure you've heard that Ms. Garibaldi was shot to death in her home, yes?"

"I watch the news. So yes. It's been hard to miss."

She assesses me carefully, taking note of my awkward posture. "Something wrong?"

Let's see. Someone well acquainted with several members of this family is dead, and there's a detective in my living room, taking notes. But that's not where I go, not even remotely. "Oh, yes. I had knee surgery not long ago. It's still hard to find a comfortable way to sit."

"Ah. Skiing?"

"Exactly. It's how I met my husband, in fact. He's an orthopedic surgeon at Barton."

She brings her eyes level with mine. "We know."

Of course they do.

Now she amends, "We'll interview him separately."

"As a suspect?"

"As a possible witness, though at the moment everyone who knew Ms. Garibaldi is a suspect."

"Including me."

"Including you."

At least she's direct.

"Can you tell me your whereabouts this past weekend?"

"Well, yes. Friday I experienced a food allergy reaction that required an EpiPen intervention. Saturday, I was in charge of a fund-raising effort that required my attention all day, and well into the evening. And Sunday was my sister's birthday. We celebrated with a *Dixie* cruise, followed by pizza right here."

"You have witnesses who can confirm all that?"

"Absolutely."

Suddenly, it strikes me. "Do I need an attorney?"

"Not at the moment. You're not under arrest."

Arrest? I'm kind of thinking I do need an attorney, and a good one. Be careful what you say, Tara. "I have no idea why I would be a suspect. I knew Sophia, but not well."

"Your husband knew her well."

Cavin. They think he did it. How much do they know about his relationship with Sophia? "What are you fishing for, Detective?"

"Whatever you're willing to tell me." She produces a small tablet. "You don't mind if I record our conversation, I hope. I'd never want to be accused of not having my facts straight."

I don't like this woman. "Sophia knew lots of men. Cavin was one of them, yes, but their relationship ended some time ago."

"Are you sure?"

"Sure enough to have married him."

"Are you familiar with a private investigator named Blaine Pederson?"

I'm starting to feel a little sick. "Yes. He's done some work for me in the past."

"Investigating your husband."

"At Cavin's urging. He wanted me to be sure about his motives before our wedding. I've got substantial investments to protect, and —"

"You didn't hire Pederson to follow your husband more recently?"

What is she talking about?

"Absolutely not. I trust my husband."

She types something into her tablet. "You know, I think I'll take that water, if it's all right."

Detective Lopez follows me toward the kitchen, lagging behind enough to give the place (and me, I assume) a once-over. Not much to see, in my opinion.

I'm filling her glass when she asks, "Do you drive a Cadillac Escalade?"

"It's one of my cars, yes."

"Does anyone else have access to the vehicle?"

"Of course. My husband. My stepson. Assorted other family members, if they happen to be visiting. Why?"

She takes the glass from my hand. Sips.

Sips again. "An Escalade has been spotted several times on Ms. Garibaldi's street."

"I'm sure there are other Escalades in South Lake Tahoe. Besides, I don't even know where Sophia lived, other than up on Kingsbury somewhere, and everyone's aware of that at this point."

"How old is your stepson?"

"Eli's eighteen. Why?"

"You said he has access to your cars."

"I think that should be obvious. They're parked on the property."

"But he also drives a black Humvee."

"That's his car, yes."

"Must be nice. Did you know he had a personal relationship with the victim?"

Oh my God. How much should I say? "I am aware of that. Do you mind if we sit back down? Standing is difficult for me."

Not that difficult, really. But at this point, I'm hoping for a little sympathy.

"Of course."

We reverse direction, settle back down in the living room. Eli? No. He might be sullen and resentful, and even righteously pissed off at Sophia, but he'd never pick up a gun and kill her.

Gun.

Shit.

"Are you more comfortable now?" When I

nod, she continues, "Did you recently have an intruder here?"

"Well, it's been a couple of months, and he didn't get inside. But yes, he tried."

"And it was a Deputy Cross who took the report?"

"That's correct."

The sense of discomfort accelerates. The top of my head is tingling, like my brain really, really wants me to shut the hell up.

"At that time, he dusted your downstairs doors for fingerprints?"

So why don't I shut up? "Yes."

"And he also collected yours for comparison."

Please shut up. "Yes."

"At that time, he advised that you might want to consider a firearm for personal protection."

Shut up.

Shut up.

Shut up.

I snap my mouth shut.

"Is that correct?"

"Yes."

"Did you purchase a Glock 19, Gen4?"

She already knows the answer. "I did."

"Do you know where it is currently?"

"Of course. It's in the closet."

"May I see it?"

Nerves erupt in my stomach. I push to my feet, go to the closet, take the purse from the coat hook inside.

Too light.

Much too light.

Still, I take it back into the other room. Turn it upside down on the coffee table. All that falls out are some ancient breath mints and three sets of spare keys. "It's gone."

"I know. We found it in a Dumpster, mostly wiped clean of prints. But we were able to pull a couple of partials from the barrel."

"I need that attorney."

"I think that's a very good idea."

"May I call my husband before you arrest me?"

"Make it quick."

This is unbelievable.

Cavin is still in surgery when I call, so I leave a message with Rebecca that this is an extreme emergency and to please check his text messages immediately. *Arrested for Sophia's murder. Best attorney possible now.*

I am arrested. Read my rights. Humiliated by handcuffs. Led to a county vehicle and stuffed into the backseat. Driven down the mountain to the Douglas County Jail, where I am processed like a common criminal and put into a holding cell. They offer the services of a public defender, which I vehemently turn down.

I don't say another word, though a colleague joins Detective Lopez to try the "good cop, bad cop" routine.

Good cop: "We understand other people had access to the gun."

Lopez: "Too bad we only found your fingerprints on it."

Good cop: "Your husband had motive. Do you think he did it?"

Lopez: "You had motive, too."

Good cop: "I don't blame you. I might lose my temper if I found out my wife was fucking around on me."

Lopez: "Losing your temper is one thing. Revenge is another."

Revenge for what, exactly? I have no idea what they're talking about, but it doesn't matter. I've never been arrested before, but I know enough not to incriminate myself any more than I might have already. I go over and over inside my head exactly what I said to Lopez. Pretty sure I gave her no information they didn't already have.

It's late afternoon by the time the attorney Cavin hired is allowed to speak to me. He's a tall, slender man of sixty or so, and I hope age in his case means wisdom. He introduces himself as Leonard Fleming but allows I should call him Len.

"How much trouble am I in?"

"I don't as yet know everything they've got, but it appears to me that their evidence is largely circumstantial."

"So what's next?"

"The detectives will present their report to the prosecutor's office. You'll be arraigned. We'll plead not guilty and ask for bail."

"Do you know what they're charging me with?"

"That will be up to the prosecutor."

"Is there any chance of bail?"

Len shrugs. "Depends on the charge and the judge. You've got close ties to the community, which reduces your risk of flight. If the judge agrees, it's liable to be a substantial amount."

"How long until arraignment?"

"They're allowed forty-eight hours. I'll do my best to get you out of here by Friday."

"I don't know if it means anything or not, and you probably hear it all the time, but I did not do this."

"Do you have any idea who did?"

I've had all afternoon to think about it. There are four possibilities.

Cavin, who maybe I don't know nearly as well as I thought I did. Eli warned me there was more to his relationship with Sophia than I believed. But Cavin, as far as I know, had no clue about the gun.

Eli, who did know about the gun, and who had a recent confrontation with Sophia. But he cared about her, and I've never suspected him to be capable of overt violence.

Kayla, who might have found out about the gun from Eli and whose mental illness might push her into a very bad decision under certain circumstances. Sophia was on her shortlist of enemies and, quite possibly, so was I.

Finally, Melody.

She knew about the gun.

She was visiting at the time.

If she got up in the middle of the night, she could have taken the Escalade, accomplished the deed, returned the Cadillac, and gone back to bed before any of us noticed anything amiss. There were spare keys in the purse where the gun was.

I remember her demeanor that afternoon on the *Dixie.*

Shaky.

Pale.

Nauseous.

Uncommunicative.

Those things could be explained by a hangover, or Xanax, or a combination of

531

the two. But then she took off without explanation or good-byes. The more I think about it, the likelier it seems.

An immense question materializes.

Why?

Why Look for Meaning

in little things:
the murmur of a sparrow's
wings, questions
asked of wind and seed
lost in autumn grass;

the stubborn reach
of surf, intent on whittling
beach and arranging
curls of seaweed
on driftwood statuary;

the copper scent
of rain on prairie shoulders,
bent by drought,
slivers of creation, wet
in shallow reflection.

Why look for meaning
in little things
when monoliths stand
square in your way
and are easier, by far,

to topple?

EPILOGUE

Crazy does, indeed, beget crazy. Turns out Melody inherited the worst kind of crazy from our dear, departed Mom. The kind that not only negates compassion but also eliminates even the slightest compunction about murdering a complete stranger, all in the name of revenge.

Revenge against me.

The motion detection cameras we had installed on the exterior of the house did trigger with Mel's leaving that night in my Escalade and returning an hour and twenty minutes later. The footage was time-stamped and coincided with Sophia's approximate time of death as reported by the autopsy.

Unbeknownst to anyone else in the house, I had nanny cams installed in several rooms, too. The one in the living room caught Melody Ann Schumacher coming up the stairs and going into the closet by the front door, then withdrawing with a holstered gun in one hand and my spare set of keys in another. She didn't even look guilty about it.

That was enough evidence to let me out, but not before I had to spend two days in lockup, wearing a baggy jumpsuit, barely eating the slop they served, and relieving myself in clear view of too many prying eyes. Beyond those things was simply the boredom, nothing to do but pace and think. I can't imagine how people survive in such an environment for weeks, let alone years. It would make me absolutely crazy.

Worst of all was the total lack of control. Not just was I told what to do, and expected to follow orders, but I was powerless to help myself find a way out of the situation. I had to rely on my attorney, a relative stranger, to gather the necessary facts that would allow the charges against me to be dropped.

Len contacted Graham, who informed him that Melody had never returned to their home in Sacramento. He had no idea where she'd gone, and there had been a total lack of communication. She did manage to make several large cash withdrawals at a number of Reno casinos.

"Put Blaine Pederson on it," I instructed Len.

He tracked Mel to Jerry's house in Glenns Ferry, where she was arrested for Sophia's murder. The last thing she asked for before they locked her up was a cigarette. Newport. I never had a clue she smoked from time to time, but she can't indulge the habit in the Ada County Jail in Boise. She's there now, awaiting extradition to Nevada.

Graham and I flew to Idaho to see her. He, to let her know he'd hired an attorney in Douglas County and to promise he'd take good care of the girls. I don't think the weight of her deed totally sank in until then. By the time they let me see her, she was despondent.

All I wanted was that one giant question answered. "Why, Mel?"

Her demeanor flipped to defiant. She gave me more than I expected. "You've always gotten your way and never had to work for a goddamn thing. I mean, all you had to do was spread your legs for the right man and the money kept rolling in. I've struggled all my life just to be a decent mother and hold my marriage together. You had no right to try and take that away. Graham was every-thing to me."

"Mel, the affair with Graham is completely in your head. It just never happened. But even if it had, why would you kill Sophia?

Why not just kill me?"

Her laughter was alien. "You always said you'd rather be dead than face years living behind bars. I didn't want to kill you. I wanted to maim you. It would have been fun to watch you waste away. Besides, the bitch deserved it. It wasn't hard at all."

Brutal.

Definitely insane.

It seems "crazy" also attracts greed, and Cavin defines the word. I should have quizzed Eli harder about the secrets he alluded to, secrets that turned up on Blaine Pederson's report. Not the one I ordered. The one Mel did, in my name, trying to set me up.

She didn't ask Pederson to follow Graham at all but rather to tail Cavin, hoping for some evidence of his dalliance with Sophia. Oh yes, they had a relationship, and it extended well after he married me. Whether or not it included sex is anyone's guess, but it started with this little underground business he conducted, selling prescriptions for controlled substances.

The oxycodone found in Genevieve Lennon's blood work after her accident? Yep, that came from Cavin, and it contributed to her intoxication that night. She should have known better than to drive under the influ-

537

ence of both booze and opioids, so I probably should blame her completely. But I can't. And I'll always wonder if that's what she wanted to tell me.

Apparently Genevieve didn't have arthritis at all, and Sophia's rotator cuff was in perfect shape. Investigators uncovered a small local network of doctors and pharmacists, and Cavin was chief among them. Not only did he supply Sophia but he also wrote prescriptions for many of her friends, including Austin Colvin. Maryann might not have known Sophia, but Austin definitely did.

And after a while, to help pay for her own habit, Sophia started blackmailing Cavin. Quite a few of his "gambling losses" were actually payments to Sophia. He has been indicted, along with his cohorts. Sophia got no more nor less than what she deserved, and neither did he.

Which puts me in a unique position. Obviously my resources were what attracted Cavin to me in the first place. Eli was right about that, too, and I am chagrined to have glossed over the assertion without more thought. I won't ever let down my guard like that again. Not like I didn't know better.

Love?

It's a myth.

As husbands go, I'm not sure doctors are worth the investment of time and energy. In the past, I've chosen to marry men who were capable of building my personal wealth, and if things had gone differently, I'm afraid Cavin would've ultimately proven himself net negative. Superlative bedside manner will never be a benchmark in the future. If I happen to yearn for a fling with a man in scrubs, there's always Cory Heinlen, though I won't be living in Tahoe much longer.

Cavin did make the mistake of putting his properties half in my name, and nothing in the prenup denies me ownership because he's likely facing prison. We'll have to sell the Glenbrook house to cover his legal expenses. I sure as hell won't take care of them. He'll never see another penny of mine, and he'll probably never practice medicine again.

Carmel is on the table, though. My thought is to trade equities in the two properties. I don't mind assuming the loan. While our attorneys squabble about the details, I plan to spend quite some time on the California coast, reorganizing my life.

Again.

Despite the insanity, Eli will graduate high

school with honors and has been accepted into Sierra Nevada College. Until then, he has asked if he can stay with me in Carmel when he gets back from Australia. I mean, after we get back. I'm joining him there for an extended vacation. Considering his relative loyalty to me, I decided to ice his cake.

"Does this information surprise you, Mom?"

I'm sitting on the fresh sod blanketing a grave in the Glenn Rest Cemetery. It's a luscious blue November morning, the autumn trees already skeletal, and that seems appropriate when conversing with a ghost.

I admit much of this story surprised me at first. I would never in a billion years have thought my sister capable of murder. I witnessed her unraveling but didn't recognize the extent of the damage until I got hold of Pederson's report. Once I discovered my name on the file, my suspicious mind started working overtime. I asked for a copy, which Pederson happily supplied. It wasn't difficult to put two and two together.

You suspected Melody had murder in mind.

"I did."

You could have saved Sophia.

"Probably. But why would I have wanted to? No. Better to help Mel accomplish her goal. I even chanced taking those bites of

540

mango strudel, knowing the EpiPen and Glock were together there in that handbag."

You set up your sister?

"Hey, what goes around comes around. Now it's Melody who'll face years behind bars or, at the very least, a padded cell in a high-security psych ward."

And you plan on having sex with your husband's son?

"Cavin's my ex-husband, or he will be soon enough. And as a sort of tribute to Sophia, why not see what Eli's made of? He's eighteen, and as far as I can tell after much dissection of memory, he's always told me the truth, or at least some version of it. Unlike his father."

How does the boy feel about everything that's happened?

"Sophia's murder shook him up, of course. It was the first time an overt act of violence struck him so close to home. But while he most definitely was in lust with her, love didn't play a role. It rarely does for sociopaths, and I ought to know.

"As for his father, Eli says he deserved to go down. A mantle of resentment roils inside the kid, hot and thick and sticky. Originally, he wanted to move in with Cavin and me to cause friction between us, but once he and I connected, he wanted to protect me. I got that straight from Eli, and I believe him.

"Well, it's been interesting chatting with you, Mom. Odd to discover it was you I've been talking to in my head. It's the most conversation we've ever shared. I suppose I should be going, though. Graham's waiting in the rental car. I sprang for a Lexus. Nice ride."

Wait.

"What?"

Was Melody Ann right about you and Graham?

"I would never have cheated on Cavin with Graham. Not my style."

What about before you met Cavin?

"I think I'll plead the Fifth."

But you always claimed you were averse to sleeping with married men.

I enjoy a long draw of sage-scented air, exhale steam into the brisk autumn azure.

"True. But I never said I wasn't a liar."

Shed of Skin

Freed within her exile, serpent
slithers boldly, strikes
without compassion,
splendor in the death dance.

Ah, patient is my sister.

No hurry now but to sup
before the meal grows cold,
she enfolds her victim tenderly,
awaits the egress.

Therein lies the victory.

Could Eve have denied her,
so beautiful in patterned scales, cool
in calculated treachery, sensuality
defined in the flick of her tongue?

Temptation is her legacy.

Enhanced by evolution,
perfected by time's passing,
she expels the weight of Eden
in gushes of sweet venom.

To grow, she must leave herself behind.

Subtle stretch. Elastic. Pinpricks
of sensation. Inner fabric gives
way in painless liberation.
Sister emerges, new.

Sin such as this commands envy.

ACKNOWLEDGMENTS

Women must maneuver this world thoughtfully. Look pretty. Act sexy. Be a good mommy, a hell-raiser in bed. But don't dare demand your place at the table. And should you be offered a seat, expect less money and an uninvited hand up your skirt, and be grateful you were invited at all. It is heartening to see women step up, push forward, gather momentum, and earn the respect they so deserve. And we must honor those who paved the way — women like my mother who survived neglect, abuse, poverty, and war, and emerged kind, creative, and full of heart. Thank you, Mama, for gifting me with words, faith, and abundant love. I miss you every day.

ABOUT THE AUTHOR

Ellen Hopkins is the #1 *New York Times* bestselling author of thirteen young adult novels, as well as the adult novels *Triangles, Collateral,* and *Love Lies Beneath.* She lives with her family in Carson City, Nevada, where she founded Ventana Sierra, a nonprofit youth housing and resource initiative. Visit her at EllenHopkins.com and on Facebook, and follow her on Twitter at @EllenHopkinsLit.

The employees of Thorndike Press hope you have enjoyed this Large Print book. All our Thorndike, Wheeler, and Kennebec Large Print titles are designed for easy reading, and all our books are made to last. Other Thorndike Press Large Print books are available at your library, through selected bookstores, or directly from us.

For information about titles, please call:
(800) 223-1244

or visit our website at:
gale.com/thorndike

To share your comments, please write:
Publisher
Thorndike Press
10 Water St., Suite 310
Waterville, ME 04901